Dead
on
Time

John McVicar

BLAKE

Published by Blake Publishing Ltd,
3 Bramber Court, 2 Bramber Road, London W14 9PB, England

First published in hardback in Great Britain in 2002

ISBN 1 85782 364 8

British Library Cataloguing-in-Publication Data:
A catalogue record for this book is available from
the British Library.

Typeset by Jon Davies
Map by ENVY

Printed in England by CPD, Wales

1 3 5 7 9 10 8 6 4 2

Papers used by Blake Publishing Ltd are natural, recyclable products
made from wood grown in sustainable forests. The manufacturing processes conform
to the environmental regulations of the country of origin.

Contents

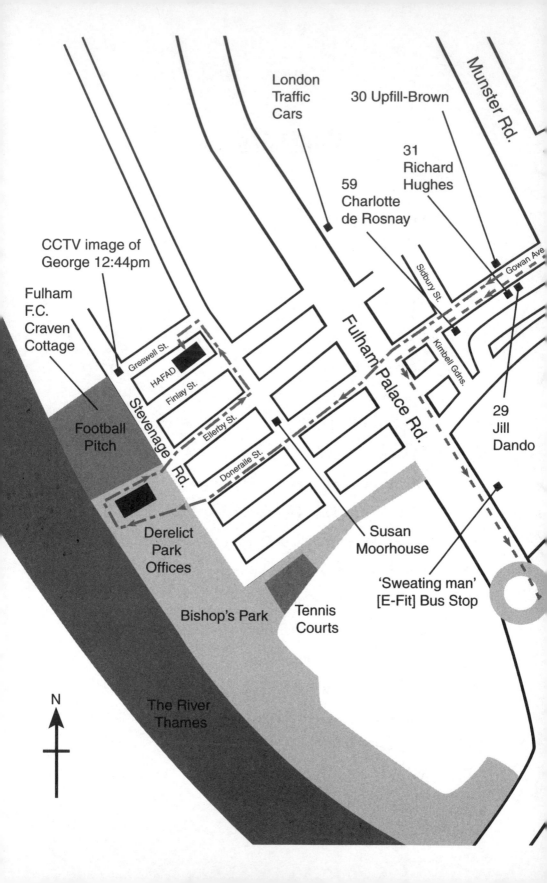

London Traffic Cars

30 Upfill-Brown

Munster Rd.

31 Richard Hughes

59 Charlotte de Rosnay

CCTV image of George 12:44pm

Gowan Ave

Sidbury St.

Fulham F.C. Craven Cottage

Greswell St.

HAFAD

Finlay St.

Fulham Palace Rd.

Kimbell Gdns.

29 Jill Dando

Football Pitch

Stevenage Rd.

Ellerby St.

Doneraile St.

Susan Moorhouse

Derelict Park Offices

'Sweating man' [E-Fit] Bus Stop

Bishop's Park

Tennis Courts

N

The River Thames

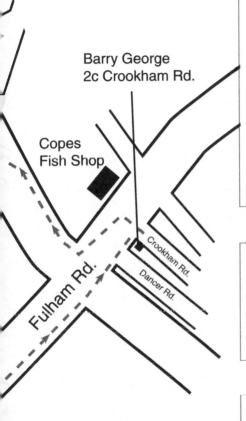

Barry George
2c Crookham Rd.

Copes
Fish Shop

Crookham Rd.

Dancer Rd.

Fulham Rd.

200 metres

THE CROWN'S ROUTE
FOR GEORGE (partial route shown)

← – – – – – –

11.33am – shot Dando

12.00pm – returned to 2c Crookham
Road; changed clothing;
walked to Bishop's Park

12.35pm – spoke to Susan
Moorhouse

12.44pm – CCTV image of George
in Stevenage Road

12.55pm – HAFAD

1.10pm – London Traffic Cars

GEORGE'S CLAIMED ROUTE

10.30 –
10.45pm – left 2c Crookham Road
11.15am – HAFAD
1.00pm – London Traffic Cars

GEORGE'S ACTUAL ROUTE

← – · – · – · – ··

11.33am – shot Dando

11.45am – changed clothing at the
derelict park offices

11.55am – 12.00pm – HAFAD

12.35pm – spoke to Susan
Moorhouse

12.44pm – CCTV image of George
in Stevenage Road

1.00pm – London Traffic Cars

Dramatis Personae

Bob the Builder – nickname for a juror who turned the tide on acquittal at Barry George's trial

DCI Hamish Campbell – operational head of the Oxborough squad set up to hunt the murderer of Jill Dando

Robert Charig – friend of Barry George

Clem – McVicar's tan terrier to whom the book is dedicated

George Coward – friend of Barry George and also of the late Freddie Mercury

Detective Constable D – the pseudonym of an officer on Oxborough whom Macnamara recruited to give *Punch* Magazine inside information of the murder investigation

Marilyn Etienne – solicitor for Barry George

Dr. Alan Farthing – gynaecologist and fiancé of Jill Dando, help set up Dando Crime Institute after her murder

Mohammed Al Fayed – Egyptian plutocrat who owns Harrods, Fulham Football Club and *Punch* Magazine

Mr Justice Gage – trial judge

DC Gallagher – the first Oxborough detective to interview Barry George

HAFAD – Hammersmith & Fulham Action for Disability

HOLMES – acronym for computer system used for logging all the information compiled by Oxborough; stands for Home Office Large Major Enquiry System

Ian Horrocks DI – second in command of Oxborough, a wily, affable Northerner

Fiona Hughes – school-teacher wife of Richard Hughes

Richard Hughes – next-door neighbour of Jill Dando

Dr Robin Keeley – forensic scientist who found the primer discharge particle that led to Barry George being charged with the murder of Jill Dando

John Macnamara – ex-DCI at Scotland Yard and at the time of the investigation, and Fayed's head of security

Mike Mansfield QC – rich, left-wing barrister who led for the defence

Benjamin Pell – known as Benjie the Binman, he was researcher for McVicar but he originated many of the ideas that led to the uncovering of George's motives

Orlando Pownall – Treasury counsel who led for the Crown

Nick Ross – co-presenter with Jill Dando of *Crimewatch* and a regular commentator on her murder

James Steen – editor of *Punch* Magazine at the time of Jill Dando's murder

Itsuko Toide – Japanese ex-wife of Barry George who left him and England because of his abuse

Nicholas Witchell – BBC newsman and colleague of Jill Dando

prologue

When Jill Dando was murdered, it was seen by many who did not know her as a national tragedy. It was almost as if Middle England was engulfed in mourning sickness. I did not know her and I did not mourn her death. Personally, I regard it as inappropriate to mourn someone whom one doesn't know and who, despite being in the public eye, made no unique contribution to public life. That does not make me unsympathetic to those who did know her and still grieve over her untimely end — not that I labour under any illusions that they need or want my sympathy.

Yet I have written a book about her murder and, in it, often refer to her off-handedly as if she was merely the token victim necessary to create a fictional whodunit. After all, to have a murder thriller, first someone has to has be murdered. And that was my attitude to her death even though I, more than most, became aware that it was a foul, merciless and — except to her killer — utterly pointless act. It would be hypocritical of me to claim that my flippant approach to her murder derived from my repulsion at the collective outbreak of mourning sickness or that it was a reflection of the surreal nature of the crime. In fact, my attitude to her murder is what I am like. I love life but I treat it irreverentially.

.Nevertheless, it is right to point out to those who will be offended by my attitude that what I learnt about Jill Dando goes entirely to her credit. She was a decent, hard-working, kind-hearted, generous woman. In fact, I did not come across anything discreditable about her, which is a claim that the reader can rely on as I am exactly the kind of journalist who, if he did find any dirt, would not have been able to resist printing it.

1

the best show in town

On 21 June 2001, when Mike Mansfield gave his closing speech to the jury trying Barry George for the murder of Jill Dando, I was sitting on the front row of the press benches alongside actor James Wilby. His producer had smuggled James into court as he was to play Mansfield in the ITN reconstruction that went out on the evening of the verdict. During a pause in Mansfield's speech, James leaned towards me and whispered, 'This is brilliant. It's the best show in town.' Anyone who wasn't deaf, blind or stupid in the Number One Court at the Old Bailey that day knew that they were witnessing a great performer at the height of his powers giving his all. When he sat down, I wasn't the only one who had to stifle an impulse to break into applause. Perhaps it is not an underworld myth that the richer and more informed gangsters see it as a wise move to book Mansfield in advance of committing any risky crime.

Mansfield was mesmeric. He occasionally looked at his notes but most of the time he held eye contact with the jury taking them sometimes humorously, often passionately, at other times dramatically, occasionally gravely through the evidence with all the timing and command of a masterful storyteller. The court was hypnotised; even the three Crown barristers, who were sprawled out on the lawyers' benches to his right, were openly watching him in awe, although Crown lead Orlando Pownall also conveyed that, while he admired the performance, to him it was like watching a magician playing tricks with his audience's perception of reality. Nonetheless, he, along with the rest of the court room, was hypnotised as Mansfield demolished and undermined every bit of evidence against Barry George. Even evidence that, when you had heard it, you had concluded was set in stone was ground into dust. Most informed observers thought the Crown had already lost the case before Mansfield stood up but, by the time he sat down, nearly everyone, including the jury, was sure that the only verdict was not guilty.

As we know, things didn't quite work out like that.

In the early part of his speech, Mansfield went out of his way to praise Jill Dando's personal qualities; she 'had a place in everyone's heart and mind', and how 'on the television screen she was a central figure in many people's minds'. Throughout the trial, however, he had been objective and even clinical in the way he referred to Jill Dando. He is not a man who has much truck with the overpaid, undertalented *glitterati* of daytime TV. Now it was different — on a couple of occasions, she even became 'Jill'.

Mansfield-watchers know that everything he does in court is directed at securing an acquittal — naturally, he does not prosecute. So if you are puzzled by what he is saying or you cannot understand his line of questioning, you have to ask yourself, 'What is he up to on behalf of his client?' Why, then, the sympathy for 'Jill'? It was to alert the jury to their natural sympathy for the people's TV presenter, then warn them that justice required that they did not let it influence their deliberations.

He told the jury, 'We ask you to be careful about the strength of feelings that there may well be. What this case requires above all, especially by you as judges of the facts, is an ability to ignore those feelings. They cannot be allowed to influence you in your approach to the case. It will do no justice to Jill Dando's memory or this case were you to allow those feelings to mould together what otherwise might be a non-existent case because there is, in some unconscious way or another, a desire to see someone pay.'

Yet, while his closing speech to the jury was spellbinding, there were small cracks in it. For example, in his preamble warning them about letting their memories and shock at Dando's murder influence their deliberations, he joked about whether or not they fell into that category of people who could remember exactly where they were when they heard of some earth-shattering event. Of course, the definitive example of this is the murder of President John Kennedy, but Mansfield shied away from this. To cue them up to remember their emotional responses to when they first heard of Dando's murder, he gave them two other examples of events that for many of us are fixed in our personal histories: the Cuban Missile Crisis and the death of Princess Diana. Of course, the reason he avoided President Kennedy was because he, like Dando, had been gunned down by a maverick loner.

Such calculated advocacy left hairline cracks in the spell that he had cast over the jury and over six days of deliberation these were crowbarred open by a minority of jurors until a majority who had believed in what Mansfield had conjured up were finally to reject not merely his tricks, but also his truths. His silver tongue was seen as forked. The jury's verdict of guilty was contrary to the facts and, while not perverse, it was a prejudicial verdict. The right verdict for the wrong reasons.

As Mansfield jogged the jurors' memories of where they were and how they felt when they heard about Jill Dando's murder, I recalled where I'd been and how something that at the time I had not reacted to emotionally at all was to claim over two years of my working life until, eventually, some of its lessons were to imprint themselves permanently on my sensibilities.

★   ★   ★

I flew out from Gatwick on 21 April 1999 for a week's holiday on the Dodecanese island of Rhodes. As with most things we do, I was motivated by a variety of reasons. I was meeting a Finnish university student named Tiina with whom I had struck up an e-mail friendship over our mutual interest in the use of performance-enhancing drugs in sport. She was going out there with a couple of her girlfriends to celebrate the conclusion of some exams they'd just sat. Although it was a holiday for me, I was also combining it with work. I had been commissioned to write a travel article for *Punch* — a magazine that I then wrote for — and so my trip was a freebie, which was another reason for going. No self-respecting hack turns down a free lunch even if he has to travel to Greece to eat it.

I'd been booked into a resort called Faliraki, which is like

Blackpool in the sun ... but a lot worse. Even with the sun and no sewage on the beaches, it is a lot, lot worse. The pleb teenagers who flock there from England, Germany and Sweden call it 'feely-fucky' because they go there to get laid as many times as possible with as many different partners as fancy takes them. When I eventually wrote up my article, I claimed on the basis of a straw poll of the local pharmacies that Faliraki is the only place on the planet where the women buy more condoms than the men. I made that up as a small fillip for the local tourist trade; but from what I saw of some of Tiina's mates, it was probably true, too.

I swam a lot, read some, scootered around the island on my hired Gillera 125 and saw Tiina a bit. On the whole, she preferred to party with her Finnish mates and compete with them on how many boys they could lay; whenever I was lonely, I found solace in the immutability of the Greeks. The ancient Greeks gave us so much that underpins Western culture that I always pay silent homage to their descendants. Maybe I'm sentimental but democracy, philosophy and sport are a heady legacy. Especially sport.

The Rhodians get on with their lives, however crass and banal the tourists to whom they pander. I enjoyed their attitude. To make a living, they have to put up with what this kind of tourism does to the accessible coast of their island. They clearly see the up side as more than compensation for the down side and who am I to double-guess them? And Faliraki was so bad, its dreadfulness gave it some merit to me. Looking at all these economically-blessed Northern Europeans, who were young enough to be my grandchildren, corrupting their bodies, minds and sensibilities always gave me a sense of my own superiority. And, to invert Chris Rock, I am not rich.

Anyway, on the penultimate day of my week's holiday, 27 April, I was sipping coffee in Vickie's Bar, which is what it sounds like — a haven for homesick Brits. Heart-shaped, over-chlorinated pool; plastic wicker chairs; 'Cor blimey' waitresses wearing unbra'd T-shirts who serve instant filter coffee; but it also had a big projection screen showing Sky Sports 2.

Now, I like watching football even more than celebrating the Greeks. This particular compulsion has its origins in being forced to play rugby at school. Rugger is bad for English males — it encourages them to get too close to each other's genitals, fosters a need to send their children to public school, breeds respect for the Royal Family and spoils the joy of watching Tim Henman lose at Wimbledon. Give me a football hooligan over a rugger-bugger any day. So, when Tiina was off, I would slope into Vickie's and watch the footie and the waitresses' tits. These were my reasons — sufficient ones for me — to sit in Vickie's Bar drinking the awful coffee.

On this occasion, I was reading the previous day's *Daily Telegraph*. Now the *Daily Telegraph* may be Middle England, but it does let its writers think in print and, most of all, it is not the *Guardian*. As a rule of thumb, the more social conscience claimed by a newspaper, the meaner they treat its contributors. But it was hot, sunny and windy, I was in the shade reading yesterday's *Daily Telegraph*, listening to Sibelius's Second on my Minidisc player and looking forward to seeing Tiina that evening and night. Life was not perfect but still pretty good.

Suddenly, a male shadow darkened my reading about how David Ginola and Nicolas Anelka had been recognised by sportswriters as huge talents.

'Is there anything in there about Jill Dando?'

It broke through the lyricism of Sibelius, which I turned off to deal with the intruder in my time-honoured fashion. He was about 24, beer-gut, cropped hair. He had on a shiny Man U strip with fraying flip-flops but the accent was Dagenham Essex.

Normally, in these circumstances, I draw on my pidgin Russian and pretend I cannot speak English. Just as I started to kick into Russian gobbledegook, I realised the import of what I was reading.

'Dando?' I replied puzzled but disinterested. It wasn't only that I wanted to brush off Essex Man; I didn't at that moment tag the name Dando to the BBC newscaster and, even if I had, I wouldn't have been that interested.

But Essex Man was ahead of me. 'Nah, that's yesterday's ...' He could read. 'It was on Sky last night. She was shot dead, midday in Fulham. Wankers, Fulham.' He also recognised that I was studying the football pages. Al Fayed money; Keegan manager. (Kevin Keegan was still manager then.) He grunted his disapproval, then capped his judgement. 'Little wankers they are, the pair of 'em. Who d'you support?'

'Hmmm ... West Ham,' I answered apologetically. You have to apologise for supporting West Ham as they play football but never win anything. This put me on my back foot, so I went on the offensive with why I support the Hammers. 'I grew up in the East End, so ... yeah, West Ham.' I eyeballed him without blinking ... meaning that I came from the East End, so I was no wanker, even though I do support West Ham. The trouble was my age was against me.

'West Ham!' The Hammers did not exist on his soccer map. My East End roots clearly hadn't impressed him — I wasn't Cockney enough; I was also reading what in his parts was a foreign newspaper.

He probed suspiciously. 'At least it ain't Chelsea. Poofs, the lot of 'em.' Then he growled, 'Ain't they?'

Chelsea were on his map, but in enemy territory. He watched craftily to see whether his put-down touched a nerve.

However, my head was on another tack as I had just put the name Dando to the newscaster.

I switched back to where we started. 'Jill Dando? The woman who presents *Crimewatch*? What murder?'

'Yeah, I just told yer. One in the nut. Hit-man ... got away clean as a whistle.'

I replied languidly, 'Just shows what you get for fronting *Crimewatch*. It'll turn out to be some nutter.' My eyes slid back to the sports page. But I was already thinking, Shame it wasn't the programme's anchorman, Nick Ross. I suffer from Nick Ross allergy. His carping, whining voice, rabbit-in-the-headlights eyes, hang-dog fearful expression ... any exposure to him wrecks my immune system. Middle England's spokesperson is a must-turn-off for me, but occasionally the calls of journalism force me to record *Crimewatch*. Never live, of course. I need the fast forward for when the germs overrun the weakened immune system. But Jill Dando shot in the head! It didn't make sense.

Essex Man thankfully took his cue from my switching back to the newspaper. 'Thanks anyway, mate,' he said sloping back to his table, beer and peanuts. I imagined him finishing off his remark under his breath '... for nothing'.

But I wasn't absorbing what I was reading for thoughts about Jill Dando. TV stars don't get murdered, especially ones like her. She was another one of those girl-next-door clones that are the stage army of lowbrow TV ... middlebrow being as high as the medium goes. Not too bright, beaming air-hostess smile, blonde, attractive but never sexy. They come and go ... Anneka Rice, Anthea Turner, Anne Diamond, Gaby Roslin ... I know them well because they anchor the kind of down-market programmes that I guest on: breakfast shows, local news, *London Tonight*.

For roughly 20 years, I have doing such 'talking head' gigs. I turn up, go into the studio, unzip my mouth about some crime topic like hit-men or the drug trade or how dreadful our prisons are, then wait for my hundred quid cheque to arrive. Most interviewers do not have a clue what the interview is about; the questions they ask are written by researchers and all they do is read them out from the autocue. Reading from the autocue is their only necessary skill ... the sufficient one is to sleep with the producer.

But even with Essex Man out of sight and mind — in fact, he was on the other side of the pool — I couldn't help stew over what he had said. 'Jill Dando gunned down in Fulham ... well, well ...' Before getting back into the sports pages, I concluded that her killer would turn out to be another nutter with some cause that makes perfect sense to him but appears mad to everyone else and, as it is constructed out of the usual mishmash of delusional beliefs, is mad. I couldn't really cast her as the victim of a *crime passionnel*. Hovering in the back of my mind, moreover, was the thought that James Steen, the editor of *Punch*, would ask me to cover the case when I got back to the office on Thursday. At that time, I had been working for *Punch* as its crime and legal correspondent for about two years, so as long as there was no arrest in the next few days, I might well get landed with the Dando case.

And, in my head, that is how the murder rested ... on hold. It was now late Tuesday afternoon, 27 April 1999; my focus was on making my and Tiina's last evening on Rhodes a memorable one. We were both going our separate ways the following day — her to Savonlinna and me to London. She was another lost cause in my attempt to play catch-up on those years in prison. Doubtless, it was all leading to an early grave but, at least, I'd go there outrageously.

My last night with Tiina certainly didn't help the life expectancy. She looked at my passport while I was showering and when I came out she was under the duvet in the foetal position where she stayed all night. I had told her I was 40, not 58, which was really not my fault. Before I left for my first meeting with Tiina, I had asked a female mate of mine what age I could get away with and, after giving me the once over, Jane had replied 50. I then added that Tiina was only 20. Jane paused before decreeing heartily, 'Forty, then. She won't know the difference. When you're 20, any man over 30 is geriatric.'

So my last night in Rhodes was a disaster and the morning was worse, with Tiina wailing on about how could she take a man old enough not only to be her father, but her grandfather! It's a memory that still trips the cringe reflex.

I looked at the papers on the flight but ducked the Dando stuff. I absorbed how big it was running — obviously we were back in Lady Di-land, mourning sickness and all — but I didn't study it. At the time, I was absorbed in composing on my laptop a 2,000-word e-mail to Tiina, which, after putting the blame squarely on Jane's shoulders, pleaded for another chance. Burdened with such a weighty enterprise, it was no wonder that I did not take much interest in the Dando murder; for what it mattered, my take was a nutter but maybe an ex. I mean, while I couldn't see anything in her that might have stirred the green-eyed monster, you never can tell if someone else had.

I got into Gatwick, whizzed through passport control and Customs — hand luggage and nothing to declare — scuttled on to the Gatwick Express and was back in Battersea in time to collect the canine love of my life, Clem, from Charlotte and John who dogsit whenever I go abroad. He wasn't that enamoured to see me. He always makes it plain that he prefers living with them, their two kids, the nanny and the garden to sharing a second-floor flat and a poky balcony with me but, as he is a dog, he has no choice. Nevertheless, I always took it to heart that I couldn't even earn the loyalty of a dog.

Back in my flat, while bribing Clem to be nice to me with some chocolate offerings, I listened to the answerphone messages. Among them was one from *Punch* editor James Steen.

'John, hope you had a great time. Now, the Jill Dando murder; it has gone galactic and unless they get someone it is going to stay that way. We need a cover on it for the next issue. Ring me as soon as you get in.'

I was still in the back-to-London decompression chamber and wondering whether my e-mail would pull Tiina's compassion strings. Her flight had left before mine, so logging on to see if she had replied took priority over contacting James. The Dando case could wait. *Punch* is a bi-weekly magazine and my thinking was that the next edition would be going to print towards the end of the following week. I had at least a week before my next deadline. Tiina was more important than Dando and *Punch*.

James Steen turned out to be an important figure in my take on the Dando murder as most of what I wrote on it prior to the arrest of Barry George was done in conjunction with James and published in *Punch*. The media interest in her unsolved murder just ran and ran and we went back to it in the magazine time and time again. Apart from these articles, in the year between the murder and George's arrest we spent countless hours brainstorming on the case whether on the telephone, in the office, over lunch or drinking far too many bottles of Pinot Grigio.

The *Times Media* section published a page profile on James Steen on 12 May 2000 headlined MUCK-RAKER, which was under a picture of James with a glass of wine in one hand, a fag in the other and a big grin on his face. The snap is accurate, the headline inaccurate. James always puts having a laugh before causing a stench. He is certainly a trouble-maker — which is right up my street — but journalists should always be looking to ruffle the feathers of the rich, the powerful and the famous. James also likes having fun while he does it, which is not a bad creed for a journalist or for a publication either.

When James was editor, *Punch* was like that but it also punched straight from the shoulder. Those who said it didn't claimed it was Mohammed Al Fayed's get-back rag. True, Al Fayed owns it; true, he writes a column in it, which when it was edited by James was ghosted by him; true, he subsidises the magazine to the tune of nearly a million a year; true, it often savages people whom Al Fayed doesn't like, but when I worked for it, Al Fayed never commissioned those attacks.

During that period, Al Fayed did not influence the magazine's content at all. He certainly put pressure on James to lose less money but he didn't order James or any of his writers to get at any of his enemies in public life. For nearly three years, I had been lashing out at all and sundry in my articles in the magazine but never at Al Fayed's instigation and only once did he ever moan about the people I attacked. This was over an article I wrote in Issue 104 (19 April 2000) on the then forthcoming Lockerbie trial.

When the mag hit the news-stands, Al Fayed was visiting Libya at the invitation of Colonel Gadaffi. My article revealed the evidence against the two accused that would be presented at the forthcoming trial and analysed the reasons why Gadaffi ordered the sabotage of Pam Am flight 103. After he'd returned, Al Fayed said to James, 'It was very embarrassing for me, James, to be a guest of Colonel Gadaffi just when *Punch* is saying he is a mass murderer. In future, can you tell me who you attack, so we can avoid these misunderstandings.'

James just cracked up with laughter. He replied, 'But you didn't tell me you were going to Libya. And how can I tell you who we are stitching up? If it is a good read and true, we want to run it. We can't keep coming to you for approval ...'

The Lockerbie mix-up showed how little Al Fayed even knew about, never mind influenced, what the magazine published. Nevertheless, that wasn't the way it was perceived by the critics and there was so much sniping the magazine never got its dues.

Anyway, the day after getting back from Rhodes, I was on parade at Knightsbridge's hostelry, the Swag and Tails, which doubled as a hospitality room for *Punch*. It's a couple of hundred metres from the magazine's offices, which are bang opposite the western wing of Harrods in the Old Brompton Road. James was cackling with laughter at my adventures with Tiina. He commented, 'I don't suppose the *Punch* readership is going to hear about your going off with a Finnish teenager ...'

I pointed out that she wasn't a teenager.

'John, come on! Relative to you she is granddaughter material ...'

At that time, any word that began with 'grand' was like being exposed to Nick Ross. I couldn't even protest, but eventually we turned to the Dando murder.

James said, 'There is something not quite right about this and the police and Fleet Street don't have a clue. There are too many whodunit theories already — Serbs, *Crimewatch* collars, exes, stalkers ... it could be anyone ... well, except you ...' James paused for another cackle, 'because you were in Rhodes with an underage Finnish teenager whom we are not going to read about in *Punch* but we won't go on about that.'

As I felt the immune system wobble, I wondered whether I would wake up tomorrow with pneumonia or something. It was no good rising to the bait and, when I didn't, James went back to Dando.

'John, read the clips, go down there, see what you think, and we'll run with it. By the way, you will like this. Dando was born with a hole in the heart and, wait for it ... died with one in the head. That's symmetry for you.'

James, like all journos, is bad taste personified. I laughed and asked where he had found out about the hole in the heart.

'The clips. When you leave, drop in the office and get them off Caroline.'

Caroline was the office's young, thin, blonde, puritanical factotum. She certainly disapproved of me. Her commonest response to my voicing even the mildest of my filthy thoughts was, 'Don't tell me any more, that's disgusting.'

Mentally, I passed on the office as, after James, I couldn't take Caroline on Tiina, too. She would be beside herself to ask. I decided once I got home to e-mail Caroline to bike them over and it meant I could check whether my long e-mail to Tiina had done the trick. I asked James how long he wanted the piece.

He answered, 'At least a spread and another page [three pages and roughly 3,000 words]. Definitely a splash [cover story]. See what you can make of it.'

When did he want it by?

'Wednesday at the latest ... and I know that you think Wednesday is Thursday but we really need it by Wednesday to give the subs time to lay it out properly ...'

What about Rhodes?

'Leave the Rhodes piece for another time ... unless you want to warn the readers about the dangers of taking a Pamela Anderson lookalike to a Greek island. So when do we see the photos?'

I groaned; all Rhodes led to Tiina. I should have known better than to blag a freebie with a young Finn. It was another story that was going to run and run.

Hacks need to know three things when they strike on a commission: how long, how much and when the deadline is for filing. With James, I didn't need to ask how much as I was a regular contributor, so in my head it was 3,000 on the Dando murder by Thursday and the Rhodes piece would never be mentioned again ... by me at least but, of course, James never left it alone.

2

it's no hitman

A week after the kill, at around the time it occurred, 11.33am, I cycled over to Gowan Avenue where Jill Dando had lived for five years until she was murdered on her doorstep. It is about four miles from where I live in Battersea. I covered the distance in 14 minutes in what turned out to be the first of many such trips. Whenever I exercise, I time myself. It's another one of my sick ways of chaining myself to the fitness treadmill. Every regular journey gets its Personal Best time. I wore my cycling gear with a knapsack in which I had my working kit: ID, notebook, pen, tape recorder and camera. I knew the location well because from Dando's house it is only another 250 metres east to Fulham Football Club, which, incidentally, is also owned by Al Fayed.

Gowan Avenue is a quiet suburban street lined with cherry

and apple trees that runs about 400 metres from east to west
between two very busy roads — Munster Road and Fulham Palace
Road. Gowan does not give 'rat run' motorists any edge and so is
spared the general congestion of Fulham and the much-beloved
speed bumps and one-ways of London's traffic engineers. This gives
its terraced Victorian houses, originally working-class but now
expensively gentrified, a tranquil backwater feel that is reflected in
their price tag of £350–500 thousand.

I cycled in from the Munster Road end with my head abuzz
with the police statements and press reports that I had studied over
the weekend. For over a year, Dando had been living with her
fiancé, Dr Farthing, at Chiswick, and only using her Gowan
Avenue home virtually as a dormant office. The house was also
under offer having been up for sale for some time. Once she and
Farthing were married in the autumn, they intended to set up
home in Little Venice, which is near Paddington Hospital where
Farthing worked. She only visited the place once a week and the
estate agent and her cleaner went there more often than her. There
was also no pattern to her visits, so the gunman either had had
inside information on her intention to visit Gowan Avenue that
morning or he had hung around and got lucky.

The latter seemed the most likely as there were a number of
reports of the gunman being on foot and hanging around near her
house for some considerable time. Moreover, it seemed highly
unlikely that he had had inside information as Dando did not plan
to go Gowan Avenue that morning until her agent rang her a
couple of hours before to tell her that her fax machine had
jammed. This is why on her way to Gowan Avenue that morning
she stopped off to shop for a fax cartridge at Dixon's and Ryman's
in Hammersmith. Thus, if the gunman had had inside information,
it could only have come from very few people. Alternatively, she

may have been followed from Chiswick or her phonecalls were being intercepted. Even a cursory acquaintance with the facts, however, made even the *how* of this murder, never mind the *who* of it, puzzling. Since my return from Rhodes, my hunch on *who* had evolved from nutter to ex-lover — either hers or Mr Farthing's. My reasoning for this was that the kill had been a bit too slick and efficient for a nutter.

My immediate impression as I cycled down Gowan Avenue was that if the gunman did hang around as the reports indicated, he must been aware that he stood out like a sore thumb. Gowan Avenue is not a comfortable plot for a criminal to hang about in. And this one was armed, so he must have been acutely worried about a possible police response to a householder who rang 999 to report him acting suspiciously. A patrol car carrying out a stop and search action would have collared him bang to rights. The only inference that could be drawn from him hanging around with a loaded gun in his pocket was that he was waiting for someone to return home whom he intended to shoot. Tell that to the judge for a community service order!

From the Munster Road end of Gowan Avenue, number 29 where Dando lived is about 60 metres down on the left-hand side. My first response to the gunman's problem of springing her without attracting attention was that he would prefer to plot up at the Munster end of Gowan Avenue where there is much more movement of pedestrians and traffic than in the avenue itself. He couldn't use the Fulham Palace Road end, which is even busier, as first of all the slight kink half-way along Gowan Avenue means you cannot monitor the roadway around number 29 from that vantage point and, second, it is too far away to use as a springboard for an attack. If the gunman had plotted up there, when he saw her car he would have had to leg it 360 metres to catch her before she entered number 29. Clearly, he could not use the Fulham Palace Road end as his bake before ambushing her.

But he had not used Munster Road either, as all the reports were of the gunman — some say wearing glasses, others carrying a mobile phone — hanging around her house for some time that morning. Oxborough, which was the operational name assigned to the Dando squad, had already issued the famous E-fit of a dark-haired man in his late 30s with a nose marked by the habitual wearing of spectacles. This tallied with one of the descriptions of a man seen hanging around 29 Gowan Avenue that morning. The E-fit, though, was based on witnesses' descriptions of a man waiting at a bus stop in Fulham Palace Road some 500 metres from number 29 and 15 minutes after the kill. He was sweating and he came to be known as 'Sweating Man'. The fact that he was sweating fitted other witnesses' descriptions that the gunman had run down Gowan Avenue, then dashed into Bishop's Park. Sweating Man came from Bishop's Park when he joined the bus queue, and he was Oxborough's main suspect.

Even as I cycled into Gowan Avenue that morning, I could not see how the gunman/Sweating Man could be a professional criminal. It did not stack up, despite the way this particular theory was being bandied about in the press. The *Independent* newspaper was especially amiss in telling its readers how contract killing is a 'growth business', with hit-men being 'hired for as little as £1,000'. This journalist wrote that Jill's murder 'closely matches the blueprint for a professional hit, in terms of location, timing and method of execution'. No professional killer recruited from the underworld would work without gloves, mask or back-up such as a getaway car and driver; no hitman would hang around for hours in Gowan Avenue where householders are sensitive to prowlers waiting for his target to show. Indeed, the one indelible impression that the Dando murder case made on me, which was confirmed time and time again over the following two years, is the appalling quality of our crime reporting. No wonder the police generally, and many lawyers, are contemptuous of 'the members of the press'.

Nonetheless, however amateurish the gunman's *modus operandi*, the hit was flawlessly clinical and efficient. One bullet to the head, fired at point-blank range. At the trial, a firearms expert, Major Peter Mead, called by the defence, agreed with Mansfield that the murder bore the hallmark of a professional hitman. He said, 'It is difficult to imagine how it could have been bettered.' Yet, while you could not improve on the kill, as I was to point out in my first article, what you could not read into it was the signature of a professional hitman.

In my article two weeks after Dando's murder, I wrote about the gunman, 'He is clearly at home with firearms. The one thing — maybe the only thing — that really was professional about this hit was the actual kill.' I also pointed out another obvious fact: underworld hit-men rarely kill at such close quarters. The reason for this is that a 'hard contact' kill means coming close to the victim who may lash out in panic or by instinct or in a bid to disarm the gunman. But any contact incurs the risk to the gunman of leaving a trace of his DNA at the scene of the crime, which is why nearly all such hits are carried out a yard or so away from the victim. Taking the kill in the round then, it was a professional job but not carried out by a professional criminal — which was why James Steen's cover blurb for my article was: DANDO — IT'S NO HITMAN. The actual kill itself, I wrote, had 'a militarist feel' to it, which a minority of journos had also picked up on.

I quickly discounted, as well, the other criminal hitman scenario — that it was an amateur who had stepped up a league.

According to this scenario, an ex of Dando's had commissioned the kill because he was jealous of her impending wedding to Alan Farthing and he had recruited a local thug for the job. Generally, the exes of Alan Farthing were not given much of an airing in the press, although, as I later discovered, Oxborough certainly did. The ex's judgement would have been so clouded that he discounted the strong possibility that his wannabe hitman would almost certainly be arrested and would name him to the police. But, eventually, the amateur hitman's name would surface on the grapevine and the murder would be solved.

But running this scenario quickly nosedived you into the sand. The ex's emotional state would not transfer itself to his recruited assassin; all that would be motivating the latter would be money and, presumably, not that much as otherwise he would have had some kind of getaway transport or, at least, back-up. How could he hang around like he did without his nerve cracking?

Another point against the amateur scenario was the implication of Jill not being a nine-to-five gal. The killer had had no means of predicting not only when she would return home that morning but also if she would. Even a mercenary, amateur contract killer with professional aspirations would not hang around Gowan Avenue for hours in just the hope that she would arrive. He is a sitting duck for a long sentence with a 9mm gun on him that only had one purpose. His nerve would almost certainly have cracked long before she had turned up. And, if it hadn't by the time she did show, it beggared belief that he would have had the coolness, presuming he was unaware of the DNA risk, to close in on her and shoot her at point-blank range. That kind of kill requires a particular kind of cold resolution — the trademark of what Mafiosi call a 'stone killer'.

The amateur contract killer stood up slightly better than the professional killer theory, but in my book it still didn't pass muster. With all his antennae on full alert, the gunman would definitely have noticed the people who were watching him. Even stupid criminals are mindful of not getting caught and no killer on a return of a few thousand pounds with all the risk to his liberty that this enterprise involved would act the way Dando's killer did. The amateur's mindset just didn't fit the behaviour of the gunman. At the time, I wrote, 'This killer was powerfully motivated either by something personal or by some cause. Moreover, the actual facts of the kill suggest the latter.'

There was a simple logic to this conclusion. Once the commissioned hitman scenario is eliminated, then it follows that the person with the motive to kill her was also the person who pulled the trigger. If it was personal, then whether the motivation was jealousy or rejection, one looks immediately to her and Farthing's exes. Given that the murderer was a man, then unless Farthing was bisexual we could eliminate his exes. Dando's exes were quickly known to the police and, if there had been any secret ones, her phone records and diary would have put him in the frame. At the time of her murder, Dando was deified as Miss Goody-Two-Shoes but, even after leaks from Oxborough showed that the butter *did* melt between her cheeks, no mystery exes were ever discovered. She was sexually active but had no dark side that could have let in, say, some gangland figure or drug-dealer. By the time I was on the scene, Oxborough had already trawled the exes route with the E-fit as their guide and had got nowhere, so the most likely personal motive didn't look a runner. If the motive was some kind of cause, then, bearing in mind the militaristic angle, the Serb scenario looked favourite.

As I dismounted near 29 Gowan Avenue, my head was full of this kind of speculation. The façade of the house and the front garden were enveloped in a white tarpaulin sheet that went up to the roof to facilitate the forensic team's examination of the murder scene. There was a big white Police Investigations Unit portakabin parked outside and nearby was a young, uniformed constable vaguely on sentry duty. He looked blankly at me as I got off my bike, leaned it against the wall of the house opposite and began fishing around in my knapsack for my camera. The constable just looked on. As I was the focus of his disinterested stare, I felt I had better establish my right to do what I intended to do. I got out my press card and walked towards him. 'Press, officer. Do you mind if I take some photos?'

He didn't look at my card and he waited before shrugging his shoulders and hamming a nonchalant expression, which suggested, 'It's a free country but if I had my way it wouldn't be for people like you to photograph murder scenes.' I accepted his grudging acquiescence and knocked off a few shots: the police unit, the constable himself, the sheeted front of Number 29 ... the flowers. There were two desultory flower shrines; one opposite the house, next to my bike; and the other outside the wall of number 27. Most of them were accompanied by condolence cards with personal messages written by members of the public who clearly thought they knew her. Many of them were written to her and not to her friends and relations. It was a mini repeat of the hysteria that we saw in 1997 over Princess Diana's death. Presumably, the mentality of the people who play this mourning sickness role encompasses images of Dando in heaven looking down benignly at their tributes.

As I walked around whacking off shots, I saw two young, respectable, plebby women in their mid-20s approach with a bunch of flowers, which one of them laid on the shrine near my bike. They were not interested in me the photographer, the constable or even Dando's home, but shuffled along the pavement, stooping over, reading the other condolence cards, pointing out to each other anything sad or touching that caught their eye. They were not honouring the shocking death of someone in the public eye with whom they had identified or respected; they were simulating the emotions and copying the behaviour of others whom the media had shown doing likewise.

They had the same distraught expressions that the mourners in The Mall had had queuing to sign the condolence books or who had massed outside Westminster Abbey in 1997. In fact, Barry George had been among the latter and had been photographed holding up a poster dedicated to 'The Queen of Hearts', which was signed: 'Barry Bulsara, Freddie Mercury's cousin'.

As I watched the scene and the Lady Di parallels went through my mind, I felt an impulse to buttonhole the two flower-layers for some copy for my piece ... ask them where they came from, whether they had taken time off work to make the trip, why they felt the need to lay flowers for someone they did not know, whether they had done the same thing for Princess Di. In the end, I resisted approaching them, probably because I cannot credit this kind of kitsch grief and, if I try, I only turn into a spitting viper. The article would have become a diatribe on fake emotional tourism and celebrity-itis.

At George's trial, we also learned that, on the afternoon of the murder, he bought flowers for Jill Dando, which he gave to a policeman then manning the cordon at the Munster end of Gowan Avenue to put on her shrine. The flowers were yellow carnations in homage to his idol Freddie Mercury — Mercury's favourite colour was yellow — but exposing yourself to the enemy soon after the crime while assuming a contrasting persona came directly from his martial arts training. The idea is for the assassin to present himself in a form that is incongruous with that of the killer in order deflect suspicion.

In his police interview 13 months after he had murdered Dando on 26 April, George was asked about the flowers he had brought to lay on her shrine. The video of the interview was played to the court on 24 May 2001.

Snowden (the interrogating detective): 'When did you lay the flowers?'

George: 'I conveyed the flowers to the gentleman on the police cordon.'

Snowden: 'On what day?'

George: 'When the cordon went up.'

Snowden: 'What date was that?'

George: 'I believe it was the 26th.'

Snowden: 'You took the flowers on the 26th?'

George: 'Yes.'

Snowden: 'How can you remember that?'

George: 'You tend to remember things like that.'

There the killer's flowers lay like a swastika hidden in a synagogue.

As I watched the scene and the Lady Di parallels went through my mind, I felt an impulse to buttonhole the two flower layers for some copy for my piece … ask them where they came from, whether they had taken time off work to make the trip, why they felt the need to lay flowers for someone they did not know, whether they did the same thing for Princess Di. In the end I resisted approaching them, probably because I cannot credit this kind of kitsch grief and if I try I only turn into a spitting viper. The article would have turned into a diatribe on fake emotional tourism and celebrity-itis.

Of course, on my first visit to Gowan Avenue when George's arrest was 13 months away, all I knew was what was in the newspaper cuttings and what I could glean from the crime scene. Although I quickly discarded the theory that the murder was the work of any kind of professional or amateur hitman, the militaristic feel to it reminded me of the executions carried out by death squads. You couldn't help but think this man had killed before and, to him, it was no big deal. Thus, I was leaning more and more towards the Serb theory as the best of those on offer. But there were plenty on offer.

The media was theory-mongering with a vengeance. As with the Diana death, the Dando murder sent the conspiracists into overdrive. Of course, with any story in which there remains a strong public interest, as the facts dry up the theories proliferate to fill the vacuum. This seems to be one of the few iron laws of journalism. A corollary to that iron law is the more theories there are, the less it matters that they meet the facts. Free-wheeling speculation and conjecture had already taken over in the press.

At that time, the main theories were jealous ex-lover; contract killer; a stalker; a nutter lashing out randomly at a victim who happened to be her; revenge over a *Crimewatch* collar that she had instigated; a Serbian revenge murder for the bombing of their own TV stations ... mixed in with all this was the police's appeal over the driver of a blue Range Rover that had been seen speeding away down Fulham Palace Road at around the time of the murder. Of course, Range Rovers always speed, especially blue ones, but this raised the possibility of an accomplice who had left the gunman to it.

At trial, Mansfield ran the Serb hitman using a Range Rover as one of his fishiest red herrings. Thus, the reason the hitman

27

hadn't been seen just before the kill was because he was being dropped off by his accomplice in the Range Rover when Dando's car was seen entering Gowan Avenue. The driver then moved off and, after the gunman had murdered Dando, picked him up down the road. The Crown lead, Pownall, missed the opportunity to souse this because he didn't know how a contract or professional killer would operate. Why should he?

If he had had vehicle back-up, the gunman would certainly have alighted outside number 29 because that would have obviated the danger of plotting up in a road where any suspicious stranger was vulnerable to a 'stop-and-search' action. However, contrary to what Mansfield ran before the jury, the driver would stay put. He would never drive off and leave the gunman. Time is of the essence in such circumstances and no getaway driver would see any percentage in driving some distance down Gowan Avenue for his pick-up. This would waste crucial getaway time and leave the gunman to run the gauntlet of possible have-a-go bystanders. Despite its provenance, this theory was another non-starter.

The other accomplice theory, which was run by a number of journalists, was rooted in the reports of the gunman carrying and talking into a mobile phone before the kill. This one had the gunman receiving details over his mobile of Jill's movements — buying fax accessories — from an accomplice who was following her. If he had had such back-up, the gunman would not have been hanging around 29 Gowan Avenue where he was obviously vulnerable to neighbours reporting his presence to the police as suspicious. He would have waited in a nearby street and only moved in for the kill when informed of her approach. More nonsense. That is not to say that the police could ignore that the killer may have made calls — perhaps as a form of disguise, in that it made him seem as if he had business in the road. In fact, the most onerous strand of Oxborough's enquiries turned out to be checking the records of the mobile phone networks to identify calls made around the time and in the area.

The conclusion I arrived at after my first visit to the crime scene was 'he was a loner', but not a celebrity stalker loner — that was a contradiction in terms, despite the fact that it was run and run by the media and, bizarrely, by the Crown Prosecution Service at George's trial. Stalkers show their obsession long before they strike so lethally. I always felt that even knocking down the stalker theory gave it more substance than it warranted. I wrote at the time, 'If it was a stalker, he would have been nicked by now.'

A related theory that it was a lone nut with a grudge against society didn't stack up either. Dando's killer was never a Thomas 'Dunblane' Hamilton without the suicide. Psychotics don't bother to cover their tracks very well; they're also too deranged to kill so clinically and meticulously. Obviously, this theory could not be completely discounted but it was such an outsider that a betting man would safely consign it to the knacker's yard.

Similarly, one could dispatch the *Crimewatch* theory. Although the then Home Secretary, Jack Straw, paid tribute to Dando on the day of the murder, saying she had been in the forefront of the fight against crime, Dando was not even an understudy for Nick Ross. When Seetha Kumar, Editor of *Crimewatch*, gave evidence, Mansfield began trawling for support for his Serb/Arkan red herring. He asked Mrs Kumar, an overwrought BBC-ite, was it not right that Dando symbolised the BBC and, as a leading reporter on *Crimewatch*, was on the cutting edge of the war against crime? It was not the answer that Mansfield wanted but it transpired that all Dando did was read Nick Ross's script from the autocue, her only input being to 'tweak the odd word or two'.

Moreover, Dando had been co-presenting the programme for

three-and-a-half years, which hardly offered the kind of time necessary for a criminal entrapped by the programme to bear such a grudge that it motivated him to murder her. Any criminal who was sentenced to more than eight years as a result of a *Crimewatch* that she had co-presented would still be in prison! The number who were sentenced to eight years or less and were capable of and sufficiently motivated to kill Jill Dando were so few in number that they were eliminated by Oxborough early on in the investigation.

Indeed, the obvious target for such an act of revenge would have been the BBC's own Special Constable, Nick-Nick Ross, who had been with the programme since its inception and who on anyone's elimination scale towers above either Jill Dando or her predecessor Sue Cooke.

Where I went badly wrong in my first article on the case was relying on press reports that a silencer had been used. It is very rare for a criminal to use a silencer in this country, so I used this in my article to shore up my argument for the Serb scenario. Access to a silencer, I argued, was further indication that the gunman drew his weaponry from the military rather than a criminal source. However, the silencer proved a bum steer in more ways than one.

★   ★   ★

About three weeks after the murder, Campbell called a press conference to knock down some of what he called the 'false theories' that were doing the rounds in the media. There was no silencer, no dum-dum bullet and the gun was a 'short' 9mm semi-automatic, not the regular 9mm that we had been reporting. Campbell said that the reason he was doing this was to dispel the misinformation that had built up around the case. However, he never said nor was he asked why the misinformation was allowed to build up in the first place.

Oxborough had no stake in waiting so long to correct these false theories. On the first day of the murder, Campbell had appealed to the public for help and, if this was to be the source of the breakthrough in the case, then it was vital that the public was not misled about the known facts of the case. It could not help the inquiry to leave mistakes on the public record that, through being reported in the media, would focus people's attention on irrelevant matters and deflect them from relevant ones. Some information for operational reasons should not be disclosed to the press — obviously, matters that may warn the murderer to take precautions and so on. However, letting the silencer rumour gain a foothold was counter-productive to encouraging information that would help catch the gunman and it should have been corrected as soon as it surfaced. Of course, the way the Dando murder was analysed and reported by the press was disgraceful, but Campbell lost the real plot in his willingness to see the crime reporters get egg on their faces.

It is not too difficult to see why he let the false theories gain a foothold, then, with the mien of an exasperated headmaster, publicly give the culprits six of the best. McPherson had reported on the Lawrence Inquiry exactly two months before the Dando murder, and the Met had become open season in the press for 'institutionalised racism', inefficiency and incompetence. The roasting that the press had given the Metropolitan murder squad detectives over the bungled investigation and subsequent Lawrence Inquiry was still rumbling on at this time. It was a devastating indictment, which no conscientious detective could shrug off and Campbell is nothing if not conscientious.

With my hardening Serb theory, I cycled off towards Fulham Palace Road following the route taken by the gunman and again I found myself thinking that this did not make sense. Just like the hanging around with a loaded gun in a burglary-conscious street, if the gunman was mindful of not being caught, he took off in the wrong direction. He could not anticipate that he would shoot Dando without anyone seeing him and maybe shadowing him. In fact, any realistic appraisal of what he faced would go towards anticipating that he would be noticed and followed. He had a gun to deter any have-a-goers but he was also on foot, so his own safety cried out for him to take the shortest route to where he could turn off and also optimise his chances of losing anyone on his tail.

When he left number 29, he either went left towards Fulham Palace Road or right towards Munster Road. Going towards Fulham Palace Road is bad news — compared with Munster Road, it is twice as far to walk before you can turn off. Moreover, when you reach Munster Road, you have the option of taking five different routes, plus you have the cover of more cars and pedestrians compared with what you face going towards Fulham Palace Road. A child — or, to use Mansfield's phrase, 'a Maigret with a mental age of seven' — faced with this choice would scream, 'Go right.' Instead, the gunman went left.

On the first days of the murder inquiry, Oxborough made two critical blunders. The first was to ignore their two eye-witnesses to the murder, which led to the wrong E-fit, and the second was not to grasp or, at least, not forget that there must have been an extremely good reason why the gunman had turned left and not right. If they had grasped or remembered this, when Barry George came into the frame they would immediately have appreciated why he went left.

He turned left because he had planned, after changing his clothes on the way, to visit a local advice centre — HAFAD (Hammersmith and Fulham Action for Disability). The route to

HAFAD is almost directly east, which is the direction he took when he turned left at number 29 Gowan Avenue.

Oxborough's review of the low-grade suspects on 26 February 2000 spewed up the name Bulsara — aka George — for action, because of the HAFAD reports. The computer system into which all the early reports had been filed contained numerous messages from HAFAD naming Bulsara. Ten months later, Oxborough decided to proof George for the murder. The detective assigned to do this only got started on 6 February and didn't make contact with George until 11 April. It was a low-priority action.

Of course, any detective who still remembered the puzzle of why the gunman turned left and not right would have gone 'Bingo' when the review threw up the HAFAD messages naming Bulsara (George). If he got there soon after the murder as the HAFAD messages indicated, it solves the puzzle as to why the gunman turned left after the murder. And once you get this, you prioritise George. But Oxborough didn't because no one with any clout on the squad made the connection.

Even if this is excused as an oversight, the way Oxborough compounded it cannot. What George could not do because of the distances involved was commit the murder, leave the scene of the crime by turning left towards Fulham Palace Road, double back to his flat in Crookham Road to change, then reach HAFAD by noon. Nonetheless, in a blunder of all blunders, Oxborough decided that George did exactly this; thereby handing him a watertight alibi, which without a couple of jurors donning a wet suit would have seen him walk at trial. Where the blunder is compounded is that, even when one puts aside the timing problem, it contradicts the imperative of George going home to change. If he intended to or did go home after the kill, he would have turned right towards Munster Road after the murder. That is by far his best route to make it back to Crookham Road and, turning right rather than left as he leaves the murder scene, also gives him much better cover and options on losing any followers.

Oxborough would never have made this blunder of assuming that he went home to change — which set up his alibi — if, at the outset, they had realised that no gunman as methodical as the murderer patently was would turn left without a compelling reason that overrode the advantages of turning right.

Why did Oxborough lose the plot? The squad was certainly not collectively stupid. The oddity of the gunman's behaviour in turning left was as obvious to any seasoned detective as it was to me on my first visit. The problem was that the insight got lost in Detective Superintendent Campbell's system — Oxborough's computer programme HOLMES. At the start of the investigation, Campbell had appealed to the public for information, then watched his squad being deluged by it. To regain control, he became fixated with organising his squad in the gigantic task of classifying and filing this information into HOLMES.

Computers don't have judgement — neither, as Mansfield pounded home to the jury in his closing speech, does Campbell. He told them, 'The last person's judgement you can trust in this case is Mr Campbell's.' Campbell is hard-working, intelligent and conscientious, but he has the classic failing — he has tunnel vision and little imagination. No more clearly was this illustrated than in the way that the oddity of the gunman's left turn was forgotten by the time George was arrested.

As I cycled down Gowan Avenue, I put aside the bizarre choice of the gunman turning left and followed the consensual route suggested by the reports. He crossed Fulham Palace Road in a panic-stricken dash, then went into Bishop's Park, before coming back on himself to stand by a bus stop, ignoring two buses until finally boarding the third. This was Sweating Man upon whom the E-fit was based. I couldn't make sense of it. As Alan Farthing was later to describe the entire murder, it was 'surreal' — and that was an understatement.

To me, this confirmed the Serb theory, which is how I wrote it up in my first article on the murder. I wrote that it looked like a cause-driven murder committed by a freelance local gunman, who had military experience, and who was so outraged by NATO's bombing of Serbia that he had acted with as much concern for his safety as a kamikaze pilot. Incensed by the bombing, the final straw was the Tomahawk attack on Milosovic's own Serbian TV station, which killed 13 journalists. He selected Jill Dando both because she worked for the BBC, and because she had fronted a Kosovo refugee appeal only a week before she was murdered. The BBC would also be considered a more legitimate target than the commercial stations because it is more identified with the State. I padded this out with reference to the fact that, while not many Serbs live in London, many of them have gravitated to the Fulham area. Thus opportunity was another factor.

I argued that that Serb theory fitted more of the known facts than the alternatives, but in my conclusion I hedged my bets: 'Of course, much more by luck than planning, the man slipped the enveloping police dragnet and is unlikely, if he is a Serb, to be arrested until and if information begins to filter out on the grapevine. What we can be sure of is that the media's passion for theory-mongering will not speed up the process. As with Princess Diana, the reporting on the Jill Dando case is likely to stand as a monument to the media's taste for letting theories drive the facts rather than ensuring that the facts always drive the theories. The Serbian connection may fall down as the investigation unfolds, but to say at this stage that it is "far-fetched" is to report in the cause of ignorance, not truth.'

By the time the article was on the stands, I was already feeling uneasy about even my hedged bet. But when anyone points out that I keep changing my mind, I always invoke Maynard Keynes — when the facts change, so do I.

3

enter mr hughes

Even before my first article hit the streets, my doubts about going for a Serb surfaced in my personal diary. On 1 May, I recorded how, the morning after I'd returned, James got me to cover the murder and I had just filed my piece '... but I have a feeling that I have backed the wrong theory — Serb. Time will soon adjudicate.' I had not realised this when I wrote the article, but the truth of the Serb theory was a hostage to a very short-term future. Even if no one was arrested or no organisation claimed responsibility, rumours would quickly circulate and, at the very least, the security forces would pick up some kind of vibe from Belgrade.

There was also another factor that I had not worked out at the time. Even Milosevic's knuckle-draggers tend to pay a bit of lip service to Serb chivalry. At Srebrnica, they separated the men from the women and children and executed only the men. Serbs tend to rape, not kill women.

By the following day, my diary records how I was back-tracking: 'I think I have fucked up big time with Dando. Everything seems to be pointing towards an ex. I sent James a long message this morning to that effect but he hasn't replied.' Of course, my piece had gone to print and it was no good agonising over it now. Meanwhile, Tiina was on the warpath. She had rejected my carefully drafted Jane defence as an aggravating offence. It was not a good time for me.

After the magazine with the cover IT'S NO HITMAN — subtext, 'It's a Serb' — was on the news-stands, a researcher from ITN's *Tonight with Trevor McDonald* rang me and asked me to do a location interview on the murder for their next show. Normally, my attitude to TV is to negotiate as big a fee as the budget will stand, turn up without any preparation, unzip my mouth and talk for my cheque. The only time I take TV seriously is when I call, cut and edit the shots, but B-list talking heads like myself never enjoy that control. Partly to compensate for the indignity of only being able to do it on the programme-makers' terms, I have developed a mercenary and 'take it or leave it' attitude to TV work. However, I wasn't like that with the *Tonight with Trevor McDonald* gig. I saw it and reacted to it as a heaven-sent opportunity to slide out of the Serb camp before I next went into print.

The proof of how badly I wanted the gig was I never mentioned money! And I always mention that; I respond to any TV enquiry with a short audition that will make them want me, then, after whetting their appetite, I ask what the fee is. After making noises that indicate I wouldn't have auditioned if I'd known it was so paltry, I proceed to jack it up. It is all part of the fun of journalism, but with this particular *Tonight with Trevor McDonald* I think I would have paid them to appear.

I turned up on 14 May for my stand-up routine to camera — my piece was going to be broadcast head-to-head with a similar piece done by an ex-Flying Squad Commander, John O'Connor. We are both media tarts and are doubtless regarded by TV producers as 'how-much' contributors. However, setting the criminal views against those of an ex-detective is typical of the sort of cliché'd thinking that passes for creativity in TV. Ironically, O'Connor was now going for Serb for the same reasons I'd originally suggested.

My ex-theory, though, only worked once you hedged in all sorts of qualifications. As I had discounted an underworld or amateur hit-man, the obvious implication was that the ex in question would have to be the gunman. Yet, that possibility had already been discounted by Oxborough. They had the E-fit — which I didn't at that stage know was a major Oxborough bungle — and access to Dando's phone records and diary, so it beggared belief that an ex could have done it and had not been arrested by now. Oxborough was not only a 'total investigation', it was an 'all hands to the pump' one, too — the then Met Police Commissioner, Paul Condon, had given Campbell carte blanche on manpower and resources.

The only way the ex theory could stand up was if he had recruited not an amateur or professional hit-man but someone with a military or mercenary background, like a moonlighting IRA or Loyalist killer. Despite changing horses very early on and not feeling too steady on the new one, I never once wobbled on the military feel of the kill. Nonetheless, although I was pleased to dump Serb, I didn't feel too happy about being pushed back to hit-man — albeit one from a military or para-military background. It felt weaselly. Plus I could knock it down myself as no paid gunman would hang around the way her killer had ... and then there was his surreal getaway! Why turn left towards Fulham Palace Road?

As I stood on the pavement along from number 29, from which the tarpaulin tent had now been removed, I felt like I was jumping from the frying pan into the fire. As I waited for my cue to begin *spieling* to camera, my head was reeling with all the irresolvable and conflicting facts and theories. Although it was only about 11.00am, I promised myself that the first call of nature after I'd finished would be the nearest pub for a large vodka. I had a radio mike clipped to my clothing; in front of me was the reporter who was standing next to the cameraman and behind them was the producer who was also using a small camcorder. The reporter said, 'Ready?' I nodded nervously. I began walking while the cameraman and reporter backed off keeping the same distance.

'Now, John McVicar, you have written about the murder of Jill Dando. Can you tell us how this crime is going to be solved?' Like, while you're at it, can you explain to us the meaning of life, too?

Apart from my turmoil at the problem of taking a safe path through the evidential minefield of this case, I could also hear James's voice ringing in my ear — 'Don't forget to plug the mag in such a way that they can't cut it.' I looked down the lens.

'This murder is one of the most perplexing crimes ever faced by the Metropolitan Police.' Around this time, *perplexing* was one of my glitter words. 'It has dominated the media and, such is our fascination with the case, it has made armchair detectives of us all ...' I knew that was a line that no producer would want to go, so now was the moment to drop in a plug for *Punch* ... 'We at *Punch* have spent endless manholes going over and over ... Fuck. Sorry.' I had fluffed 'man-hours' but it was hardly Dennis Norden out-take material.

We cued up again. As I ruminated on what I was going to say again, in my peripheral vision I saw a guy come out of the door next to Dando's place. He stood there looking at the shoot — well, spectacle, more like. Early-30s, stocky, jeans but an expensive leather jacket; dark unruly hair over a typical public school face; pampered, confident, self-aware, supercilious ... however, the overriding impression was that this man had the world on his shoulders. He was worry personified.

'OK.' The reporter caught my attention as he cranked up to shoot again.

My second take went well and we moved off down the route the gunman had taken, stopping every now and again to do a piece to camera. I got in all the qualifications I had for thinking it was an ex, some of which were broadcast, but now that I had come off Serb and I was toying with what seemed the best of the alternatives, I was actually more confused. In some respects, Serb still fitted more of what was known than any other theory. The trouble was that it was fatally flawed by there being no confirmation either in a propaganda claim or through the grapevine. We were over three weeks on from the kill and nothing. Time had put Serb to proof and scratched it as a runner. Alternatively, I could not see how anyone recruited by an ex could commit such a surreal yet clinical murder.

Once the shoot was over, I bade my goodbyes to the *Tonight with Trevor McDonald* crew, then cycled back to *Punch* to drag James out to the Swag & Tails ... not that he ever needs much dragging. I had forgotten about Dando's neighbour, and all that was on my mind was to get some alcohol down me and escape a tongue-lashing from Caroline for my jaunt with Tiina. As I hadn't visited the office since returning, she still hadn't had her pound of flesh on that, but I knew she would ... with interest. When I was outside

Harrods, I rang James on my mobile saying I'd see him round the Swag. However, he said to come up as he wanted to show me the flat plan (the proposed layout of the mag) for the next edition. I agreed, mainly because I knew I would have to run the Caroline gauntlet some time and fate seemed to be decreeing that I face it now.

I locked up my bike on the railings on the elevated section opposite Harrods and, after greeting George the doorman, I trudged up the two flights of stairs. I knew Caroline would be sitting at her screen by the door to the *Punch* complex waiting for me to make her day. She was only the office secretary but I, like everyone, sucked up to her as she handled all the journalists' routine enquiries, managed payments and travel. Just as Campbell had a mantra — the 'system' — James's was 'Ask Caroline'.

I had dressed casually but smartly for the *Tonight with Trevor McDonald* gig, which was a noticeable change from the usual sweatshirt, cycling leggings and baseball cap. As I walked into the open plan office with its 14 or so big-screen computers, printers and photocopiers manned by around nine or so staff, I saw Caroline's eyes swivel as she picked me up. She kept her head facing the screen, her straight, straw-blonde hair hanging down to her shoulders. I could hear her meagre supply of brain cells whirring as she tried to compose a sarcastic greeting.

As I walked past in the direction of James's office on the far side, I said breezily, 'Hi, Caroline.'

'Hell-o, stranger,' she oozed in a slight country burr. 'Are we all too old for you now?'

I kept walking.

She shouted so that everybody heard it, 'It's all right. James has told me not to mention her.' A couple of the other female staff had tuned in to her number and they sniggered.

I stopped and turned my head. 'Caroline, I know who killed Dando but I am not going to tell the cops until he kills one more blonde.'

'John McVicar,' she said indignantly, 'what a thing to say. I've a good mind to report you to the Parole Board.'

As she spoke, I suddenly remembered the neighbour and realised that he lived right next door to Dando. Although I had seen him come out of number 31, I had been too absorbed in what I was going to say to camera for it to register. I grinned at Caroline and continued towards James, my mind racing to recall my impressions of him. Before I had turned into James's office, I was sure that I had seen the face of a very worried man before it registered that he was Dando's neighbour. As that passed the reality check, I felt the hunch of a new theory. I felt it — and had bagged the reward.

James was leaning back in his leather swivel chair with his feet crossed neatly on his desk, while he spoke into the phone in his right hand. As he saw me, he clasped his left hand, which was holding a burning cigarette, over the mouthpiece. 'Hi, Johns. It's Mo'. I'll be with you in a sec.' He continued talking to the Chairman, while I wandered over to look at a flat plan for the next edition. I saw that my column was up at the front end of the mag, which meant that I would have to file early — something that I hated nearly as much as the actual writing of it. I scowled, wondering what excuse I could come up with to go to the back of the queue.

James finished with Mo'. He turned to me. 'How did it go this morning? Did you manage to get a plug in for the mag that can't be cut?'

As Al Fayed would not give any more cash to promote the mag, James fought a constant battle with the national press and TV to plug it on the fly. No media outlet wants its contributors to advertise other publications, but *Punch* in particular, because it is owned by Al Fayed. The media generally saw Al Fayed as just a rich scallywag on the social climb. The argy-bargy that went on around trying not to give *Punch* credit for anything because of Al Fayed was one of those games that everyone knows everyone else is playing without any of the players acknowledging what is going on. I started to explain what had occurred that morning and why I thought my plug would be screened.

'Let's discuss it over a glass of wine,' James said. Glass! Couple of bottles, more like. We walked out of the office and, as we passed Caroline, he told her that if anyone important called, he was on the mobile. She eyeballed me but didn't say anything. We strolled along the Old Brompton Road chatting about the magazine, but once ensconced in the corner of the Swag with a bottle of Pinot Grigio in the ice bucket and two half-filled glasses in our hands, I took him through my piece to camera, including my impression of the neighbour. I stressed how I'd seen the worried look before I connected it to the guy coming out of the adjoining door to Dando's.

James remembered him from the TV coverage of the time and said there were references to him in the papers. He said, 'There was something that struck me about what he said at the time that didn't make sense. He heard her scream and passed it off as a joke or something but he didn't hear the shot. I can remember thinking — that doesn't add up. In fact, a lot of people must have wondered because it was odd. I'll get Caroline to dig out the cuts on him ...'

I had missed this in my reading of the reports, but then I had been more concerned with proofing the different theories that were being touted. I pointed out to James that we had dismissed the celebrity stalker because it didn't stack up and, anyway, given that that was the hot favourite with the tabloids, it was bound to be wrong. Yet, you could have an obsessive who had secretly become fixated on her, not through the media, but through living next door to her. And this would sidestep one of the uncanny features of the case in that, as there was no pattern to her rare visits to number 29, how could the gunman know she was going to show that morning? It left out to dry the reports of the guy hanging around, but it fitted more of the facts than a moonlighting paramilitary hired by an ex.

James threw the spanner in my new works. 'But the killer did hang around, so it couldn't be the neighbour. And he did bolt off and end up waiting for a bus in the Fulham Palace Road and *he* could not be the neighbour, either.'

There was an irrefutable logic to this, which I ruefully conceded. But I added, 'James, this guy looked worried out of his life. It really hit me on the head.'

'So what? His wife is on to to his call girl habit ... his business has crashed. It could be any number of things. It doesn't have to go to Dando.'

Again, I had to accept I was snatching at straws. I confessed, 'I am getting addicted to this case. It's a conundrum that, in some respects, must be for the cops to solve as they know so much more than anyone else. Yet, you feel they are missing the plot somehow. They can't even work out the motive, which means that while they know more, it ain't doing them any good. Why kill her? Serb is no longer a runner but ex is equally fraught. The ex can't have done it himself, which means he has recruited someone — someone with a military background.'

James followed me, nodding, as I ticked off the points.

'Now let's put aside the hanging around and the bizarre getaway. Let's look at the police checking this out. The ex has to have some contact with the guy, he has to have paid for the hit. It beggars belief that with the powers the cops have — phone records, bank statements, credit card details — that they couldn't pick up some suspicious tell-tale leads. They have virtually third degree'd these guys — even Farthing — because ex is the obvious favourite, and come up with zilch. It is weird this, James.'

James listened carefully. 'I know what you mean, John. But once ex and Serb go, where do you look? Stalker? But as you've said — and I agree with you — stalkers show themselves before they strike. But maybe someone in her circle developed a secret obsession with her and when she was going to marry Farthing he flipped? What about that?'

'Like the neighbour?' I grinned. He shook his head and turned down his mouth. 'OK,' I continued. 'The problem is that she is not the sort of woman who, if you knew her, you could dislike. I am getting a feel for her. She may have been just another face of dumbed-down television, but I bet even I would not have disliked her.'

James laughed as it is a standing joke that I dislike far more people than I like.

'No, really,' I concluded, 'she was a genuine woman who everyone seemed to like, which is why Middle England loved her.'

'Jealousy, John. The green-eyed monster can neutralise anything ... She is marrying Farthing and that week she is on the front of the *Radio Times* in leather and straddling an Aston Martin. The object of his secret love is leaving him for another man, rejecting him.'

I screwed up my face and wondered to myself how anyone but a retired bank manager could fire up a passion for Jill Dando. But a lot of commentators had seen this connection and made it the trigger that flipped the killer.

Although the *Radio Times* cover was only to promote a new

antiques programme that she was fronting, Dando had thrown off the Laura Ashley summer frocks for the leather look, all raunchy and Avenger-ish. To my eyes, the shot shows a woman who is clearly not raunchy not only trying to be raunchy but also looking desperately self-aware that this is all a ghastly mistake. Her expression is of a woman who is fighting to hold back her embarrassment. The photographer who did the shoot, Barry Holmes, was later to say, 'She had worn leather before but she was rather coy asking, "Is this really me?"'

Nevertheless, it figured in a lot of the theorising revolving around stalkers, obsessives, erotomaniacs. What made this area even more engaging for the commentators was that on the back cover of this edition there was a full-page book ad for a thriller, which asked rhetorically: 'Couldn't you just murder?' This was another feature of the case that I hadn't gone with, but you couldn't entirely discount it. Perhaps the most eloquent proponent of it was a US lawyer named Rhonda Saunders whom Oxborough consulted about celebrity stalking. The *Mail on Sunday* quoted her on 9 January 2000:

> *Most stalkers who haunt famous people suffer from a syndrome called erotomania. They believe they are totally in love with the celebrity and that person loves them back. Very often, they amass huge private collections of material related to their obsession … In most celebrity cases, the stalker builds up a false idea that they have a relationship with the star. They see the celebrity on television and in magazines and they think they have a connection. When that connection is thwarted or when their romantic overtures are snubbed, the obsession turns to rage and anger and, occasionally, cold-blooded murder.*

Of course, I had rejected celebrity stalker from the beginning, mainly because stalkers reveal themselves to their victim in such a way that, if they strike, it makes them easy to catch, but also because Jill Dando was just not the sort of woman who could incite cold-blooded murder in a would-be stalker. In response to my turning up my nose at the jealousy motive, James retorted, 'John, what you have to remember is someone did it and he will have his reasons. He may be mad, but you can bet they will make sense to him.'

Later on during the trial of Barry George, I was reminded of this conversation with James. By then, I was studying — at the urging of my colleague Benjamin Pell — the lyrics and albums of Queen, when I noticed that 'Jealousy' and 'Dead on Time' were on the same album. It was coincidental that the early favourite on the motive for the kill — jealousy — and my title for this book — *Dead on Time* — were both song titles on the same Queen album. It was just a coincidence that also had no significance but, as these things do, it still caught my eye.

Benjamin Pell who assisted me at the trial is extremely good at spotting and developing such coincidences into what we called 'symmetricals'. For instance, Barry's George's trial overlapped with that of Jeffrey Archer. They both began their sentences in HMP Belmarsh and were there at the same time. They both share the same birthday — 15 April, with a 20-year gap. He is Lord Archer of Weston-Super-Mare, which is where he was born; so was Jill Dando and she is buried there, too. She started out her career working for the *Weston Mercury* newspaper, for which Archer's mother, who died at the end of his trial, wrote a column during his childhood. George changed his name to Bulsara, the real surname of Freddie Mercury — *Weston Mercury*. Boom, boom ... Dando shared a dance with Archer at a charity bash at the Natural History

Museum two days before her murder; before he shot Dando, George, in a macabre dance of death held his arm around her to force her on to the ground. With Farthing in between, they were probably the last three people to put their arms around her!

OK, so what? Well, just as some people, like Mansfield, sniff conspiracy behind any coincidence, there are others who read or, perhaps more accurately, attribute significance to any such chain of coincidences. We all encounter coincidences and people differ as to how readily they assign irrational significance to them, but some of us are highly susceptible to invoking superstition or even supernaturalism. Traditionally, this kind of mystical interpretation is called cabbalism, which involves using esoteric methods and ciphers for extracting meaning from sacred texts. Writers still use cabbalism to interpret the Bible and demonstrate, for example, how it predicted all the apocalyptic events of the twentieth century. Such books periodically enter the bestsellers lists, which shows that a lot of people entertain this kind of thinking. Indeed, in the modern world, cabbalistic thinking is very common in secular matters and is sometimes referred to as 'magical thinking'. You see it in people who, when they can't work out how the magician makes the lady vanish, are quite happy to attribute it to magic. But such people also act on the basis of their magical beliefs.

Gamblers, for example, often pick up on coincidences as mystical symbols of luck, then make bets using these magical beliefs. They have lucky numbers or they observe certain rituals, like stroking a lucky coin to influence the future, or they will have an esoteric system for willing the dice to roll a winning combination. In a dramatically different context, but expedited by the same type of magical thinking, a militant Palestinian will hijack a plane or strap a bomb to himself and blow him and everyone else into kingdom come. Such kamikaze martyrs will go to their death serene in the belief that they will awaken in paradise with their 40 virgins. From one reference in the Old Testament, extreme Zionists see it as their God-given right to colonise the whole of the Holy Land, 'Terra Sancta'. Both these examples are strictly cabbalistic, but the point I am making is that magical thinking makes perfect sense to those who practise it.

The reason I am now flagging the issue of magical thinking is that it is critical to understanding George's motives. As Benjamin and I plotted the fault lines in George's head again and again, one of us would use the phrase 'You couldn't make it up'. Naturally, this was accompanied with the obligatory shaking of the head in the face of some astonishing fact that in a novel or a play would strain credulity. George is a magical thinker, as was his idol-cum-alter ego, Freddie Mercury. Moreover, the murder of Jill Dando was driven by George's magical thinking and cabbalistic interpretation of Queen lyrics, Ninjutsu mythology and evangelical Christianity.

In May 1999, James and I did not have the imagination or the clues to move beyond speculating about emotionally-driven delusions to even considering the esoteric delusions of a magical thinker. We petered out in trying to make sense of it all, fell silent and poured wine on our confusion. James shifted the ground slightly and asked me what was coming out of the Dando squad. I told him not much; Campbell was tight-arsed and aloof from the press. He didn't like his squad fraternising with hacks. Most of the purported leaks, like the silencer, seemed to have been invented by crime reporters. James thought about it and added, 'Look, I'll talk to Macnamara and see if he can dig around for us. He is bound to know someone on the squad.'

John Macnamara was Al Fayed's head of security and another

high-ranking ex-Scotland Yard detective who went during one of the periodic purges of the Flying Squad. Macnamara was Mo's Mr Fix-It. That was what he was paid for and that was what he did. He paid off the squawkers, cajoled the journalists, briefed the lawyers and, not least, kept his Big Brother-ish eye on Al Fayed's staff.

For £10,000 he bought, via Benjamin Pell — who, apart from helping me, is a celebrated bin-raider — a draft copy of the questions that Neil Hamilton's barrister put to Al Fayed when he went into the witness box during their libel trial. It enabled Al Fayed, who had never gone into the witness box before, to put in a bravura performance, which won over the jury.

The person who passed the documents to Macnamara was a journalist. In Tom Bowyer's exposure of Al Fayed in *Fayed: The Unauthorised Biography*, Bowyer exposes not only the organ grinder, but also his monkeys. The book shows why of all Al Fayed's hirelings, Macnamara was the one you didn't cross: as a close associate of Al Fayed's once told me, 'He just lets you glimpse the grief he can cause you; I think even Mo' fears him.'

However, Al Fayed's 'cash for questions' scam unravelled because the intermediaries fell out. At the end of 2000, 12 months after the libel verdict, Hamilton's appeal was heard in the High Court. Hamilton's case was mainly based on the cash for questions abuse of due process that had occurred at the trial. Al Fayed had to give evidence again. It was a different story this time. He was humiliated and broken by cross-examination — his only answer to questions about how he had benefited from Macnamara's abuse of due process was 'I don't remember'. He said it 43 times. Although the panel headed by Master of the Rolls Lord Phillips upheld the libel jury's verdict, it condemned Al Fayed. It came out during this appeal that Macnamara had left Harrods employment and was in

South Africa. It is rumoured that Al Fayed paid him a half a million bonus on top of his £100,000-a-year salary for his fidelity.

Needless to say, Macnamara is a marvellous contact for a journalist.

4

the system's man

While James put the feelers out in Macnamara's direction, Oxborough's 50 or so officers were out on their allotted wild goose chases. It was about three weeks after the murder. Campbell had his system up and running, which was a computer system running HOLMES 2 (Home Office Large Major Enquiry System). Blue Range Rovers were being tracked down; more than 80,000 mobile phone owners who had made calls in the Gowan Avenue area around the time of the murder were being traced; footage from 191 public and private CCTV cameras in the Fulham and Hammersmith area was being examined and logged; statements were being taken from an eventual total of 2,400 people; firearms experts were examining the cartridge and bullet with its bizarre markings; public reports about men resembling the E-fit were being checked out; visitors to websites featuring Jill Dando were being tracked down; her own e-mail records, plus 14,000 received by the BBC after her death, were being scrutinised; any man who had shown an obsessive interest in her was being investigated ... this was 'total investigation' by Campbell's system.

John Macnamara has a steely presence. He is a no-nonsense, 'let's get down to business' sort of man, but also one who is used to wielding power over others. He has broken far more people's careers and lives than he has made, although that is more to do with the kind of authority he has exercised rather than any psychological malevolence. He comes over as a man who does not place much faith in human beings; a lifetime of looking for and seeing flaws in people would hardly do otherwise. Yet he has led a successful life both as a detective and as Al Fayed's head of security. He is a good judge of people and places his trust in those who pass his scrutiny.

About a week after my conversation with James, I wandered into the Swag around midday to meet up with him and Macnamara. The place was packed but I spotted Bernie Ecclestone in a huddle with someone and thought how, despite being far richer than Mo', he had none of the security apparatus around him or the paranoia that Macnamara provided for our Chairman. As always when he saw me in the Swag, he stared at me with daggers drawn. Yet, over Battersea Park, he was quite happy to let his kids and his bulldog Fudgie play with Clem, my dog. *Punch* had turned him over some time back, but tell me what public figure hadn't been given a good pasting in the magazine when James was editor! Thankfully, he and Macnamara were tucked well away from Bernie.

James greeted me with the usual humorous rebuke at my unpunctuality. 'I was laying a sweepstake with John that you'd be at least 15 minutes late, so as it is only five I'll get them in.'

As James ordered me a beer, I mumbled some sort of apology to Macnamara who was smartly dressed in a grey suit with a black leather briefcase at his feet. I shook hands with him.

'I've been reading your column,' he began, his eyes watching me. 'Good stuff. Very interesting. You're getting a lot of inside information.' He was in his late 50s but, although he had worked all his life in London, he still retained a slight Scottish burr. I shuffled around, alternatively making appreciative and self-deprecatory noises, aware that he was assessing me.

However, I did add that the reason I was getting inside stuff was more to do with Benjamin Pell than me. Pell was supplying me with a lot of griff around that time. He looked puzzled at the mention of Pell and I told him that Benjamin made his living hitting the binbags of agents and solicitors of the rich and famous, then selling the newsworthy stuff to Fleet Street. As I told him, it rang a bell ... Pell was creeping into the press but I could also see Macnamara mentally noting that he must check if Harrods' rubbish was vulnerable to such a sting.

James gave me my beer and began to explain that Macnamara might have a lead for us. I was startled at such an early result as Macnamara had not even hinted as much to me, but James dampened my enthusiasm. 'Hold on, John, it is early days but John has something that ...'

Macnamara took over. 'I couldn't find anyone on the squad but, as luck would have it, I have a woman who does some legal work for us who has. It's her brother. He's only a DC [detective constable] ... I am going to *talk* to him tonight.'

His intonation and his use of 'DC' suggested that, while it had been ten years since his Detective Chief Superintendent days at the Yard, he was quite confident that he could pull rank. There was probably the carrot of work for his sister, too. Macnamara is an operator.

I was beside myself. 'That would be marvellous, John ... we're stuck because we are out of Campbell's press loop and, anyway, he keeps most of it under wraps. Most investigating officers running a high-profile inquiry know that you have to keep the press informed if only to stop them making it up. Campbell doesn't.' I shrugged.

Macnamara explained, 'This is the new breed, John. They are entirely different from the old school that you knew when you were at it. These are detectives who don't learn the job solving crimes but at Brahms Hill or university *studying* how to solve them. They rely on computers, not their contacts or their hunches. They work by collecting and collating information, not getting out to the crime scene and talking to witnesses. As for putting their foot in a door or cutting a corner or two, that isn't what the book says. You've go to understand that Hamish Campbell is a system's man.'

It was left there, but on the way back home to collect Clem and go for a run around the park, I thought about the remark 'system's man'. It smacked of methodical attention to detail, but also obsessiveness. The first time I saw Campbell in the flesh was when he gave evidence at the pre-trial in February 2001. As many of his answers to questions referred to 'the system', he soon launched into a description of it. After listening for a bit, I turned to another Dando book author, Brian Cathcart, who looked as gobsmacked as me at Campbell's labyrinthine and multi-layered system for storing information. I said quietly to Brian, 'Talk about setting an obsessive to catch another obsessive!'

The pre-trial is a vital prelude to any long or complex court case as it clarifies and tests the Crown's case in law. It is when the defence and the Crown argue before the trial judge about the admissibility or inadmissibility of evidence, whether there is a case to answer, whether rights have been breached that are an abuse of due process, whether publicity has made it impossible for the defendant to receive a fair trial, whether irregularities in procedure renders evidence unreliable and so on. Although the major issues are dealt with in the pre-trial hearing, other legal issues generally crop up during the trial. In those situations, the jury then retires, and they are thrashed out in a *voire dire* or trial within a trial. As all such legal argument takes place in the absence of the jury, it cannot be reported — not even the judge's rulings. This form of legal argument is an integral part of the adversarial system.

This is nothing to do with not trusting juries. It is applying the rules of evidence to ensure that the facts the jury are asked to deliberate on pass the rules of admissibility and, ultimately, meet the requirements of a civilised society.

The advantage for anyone monitoring a trial is that pre-trial proceedings tend to be far more rigorous and frank than anything that occurs before a jury, so one gets a comprehensive briefing on most of the evidence that will figure in the trial itself. Indeed, it is impossible to fully understand fully a long and/or complex trial without attending the pre-trial. However, the prohibition on reporting until after the trial means that such hearings are not that popular with members of the press, especially the run-of-the-mill crime reporter. In fact, it was glaringly obvious in the press coverage after the verdict that, with the odd exception, most of the crime reporters either did not attend the pre-trial or, if they did, did not understand it.

The contrast between the use of pre-trial evidence in reports of the George and Archer trials — the latter ended two weeks later — could not have been greater. Those who wrote about the

Archer trial after the verdict invariably used pre-trial evidence and arguments to inform the reader of the wider picture of some aspects of the case. The reason for the discrepancy in the two trials is simply that the Archer reports were often done by heavyweight journalists who know how to cover a trial properly.

The one exception to use of pre-trial evidence in the Dando case that I spotted was Mike Sullivan of the *Sun* (editor David Yelland calls it 'the copper's paper'). Headlined WHY TAKE 395 DAYS TO ARREST THIS MAN? THEY KNEW OF HIM FROM DAY 1, Sullivan, who covered some aspects of Campbell's system, including its inception just after the murder, wrote, 'A huge squad of 47 detectives was assembled over the [next] few days. They had back-up from a computer analyst and civilians to log details into a computer. One officer said, "There was more work on this job than all the other murders in Central London put together."'

What Sullivan did not point out was that the unavoidable consequence of the 'failure' of the system to identify George early could have meant that many other murders were not investigated properly because trained murder squad officers were tied up in the unnecessarily prolonged Dando inquiry. Thus, murderers who might otherwise have been convicted slipped the noose.

The pre-trial hearing opened on 26 February 2001. Campbell went into the witness box to answer questions about why, after having witnesses name him from day one, it had taken so long to arrest George. Aged then 44, he is a balding, stocky man with shortish legs, which gives him a low centre of gravity — a big advantage in his preferred sport, judo. He is, as his name suggests, of Scottish extraction, but grew up in England. Like Barry George, he has an interest in martial arts but, unlike George, successfully practises one, in that he is a judo black belt. Curiously enough, the jury was told that in 1988 when he was a detctive sergeant, he stopped George at Shepherd's Bush on suspicion and took down his details, but the jury was told that he could not remember the incident. His voice is soft and well modulated. He certainly does not look like a detective or someone who is successfully climbing the career ladder of his chosen profession. The image he presents is more that of a bland, tidy, self-employed small businessman.

Policemen invariably swear on the Bible when they give evidence, often with a theatrical flourish on words like 'swear', 'truth' and 'almighty God'. Yet, witnesses who affirm are consistently more truthful. Campbell affirms. He stood in the witness box with his hand on either side of it and explained that the tidal wave of false clues was 'one of the key features in the investigation'. There was so much information that it 'approached unmanageable proportions'. The *system* was installed to manage it.

Information came in as 'messages', which were taken down by 'receivers', then, after being fed into the computer running HOLMES, was assessed by the receiver or an 'intelligence officer' for 'actions' to be taken. 'Research officers' would take a more analytical approach to the information coming in, and overseeing the whole system was an 'office manager' with Campbell in overall charge. As Campbell explained at trial, 'It was an attempt to try and organise a large amount of information coming into what I call "stranger homicide" investigations, where there is no immediate motive and no immediate suspect and it was following a simple strategy of dealing in the first instance with eye-witnesses; what happened to the victim? How was that person killed? Where were they killed? When were they killed?'

Obviously, messages naming suspects were vital and, at pre-trial, Campbell explained how there were three categories of suspects. 'An inner circle of friends, family and lovers or ex-lovers

... people who knew Miss Dando ... and third, people who didn't know Miss Dando.'

Within these three categories — 'the suspects pool' — points were given to each suspect so that they were prioritised for investigation. This was called 'the queuing system' and, on the basis of how they were queued, each suspect was put into a hierarchy of 'five boxes'. Receivers would then allocate 'actions' on the basis of the message's position in the queue in the particular box. An action could be to check out a suspect but it also included 'any instruction to an officer to complete a piece of work, whether it is to take a statement, to trace a witness, to find a car, anything that is recorded and given an action number.' The problem with Campbell's system is that it became more important than what it was supposed to do.

This was head-banging time and even Mansfield, before he began turning up the heat, looked slightly nonplussed as Campbell's train-spotting mind revelled in the details of the system. Justice Gage, who behaved with impeccable neutrality and respect for the law throughout all the proceedings, looked askance at the normally reserved Campbell's animation. Mansfield, however, swiftly cut to the quick. The issue was why, given that George was in its system from day one of the murder, Oxborough hadn't checked him out until ten months later.

After the kill, George walked to a local advice centre, HAFAD, where he made himself busy in order to be noticed before leaving and talking to a woman, Julia Moorhouse, in a nearby street. She was the first witness to report George to Oxborough. George then went to a minicab office on the Fulham Palace Road, where he attracted so much attention that the controller, Ramesh Paul, also reported him to Oxborough on 26 April. He added that the driver who had driven George to his destination said that he had been 'agitated'.

The day after the murder, a woman along from George's flat, Susan Oddy, also rang in anonymously to say that the police should look at the oddball in number 4 (actually, he lived next-door in 2b) who used air guns and a crossbow. She followed up this call on 15 May, giving her name and saying that the oddball was called Barry Bulsara. On this occasion, Oddy actually queried why no one had linked George to the murder.

Two days after the murder, George returned to both HAFAD and the minicab office, this time mentioning Jill Dando and saying that he was worried about people saying he fitted the description of the murderer. HAFAD began ringing up, eventually pleading for the police to investigate George.

Mansfield composed a 12-point matrix of why Campbell's system should have been making very loud wake-up calls.

- All of the reports — 'messages' — put George very near the scene of the crime
- he was asking for a taxi at HAFAD
- it was at the relevant time
- he went in there on the 26th, the date of the murder
- he went back in there on the 28th, referring to the murder;
- by 12 May, the police would have known that he lived in Crookham Road which is near the scene of the murder
- he also said that he may have witnessed something pertaining to the murder
- HAFAD rang up four times in all
- the description given by HAFAD is not inconsistent with the descriptions that the police already had of the person at the scene of the crime

- the people at HAFAD thought he fitted the E-fit
- HAFAD gave not only his name, but also his date of birth
- finally, he was talking about Jill Dando when he was there on 28 May

Mansfield took Campbell through all this. In his inimitably sarcastic tone Mansfield commented at the time when Crookham Road was confirmed by HAFAD, 'If someone is doing their job, you now have Crookham Road ... the matrix of relevant factors is building up quite well, isn't it?'

'Not at the time,' Campbell answered dolefully.

Mansfield now put the complete 12-point matrix to him and then pointed out that on 15 May, an officer processing some of these messages decided to raise an action to check out George. Campbell did not know the name of this officer but Mansfield put to him, 'So, whoever that was also spotted that the message needed to be looked at. And that person did get it right, didn't he?'

Campbell replied evasively, 'There would then be full analysis of the queuing.' The point was that this officer had given it top priority, so Campbell was using the esoteric criteria of queuing to excuse the failure to follow up the recommendation.

Mansfield became exasperated with Campbell and said bullishly, 'But that is where the system becomes nonsense. It gives it a nominal number; it is given priority number 1; it goes into a queue as priority number 1; yet no one does anything about it.'

Campbell again tried to muddy the waters by invoking the dark arts of queuing but when Mansfield asked who the 'action George' officer was, Campbell replied lamely that he didn't know and would have to look it up. He never did and we never learned the officer's identity. Mansfield then turned to another HAFAD message, phoned in on 12 May, about Barry George being there and acting oddly at 11.00am on the morning of the murder.

The four HAFAD women came over as a topsy-turvy lot and were somewhat at sea with their timings. Nevertheless, the woman who rang in on 12 May spoke at length about George coming back on 28 April asking about what clothes he was wearing when he visited on the day of the murder because he fitted the description of the murderer and people suspected him. Prior to this message, they had stood on their policy of confidentiality to their clients, but in the circumstances that went by the board. She gave the Oxborough receiver George's address, name and date of birth. This was all taken down by Oxborough and fed into the system, but no one acted on it.

The point about HAFAD is while it was nothing in terms of evidence, it was everything as far as the investigation was concerned. Once George was investigated, then he fitted the bill to a T. However, the evidence that could convict him was like an organic substance that deteriorates over time, which was one of the few things Mansfield and Campbell agreed on.

Mansfield: 'Do you agree that time is of the essence in this case? The longer that something goes on, the greater the chance that evidence will evaporate.'

Campbell: 'Yes, I do.'

Confronted with the first HAFAD message (28 April) and its 11.00am time, Campbell replied confidently, 'That would not have been a priority for any action at that stage. 11.00am was half-an-hour before the murder — an individual attending an advice centre. Nothing to warrant attention.' Another message then that went into the queue for ten months.

Mansfield did not bother to rub Campbell's nose in his misplaced confidence as he had lots more of the same fish to fry.

However, Campbell was being obdurate. If the suspect was there at 11.00am on the day of the murder, nothing prevented him from committing it *after* attending the advice centre. HAFAD is six or seven minutes' walk from 29 Gowan Avenue.

It was obvious that in the early stages of the investigation, Oxborough either had information overload or they were inefficient — whatever the explanation, they missed the plot on all these messages about George. Too blinkered to see that he was defending the indefensible, Campbell kept obfuscating and prevaricating in the face of Mansfield's open contempt.

Now that he was champing at Campbell's failed system, Mansfield was like a dog with a bone. What went wrong with it? Campbell replied, 'I am not saying anything did go wrong with the system ... I do not believe there was any inaction on our part. That is the choice made in the framework of the investigation. This message was put into the queue.'

Mansfield now moved back to the unknown officer who had spotted the relevance and called for an action. He asked what criteria were used when it was queued but lost in the system. Campbell replied, 'I do not think it was lost in the system. We were assessing priority. The officer made the choice that it was one that should be queued. And that choice was put into the system.'

Campbell was visibly wearing down by now. A man who prides himself on being rational, he must have felt the psychological strain of being doggedly irrational. The point was, queuing with top priority meant, *as it had not been acted on*, that by definition it had been lost in the system.

Mansfield then moved on to another HAFAD message fingering George, this time on 19 May. This woman reported George as being very flustered and, when he came back two days later, said that he may have witnessed something. When Mansfield pressed him on the significance of this, Campbell wearily, but with a leavening of wit, replied, 'It doesn't make it very significant when one looks at it then. It only makes it look significant now.'

This spark of resistance seemed to inflame Mansfield who suddenly shouted at him, '**Then**, Mr Campbell, **please**, I suggest you should have been round there in a flash. Never mind queuing.'

'You would have actioned it,' Campbell replied with a touch of sarcasm, 'but that is not what happened.'

Mansfield then moved to the final HAFAD message, received on 14 June, and said to Campbell, 'If you needed the final nail in the information coffin, this is it. If you need it spelt out any further, this should be the call. Elaine Hutton rang up; she spoke to DC Souza — was he a retriever or an intelligence officer?'

Campbell feigned boredom. 'I don't know,' he replied. He had lost this battle but he wasn't going to give Mansfield any openings to decimate further his battered forces.

Mansfield was leaning forward on his lectern toying with a pen in his right hand — he looked like he was giving up on the bone and preparing to sink his fangs into Campbell's jugular. Where he'd been bullish, he was now wolfish. His soft, menacing tone was a mock version of a beguiling Little Red Riding Hood. 'They want to know if you will be taking a statement. Does it not matter to you; they appear rather keen and they are deeply concerned? They are constantly ringing up. No one even thought to ring them back or go down there. She repeated that he had kept on talking about Jill Dando. You wanted a link with Jill Dando. You have a man in an agitated state in a place that is not far away and he mentions Jill Dando.' He paused for Campbell's response to this rhetorical ambush.

Campbell replied calmly from inside the mental redoubt to which he'd retreated, 'On 14 June, that was not a priority action.

With your view and our view a year later, it is a shining light, but not then.'

Mansfield snapped back, 'But you do accept that there was failure.'

Campbell refused to be drawn. 'I have explained my interpretation of that failure.'

But both of them knew that this was just the stalking, the spring for the jugular was still to come. Mansfield led up to it with a general point about how it was vital that Campbell must have ensured that information was being correlated. He said, 'You don't want an officer with tunnel vision. At the end of each day, surely someone should summarise the messages and see what is relevant. Did the system allow someone to do that exercise?'

Campbell replied warily, 'There were various officers dealing with the information coming in.' Then, in reply to Mansfield's comment that surely someone was doing that at least by 28 April, he answered, 'I don't know.'

Mansfield then turned to one of the 20 or so lever files which were propped up like a shelf of books right across his bench. This one was already open at the relevant page. He read from it: 'In a report of November 2000 in Assessment Barry George, on page 51 you say, "Judgement with hindsight will not help at this time. There was a failure with regard to the Gresswell Centre (HAFAD), but the call from London Traffic Cabs was dealt with properly."'

It was just another Mansfield try-on, but Campbell reacted as if someone had been reading his diary behind his back. He replied indignantly, 'These were notes made for me, the Inspector and Sergeant and ultimately for a meeting. It was not an acknowledgement of fault.'

Mansfield stood looking at him, sighing, like one might at a child who is caught with his hand in the jar but denies trying to steal the cookies. It was a Category A act, but one that was never going to wash with the only audience that mattered, Justice Gage. Mansfield knew this, of course, but that would never have deterred him from trying — the hallmark of his advocacy is to challenge everything and anything relentlessly. This kind of comprehensive thoroughness can and does yield dividends from the most unexpected of sources. It also imposes an astonishing workload and requires a daunting attention to detail. Campbell, on the other hand, did not understand that this push by Mansfield was a phoney battle that he did not have to fight. Instead, he dug in behind his system and was pounded by Mansfield for it.

Mansfield spoke forcefully to Gage when summarising his 'justice delayed is justice denied' application. 'The trial process in this exceptional case will not be able to overcome the delay.' However, this argument depended on the delay in George's arrest being not merely a failure of the system but the fault of Oxborough. Mansfield put it to Gage, 'At first, Mr Campbell told me that it was a failure, not a fault, whatever that means. That is total nonsense.'

But in his ruling, Justice Gage dismissed it out of hand. It wasn't a fault, he ruled: 'What at the time seemed to be the most important lines were followed. It has not been demonstrated that there has been a failure in the system. If I am wrong, it was only a minor failure.'

One can split hairs over whether it was a fault or failure but clearly something went badly wrong. Again, it is a moot point whether what went wrong was due to the system or the Oxborough officers. The latter really means Campbell, who was in day-to-day charge of the inquiry, which in his case, given that he is a workaholic, meant most of the night, too. Yet, in all this, the biggest nail that could have been hammered in Campbell's information coffin, Mansfield, ironically, could not use because it might have damaged his client's case far more than it would have discredited Oxborough. But come the post-verdict, not one commentator on the case had picked up on it.

On the day of the murder, Campbell was called out to Gowan Avenue as news of what was first reported as a stabbing broke. He only learned it was Jill Dando, whom he knew from *Crimewatch*, en route; he arrived at the crime scene as her body was driven off at 12.30pm to Charing Cross Hospital. Her death was not announced until 1.00pm, but Campbell learned at the crime scene that it was curtains for her. He oversaw the setting up of police procedures for investigating a serious crime: the closure of Gowan Avenue; the sealing off of the area around number 29 for forensic analysis; uniformed officers were despatched to search for a weapon in the immediate vicinity; others conducted house-to-house enquiries for witnesses; some witnesses already at the scene were questioned; and so on.

Campbell stayed at the crime scene, and even briefed the press at 2.30pm in a characteristic, clipped fashion. He already knew that Dando had been shot but he kept it back, telling the press that the cause of death would be announced after the post mortem. He had already ordered police officers, even hospital and ambulance workers, not to reveal what they knew to the press. As always with Campbell, the knee-jerk reaction was to keep control. He expressed his personal concern about this 'terrible' murder and appealed for information from the general public. In fact, this constant refrain from Campbell — 'It is imperative that people come forward with information, however insignificant they may think it is' — was responsible for the tidal wave of calls that engulfed Oxborough.

However, despite what he was later to claim, the one thing he did not do was follow the Macnamara rule book — go to the heart of the crime scene. Go where the clues are to the killer. After securing the crime scene and ensuring that it had been preserved for forensic analysis, he should have gone to the two eye-witnesses. He interviewed neither, even though he found time to speak to the media. At the very least, he should have ensured that the eye-witness statements were taken by competent detectives and he should have scrutinised them as soon as he returned to the incident room.

There were two sure eye-witnesses to the gunman — Richard Hughes next-door to Dando in number 31 Gowan Avenue, and Upfill-Brown opposite in number 30. Hughes was in his master bedroom preparing to get ready for lunch when he heard Dando's car alarm; he was getting ready to take a shower by the slatted window above his own porch. As their porches adjoined in these terraced houses, he was actually only a metre to the west and a storey above where Dando was killed. He then heard her footsteps to the front door of number 29; next, he heard her scream. He interpreted this as if someone she knew had startled her, not as her being in distress. Next, he heard her wrought-iron gate click and he decided to look out through his slats at who was leaving number 29. He saw two people.

One was the gunman who was walking across his line of vision, roughly in front of his own front garden gate, going down towards Fulham Palace Road. The other person was Geoffrey Upfill-Brown coming out of his house opposite. Whatever qualms he harboured at hearing Dando's scream were allayed by Upfill-Brown who was unperturbed in his expression and manner. His eyes went back to the gunman who, a couple of metres on, turned his head to the left and looked in the direction of Dando's porch in a kind of goodbye glance. He saw the man's face three-quarters on.

The gunman then passed out of sight and Hughes went back to his ablutions.

Meanwhile, the gunman broke into a trot, which caught Upfill-Brown's eye and he looked carefully at this man hurrying down Gowan Avenue, conscious that he may later have to describe or even recognise him. The man looked back a few times only confirming Upfill-Brown's suspicions that he was up to no good. Both their descriptions matched, although Hughes was more detailed on the man's facial features and Upfill-Brown, as he had seen the man hurrying, thought from the unnatural movement of the man's hair that he was wearing a wig. Thirteen months later, both witnesses turned out to have formed accurate impressions of the gunman but neither picked out George, now sporting a goatee and moustache, on identification parades.

Campbell didn't speak to either Hughes or Upfill-Brown, leaving them to be interviewed by the foot soldiers who then fed their statements into the system. Meanwhile, Campbell went back to the Kensington headquarters to oversee the setting up of the system. What was plaguing him was ensuring that he was not swamped under the tidal wave of messages. The fact that it was uppermost in his mind and that he had to do it is the nature of the man.

The significance of what Hughes and Upfill-Brown saw — especially the former — was lost in the system. In the process, Campbell took his eyes off Macnamara's ball — the crime scene and the witnesses to the killer. Instead, what overlaid itself on those looking to catch their man were later reports of a man running across Bishop's Park, backed up by what seemed like the same man coming back to stand by the bus stop opposite the corner of the park on the Fulham Palace Road. Running Man had a continuity with Sweating Man at the bus stop. Another man at the bus stop,

Joseph Sapleton, clocked him with the same kind of attention to detail as Upfill-Brown had the gunman.

Sapleton's description was compelling and this was reinforced by the circumstances in which he saw Sweating Man. Other people who were also at the bus stop also noticed Sweating Man. He let two buses pass before getting on a third — its CCTV footage had been erased by the time Oxborough got round to locating it — and some bus passengers and the conductor also saw him. Where he alighted pointed to him having gone down Putney Underground where there were also CCTV cameras. No wonder Oxborough got into a lather. And no wonder, once they took their eyes off the scene of the crime, Sweating Man became the model of the only E-fit issued of the prime suspect in the inquiry.

5

detective constable d

For some reason, Macnamara took a long time to come back to James on his mooted recruitment of the Dando cop. I kept pressurising James, who, in turn, would occasionally pop into Macnamara's office when he saw Mo', which, as he was ghosting his column, could be several times a week. The year before, James had prevailed on Mo' to make a contribution to the magazine; it was titled THE THOUGHTS OF CHAIRMAN MO. He took to rabid, back-biting journalism like the rich to the Paris Ritz, which he also owned. Oddly enough, Mo' seemed to find that being able to sound off about all his enemies and the things he hates was rather more interesting than running 'the shop', as he calls Harrods. He was always discussing it with James and, often when I walked in his office, he would be on the phone fielding some enquiry or fending off some suggestion from

Mo'. He could be sailing around the Med on his yacht and still the phone calls and faxes would come in. At one time, when James hid behind his mobile, Mo' brought him a satellite one especially for him so he could always bend his ear.

For James, what began as a gimmick that might deflect Mo' from noticing the million a year the magazine was losing, turned into a millstone round his neck. First, he had to drag out from Mo' what was interesting rather than what he wanted to rant and rave about; then came the easy bit — writing it up; next came the razor-edged business of securing Mo's approval for a column that went out under his name but, as the rant and rave stuff had gone, didn't include what he wanted in it; finally, after he had earned Mo's approval, there was the rearguard action from all his advisers who would all flinch in horror when they read it. Whenever I saw James in the Swag sipping at the Grigio without his habitual grin, I knew it was 'the column'. THE THOUGHTS OF CHAIRMAN MO was his fortnightly cultural revolution; even the po-faced Caroline used to giggle at the amount of angst it cost James.

Mo's office is on the fifth floor in the west wing of Harrods. One of Mo's cultivated eccentricities is the life-sized white teddy bear, which he positions on the swivel leather armchair behind the desk. He prefers to sit on the other side where visitors normally would; it is the egalitarian move of a plutocrat in his plan to make himself richer at your expense. James would sometimes greet the stuffed animal with a cheery, 'Hello, Chairbear,' which always amused Mo'. However, he invariably saved the joke for when he knew he had a job on his hands to dissuade Mo' from insisting that his latest pet diatribe went in his column.

Mo's advisers — press, legal, security, PR — are located in the string of offices in the same wing as Mo's. As these advisers are always popping in and out of each other's rooms, rather like the head boys of a public school, James dubbed the corridor 'The Dormitory'. However, instead of being bent on tampering with each other's bottoms, the Harrods head boys were plotting to make sure Mo stayed headmaster.

Macnamara's office was only two along from Mo's and during this period, he was engaged in getting the griff on the MI6 plot that was behind the Paris crash in which Dodi and Princess Di were killed. Mo' first blamed the paparazzi but, as he became consumed both with anger at the way the Royal Family had snubbed him and rage at losing his chance of becoming grandfather-in-law to the future king of Britain, his conspiracy-mongering inflated to match the grandiosity of his ego. He required rather more important plotters to blame for the crash than scooter-riding press photographers.

This was Macnamara's task: confirm Mo's paranoia about spooks, conjure up evidence on the MI6 plot. Another day at the office. Of course, the irony here was that Macnamara, as much as anyone, had fed Mo's ego to fund the level of security at Harrods and the Paris Ritz that you need to take a holiday in Chechnya. Dodi and his last girlfriend died because one of the people running this showcase to Mo's ambitions knew that it was all a charade and got drunk on duty. Nonetheless, it was no wonder that Macnamara was a bit late pulling strings on James's behalf.

In July, James got the nod from Macnamara that he had hauled in our man and proposed that we three meet again in the Swag to finalise the meet. Macnamara wanted to see James before I came along, so I didn't turn up until half-an-hour later. James told me afterwards that before they got down to business, he had told Macnamara one of my bank-robbing stories from the '60s that James thought was a hoot. We used to take out the pellets of shotgun cartridges and re-fill them with rice, so we would shoot people in the leg and they would fold up as if their leg had been blown off but it was just phantom pain shock. James loved this story, but when he told Macnamara, the dour Scot said, 'Well, it might be funny listening to John tell it but I have interviewed victims of such rice-shootings and they never thought it was funny at all. They were terrified out of their lives.' Touché.

He'd then gone on to take James through the drill. The Dando detective was a DC and would talk, but the briefings would 'be off the record' and non-attributable and his identity would be protected. There was to be no tape-recording or even note-taking, as it could substantiate contact. Macnamara was on the ball here, as shorthand is considered as being far more accurate by the courts than notes written up afterwards. There was also the consideration that shorthand would enable us to reproduce the pattern of his speech that could unmask him if we at *Punch* decided to set him up. Macnamara especially wanted James's assurance that I would not secretly tape the meeting. James, of course, did reassure him but he also invited him, as he knew I would not mind, to rub me down before it. Macnamara shook his head and said that he trusted me but wanted there to be no misunderstandings.

By the time I arrived, the drill had been settled and they briefed me on it. This whole palaver, however, was just an offspring of the same security paranoia that ruled in Harrods. But we had to collude in it. When people employ bodyguards not because they need guarding, the seeds of madness are sown. The madness germinates when everyone involved begins to act out the charade with such conviction they end up fooling themselves that their delusions are real. It certainly made no sense to think that James and I could sell out the Oxborough cop in *Punch* because, not only did Al Fayed own the publication, but also Macnamara had far more influence over Al Fayed than James. Even if it made it into the magazine, both of us would have been out on our ear. But Macnamara manned the gateway to the Oxborough cop and so we could not question his entrance price, which was to go along with his security for its own sake.

The fundamental point was that neither James nor I would betray a confidential source anyway, which was borne out by subsequent development. James and I resigned from *Punch* in November 2000; the following month, I was instrumental in humiliating Al Fayed in the High Court during the appeal by Neil Hamilton. I then joined the long list of 'traitors' who have double-crossed him but I still would not — and do not in this book — reveal the identity of our Oxborough source.

My first meeting with the Oxborough cop was at 2.00pm in an office in the *Punch* building, but on the next floor up to ensure that none of our staff saw the comings and goings. I was already waiting in James's office when we were alerted by the desk that Macnamara and Mr D (as James nicknamed him in homage to Dando) had arrived downstairs. While they took the lift, I ran up the stairs to our designated office. When they came in, Mr D seemed rather chuffed to meet the old bank robber-turned-journalist. He shook his head in wonderment and said, 'This must knock you over, John. Talk about poacher-turned-gamekeeper — you've turned a sawn-off into a typewriter.'

I laughed, even though I could sniff the midnight oil in his comparison. Still, it was reassuring that he had bothered to try. I told him that even though the pay wasn't so good, I didn't have the Flying Squad on my case. I had wanted to say 'nicking most of it', but censored that in the interest of being politic.

There was some more of this type of banter as we felt each other out. Macnamara stood back from us as the two of us sprawled on chairs around a table on which Caroline had put a large thermos flask of coffee with milk, sugar and cups. I did mine host. Mr D and I had coffee. Macnamara declined, pulled a chair away from us, put his briefcase on the floor next to him then sat watching like an invigilator at an examination for any cribbing. I had deliberately put on cycling leggings and a T-shirt so it highlighted that I wasn't wired up, but that didn't stop Macnamara's eyes tape-sweeping my body.

I asked Mr D why the investigation was called Oxborough ... I had always been puzzled why it had adopted the name of a village in Norfolk. I couldn't see the connection. He looked at me as if I had asked him why we drive on the left-hand side of the road or some other 'just is' fact. It was so obvious, he couldn't answer it. He um'd and ahh'd before saying, 'It was just the next town on the list. They have a list of places and, as an inquiry is started, they give it the name of the next place.' Of course, I wanted to know who had compiled the list but from the look of utter disinterest on his face I thought I'd better pass to more relevant topics — how the investigation was going.

'It's a sticker. It has got nowhere and it looks like that is where it is going to stay. No real leads at all.' Mr D was one of those people who said what they had to say then shut up. I asked about the mobile phone clue. He explained that that wasn't his bag but it was nothing like as easy as people would think. In fact, one of the detectives on it had told him that, like the needle in the haystack, tracing a definitive call that identifies the killer is probably impossible, even though it is there to be found.

I said that, as far as I knew, this was just a methodical but manageable task that would eventually deliver a result. He shook his head but also added that he wasn't so sure that the gunman had used his phone. He said a lot of the people on the squad felt it was a strand of the investigation that wasn't worth the priority it had. Nevertheless, his expression indicated that prioritising the various strands of the investigation was a hit and miss affair.

I nudged in to how Campbell was seen by the rest of the squad. Were there dissenting voices? He turned out to be a Campbell fan and said nothing dramatic. He told me that he thought Campbell was doing the best of what was an impossible job. He said that the one difference on this inquiry as compared with others was that Campbell did not explain to everyone what everyone else was doing. He likes to keep his cards close to his chest and had a kind of divide and rule policy. This was as critical as he got.

I asked if Dando's background had thrown up anything. He said that it wasn't any of her old boyfriends. He explained that you can never entirely eliminate it, but nothing had come of it and they had all been checked out. When I asked, 'Serb?' He just shook his head dismissively. Then he began talking about Dando and how surprised the squad were that she was a lot more 'raunchy' than any of them would have guessed. 'But it is always the way, isn't it?'

I assumed that this had come from her private diaries, but it turned out that analysis of her mattress had thrown up some surprises. I asked how many men, thinking that he meant she was a real goer, but he just said, 'I think three or four.' When he picked up my 'Is that all?' expression, he added, 'But that's not the image that comes over.' He also told me that the post mortem had shown that she was pretty liberal-minded. This post mortem had not been reported and it provided the basis of our first scoop. He explained that she had been pushed on to the ground and her face was very near the floor when the gunman killed her. I asked why someone would do that and he just shrugged his shoulders, 'Your guess is as good as ours. No one knows. But the gun was right on her head. One behind the ear. OBE.' He nodded reflectively.

I posed the question, 'Northern Ireland?' which is where OBE assassinations have occurred. Again, he indicated with open hands and a 'Who knows?' expression that Oxborough had gone through the same speculation and, after it had failed to deliver, passed.

He also confirmed that the E-fit was the wrong man. This had already slowly filtered out without anyone making it absolutely explicit. However, he didn't think Campbell was at fault on that; nonetheless, with 'hindsight' — one of his boss's favourite words — it would have been better to have built it on the eye-witness accounts. When I asked who he meant, he said her neighbour [Hughes] and the guy opposite him [Upfill-Brown] who had come out at the same time. He explained that they both saw the killer and it seems that they shared common descriptions of him. But Hughes said that he reminded him of ____ (a well-known TV personality, who for legal reasons cannot be named). This was new to me, but any mention of Hughes intrigued me. I pressed him on Hughes and he said there were problems with him but not at the time that the E-fit was constructed. All he said was that he was a 'bit of a playboy' but as I was badgering for more, Macnamara called time.

My allotted half-an-hour was up, so I had to call it a day. He said he'd explain Hughes to me another time. They left and tore down the stairs and went in to see James who was still round at the Swag. I went round there just as quickly and, as I told him, began writing out my notes. We ran Mr D's first briefing big time in *Punch*. Oddly enough, none of the nationals picked up on us and it wasn't until the end of the year that I saw an article in the *Sunday Times* that summarised all the post mortem details that we had printed five months earlier.

Meanwhile, Tiina had come back on the scene because she was now studying to be a journalist, which meant she was prepared to forgive me for being so old. She wanted my advice. The upshot was she invited me to Finland. Ever the freebie journo, I went cap in hand to Caroline to book me a cottage holiday near Tampere, which was where Tiina was studying. This got the blonde factotum all aquiver. 'Finland ... oohhh ... so it's back on, is it? She's forgiven you, has she? Viagra's banned in Finland. What are you going to do?'

It went on and on. My private life was an office soap opera but I suppose that is one of the prices for not acting your age. Ever since I went to infants' school, people have been telling me that, but all they have done is confirm in me the wisdom of doing the exact opposite. However, given that Tiina's lifting the ban on me was hedged with all manner of reservations, I thought I'd try to ingratiate myself by coming up with something that might earn me a full pardon; so I asked James if he could swing it for Tiina to interview Mo's wife, Heini, who is also Finnish.

I had been struck by a remark she made to Mo' soon after the funeral of Princess Di. Mo' had been gushing on about how he believed they were 'living in heaven together' and that kind of cringe stuff. Heini had reminded him of when Diana had been doubled up with laughter in St Tropez not long before the crash. She recounted a Finnish saying to Mo': 'After too much laughter, tears.' This made me think that she would make an interesting interviewee and a perfect one for a cub reporter like Tiina.

She had told me in Rhodes that the Finnish papers are always speculating about the state of her marriage to Mo'. She said, 'There are not many famous Finns in the world, so the press print endless articles about Mika [Hakkinen] and Heini.' I asked James if he could do anything but he said that the answer would be no as Mo' never let the press near her. He said, 'Ask him yourself,' but I didn't follow it up.

James had Clem while I was in Finland. Charlie, his young son, had become enraptured with Clem's party trick. He picks up a tennis ball, rolls it at you, then waits expectedly in the crouch position for you to throw it. When you do, as even dog-haters end up doing, he catches it, does a little prance round in triumph, then repeats it all over again, again and again. After a while, adults tire but children never do and, when parents intervene to break up the ritual, they start asking for a dog like Clem. Anyway, he was happy while I enjoyed everything Finnish, except the mosquitoes.

We idled around a lake, often boating out to little islands for a picnic and a swim, then coming back in the evening to sauna and supper. The sun never really set; it was idyllic. But we had become mates without it being discussed. I decided it was time to grow up ... a bit, but not entirely.

I came back to London determined to install a sauna in my flat. In Finland, there are nearly more saunas than people, whereas the English think a shower is a luxury. Somehow, that crept along the grapevine into the office culture and so I had Caroline asking me what I got up to in the sauna. 'Bit too steamy for you, Caroline,' was my retort, which I thought was a bit too quick. The trouble was when I came up with a sharp retort she would broadcast it round the office — 'Listen to what ...' — which would turn it back on me.

Meanwhile, the investigation was still surfacing in the press but, as Mr D had predicted, nothing promising was emerging and the investigation looked grounded. After we ran on the post mortem story, I began nagging at James to have a crack at Hughes. He didn't need much persuading and, in early September, we both went round to number 31 Gowan Avenue, which I describe later.

Meanwhile, we restarted the Macnamara rigmarole to see Mr D again. This time, James said to him that we would like to give Mr D a drink as what he was giving us was gold dust. Macnamara nodded. He said to James, 'OK. But the way John does it is to put it inside an envelope and, in the middle of the conversation, just take it out and put it on the table. But tell him not to say anything or even look as if anything unusual is happening. He will pick it up and nobody notices or mentions it.' James looked puzzled.

Macnamara explained, 'We know that John is not taping, but it is just a little bit more risky for my man and he would be out if anything did leak. It is just a bit more protection because he is more vulnerable to a sting. It is the way we do things.' James then asked how much but, thinking that he didn't want to bust his budget, suggested £500.

Macnamara shook his head, 'No, don't spoil him. Three hundred.'

So that was planned for the next meeting in September. We followed virtually the same procedure as before, except it was later in the afternoon. I had the envelope stuffed with 15 twenties in my T-shirt pocket. It was sticking up and quite visible but neither he nor Macnamara looked. I wanted to ask about Hughes, but first I asked about the gun, which was something that James had become interested in. By this time, not much had been disclosed except that it was a 9mm semi-automatic short. The short is the baby version of the conventional 9mm, less accurate and powerful but, at close quarters, no less deadly.

He grimaced slightly and nodded his head. 'I can't give you any more on that than what is already out there as some info we are keeping back for obvious reasons.' He meant, of course, that it might assist the gunman if he knew how much Oxborough knew.

I quickly conveyed my understanding and he moved on ... to Hughes.

But I interrupted him and explained that, on the basis of what he said last time, James and I had already been round to see Hughes. I told him the gist of how Hughes had met us and afterwards how James and I had walked away and each of us had kept asking the other, 'What do you think?' until James broke the deadlock saying, 'I bet Richard has gone straight into the Pig and Pen for a large G and T.' I told Mr D that we both formed the impression that he was involved and that the article on the interview was in the next edition. Mr D looked slightly confused but said he'd read it with interest.

However, he then explained why Oxborough was interested in Hughes. It was all to do with the Fiona Hughes lookalike theory. It seems that Hughes's wife, Fiona, looked like Dando and drove exactly the same model car, a black convertible 3-Series BMW. Oxborough had speculated that Hughes may have decided to have his wife bumped off but the hit-man had got the wrong woman — blonde, driving the same car and living right next door. It was over this possibility that Hughes had been interviewed a number of times and was still a suspect. I then pressed our theory that Hughes could have got the hots for Dando and flipped. Of course, Hughes was totally innocent — his only involvement was that he was unfortunately a neighbour.

Mr D screwed up his face. 'We haven't eliminated that possibility but it is not top of our list.'

Needless to say, this was all dynamite as far as I was concerned, especially as Richard Hughes had not mentioned it when James and I had spoken to him. I told Mr D that in two interviews, Hughes hadn't mentioned this. He shrugged, 'Well, why would he?' Some stories are too good to listen to despite the evidence that knocks them down. I replied that while a detective may be sceptical, that doesn't mean it can't make a belter of a story.

But then he continued, 'There are some interesting stories that you might like about some of the people we have eliminated.' The promised 'drink' was definitely plucking some plums from the duff.

He then told me that Dando's fiancé, Alan Farthing, had been married before and they had to look at any men his ex-wife had hooked up with since they parted. Oxborough had looked carefully at her boyfriends. But the biggest scoop of this meeting was that a lot of time had been spent investigating the bisexual ex-boyfriends of one of her former lovers. Of course, at the time when Mr D told me, I was bowled over. As Dando had consistently been portrayed as the golden girl, it just was difficult to adjust to.

He explained that Oxborough got all in a lather over this as some of the lover's boyfriends were medics, which fitted the clinical nature of the kill. I had been puzzled by the gunman going in so close to the victim but, while it did not cover the DNA problem, a medic would be much less squeamish about getting in close, spilling blood and even getting it on him.

Thus, in the early days of the investigation, a gay pride gunman avenging his former boyfriend's betrayal of the homosexual cause was a big runner. However, like Farthing's ex-wife, it was eliminated. When we ran this in *Punch*, we decided to omit the lover's name — he became 'a recent lover' — which meant we could not milk the medic aspect that gave some explanation for the close contact, clinical nature of the kill. As I knew that this was definitely the story for the next edition, I decided it was envelope time.

Of course, in tribute to Mo', it had to be a brown envelope.

The conversation with Mr D became quite animated as he elaborated on the gay pride investigation, with even Macnamara grinning and joining in. All policemen, journos and ex-bank robbers are a bit homophobic. I slipped the envelope across the table without breaking the flow of the conversation or eye-contact with Mr D. He did exactly the same as he picked it up and we carried on talking as if nothing had happened.

Soon after this, we broke up and I bounded down the stairs so fast that I zoomed past Caroline like a bat out of hell. I was electrified as I told James the latest from Mr D. There is a test that libel readers apply in issues of contempt that is colloquially known as the 'Fuck me!' response. If the new information provokes such a reaction, it is contempt to print it. That Oxborough was investigating Hughes was definitely 'Fuck me!' news. Especially as we gave much less credence than Oxborough to the hit-man scenario — I never faltered on the gunman's MO being incompatible with a hit-man unless he was a freelancer with a paramilitary background.

Thus we had already discounted the way Oxborough was shaping up on Hughes. Our take on Hughes — which turned out to be as equally without foundation as Oxborough's, and which was based on my first impression and our interview — was that he lived next door, could have developed an obsession for Dando, then flipped when she decided to leave and get married. His closeness to her meant that he could circumvent what seemed the insurmountable difficulties that an outsider ran in dealing with her infrequent and unpredictable visits to number 29 Gowan Avenue.

When we ran the Hughes stuff, it was picked up by the nationals. However, in our next edition, we ran on the gay pride and the Fiona lookalike theory. This confirmed to Campbell that we had a source in his squad. He was furious and even next

February when we linked up with Oxborough he was still asking his detectives to identify our source.

I met Mr D one more time in October, which was after the article on Hughes. I asked him what he'd thought as he'd read the piece. He replied, 'I don't think you're wrong.' But he showed without actually spelling it out that the bosses were not enamoured with our Hughes scenario — that he was responsible not for a mistaken hit on his wife but was behind the actual plan to kill Dando. Generally, he was less forthcoming on the third meet, although he didn't seem worried about Campbell sniffing him out as the *Punch* source. He pocketed the drink as before but he showed only polite interested in my enthusiastic speculation and hunches about Hughes.

The only edge he gave us at this meeting was when I raised one of the leaks that had appeared in the press. A couple of the papers had been fed a story from Oxborough about there being significant new developments in the Dando case. Mr D just shook his head. 'It's just PR. It's the Range Rover; but it is a load of bollocks. The guy is nothing to do with the murder.' From his dismissive manner, I formed the impression that he had become disillusioned with the investigation ever detecting, never mind convicting, the killer. I ran a piece to the effect that even if Oxborough detected the killer, there would be problems convicting him.

6

meet mr hughes

After some discussion about how to approach Mr Hughes, James and I decided to doorstep him at number 31, Gowan Avenue. We just caught a cab from Knightsbridge and went to Gowan Avenue around noon on 8 September and rang his doorbell. Richard, as I came to know him over the next few months opened it. He looked nervy, edgy, as James, ever the charmer, explained our purpose.

'Sorry for bothering you, Mr Hughes, but we are from *Punch* magazine. We just wondered if we could have a chat. I'm James Stein the editor ... ' Out went James's paw, which Hughes, like any well-trained public school boy, instinctively shook, 'and this is John McVicar, who is our crime writer.' I did the same as James. 'We know you must have been pestered and pestered by the press and we do appreciate that, but we just wanted to run a few things through you concerning the Dando case.'

Hughes looked ambivalent and I wasn't sure whether James would land him. 'I have already said lots, that is all I have to say,' he replied. 'There is nothing else I think I can add that hasn't already been said.'

James intervened. 'I realise that, Richard ... can I call you Richard?'

Hughes looked nonplussed, 'Err yes ... I don't mind.'

'What we are looking for is just to have a chat over a drink or something because sometimes with the passage of time, people do recall things that they don't know are significant.' James continued subtly to twist his arm until he agreed.

'I don't think I can help but I will if you chaps think I can. Anything to help. But I can't do it today,' he answered.

James was straight in. 'No, we didn't expect you to — we were just passing by and thought we'd just knock. But what about tomorrow ... say, lunch on us?' James beamed at him affably. James genuinely is a very nice man whom even his enemies find difficult to dislike. Hughes was too polite and insecure to withstand his charm offensive. We agreed to meet at a restaurant near the Fulham Palace Road the next day at noon.

We arrived slightly early and James took one look at the place — 'Can you imagine the wine list?' — and went off to recce for something more appropriate nearby. He returned after about ten minutes smiling, 'Perfect French bistro just over the lights.' 'The Café' is supposed to be that too, but is actually one of those ghastly chains that market microwaved Franglais food and winelake Piat D'Or. We sat in there waiting for Hughes, ordering only a couple of Michelobs until we transferred to a more acceptable venue. It was a heatwave September and the beer was an apéritif for wine. Hughes had other ideas and the writing on that particular wall was signed, sealed and delivered in the way he and the manager greeted each other. James groaned, 'He's a regular.'

'Richard,' James stood up greet him, 'how nice to see you. You well?'

Richard assured us that he was. Then, acknowledging our drinks, added, 'A good day for drinking beer.'

James picked up on this, 'A starter for the wine, Richard. What I thought — but it is entirely up to you — is that we could have a spot of lunch along the road in a place I know. We are lucky at *Punch* in having a proprietor with very deep pockets ...'

However, Hughes looked like he was being backed into a corner and I knew he wasn't going to acquiesce on this one. James also picked it up and, while Hughes spluttered and muttered about preferring to stay put, he accepted gracefully.

'Richard, we are happy where we are. You're our guest ...' I could see James's slightly panicky eyes scouring the wine list and I thought he might have one more crack at getting Hughes somewhere more civilised but he clearly thought better of it '... and this is fine. You must excuse me; it's just that I delight in spending Mohammed's money.'

Drink, food and *bonhomie* are the journalists' little helpers; they open up the vocal chords of gossip, indiscretion, even confession. Some journalists become so caught up in the means that they lose sight of the end; others are so focused on the end, they can't enjoy the means. Indeed, the latter often get less than the former because at least an unfocused conviviality does not make the interviewee tighten up, perhaps become resentful, feel exploited. James is that rare journalist who manages to enjoy the means while never losing sight of the end.

Hughes sat down at our table. He is a small Celtic man in his early 30s with very dark eyes and an expression that is an intriguing mixture of public school over-confidence and little-boy vulnerability. But his manner is upbeat and hearty; he is an engaging man. He tends to wear expensive, sporty leisure clothes: golfing sweaters, polo shirts, chinos and Deckers. A luxurious, blue-faced Omega watch touches up his financial status. He put down his Silk Cut packet and lighter on the table but did not light up straight away.

We began ordering a variety of snacks but he passed on wine. James and I deigned not to notice but inside our heads there were flashing arrows pointing at the thought bubble — 'Doesn't want a drink!'

Afterwards, James concluded, 'He loves a drink. You can tell. But he doesn't drink with us. Now what does that say? And he took his time lighting up the first fag, but did you see him draw on it when he did? Nervous. But he didn't want to light up because he wanted to exercise control over his weaknesses.'

Unfortunately, we analysed all Richard Hughes's supposed psychological quirks and always found they led to a suspicion that he was involved in the murder. Another one of the spectacular mistakes I made in this case. However, even when they are playing armchair detective, journalists are not policemen, nor are they on the same standard of proof. Journalists are obliged to put any allegations and to report the respondent's answers accurately and fairly, but they work 'on the balance of probabilities', not 'beyond a reasonable doubt'. One of the consequences of this is that, while journalists have fewer powers than policemen, they have a lot more licence, which detectives themselves sometimes exploit.

It is assumed that suspects read stories about the hunt for them more avidly than the ordinary reader and detectives harness the greater licence enjoyed by the press to talk to a suspect through an article or a TV programme. This usually only occurs where they are dealing with serial killer or rapist or a difficult murder like the

Dando inquiry. They will plant stories with the collusion of particular journalists working on the nationals with the express purpose of unnerving or flushing out the suspect. It never works but that doesn't stop them doing it. Thus, the reader is an *en passant* pawn in the chess game that the police and lickspittle journalists are playing with the suspect.

In the case of Hughes, there was no police encouragement, but that didn't stop the 'wink-wink, nod-nod' *hedunit* stories that *Punch* published being followed up by two nationals, both of which added a bit more bite to the accusations. In all, James and I inaugurated a bit of a Hughes witchhunt, which eventually galvanised Oxborough enough to decide to take a much closer look at him long after he should have been eliminated as a suspect. By coincidence, just as they were preparing to do this, George popped into the frame and, once he did, all the other runners, including Hughes, were scratched. Nonetheless, Hughes was crucial to my understanding of the Oxborough investigation and he gave me an edge on Campbell's limitations that stood me in good stead at the trial.

Hughes is a financial trader who works from home from a commercial TV feed on movements in stocks and shares. This is backed up with reading the financial journals and papers. 'You either make a few bucks or you lose a few bucks. You've just got to make sure you get more than 50 per cent right. It can be obviously heart-stopping sometimes. But that is the name of the game, unfortunately.' Hughes's diction is, from time to time, invested with clichés.

He, like us all, had thought a lot about the murder but now, over four months on, was sceptical about Oxborough making an arrest. 'It is very difficult. Without a primary motive, I think it is going to be very difficult, especially for the police to follow any particular lead. They have got to suddenly find out why. I mean, if it was maybe a drug-dealer living next-door to me, then, fair enough, you could understand. But, I mean, how she was portrayed on TV — she was like that in real life. There were no airs and graces with her. She was just very simple.' He stumbled to correct himself as he realised the import of his words. 'Not simple, but a very normal person. It's so bizarre. It was such a calculated killing, if you want to call it that. I mean, she must have pissed off somebody big time. It must have been massive motivation to have done it in that method. I mean that was a massive hit. And for it to be undetected four months later ... it just shows the professionalism of who's behind it.'

The elephant trap for James and I was that, whenever he spoke about Dando, he showed that he wasn't a particular fan of hers — his tone belied his words — and he also revealed an interest in hitmen. The terms and comments he used revealed this: 'massive hit' and, later, 'If the guy had popped her from the back without giving any arm contact there would have been no scream.' Professional criminals will talk about 'pop one in his nut' for shooting someone in the head, but this is hardly the *lingua franca* of a city slicker. To repeat, all I can say in our defence is that our job is not to detect a killer but to stand up a good story. And Hughes was fitting that objective very well.

When she was killed, he was above his porch which was adjoining hers, so he was only about three metres from where she was murdered. He heard her car alarm, which he knew, then her footsteps up to her porch, then her scream ... 'It was definitely a surprise shriek. It wasn't like, you know, a causal scream. I don't know but I presume he had probably held her somewhere, maybe the arm or something. I'm presuming.'

The trouble is, Detective Constable D had told us that there was bruising on her right arm, which indicated that she was probably held when the gunman forced her on to the ground. This hadn't been made public, so we felt it was odd that Hughes put it into his scenario. And he never heard the shot but he did hear the click of the gate as the gunman observing the proprieties of Middle England shut it behind him, even though a curlicue wrought-iron gate could not hide the body.

But Hughes did not hear the shot. 'I heard the scream, the footsteps and definitely no shot whatsoever. I mean, I was shocked when I head that it was a gun. If she was stabbed, fair enough, she would have made more of a noise anyway. No, I'm still bemused why there wasn't a sound of a gunshot.'

We went into the minutiae of the scream. 'It was quite long. But it was not just an "Aaaahh". It was quite a long shriek. But it was more a surprise scream, which obviously it turns out it wasn't. It was obviously a surprise scream. Ahem ...' Hughes often muddles his syntax and what comes out is often not what he means, unless you thought, like James and me, that it is all a big Freudian slip. 'And that was it. No more Jill.'

Of course, our minds were already closing around the conclusion that Hughes was involved, which meant that our interpretations of his manner and words were loaded. Some stories are too good not to be true and journalists begin to move towards standing them up rather than seeing if they are still standing after doing one's damnedest to knock them down. I plead 'Guilty, m'lud,' for stitching up Richard Hughes.

Later, James and I worked out that he might well think it sensible to hear the scream but not the gunshot as that would put the onus on him to investigate. It's generally the case that when killers or conspirators to a murder join in the search for the body, they take care not to be the one to find it. Thus, our reasoning was that he could live with hearing the scream but not the shot, too.

Policemen and journalists often talk to people merely to gain information, but the focus shifts when the interviewee is suspected of hiding something or being involved in wrongdoing. The questioning is more cagey but, ideally, the questioner should be looking to eliminate the interviewee from suspicion. However, once it proves impossible to eliminate the interviewee from wrongdoing, then the questions shift more towards entrapping him with the evidence and, obviously, even getting him to come clean. Throughout my interviews with Hughes, the questioning was unmistakably towards trying to trick him, but only once did he acknowledge this, when he commented, 'I know where you are coming from.' Otherwise, we just colluded in the fiction that I was asking him questions in order to dredge buried facts up from his memory that Oxborough had missed.

After he heard the scream, Hughes next heard Dando's gate clink, which prompted him to look out to see who was leaving her house. Again, James and I independently wondered how he could hear the alarm, the footsteps, the scream, the gate click as the killer left number 29, but not the shot. Hughes explained, 'The scream didn't make me look out. It was the clink. The gate. I saw the gate, just ... err ... it was sort of ... err. What's the word for it?' Hughes struggled with why he looked out. James supplied it to him — nosiness.

'No, not nosiness. You are just sort of looking out to see who is walking in this area. Bearing in mind, her house was for sale. Well, it had been. But the house had been sold to my brother-in-law. I can't remember how many days before she was shot. And I was curious to see on their behalf whether the estate agent had been showing other people afterwards. So I'd always have a look to see if anybody ... do you follow? I mean, estate agents are always up to something; maybe they are trying to get somebody or other to give 'em more money. So that was what really made me look out. In fact, I even thought it could have been a valuer — the guy we are talking about. Or something to do with the house sale. That was another conclusion, when I saw him. And I thought nothing more of it.' Hughes stutters, which doesn't help his mangled syntax.

It seems he looked out of his wooden shutter-blinds and saw the man walk across his line of vision, at the same time he saw Upfill-Brown opposite coming out of his home on the way to visit the Post Office. Any residual alarm planted by the scream was allayed by Upfill-Brown's unperturbed manner. The gunman continued left from Hughes's vantage point and in his right hand he had what Hughes thought was a mobile phone but could well have been the butt of the gun. The gunman then looked back.

Hughes said, 'He looked around, he looked back, he looked back at the scene ... ahem. I think he looked back to see whether or not she got up. Maybe, I don't know. He's the only person who can answer that question. He wasn't running. And he didn't seem to be in any panic or he didn't seem to fret. I mean, literally it was as if he was saying goodbye to somebody. If I'd had a conversation with you, then I was on my merry way — that was exactly how it looked and felt. If he was doing all this, you would have thought from his movements that he'd stolen something. He'd have had body movement, I'd thought, of panic. He did not have that whatsoever.'

The gunman was wearing a conventional Barbour and had a mop of dark hair, which was longer than the person's depicted in the E-fit. To help Hughes, we showed him a copy of the E-fit.

'No, err ... this was far more ... all this.' He indicated with his hands a full head of hair. 'The hair would have been over his ears for a start. He looked like he was a rugby player. He looked well groomed, well put together, like an ex-SAS guy. Like he could have been an estate agent. He didn't look like ... I don't know what you want to call it. I don't know what a typical hit-man looks like. But he was very tidy looking ... No,' he said, indicating the E-fit, 'it doesn't look anything like him, like that guy. If he was that professional, he is probably laughing at the E-fit. In fact, if anything it did him a favour ... I've said that to the police. I've spoken to the guy in number 30 [Upfill-Brown] who, you know, also feels that it is not the same guy.'

Of course, this was the *story* — it wasn't so much that the E-fit was based on the wrong person; it was that Oxborough's best witness had told them this and they had not acted on it and produced another E-fit. James and I knew that this alone was sensational. In fact, I went back to Hughes a few days later after our session in The Café to confirm some of the things that he had said. On this occasion he took me up to his bedroom so I could see exactly the angle from which he'd seen the gunman. It was quite obvious that, although he had seen the gunman from the first floor, he saw him virtually full faced, which was not how it came over when he told James and me. Then, he had said it was more a sideways-on sighting.

When I was in his bedroom replicating what he had seen, I pointed out the contradiction to Hughes. He explained, 'I know. But that's putting me in the spotlight. I don't want this guy thinking that I know exactly what he looks like. I didn't want to emphasise that for obvious reasons. I have censored that for my own reasons in the past. The last thing I want is this guy thinking, He has got a complete look at me. I've got to be careful.'

I then asked if he would recognise him now [it was then September 1999]. He nodded. 'Not a 100 per cent, but it hasn't faded. I would know that face.' However, to placate his concerns about the gunman coming back to bump him off, I put in the article that Hughes would not be able to pick out the man as his memory had faded. I explained that, to obviate this handicapping any future prosecution in which my article could be used to undermine Hughes's identification, I told him that I would explain to James that I would lie in the article and why. Hughes thanked me, but I just did not believe him and interpreted it as another part of the elaborate game that he was playing to hide his involvement in the murder. Nevertheless, I quoted him in the article as saying that his memory has faded and he would not now be able to pick the gunman.

In The Café, however, after telling us about his sighting of the gunman and the botched E-fit, he went on to explain what happened next. According to him, he faffed around in the bathroom for around 15 minutes until he heard voices. Again, he peered through the shutters and this time saw three sombre-faced women on the pavement outside Jill Dando's talking as they looked at her porch. Hughes explained his reaction.

'I could put that and then, yeah — it all clicked into place. Suddenly, I realised when I saw this group. I was already undressed and I was probably in a pair of boxer shorts. I put on tracksuit bottoms and sweat shirt and I ran straight downstairs. I could tell something was wrong and the alarm bells struck me then. The minute I walk out, one of the women says to me, "Is that Jill Dando?" I look over [the metre-high dividing wall] and said, "Yes it is."'

The trouble with Hughes is that sometimes when he repeats something the details change. In fact, all three women knew that it was Jill Dando and Helen Doble, who discovered the body and called the police and ambulance services, had named the victim. James and I logged 23 contradictions in Hughes's account of what he saw that morning. Some were between the first interviews we had conducted with him, others were between what he had said to us and what he had said in interviews on the day. Sometimes, he looked at the body and saw blood, other times just her red coat; sometimes he did not even look at the body. He thought she had been stabbed, had a heart-attack ... it went on and on.

Soon after the murder — and he repeated it at one stage to us — he said that one of the three women who were in vigil over Dando's body had told him that Dando may have had a heart-attack as she had had a history of cardiac problems. This could only have referred to the third one on the scene, Sue Convoy, who was a doctor's receptionist.

Dando was shot at around 11.33am; ten minutes later, her body was discovered by wannabe TV star Helen Doble. She rang the police and ambulance services, then she recruited Vida Saunders from the de Rosnay home at number 55 Gowan Avenue. Saunders, in turn, went to the doctor's surgery at 25 Gowan Avenue, but only Sue Convoy was there, not the doctor. All three not only knew that it was Dando but also that she was dead. Given that they could see blood on her face and a pool of it on the porch, none of them thought it was a heart-attack. Nobody mentioned a heart-attack until Hughes did so in one of his interviews. Sue Convoy was so annoyed by Hughes's statements that she instructed her solicitor to write Hughes a warning letter.

The detectives nicknamed these women the 'Witches of Eastwick'; Sue Convoy didn't really fit the 'Witches' mould but once it was coined it was too good to drop because of the one exception. When I told Hughes about Oxborough's informal name for them, he immediately said eagerly, 'I'd love to hear what they say about me. Mind you I've been as co-operative as I can.' Again, this was more hedunit points. Later on when we went over our impressions, James and I asked each other rhetorically, What does he mean by 'as co-operative as I can?'

I remembered what Detective Constable D had said. I replied, 'You're a playboy.'

He said grinning, 'Haaa, I'm married.' I repeated the playboy tag.

'I'm married,' he said again.

I said, 'You might be married but in their book you're still a playboy.'

He stopped the banter and said reflectively, 'Tell me anyone who is a playboy who is married?'

James and I interviewed Sue Convoy around the time we were sniffing at Hughes and it transpired that she hadn't ruled out Hughes. His manner had been so odd when he came out of his house that morning that she immediately suspected him.

'It was just the way he acted. I just thought he was guilty,' she told me and James in early November. 'He certainly did not look at the body but muttered something about hearing a scream and seeing a man before rushing over the road to consult with the man opposite.'

Of course, this was grist to our Hughes mill. We read his confusion as panic that his part in the murder would be discovered; he couldn't look at the body because he felt guilty; he rushed over to Upfill-Brown to check out his description of the gunman in order that his own description tallied or to see if Upfill-Brown would recognise him. Our reasoning was that he could have disguised himself, then walked round the block and come in the back entrance in time to make his appearance when the body was discovered. Maybe we had watched too many Miss Marple whodunits, but that was our theory.

Sue was the last straw for James and me and, later that month James rang DI Horrocks, Oxborough's second in command, and took him through some of the Hughes contradictions and told him of our suspicions. It was in James's office and I was listening in. Horrocks let James have his say, then replied wearily, 'Yes, I know. Richard Hughes gets muddled but he is just another rich young man. We've 'ad a look at him and, well, we don't think there is anything there ... If you have got anything interesting, we'll look at it. We'll look at anything.'

Horrocks obviously didn't share our suspicions, even though we knew from Mr D that, in September, Campbell had told the squad at one of his briefings: 'What are we looking at, then? We have three possibles: one, stalker; two, contract killer; and there's the neighbour, Mr Hughes.'

My reaction was like James's to Horrocks's blasé dismissal of all our laborious work and theorising that this was just another thicko cop. I got to know Horrocks a bit at the trial; he is a Macnamara-type cop, not a system's man. Northerner, bristly walrus moustache, shock of unruly grey hair, 45-ish, likes a drink, a joke and his grub, no intellectual but very shrewd. He trusted his gut feel and, on Hughes, it was right. I credit him and, now the dust has settled, appreciate that his exasperated attitude towards us was justified.

One of the problems for the Oxborough cops was that, as the inquiry lasted so long and public interest never really waned, people naturally indulged their own whodunit theorising. At one stage, Campbell even appealed to people who were thinking of ringing in with information on the helpline not to tell him theories. The armchair detective was the bane of Oxborough.

Yet, as we already know, Oxborough would hardly have won their Conan Doyle badge for the E-fit, although at that period in Autumn 2000, James and I thought that their worst blunder was not giving Hughes a run. Instead, the first officers on the crime scene investigation actually used Hughes's home as a temporary office. The police arrived just before noon and Hughes told us, 'So they started to cordon off everything. The women who had found her came into my house and the police came in, too. They used my house as a bit of a base, taking statements off the women, but only for about half-an-hour.'

I remember Macnamara's reaction to this when we told him

about it. He commented, 'I would have immediately treated the neighbour as a suspect. He was one of the last people to see — no, hear — her alive; he was on the scene soon after the murder; he came over as nervous and confused. I can remember thinking that from what I saw of him on TV at the time. Something wasn't right. What I would have done is treat the two houses — hers and his — as the scene of the crime. It would have been quite legitimate. Their doorways were side by side and the murderer could have come out of Hughes's house or could have hid in his front garden. By doing it like this, we would have been able to check out any possible involvement. That's the way we would have done it.' Macnamara's 'we' was his old school at Scotland Yard, not the new Campbell-like system breed.

Hughes gave two or three statements that day to plain-clothes detective constables. Then a fortnight later, Campbell saw him. He told James and me about Campbell. 'He interviewed me I think two weeks afterwards. He rang me to see if he could come and interview me. I had the interview and I haven't spoken to him since. He took me through the statements that the other police had taken. I thought his manner was polite ... ahem ... and obviously a thoughtful manner. There seems to be a lot more of him than he makes out. He seems to be very intellectual ... that's the impression I got ... sometimes, even when you see him on TV, he seems to have that smile on his face and what have you, but I'm sure behind all that he is a lot more calculated and intense than maybe he makes out.'

Campbell also asked Hughes for his own theory on the murder and he replied, 'I told him basically what I've told you. I don't have a theory because without a motive it is difficult to conclude any sort of theory.'

But even though Campbell never came near Hughes again,

other Oxborough detectives did; in all, he was interviewed about ten times. He said, 'They have just come over and really just say, "We have been going over the statement ... We have been going over this information." They are just trying to cross-check various things that they may have picked up recently ... with what, what I've said. Obviously cross-checking, I presume, against any new information that they may have that could ring bells. But in nothing like the detail you are. They are polite. I mean, at the end of the day, they are not going to make me do any spread-eagles on the walls, are they. Unless I was a suspect, I suppose.'

Of course, he was a suspect at that stage because of the Fiona lookalike theory and that is why the cops kept coming back to him. They thought he may have commissioned a hit on his wife or that someone else decided to take her out and the gunman got Dando instead. The trouble is, we did not know about the mistaken identity theory on our first meeting with Hughes and he never volunteered it. So we read the continuing interest by Oxborough in him as further confirmation that they suspected him to be the killer.

It was only during my second talk with Mr D that I learned of the Fiona lookalike theory, so, naturally, after it I contacted Hughes again and met him on my own at The Café. I repeated what we had put to him at our first meeting. 'Did you know you are a suspect?'

He feigned ignorance but, as with everything, he qualified it. 'No. I presumed I was. When I say ... I didn't know that they were aggressively saying I was a suspect but I assume everyone was a suspect.'

I then asked him if he knew the reason why. He shook his head and his expression indicated that he had no idea. I told him that it was because of his wife. He just replied neutrally, 'Right.'

I clarified, 'Because, from behind, she is sort of a Jill Dando lookalike.'

'Right.'

I had him by the balls, of course, so I just squeezed a bit. 'You didn't know anything about that?'

Hughes answered, 'No.'

I elaborated, 'For a while, they thought that someone may have tried to kill Fiona because her car is the same as Dando's, she looks a bit like her, blonde ... the gunman makes a mistake in the heat of the moment.'

'Why would I want to be shooting my own wife?' I thought he was deliberately misreading the theory. I explained that the scenario was that he had commissioned someone to kill Fiona for insurance or something.

He prevaricated, 'I can see that, but my wife does not come home until 12.30 and that happened at 11.30 ... I can understand them running that. It did cross my mind that it could be mistaken identity.'

I mocked up a surprise reaction. 'It did?'

'Yeah. But I am not going to say that in public. It crossed my mind that the police may think ... but they never actually said to me specifically "Do you think it is mistaken identity?" They've never said that to me. But it's like anything. I know that she has the same car as Jill Dando. That, incidentally, I'd rather keep as quiet as possible. The minute that car was in the same street ... I ... err ... got rid of it straight away.'

I knew from Mr D that he had actually driven it down to his father's place in Wales! But I let him whitter on.

'I didn't want the mix-up. I didn't want people to put ... put ... to-to-to think that even could be the case. I can and have thought about it, John. And I've thought about it and if it was a mistaken identity, OK. Ummm ... and someone wanted to shoot my wife, whatever the reason was. Forget me for a second. Say it was someone else trying to kill my wife. I mean, Jill Dando has got

to be at least three or four inches taller than my wife. They
certainly don't wear the same clothing. Say it was someone else.
OK, for one, she never drives to work. And the car wasn't used.
The car was opposite Jill Dando's that day ... in the same street. So
as far as I am concerned ... straight away, do you think that
someone that good — who obviously was who shot her — would
have got something that wrong? He's done everything right and I
cannot see him ... What I'm trying to say is that the guy knew
what he was doing all the way along the line. He would have
known that was her ... and again what-what motive does anyone
have to-to-to kill my wife? I certainly don't.'

The detail of her car being parked opposite was more grease
to our elbow. When I briefed James on it, we integrated it into our
version of how he killed Dando. If Hughes had commissioned
someone to kill her — say from Northern Ireland (he also let drop
he had visited Ireland) then the plan might well have been for him
to assist the gunman by setting Fiona's alarm with the remote from
his bedroom window to cover the shot. The gunman could even
have come out of the Hughes house as she drove up and before he
pounced. We speculated that perhaps she screamed as the gunman
approached her, then Hughes set off the car alarm a bit late but
sufficiently early to drown the shot. He had to hear the scream
because others may have heard it, but not the shot because of the
alarm and because it would have meant him going downstairs and
being the first to find the body.

The only problem with this scenario was that if he had
developed a private obsession with Dando, he would want to carry
out the kill himself. Despite the holes, we were convinced that he
had something to do with the murder. We were *Cracker* with the
bells and whistles. And we were not the only ones. After this
meeting and, using some of my *Punch* articles, the *Mail on Sunday*

had also jumped on the Hughes trail.

The *Mail on Sunday* piece on 26 September 1999 was titled THE SEVEN QUESTIONS THAT DEEPEN THE QUESTION OF JILL DANDO'S MURDER, and written by some in-house *Mail* hack named Thomas Penny. It began portentously by stating in typical *Mail on Sunday* dolorous style, 'Today would have been the first day of Jill Dando's honeymoon ...'

The article was mainly drawn from the *Punch* article and focused on a number of the changes that Hughes had given in his various accounts. The only new fact — well, speculation — introduced by the *Mail* journo was that, as her bag was open, the gunman may have stolen her diary! The article's subtitle trailed, 'As friends remember the star's life, is her killer's identity revealed in a stolen diary?'

The passage dealing with the stolen diary is pure English crime reporter-ese: 'Police say they are satisfied that Miss Dando had decided not to start a diary for 1999, but they have no direct evidence of this. Could it be that, living between two addresses, she kept her diary in her bag and it was stolen because the killer believed it contained details of his or her identity?'

I mean, James and I may have conjectured more than the facts warranted, but we didn't lose our marbles. Two addresses! She wasn't living at Gowan Avenue, she used it as a holding address for mail and faxes. No one has ever suggested that the gunman could have been a 'her'! He killed her and at the same time took her diary because it could have identified him!

By all means speculate about a diary to spice up a story, but if one is going to integrate it into the kill, it must meet some basic reality checks. Even if the gunman had known that she carried the diary in her handbag — something her fiancé, Mr Farthing, didn't as he would have told the police — it just beggars belief that he could rely on retrieving it. The gunman cannot kill her in circumstances of his own choosing. He cannot predict that he won't be spotted in the act or that the shot would not be heard, which would deny him the opportunity to rummage around in her bag for the diary that could identify him. This gunman was already riding his luck. He may have had a gun but he was on foot, in an ordinary suburban street with no back-up. He was just a phonecall away from a full-scale manhunt. However unusual the kill, it was still organised and professional. The idea that after shooting Dando he looked for her diary was utterly at odds with his *modus operandi*. Moreover, if his purpose was simultaneously to kill and take the invented diary, he would have just taken her handbag!

The basis for this crackpot theory is Dando's open handbag, but the gunman could not predict or anticipate that happening. Just a moment's critical thought renders this reporter's diary scenario untenable. This selling out of the reader is rightly returned with interest in the contempt cops like Campbell have for journalists.

When I put this diary theory to Hughes, he said, 'I don't think anything like that does any favours to the cause of the situation. I know they have got to sell newspapers and they have got to sell the article, but that doesn't mean you don't write the facts. I'm sure if he'd done more homework, maybe he would have found something.'

Hughes's overall problem with the article was that it went a lot further on him than *Punch* had. 'I was a bit pissed off. They made me look either that I did it or I've got something to hide — which I haven't.' He was also annoyed about the way in which Thomas Penny, the *Mail* reporter, had decided that 'perhaps the most significant change in Mr Hughes's statements is that he told reporters on the day of the murder that he was the first person on the scene ...' As Hughes noted, 'I have never said that.' Which is true.

However, over the following weekend, Hughes's press coverage went from bad to worse. The *News of the World* got in on the act with its particular 'exclusive'. At the time, the *Screws* was edited by Phil Hall. The article was headlined: WHY DOES JILL DANDO'S NEIGHBOUR KEEP NEWS CUTTINGS ON HER MURDER? and the subtitle was 'Police will question broker Richard again'. It went over some of the contradictions that *Punch* had covered earlier, but even I winced for Hughes — and I thought he was guilty! The article ended up with a quote from him in italics: '*I've no idea why anyone would kill Jill.*' Sadly, mate, the *Screws* has a very good idea.

I rang up Hughes under the guise of commiserating with him to see if I could get some kind of newsworthy reaction, but he had really had enough of the press. 'John, people are asking me straight out, "Did you do it?" because that's what this article says. And in so many words ... that's the only interpretation ...' At the urging of James, who found it all hilarious, I offered him the services of our libel lawyer, David Price.

Hughes replied, 'It's very kind of you, John, to make the offer, but I can't be bothered. It was just a bit embarrassing, that's all. I mean at the end of the day, nobody believes what they read in newspapers anyway.'

This made James crack up and he said to me, 'But you started it by nobbling him in the first place. Poor Richard. He was quite happy playing with his stocks and shares until you came along.'

James is more than a bit pronto when it comes to rewriting history. I gasped, 'That's a bit rich. Don't you remember what you said after our first interview?'

'True. But you started it when you kept going on about how guilty he looked the first time you saw him.'

I corrected him, 'Worried. I said worried.'

'Johnnnn ... are we going to quibble over the difference

between guilty and worried? The fact is, you unleashed the press bloodhounds without a thought for Richard, his poor wife Fiona — who, don't forget, is a schoolteacher — and his family.' So it rested, with the persecuted Hughes now becoming Richard.

Meanwhile, Horrocks had not followed up his vague commitment to look at what we had on Hughes, and the articles in the *Mail on Sunday* and the *News of the World* were also ignored. I did a puff piece on the intrepid Campbell getting his man, but there we let sleeping dogs lie. In January, James decided to chase up Horrocks again and, this time, Oxborough did send someone to look at what we had. By now, of course, the squad was scraping the bottom of the barrel where leads were concerned.

In mid-February 2000, we got a call from Detective Constable Mick Hulme, whom Horrocks had actioned for investigating what we had. However, he first requested to see James alone because there was a problem — me! Campbell had a bee in his bonnet about my articles.

They met in a pub — not the Swag but the Bunch of Grapes in the Old Brompton Road — and he told James that Campbell did not like what I had written and Oxborough was under orders to treat me as a criminal. An inactive criminal, but as my past offences were not spent under the 1974 Rehabilitation of Offenders Act, still a criminal. James was bemused to say the least and pointed out, first, that my last crimes were over 30 years ago and second, other detectives who had followed up my articles had never raised this. Hulme just shrugged.

Later on in that month over a few beers, he told James that Campbell was incensed by the leaks about the bisexual ex and the Fiona Hughes lookalike theory. Mick Hulme also had a stab at getting James to divulge my source. He even trailed ex-Commander John O'Connor — with whom I had gone head to head on the *Tonight with Trevor McDonald* programme — as a possible intermediary to someone on the squad. James just laughed at him. 'Mick, you're only doing this because you have been ordered to — you know there isn't a cat in hell's chance of me betraying a source. Hasn't Campbell got better things for his squad to do?' To his credit, Hulme did not defend his boss and spoke volumes by staying inscrutably silent.

However, at this first meeting, James made it clear to Hulme that he would have to deal with me as I had written the Dando articles and had recorded all the Hughes interviews. Of course, James would say that, as the last thing he wanted was to have go through hours of interviews with a detective. After some consultation — presumably with Campbell — the conditions for Oxborough to meet me were that there would always be two detectives, we would not attend a public place, especially any public house, and the conversations would be a 'one-way exchange of information'.

It was all very anal but we could hardly not co-operate. After all, we thought that we had information that could lead them to make a breakthrough in their murder inquiry. It was arranged to meet up at *Punch* and for us to use James's office. I agreed to supply transcripts of the tapes, which they could read while listening to mini disc copies on some small speakers that I temporarily disconnected from my computer. James was there for the introductions before going over to see Mo'.

Mick Hulme arrive with another detective constable, a hatchet-faced Scot named Jim Sword. Wiry, with swept-back, straight dark hair, Sword was eventually to play the hard man in the hard man/soft man duo that Campbell used to interview Barry George after he was arrested.

Hulme is a cheery baldy, about 34-ish, with an infectious grin. He saw my eyes clock the pink shirt and said pointedly, 'My wife ironed this shirt only this morning, so I had to wear it.' He had only just recovered from a rugby accident but he didn't come over as especially athletic, although few rugby players do.

Before we got down to business, I said, 'Look, I know you all think we are just looking for anything sensational that will sell copies of the magazine, but even for us there are more important things than *Punch*. We don't carry a torch for the people's presenter but, at the same time, we do happen to think that catching her murderer comes before the sales of our magazine.'

They both listened politely but clearly were not convinced.

I blathered on a bit more in this vein, then Hulme said, 'I suppose James has told you that this is strictly a one-way exchange of information.'

I nodded. 'We are not looking for any return, I mean we would like to think that, if something comes of it, Campbell will give us an interview or something.'

Hulme eyeballed me. 'I may as well tell you, John, that he won't give you an interview.' It was said honestly and bluntly; Mick Hulme is OK.

The attitude behind the blank was pure Middle England. Whatever low spot you hit in your life, that is where you stay. There was nothing I could do except move on. I explained that what we had on Hughes was fine journalistically, but evidentially it didn't amount to a bag of beans.

We had two sessions of about two hours each, spread over a couple of days during which we ploughed through the tapes. James tended to absent himself but came in every now and again. I would play sections I thought were significant parts; I would then explain why I felt they were worth noting and they would take notes. At one stage, when the bisexual ex-lover stuff came up, I said that, as they knew, we had had some help from a guy on the squad but I trust they were not going to hold that against me. It was a bit embarrassing. I had used it with Hughes to put him on the back foot — the theory was that if he thought that I knew what the squad were doing, he might be nervous. Jim Sword, who hardly spoke during these sessions, grinned and said, 'You use what you have. There's nothing wrong with that. We'd do the same.'

Near the end of proceedings, Hulme, who definitely did suspect Hughes, said there was a section of the squad that believed he was guilty. He added, 'That's not how I work. My method is to set out to do whatever I can to eliminate a person from the inquiry. I don't approach somebody thinking the guy is guilty.'

I suspected that all this stuff about elimination came from Sherlock Homes. 'When you have eliminated the impossible, whatever remains, however improbable, must be the truth.' I somehow fancied that Campbell was a Holmes fan and the source of the method that Hulme was touting. The trouble was that Barry George was so improbable that Campbell was not able to see him until his HOLMES computer programme put him in the frame. But James, who was there when Hulme was spouting this elimination guff, was having none of this. He laughed, 'Mick, you are with us now. We all have the same gut feel about Hughes. Come on.' Hulme acknowledged James's point by laughing, too.

I then added, 'The issue with Hughes is that he should be proofed because if he is eliminated he becomes an important witness of truth. He got a much better look at this guy than you lot realised. It is still not too late to go back to him and work from his description.'

Of course, at that stage none of us knew that George not only fitted Hughes' TV celebrity comparison, but also modelled himself on an SAS man of action. Indeed, he had an SAS dagger tattooed on his right bicep with the motto 'He who dares wins', which he had made his own.

In the end, Hughes's sighting and potentially damning testimony never influenced either George's arrest or conviction. What could have fingered the culprit and convicted him fell by the wayside because of the E-fit bungle and the way the early reports naming George lay in the system for ten months. At trial, Hughes was in the witness box for ten minutes. He just described what he saw in general terms and that was it.

Nine days day later, I cycled over to Fulham to track down Barry George's drop — where he had changed his clothes before going on to HAFAD. On my way back, I went back up Gowan Avenue and I chanced upon Hughes who was carrying some shopping from his car to his home. He was friendly but reserved.

I felt tempted to apologise for the trouble that I'd caused him, but thought I may as well let sleeping dogs lie. Instead, I said, 'It's a fascinating trial, but George could well be acquitted because the Crown have given him an alibi on a plate. They claim that, after the murder, he went home to change his clothes before going on to a disability advice centre in Gresswell Street.' I pointed back towards Fulham football ground. 'But he was there at noon and he could not cover those distances on foot in the time available.'

He asked, 'Did he have a car?'

I said, 'No.' Then I added, 'He had a drop in Bishop's Park where he changed before going to the advice centre.'

'What, you think he did it?' He looked sceptical. So I said that George certainly did it but whether he was legally guilty was another matter.

He wasn't convinced.

I said that I'd get his email address and send him photos of a clean-shaven George. He expressed a polite interest, but I never did. I think he's had enough of journalists — especially me — to last him a lifetime.

7

dc gallagher coats barry george

As Mick Hulme and Jim Sword were putting the Hughes tapes into the system, a review of the low-grade suspects had thrown up the name Barry Bulsara. DC Gallagher was asked to TIE him — trace, interview and eliminate — on 24 February. In keeping with the low priority of the action, Gallagher went first to HAFAD, the original source of the reports that the review had picked up and which it was his task 'to activate'. He went there on 2 and 6 March but he didn't take a notebook.

Gallagher is a bit of a curate's egg detective — a dark, tall, overweight, lumbering man who wears undertaker suits and a lugubrious, introspective expression that doesn't fit his job. That is not to suggest that there is a detective look, merely that, as with many jobs, there is a non-detective look. Gallagher has the look of

115

a man who is too immersed in his own internal problems to be interested in others, which tends to be as much a *sine qua non* of a detective as it is a journalist.

During the trial, he went into the witness box three times and spent quite a lot of time there. Mansfield hauled him over the coals but, while he was burnt, he escaped a roasting. I would often see him outside the court room pacing up and down drawing deeply on a cigarette and looking like his next port of call was before the Grand Inquisitor. He was not the most impressive of witnesses, yet for all the bungling that Mansfield got him on, he still conveyed to the jury not only that he knew that George was guilty, but that he was right, too.

He began trying to contact George on 6 March 2000; by then, he knew from Criminal Records that Bulsara was Barry George with a criminal record for attempted rape, sexual assault and impersonating a police officer, and that he'd been questioned over the Rachel Nickell murder. He approached George by ringing his doorbell and, when there was no reply, putting a card through his letterbox asking him to contact DC Gallagher at Kensington Police Station.

Gallagher put six such calling cards through Barry George's letterbox. On one occasion, George was there but he took care not to reveal his presence. As luck would have it, he was not playing Queen albums at full amplitude, a habit that was not to endear him to his neighbours in Crookham Road. Gallagher did not know at that stage that the Bulsara pseudonym used by George was taken from Freddie Mercury's real name, but he did notice the Mercury and Queen posters in the window.

Eventually, after a month of unanswered calling cards, Gallagher relied on an old ruse for cornering an elusive suspect who signs on for welfare benefit — he sprang him at the Benefits

dc gallagher coats barry george

Office on 11 April 2000. Although Gallagher told George that he wished to interview him over the Dando murders because he had been reported as being in the area when she had been killed, George played dumb about the reason for the cards and told him that he had not responded to them as he thought they were to do with a cycle accident that he had suffered in December in the King's Road. Gallagher had already observed that he had a slight limp.

George went on and on about this accident in the belief that the more he harped on, the more Gallagher would accept him as an urban idiot. One of George's problems was his inability to appreciate that, by the time Oxborough got around to him, they did not see the murder as the work of some criminal mastermind, but a nutter pretty much like him.

Gallagher was suspicious about George — what detective would not be? While the sexual offences were committed in the early '80s, he lived close to Dando and, even from the outside, the flat looked to be the home of an oddball. Gallagher also registered that George was wearing a camouflage combat jacket. There was enough there to think 'Maybe ...'

George agreed to be interviewed, but it quickly transpired that, because of his epilepsy, the interview had to be conducted with 'an appropriate adult' present. An appropriate adult is there to protect the interests of someone who might be suggestible or could misunderstand questions. This protection was introduced in 1984 to protect vulnerable suspects and usually it was a social worker of some kind. Gallagher rang Hammersmith Social Services but they were unhappy about George not being seen first by a doctor who could confirm that he needed such protection. To cut red tape, Gallagher suggested to George that he could use his mother, to which he agreed and, after Gallagher rang her, she agreed as well.

Gallagher was at the Job Centre in Waterford Road and George's mother lived in Fitzneal Street. The direct route should not use Munster Road, but Gallagher decided to take him that way to see if George reacted to passing by Gowan Avenue. Doubtless, he would have liked to have taken George down the avenue itself, but it would have smacked of set-up that might backfire on him, so he took this less obvious detour. Unusually, Mansfield missed using this in his pre-trial challenge to the admissibility of the Gallagher interview.

The circuitous route via Munster Road, though, did bear fruit as the ever-talkative and inventive George told Gallagher that he had seen a Range Rover on the afternoon of the killing backing out of a street, Vera Avenue, near Gowan Avenue. He told Gallagher that he had reported this the next day to the police at the cordon. This was fabricated by George on the spot, but it shows how his mind works. He is invariably attention-seeking and likes to get into any act that that is being played out around him. He also gabbles when he is under pressure. But in his eagerness to get a piece of the action and also to tease Gallagher, he missed that Gallagher had taken him by a circuitous route to his mother's.

When he was actually arrested and being formally interviewed on 25 May, he revived his Range Rover story, but this time he said he saw it 'on the way to my mother' on the evening of the killing. In fact, he invented seeing a Range Rover and he did not go to his mother's by that route on the evening of the murder or any other evening. The only time he went by such a circuitous route was when Gallagher drove him to his mother's.

At his mother's home, George answered questions and Gallagher took down his answers in longhand; although it is a fairly innocuous statement, it tied George into a number of positions that were to have serious consequences for him at trial. He claimed that he was in his flat on the morning of the killing and left for HAFAD at around 12.30pm; his vagueness about times he excused on the basis of not having a watch. He said that he was wearing a three-quarter-length coat and a red tie or a leather jacket and jeans.

Gallagher, of course, already knew from his talks with the HAFAD women and Ramesh Paul at London Traffic Cars that, two days after the murder, George had returned to both places eager to establish the time he had arrived on 26 April and, especially, what colour jacket he was wearing. The reason he gave in both places was that he was suspected of the Jill Dando murder. With cab controller Ramesh Paul, he made such a song and dance about his yellow jacket that Paul was sure that he was up to something. George could not have forgotten all this, so his clothing details did not add up.

His memory of events was also uneven in the depth of detail, which is a characteristic of a constructed account. He could not remember times and had to consult a map to remember his route but he could recall 'on the day in question, I think I was wearing several days of beard growth'.

The statement also recorded another one of George's teasing lies. After the murder, he changed clothes at his drop in Bishop's Park, went to HAFAD, then on to London Traffic Cars, where he asked for a free ride to Rickett Street, which is a small cul de sac off Lillie Road. In the minicab office, he pestered Paul for a freebie ride with such persistence that the controller suspected that George had a hidden agenda. People don't go into minicab offices asking for free rides unless they are crazy or are using the encounter for other purposes.

As luck would have it, though, while he was there another

customer rang the minicab firm and asked for a package to be picked up from Rickett Street; when Paul gave the job to one of his drivers, he told him to drop George off for free. So, by a fluke, George got his free ride.

Aside from the suspicion that he had aroused in Paul, who reported him to Oxborough that day, George clearly knew where Rickett Street was. In his statement to Gallagher, though, George amended his comment on this point to say that the place he went to was in a side-road off Lillie Road, which he did not know the name of. Gallagher had written Lillie Road, but when the statement was read back to George for him to sign, he insisted on clarifying this. It duly was and he initialled the change.

Now it was obvious to anyone who listened to the evidence at trial that George had been lying and was being pedantic in recording his lies to boot. But so what? What did his lies over Rickett Steet have to do with the murder of Jill Dando? Nothing, except that some jurors thought they indicated what kind of person George is — the kind of 'nutter', as Paul described him, who had murdered Dando. George's feigned ignorance of Rickett Street was another one of George's affected teases, which, while it had no bearing on his actual guilt or innocence, did go to more than his credibility. It wasn't merely that it showed George to be a liar, but a liar who lies for the pleasure of manipulating others; a devious, scheming liar and not the bumbling simpleton that the medical evidence and the defence claimed. After all, he was deliberately lying contrary to a presentation of himself as someone who wanted to help the police solve the murder. Perhaps the reasoning of the Dando jury was as surreal as the murder but, as we shall see later, that is what they did.

When Gallagher drove George back from his mother's to Crookham, he also had the nous to ask if he could look at the three-quarter-length coat that he said he may have been wearing on 26 April 1999. Gallagher's lack of interest in the leather jacket and jeans showed that he was up to speed on the witness statements in that some of the people who saw George hanging around Gowan Avenue described him as wearing a dark, three-quarter-length coat. At Crookham Road, Gallagher waited at George's flat door while he climbed over the piles of rubbish in the hallway to retrieve and show him the coat that he referred to in his statement. He looked at it, then left George to his own devices.

George showed him a cheap, imitation Barbour-type coat that certainly was not the navy-blue Cecil Gee coat that, with its secreted firearm's particle, was to provide the longest *Carry On Up the Old Bailey* theme at the trial. This 11 April incident should only have been a sideshow to the particle but, quite unpredictably, it produced one of the turning points in the trial.

On 18 April, Oxborough swooped on 2b Crookham Road with a search warrant and among other items impounded was the dark-blue Cecil Gee coat as it matched the clothing, as described by witnesses, worn by a man seen hanging around Gowan Avenue a couple of hours before the murder. This garment, along with others went away for forensic analysis but the particle was not discovered in its right-hand inside pocket until 2 May. The discovery of this particle tipped the scales in Oxborough's decision to arrest and charge George for murder.

The particle was not conclusive as, while it was the same type as those from the bullet that killed Dando, roughly 20 per cent of manufactured bullets use the same kind of primer that, on firing, deposits such particles. Nevertheless, the particle was a hot potato for the defence and, as I describe in the next chapter, Mansfield's sustained attack on it was to dominate the trial. However, he also thought he could make hay with the fact that the coat George showed Gallagher on 11 April was not the Cecil Gee coat.

When Mansfield began cross-examining Gallagher about the 11 April production of the coat, the detective's habitual hangdog expression went positively bloodhound. He knew what was coming.

Mansfield asked, 'Did anything strike you about the coat?'

Gallagher conceded, 'I thought it was different to the one I had seen previously.'

Mansfield countered with mock theatrical disbelief, 'Did you?'

Gallagher just looked at him even more doggedly.

Mansfield continued, 'I want to ask you carefully about this. Have you ever indicated to anyone before the day you first gave evidence in this case that the coat was different to the one shown by Mr George in his premises?'

Gallagher replied, 'Yes,' but he wasn't very convincing.

'When?' Mansfield asked, eyeing Gallagher as if it was obvious to all non-policemen that he was lying.

Gallagher looked like he was, but decided that passing the buck was better than having Mansfield at his throat. He replied with even less conviction, 'When I went back to the station, I told DS Rowell about it.'

Mansfield knew that neither Rowell nor Gallagher had put this in their witness statements. He asked at his most incredulous, 'Did you not put that in a statement? In all the statements that you have made, that is not an observation that you have recorded, is it?' Mansfield doesn't waste time with the theatricals when the jugular is exposed.

Gallagher mumbled, 'No.'

Mansfield asked matter-of-factly, 'Why not?'

Gallagher drew on his fall-back position. He replied,

'Statements are purely an account of what I have done and the times that I handled exhibits and so on.'

Mansfield leaned forward, his right hand clasping a pen like a conductor's baton to orchestrate the thunder in his voice. 'But it *was* of great importance and may *still* be. It is in none of your statements that this coat may not have been the one you saw before. There has been no suggestion up 'til now that the coat you saw on the 11th is not the coat that we are discussing.'

Gallagher looked resigned.

Mansfield snapped at him, 'When did you tell DS Rowell that the coat was not the same?'

Gallagher replied, 'When I got back to the station.' Then he added an incongruous afterthought. 'I did not see it as significant.' He should have known that everything is significant to Mansfield.

Mansfield looked at the jury with exasperation. 'But soon afterwards, a particle was found, so it *may* be significant!'

Gallagher kept to his *significant* guns. 'Even then, I didn't think it was significant.'

Mansfield bellowed with rage, 'WHAT? Even after finding a particle?!'

Gallagher looked safer. He had weathered the storm. 'Not really.'

Mansfield pulled out all his sarcasm stops. 'Because it was a very small particle?'

Gallagher started to fight back. 'I did not see any relevance as to which particular coat it was found in.' He had already done significant, now relevance. Relevance is another red rag word that you don't wave lightly at Mansfield.

Mansfield rolled out another wave of thunder. 'It doesn't *matter* which coat it was found **in**?!' Sometimes it is difficult to divine whether Mansfield is asking a rhetorical question or declaiming, but he is a dab hand at combining the two.

Gallagher seemed to regret that he hadn't used *significance* and *relevance* together. He muttered with more than a little of what army wallahs call dumb insolence, 'Yes.'

Mansfield snapped at him again. 'What do you mean?'

Justice Gage decided that Gallagher had taken enough punishment on this point and intervened urbanely, 'I think that he is agreeing with you, Mr Mansfield.'

But a battered Gallagher decided he had had enough of playing possum while Mansfield kicked the life out of him. With justificatory brio and a flourish of his left hand, he retorted, 'It made no difference as we found the particle anyway.' The court collectively gasped at this breathtaking rationalisation of Oxborough's methods. Even Mansfield was flummoxed by its boldness. His slightly hyperthyroid eyes blinked rapidly and the surprise of it silenced him.

But '... we found the particle anyway!' went down well with some of the jurors. One of them was dubbed 'Bob the Builder' by Dando's BBC colleague Nicholas Witchell who attended most of the trial. Bob the Builder was always pleased when Mansfield got a bit back in kind and he smirked openly at Mansfield when Gallagher landed this sucker punch. Gallagher, though, was suddenly no longer a detective in the witness box at a murder trial but the guy propping up the bar saying, 'Of course he did it. We have got to have a trial and prove it and all that, but he did it all right.' Gallagher's expression, body language and tone shrieked this out. Verdicts can turn on moments like this, and no amount of reading the transcripts of the trial can recapture the effect this one had on certain members of the jury.

Mansfield pegged some of this back when Rowell went into the witness box. Rowell said that he could not remember

dc gallagher coats barry george

Gallagher mentioning that on 11 April George had shown him another coat and had not shown the Cecil Gee one.

Detective Sergeant Andy Rowell came over as a truthful witness and replied to Mansfield, 'I do not remember that. No.'

Mansfield milked Rowell's contradiction of Gallagher by pretending that he had not understood it. 'I am sorry?'

Rowell again repeated what he had said previously. Mansfield, not believing that experienced detectives cannot even sing from the same hymn sheet, played the detective's words back to him. 'You do not remember that, no?'

Rowell replied explicitly, 'No.'

Nevertheless, Gallagher had done the damage with his 'we found the particle anyway'.

But poor Gallagher was cast as Oxborough's patsy. Before the Cecil Gee coat was taken to the forensic laboratory to be examined, someone had had the bright idea of having it photographed, so that Gowan Avenue witnesses could be shown the photographs to jog their memory. Gallagher was detailed for the job. He collected the coat from the exhibits room and took it, together with one of his own shirts, to a photographic studio where he put the shirt and the coat on a tailor's dummy and the photographer whacked off some shots.

There were two problems with this. One, no witnesses were ever shown these photographs, although they were made exhibits at the trial. Two, the photographic studio had previously been used to photograph firearms used in other cases. Quite apart from this being contrary to all the guidelines about handling exhibits that are to be examined forensically, it also handed the defence the perfect explanation for the later discovery of the particle — it had been contaminated in the photographic studio.

Naturally, Mansfield conducted a full-scale witch-hunt into

who ordered Gallagher to take the coat to the photographic studio and this line of enquiry turned into a classic *Carry On Up the Old Bailey* scene. Gallagher fingered Rowell again, but instead of turning it back on Gallagher, Rowell passed the buck to Campbell!

To Mansfield's question 'Who ordered that the Cecil Gee coat be photographed?' Rowell replied, 'I would imagine it would have been between myself, DCI Campbell and perhaps some other officers.'

Mansfield doesn't need much aroma to smell a rat and this one stunk. He asked, 'I want to be clear — who actually took responsibility for the decision that any clothing that was relevant would be photographed?'

Rowell tried answering another question. 'It would have been myself who told DC Gallagher to have clothing photographed.'

Justice Gage graciously pointed out what Mansfield was never going to miss anyway, 'That is not quite what you are being asked.'

Rowell began to unload this now very smelly rat on to Campbell. 'I think it would have been borne out of the discussion, a general agreement between myself, Mr Campbell and any other officers.'

Mansfield wanted the dead rat just where Rowell was putting it. 'Mr Campbell was the officer in charge, so did you understand that he was taking responsibility for the decision which you communicated to DC Gallagher?'

'Ultimately, if he is in charge, then it is his decision. Yes,' Rowell conceded.

Mansfield still had a way to go but, for sure, he was going to get there. 'But he was in charge, was he not?'

Rowell had done the deed. 'Then it would be his decision. Yes.'

Mansfield wanted it in spades, though. 'Sorry, I am not

dealing in hypotheticals. He was in charge on the day on which you had the discussion. Yes?'

'That is correct, my lord, yes.' Rowell was slightly rattled at making his boss the fall guy and replied as if he was addressing Justice Gage.

Mansfield clarified what had taken place. 'So he takes responsibility as a result of this conversation for a decision that the clothing that is relevant should be photographed?'

Rowell capitulated. 'That is correct. Yes.'

An anguished Campbell at the back of the court looked on. When it was his turn to take the stand, he decided that he wasn't taking responsibility for any of it.

He claimed that he was unaware that the coat had gone off to the photographic studios, which Mansfield delicately derided. 'I suggest that is inaccurate ... Do you remember Mr Rowell giving evidence?'

As he had been in court, Campbell had to agree that he did.

Mansfield asked, 'Do you remember what he said about the giving of the instruction?'

Campbell bit the bullet. 'He indicated that I had given the instruction.'

Mansfield nodded approvingly. He encourages police officers to be truthful, although he prefers to catch them out. 'That is right. Is he right?'

Campbell, as is his wont when his back is to the wall, went on a verbal walkabout. 'No. I have said in my statement that I think there is a misunderstanding by that officer in terms of me giving him the instruction to photograph that coat, because I am more than happy to admit to anything and claim responsibility for anything. But I did not tell DS Rowell to have the coat photographed.'

jȯhn mcvicar

He was very emphatic but, unfortunately for Campbell, he could not unload the dead rat back on to Rowell without implicating the scientist, Dr Keeley, who found the particle. Keeley gave evidence that he did not know that the Cecil Gee coat had gone to the photographic studio until nine months after he had discovered the particle. Campbell had made a statement that he told Keeley at the time, so he had Rowell and Keeley against him.

When Campbell said in cross-examination that he had told Keeley at the time, Mansfield put on his disbelieving expression and asked, 'Are you sure?'

Campbell replied steely, 'Yes.'

Again Mansfield asked, 'Are you sure?'

Campbell did another verbal walkabout. 'I am. This is one of the areas of puzzlement to me because I have the records of times I have spoken to the Forensic Science Service over issues and I know that it was a matter which was raised ...'

Mansfield waited until he petered out, 'You have been in court, so you know what is behind the question?'

Campbell replied, 'Yes.'

Mansfield then summarised what Keeley had given in evidence. Keeley had quite specifically and surely said that the first time he knew the coat had been in a photographic studio before he examined it was in February 2001. It was on the day that he had gone to the studio with the defence expert on firearms particles to investigate the possibility of contamination.'

Campbell listened as Mansfield tolled off the evidence of Keeley interjecting the odd 'yes' or 'I heard him say that'. Then Mansfield asked, 'Do you have a record of telling Mr Keeley a year before that you were worried about contamination?'

Campbell again went on a verbal walkabout. 'I certainly had a number of conversations with Mr Keeley. And I have the notes I have made, having listened to this issue. I first spoke to Mr Keeley about this issue for the four days that I was at Hammersmith Police Station dealing with Mr George. The conversation with Mr Keeley was over a number of days and this was one. It was not a major issue, but it was one of the matters I raised.'

'I am sorry to be precise,' Mansfield said disingenuously. In fact, he revels in being precise, especially with detectives impaled on the horns of their contradictions. He continued, 'But the question was — "Do you have a record?" If you do not mind, I would like to see it in a minute if it is relevant. Do you have a record of what you said and when you said it to Mr Keeley?'

Campbell flushed as the horns on which he was impaled ripped through his mind. 'No. These notes certainly are notes made during the court ... It is a diary for the court proceedings, so when I have listened to that, I have always maintained that this is not correct ... So I can explain the chronology so far as I am concerned and I know Mr Keeley is mistaken ...'

Mansfield let Campbell's incoherence speak for itself before interrupting, 'Yes, I do not want to stop you. I really do not.' No, not much. 'The question is whether you have in front of you a record, something you have written down, saying, "discussed with Keeley, contamination?"'

'I am saying ...'

Mansfield cut off this verbal walkabout. 'What is the answer to that?'

Campbell sucked the lemon, then replied sourly, 'No. I have not got that written record.' It wasn't his finest moment as head of Oxborough.

Amongst all this knockabout coat stuff, however, Gallagher made his impression on the jury. He was also the first officer who got George to condemn himself with his own lies. The proof of that particular pudding is that when the Dando jury retired, the first new exhibit they asked to examine in the jury room was the original handwritten statement that Gallagher had taken from George. They already had a typewritten copy but they requested the one that showed George's corrections, which he himself had initialled. Gallagher was one of the few Oxborough detectives who advanced the conviction of Barry George.

8

the particle that tips the scales vanishes

After taking George's statement, Gallagher reported back to Oxborough ... and suddenly George leapt into the frame. Campbell had the feel that they had their man. George fitted all that was left. The exes and Serbs had long gone, the Sweating Man dismissed, the Range Rover virtually eliminated, the mobile phone enquiry still there but more a ritual than a serious line of investigation; all that was left was the obsessive loner, 'nutter' theory. Certainly, George's actual motive turned out to be slightly more obscure than the undeclared stalker or obsessive, but for the purposes of Oxborough he was their man. He had a criminal record for offences against women; he was clearly an oddball loner — part of his statement to Gallagher read, 'I believe I was suffering from a mild personality disorder ...'; he had an interest in the military and, as Gallagher had ascertained, he had been in the

Territorial Army in the early '80s. George told him, '... but I don't recall doing any training with real ammunition ... and have not had access to any firearms since that time.' That was his claim but, given that he otherwise fitted the bill, Barry George was the only suspect now.

Exactly a week after Gallagher had taken a statement from Barry George, Oxborough moved on 2b Crookham Road, and with a duly authorised warrant, searched the place. Among the specified items that they were looking for were clothing, documents, firearms and wigs! They impounded a number of items, the most significant being the dark-blue Cecil Gee three-quarter-length coat, part of a shoulder holster, a handwritten list of replica guns and a number of undeveloped rolls of film. Barry George was still allowed to live there, although after the second search on 11 May when they took the place apart, they barred him from the flat and he had to go into temporary accommodation.

Two days after the first search, the BBC broadcast a *Crimewatch* special on the unsolved Dando case in which Campbell appeared live answering questions put by Nick Ross. It was an intriguing performance which no one in the post-trial euphoria of George's conviction or even those who felt grave doubts about it have analysed properly.

When he made that programme, Campbell knew that Barry George was in the frame and while he diluted some of his comments about the loner/stalker/interest in the military with general appeals for witnesses, he offered a profile of the killer that fits George like a glove. He tells the viewers 'to look at one very strong possibility: that Jill was killed by one person working on his own ... This man clearly has an interest in guns and firearms and an interest in specialist magazines that cater for such an interest. There is something odd about him; he might be alone but isolated ... not married, having difficulty with previous relationships ... separate, away from society and groups of people. Perhaps a loner ... very likely to have had an interest in Jill Dando, or if not Jill, an unhealthy attraction, infatuation or obsession with women.'

In fact, after the HOLMES system review spewed up Barry George leading to Gallagher's action to TIE him, Campbell had given a press conference on 8 March 2000, two days after Gallagher first tried to contact George. This was the first time that Campbell enunciated his loner theory — he said it was based on 'gut feel'.

Everything he invokes in the *Crimewatch* profile is derived from the interview of George and the searching of his home, especially the reference to firearms magazines — these were found in George's flat! Hundreds of photographs of women that George snapped in the street were also discovered. Campbell's manner on the programme is odd. In contrast with his previous year's performance, he is nervous, halting and, when he has George in the frame, seemingly still in the dark as to the identity of the murderer. Yet the previous year, when he really was clueless, he was quietly confident.

What was going on? Well, Campbell was priming the media.

Anyone attempting to understand the jury system, especially in a sensational murder, should always bear in mind the words of a now discredited but once famous American trial lawyer, F Lee Bailey: 'A trial is a show for the jury, not a search for truth.' I don't know any trial lawyer who would disagree with this. Sophisticated players like Mansfield play out their theatricals in court, but just because they can't strut around on stage doesn't mean that seasoned detectives are any less skilled in shaping the production. Campbell did not make it through the ranks of the Detective Constable also-rans without learning a few tricks of the trade.

Any smart detective at the *Crimewatch* stage of the investigation into George would know that they are in a long game in which every edge may count and therefore should be honed to cut their way. Campbell knew when he appeared on *Crimewatch* that his comments would — as they did — receive wide publicity; he also knew, as any experienced detective would, that the arrest of George would dominate the headlines. He was laying the groundwork for the arrest. To hardened legal players, these are conventional trial tactics.

Potential jurors are public opinion and, in a sensational case like the Dando murder, any pre-trial publicity, no matter how circumscribed by our laws of contempt, is managed by the police to suit their interests. Generally, at this phase of the show, the police hold all the trump cards as they know the reporters and can brief them off the record. The defence usually holds no cards at this stage, although Neil and Christine Hamilton when they were arrested over rape allegations in August 2001 did utilise the press extremely effectively to offset the negative prejudice that would probably be created by their arrest and questioning. Generally, though, all the defendant's advisers can do is monitor the publicity with an eye to making a pre-trial application that their client cannot receive a fair trial — which usually fails — and to ensure any media outlets that breach the contempt laws are reported to the Attorney General for prosecution.

The publicity that occurred after George's arrest was massive and much of it went towards upholding the profile of the murderer that Campbell had run on the *Crimewatch* programme. Reporters were briefed off the record that Oxborough was 'absolutely confident' that they had the right man and the subsequent publicity was a PR triumph for the squad. This was not an accident but a skilful tactic of Campbell's that goes to his credit as a detective.

Barry George was not actually arrested until 25 May, some six weeks after Gallagher's first visit. During that period, he began, as he always intended, to traffic in being suspected of Dando's murder. Sometimes he would make comments to acquaintances and neighbours such as Emiko Okoturo. 'The police are after me but I didn't do it.' At other times, he would enjoy teasing people with his possible guilt. One neighbour, who did not want to be named, asked him if the police activity had anything to do with Jill Dando and he smiled. 'I can't say anything because the police will arrest me.'

One of his regular pit stops where he pestered women was Jazzy G, a hairdresser's on the Fulham High Street. There he spoke to a young, streetwise black girl named Lenita Bailey, and she heard him repeat his Range Rover story, but this time he admitted making it up. She told him that he was asking for trouble and, on an impulse, she asked him if he did it. In fact, she asked him three times, and each time he stared guiltily at the floor rather than answer.

Just after the broadcast of the second *Crimewatch* appeal, he also told Sally Mason, a neighbourhood friend, 'I was there, you know.' She told the jury that she dismissed it 'as Barry being Barry'.

Meanwhile, Oxborough was stepping up its investigation of George and, on 2 May, they began to shadow him, engaged an undercover detective to befriend him and also installed a hidden video camera trained on the house in which his flat was located. George responded by beginning to grow what turned into a goatee and moustache. As he had in the past periodically grown facial hair, at trial the Crown had to concede that no significance could be put upon this and, even though a number of witnesses on the various parades expressed frustration at being confronted with a line-up of people with goatees and moustaches, it was not held against him. Unfortunately, Campbell didn't request that George remove his facial hair for the parades, which, if he had refused, would have given Pownall licence to accuse him of deliberately misleading potential witnesses.

During this period, George made no attempt to curb his stalking hobby and, on his travels around London, he continued to pavement-crawl women. He also knew he was being watched and followed and let the observation team know that he was aware of their presence. He may have been the mouse, but he liked showing the cats that he didn't think they would ever get the evidence to pounce.

*   *   *

At *Punch*, James and I knew very little of these developments, but rumours of them were circulating among various crime reporters who had been contacted by George's neighbours. Certainly, the 19 April *Crimewatch* appeal left us with the unpalatable conclusion that our Hughes suspicions had not stood up. We bounced what little we knew around and, eventually, in mid-May James rang Mick Hulme to test the water. It was early evening and Hulme was all cloak and dagger. 'I can't talk now, James, as I am on observation duty.' He was on the move, presumably following the suspect, but his excitement alone spoke for itself. James asked him directly if they expected to make an arrest soon. 'James, you know I can't say anything but expect a major development soon.'

James switched off his mobile and said to me, 'They are on to him — whoever he is. Mick [Hulme] is giving me as good a steer as he can without telling me. I know him. I bet they make an arrest soon.' I felt sidelined as I knew with Hughes out of the frame, Campbell — and through him, Oxborough — would not give me the time of day.

On 2 May 2000, the Cecil Gee coat went to the Forensic Science Laboratory and Dr Robin Keeley examined it. In the inside right-hand pocket he found a firearm residue particle that had the same chemical elements as those from the bullet that killed Dando. By the nature of these compounds, chemical analysis cannot tie any single particle to a particular cartridge. Even though it was the same, the particle could have come from any cartridge that used that particular brand of primer. The manufacturers of commercial cartridges use five types of primer and the best the ballistic scientists can do is say which of the five types a particular particle belongs to. The cartridge primer of the Remmington 'short' bullet that killed Dando constitutes 20–30 per cent of the market, so there was roughly a 5–1 chance that the particle from the Cecil Gee coat came from the same brand of cartridge used on Dando.

The particle tipped the scales in the decision to arrest George for the murder of Dando and, at trial, it began as the foundation of the case against him. In his opening speech that summarised the case to the jury, Pownall said, '… this defendant happens to have a particle in the inside of his coat, which he admits he might have been wearing that day. This aspect of the case provides compelling evidence of his guilt.'

That week, *Private Eye* published a spoof on Pownall's opening:

> *The Prosecution in the Dando murder trial today produced the final conclusive piece of evidence which will nail Britain's most hated killer to the tragic death of the most popular TV personality in history.*
>
> *The courtroom hushed as the jury were asked to 'look very closely indeed' at a tiny particle of household dust, barely one-billionth of a millimetre long.*

Particle of Faith

It is on this microspeck of domestic detritus,' said Inspector Knacker of the Yard, 'that the whole of our case against the killer rests.'

The court then heard evidence from forensic experts that the piece of dust found in the sole of the accused's shoe was 'of exactly the same type, more or less' as dust found on a pavement close to the murdered TV star's West London home.

'I think you will agree,' the Inspector told the jury, 'that finding this key piece of dust is as good as putting a noose around the guilty man's neck.'

Dust Proof

The press gallery, packed with fearless and unbiased investigative reporters, burst into spontaneous applause as the journalists began tapping into their laptops headlines such as DANDO MAN DEFINITELY GUILTY. (To be continued.)

Brian Cathcart, the author of *Jill Dando: Her Life and Death*, passed it on to Mansfield while the case was in recess, thinking he would go ballistic as the article was so flagrantly in contempt of court. Mansfield just guffawed openly as he read it and looked up to us on the press benches. 'It's not contempt enough.'

Yet, presciently for *Private Eye*, the particle evidence did end up if not exactly a joke certainly not bearing any of the weight that Pownall gave it in his opening. Mansfield had to and did conduct a war of attrition on its presence. He was at his most brilliant, commanding, relentless and detailed — as well as boring — in the way in which he mercilessly examined how the coat was found, stored, sent to a photographic studio first, then on to to the forensic laboratory for analysis, the examination procedure used by the

the particle that tips the scales

forensic scientist who found the particle ... The provenance of the particle was subjected to the same scrutiny as the discovery of a new Michelangelo masterpiece. In terms of time, this evidence dominated the trial as probably a third of it was spent dissecting the particle's significance as Mansfield and Pownall went head to head on it.

There were all manner of possibilities whereby the particle could get inside the pocket of George's Cecil Gee coat and Mansfield ran each one *ad nauseam*. Sometimes, the particle from whatever source seemed to have a life of its own, having been genetically programmed like a homing pigeon to do everything possible to return to its place of release — Barry George. It was often hilarious but, evidentially, nonsense. The trouble with getting the truth on the particle to come through was threefold: Mansfield's brilliance; Pownall's inability to counter his ingenuity and resourcefulness; and Oxborough's problems.

Pownall, though, does rather plod for the Treasury. He is effective but over a long trial his earnest, ponderous single-key style kills off the brain cells. For me, Pownall lost it in two fundamental ways: if you are up against Mansfield in a case in which he pulls out all the stops, you just have to burn the midnight oil and Pownall self-evidently didn't. Time and time again, the court saw how Mansfield had mastered the fine print and Pownall hadn't, how Mansfield had primed and tuned into his expert witnesses and Pownall hadn't. Second, there was Pownall's inability to undermine the way Mansfield continually pushed the argument beyond the criminal standard of proof and into the scientific.

Days were spent listening to Mansfield debating issues that were not dissimilar to considering the possibility of being hit by a meteorite if we go out for a walk — doubtless such things happen somewhere in the world, but the possibility does not influence our behaviour. Although Pownall is an able and distinguished Treasury counsel, as well as being more likeable than Mansfield, he failed to keep the arguments over the scientific evidence in the realms of common sense.

Mansfield ran riot over how the particle in the Cecil Gee coat could have got there through contamination. One ballistic expert called by the Crown did lampoon Mansfield's argument. Dr Renshaw, a thin, dry, whiplash of a man, put one of Mansfield's possibilities of contamination succinctly: 'An ambulance man called to the scene of the murder touched the body and picked up a particle that he then deposited on the gate as he left. A passing dog brushed up against the gate and the particle clung to his coat. A detective at the scene stroked the dog and the particle transferred to his hand. He then went back to the Kensington incident room where he touched the table on which the Cecil Gee coat was in its exhibit bag ...' Eventually, with every possibility you could get the particle in the pocket of the Cecil Gee coat. However, some of the exchanges were so remote as to be laughable and, when you strung them together, the odds against this occurrence were stacked up so high that they became ludicrous and, even at a scientific standard of proof, discountable.

Nevertheless, there was something iffy about the particle. Pownall was the only one to actually to raise the issue of planting by pointing out that a particle of about 10 microns, which is about a ten millionth of a centimetre, was too microscopic to plant. He told the jury, 'Bearing in mind the size of the particle, it would be difficult for somebody to deliberately contaminate the garment.' It is difficult to gainsay this. Could even a sophisticated planter detect and lift one particle from Dando's effects then transfer it to the Cecil Gee coat?

Yet, the evidence seems to point to George making a mistake and accidentally contaminating his own coat himself. He was not wearing the Cecil Gee coat when he shot Dando nor did he change into it before he went to HAFAD. Hughes is emphatic about the gunman wearing a Barbour coat. He is far too precise and sure in his description to be mistaken. The HAFAD women, another woman in the street whom George spoke to when he left HAFAD and Ramesh Paul are all conclusive about him having changed into jeans and a yellow blouson or shirt after the murder. However, all the descriptions of the witnesses who saw him hanging around Gowan Avenue between 7.00–10.15am mention him wearing the coat.

There is also other evidence that the Crown did not call. Just before she drove to Gowan Avenue that Monday morning, Dando bought two Dover soles in a fish shop in Fulham Palace Road called Copes. It is more or less opposite Crookham Road where George lived. George hung around Gowan Avenue on his murder watch from before 7.00am. However, at around 10.00am his nerve began to crack. Terry Griffin, the postman, was the last straw. Griffin thought that George was shaping up to steal a package from his trolley and looked suspiciously at him, which made him bolt home to his address in Crookham Road at around 10.15am. However, George was probably too hyped up to stay indoors and was hanging around where Crookham Road intersects Fulham Palace Road wondering whether to resume his Dando watch or take it up another day, when he spotted Dando at Copes.

The fish shop assistant, Said Djemil, saw George hanging around outside not realising, of course, that he was not a rubbernecking fan but her putative killer checking out that it really was her. Unfortunately for the Crown, a year later when Djemil attended the ID parade, although he picked out George he conceded that he wasn't sure. It wasn't a positive identification. The Crown decided not to use his evidence because Djemil was sure that George was not wearing a coat. This meant that to tally with the evidence of Hughes and Upfill-Brown, George would have had to have gone back to his flat, put on a coat, pack his gun and leg it to 29 Gowan Avenue in order to arrive before Dando drove up in her BMW.

The logistics looked dodgy. It's about 700 metres and she found a parking spot right outside number 29. The Crown decided that this would open up a Pandora's box for Mansfield to plague their case and they decided not to use it, even though a number of the squad, including Horrocks, believed that this is what happened. In one of the breaks during the trial, I asked Pownall why they did not go for this scenario. He admitted it was a 50–50 decision but, on balance, they decided it was simpler to stay with the version they ran at trial, which was that George stayed in the vicinity of Gowan Avenue until she turned up. But, obviously, George did not.

Aside from my chat with Pownall reminding me of the stark difference between my understanding of the trial and the jury's, his explanation of why the Crown did not call Djemil brought home to me how unbelievably unlucky Dando was. On 26 April 1999, George got lucky, while Dando was supremely unlucky. In a sense, she died like the victim of a fatal collision between two cars, which would not have happened if both drivers had not made critical mistakes at the same time. If she had not bought fish or if he had decided to stay indoors, there would have been no murder. As George was later to say cryptically to people in prison, 'She was *dead on time.*'

He often describes significant events in the holy text of Queen lyrics, but the timing was so fluky no wonder he saw it as preordained. The poignancy for those who loved and knew her is that he may well have never got another opportunity to kill her. He chose to stake her out during the one and final period when she would frequent Gowan Avenue. George was used to failure and would have soon passed on his plan to kill her if he'd kept drawing a blank on his Dando watch. He literally got her the first time because of two Dover soles.

Yet, I know from conversations that George had with inmates in Belmarsh Prison that he was ballistically clued-up enough to get rid of the clothes he committed the crime in, as well as those he changed into before he went on to HAFAD. However, he almost certainly tested the gun before the day of the murder and clearly had it on him when he was wearing the Cecil Gee coat earlier that morning. The likeliest explanation for the particle, then, is that it had come from another test-fired bullet from the same batch as the one he used on Dando. He deposited the particle during his early aborted watch on number 29 but was not ballistically clued-up enough afterwards to realise that he could have contaminated the Cecil Gee coat with particles from his test firing. He got rid of the Barbour but was shrewd enough to show Gallagher a similar coat when he was asked on 11 April.

The particle started out as the foundation of the Crown's case but, by the time evidence had closed, it was relegated to a corroboratory role. Before the closing speeches, Justice Gage asked Pownall in the absence of the jury if the particle was now the foundation of the Crown's case. Justice Gage's tone was unmistakable — he would not support such weight being put upon it. Pownall blanched as if he was before the firing squad and asked what were his last words. He turned and consulted with Allison Saunders of the CPS before requesting from Gage time to consider his answer. This was granted. He conferred over the lunch break and came back and said, 'No, the Crown now looked to the particle only as corroboration of evidence of identification and HAFAD.' Mansfield's face didn't flicker. He just looked rock solid at the papers in front of him; he knew he held an unbeatable hand.

At this point, all the lawyers and legally clued-up spectators — which included few journos — knew that the Crown had all but thrown in the towel and that George had to be acquitted. The identification evidence went only to George lurking suspiciously around Gowan Avenue prior to the murder; it did not go to anything that was directly linked to the killing. HAFAD went evidentially to George being unable to have been both there and having killed Dando. Thus the two main planks of the Crown's case were pulped. On the evidence, the jury had to acquit.

Pownall lost his way completely when the particle went but, curiously enough, a rational appraisal of the evidence on the particle still left it securely in George's pocket. Mansfield had battered it into oblivion, not by rebutting the evidence on it, but by the way he beleaguered it from so many angles that it appeared that all that Pownall could do was surrender it. And he did. Yet Mansfield's barrage was all smoke and mirrors; if Pownall could have waited until the dust had settled, he would have seen that the particle was still *virgo intacta* in the pocket of that Cecil Gee coat.

Nonetheless, the particle found in George's Cecil Gee coat, which began the trial as the foundation of the Crown's case, only to be abandoned at the end, was the critical factor in arresting Barry George for the murder of Jill Dando. This was hardly DNA or fingerprint evidence but, with a wealth of circumstantial evidence building up against George, the positive on the particle tipped the scales. On 25 May 2000, in a dawn raid, Oxborough swooped on 2b Crookham Road and arrested Barry George on suspicion of murdering Jill Dando.

9

barry george is charged

Barry George was woken by policemen hammering on his door at 6.30am. He thought that they had come to search the place again — the last one on 11 May had begun at 7.00am. This time, though, it was to arrest him on suspicion of murdering Jill Dando with a view to interviewing him formally under caution. As is increasingly the practice in serious cases nowadays, the interviews were videoed. However, they also came to search the flat in the most meticulous fashion possible: specialist search officers removed all his possessions and then probed under floorboards and into wall cavities.

He was cautioned, handcuffed and swagged off to Hammersmith Police Station, where his own clothing was taken for analysis. He was issued with a forensic white paper suit — the sort that police officers or scientists wear on searches or while examining evidence when every precaution is being taken against contamination. He wore it in the interviews conducted that afternoon and evening. This tactic of removing the detainee's clothing also helps disorient him and makes him slightly more vulnerable to questioning.

George was surprised by his arrest but not flustered and began asking for his solicitor, Marilyn Etienne. She had refused to attend the last search at his home but now he had been formally arrested for murder, and legal aid was automatically available, she attended. She is the senior partner in a small legal firm in West Kensington. She is black, slight and glamorous, with elaborately straightened, slicked-back hair. At the trial, she invariably wore stylish black clothes with half-raised Cuban-heeled shoes that tipped her forward slightly and contributed to her permanently hurried look.

She is very industrious and keen to appear so. If she wasn't sitting behind Mansfield taking notes, she was rushing around either the court or its environs with papers in hand on some do-or-die mission for her client. Her busy-bee number was also used to brush off enquiring journalists and none of us attending the trial got anything from her. The only time I saw her give one the time of day was after the verdict in the impromptu press conference outside the Old Bailey, when she read a speech prepared by Mansfield, announcing that George would appeal and extolling his innocence. However, when she finished, a journalist who had come along just for the day asked her for her name. She said, 'Marilyn Etienne.' Then moved to return back inside the building. However, the journalist, with notebook poised, asked her how she spelt it. She stopped and, leaning forward, spelt out her name letter by letter, checking as he wrote it down that it was accurate. Then she stomped off.

George was also medically examined for fitness to be

interviewed. During his period at Hammersmith Police Station before being charged, he saw ten doctors! Nonetheless, he gave eight hours of interview, which was recorded on video tape and played to the jury at the trial. He agreed to the interviews, even though Etienne questioned the wisdom of him doing so, but he brushed aside her reservations. There was little Etienne could do except attend them and intervene whenever the police, in her view, overstepped the mark.

At the first interview on 25 May at 5.30pm, she portentously introduced herself from a drafted statement. 'I'm Marilyn Etienne, solicitor with Kean Etienne. I'm now required to explain my role. It is to protect my client's basic and legal rights. I shall continue to advise my client throughout the interview. My client has decided to answer questions which you may raise that are relevant to his arrest. I should intervene if my client requests or requires legal advice or your questioning is inappropriate or you make statements which are not based on evidence of which I'm aware.'

The next day, between interviews, George was driven to Kilburn Police Station where he participated in a live identity parade which was attended by five witnesses, including Richard Hughes and Joseph Sapleton, the source of the 'Sweating Man' E-fit. For all five parades, George stayed in the second spot — the same number as his flat in Crookham Road. Two, like six, is a lucky number for George; he didn't know that on the 26th he would get lucky on his Dando watch but, afterwards, this reinforced the numerology side of his magic thinking. Generally, suspects on parades choose to stay in the middle, so that the witnesses have to look at more people before reaching them. The other seven people on the parade had goatees and moustaches applied by a make-up artist. No one picked George out; Sapleton actually picked out a member of the public; Hughes did not pick anyone out, but did have a look at one civilian on the parade from the side.

Back at Hammersmith, the interviews continued. They were probably the most effective part of Oxborough's investigation. They were all led by Detective Constable Michael Snowden, backed up by DC Jim Sword, who made formal announcements concerning times and who was present, but it was Snowden who did all the questioning. The interviews were monitored by Campbell through a one-way mirror and, after each session, he, Horrocks and other senior officers would confer and discuss tactics. Nonetheless, whatever back-up he had, Snowden was impressive both in his questioning and when he gave evidence at the trial.

Around 45-ish, Snowden is tall, rangy and co-ordinated in his movements; in fact, his bearing has something of the ladies' man about it. He has an unaffected London accent but he speaks in a strong, slightly hypnotic voice. The most dramatic part of the series of interviews was the tenth and the last one in which George co-operated when Snowden sprung George with Oxborough's discovery of the gunfire residue particle. At this stage of the questioning, Snowden kept dropping into whatever questions he was asking a refrain-like 'Did you kill Jill Dando?' to which George nearly always replied, 'No, sir.' In the rundown to Snowden putting the particle to George, he asked him about the replica guns that he had in his possession around 1987.

Snowden: 'It seems to me, Mr George, you certainly possessed at least two weapons, two firearms, if not three, whether they be replica, blank-firing or imitation firearms. That's right, isn't it? At least two, if not three. Is that right, Mr George?'

'Only those two, sir,' George answered.

Snowden: 'Did you kill Jill Dando?'

'No, sir,' George replied in counter-chorus.

Snowden: 'Since this list was made, since you've bought these firearms, have you bought any other guns of any description?'

The list of replicas that Snowden was referring to was recovered from the debris in George's flat on the first search.

George: 'No, sir.'

Snowden: 'Have you had in your possession any other guns of any description?'

George: 'No, sir.'

Snowden: 'Have you ever bought or had in your possession any firearm, ammunition, whether it be blank-firing, real or of any other description?'

'As I said, only when I was under supervision in the Territorial Army and the gun club that I mentioned under supervision,' George answered equably. He rarely showed any exasperation when asked a question that he had been asked many times.

'You obviously bought firearms,' Snowden accused him confidently.

George: 'I didn't, you know. Obviously you have to pay for what you use in the club ammunition.'

One of George's techniques for playing off people is to answer a question slightly differently from the one put. Superficially, it appears as though he hasn't really understood the question, which fits his urban idiot number, but actually he has and it is something he does consciously, deliberately and habitually.

Snowden: 'You obviously had firearms ammunition to use in your blank-firing gun as we've discussed; is that correct, Mr George?'

'They were just capsules, sir, but, as I said, to go bang and that's all they do.'

George liked to emphasise the word 'bang' in his otherwise

flat, monotonous style of speech. He was born with a cleft palate, which after the operations to correct it left him with a slight speech impediment and accounts for his sibilant tone and halting delivery. He grimaces slightly, too. Those with cleft palates adopt a wide variety of compensatory mannerisms in an attempt to circumvent ineffective pronunciation.

Snowden: 'But if you put a bullet on the end of that capsule and put it in a gun, that could fire with a smooth barrel.'

'It couldn't do nothing, sir. It would blow up in your ... your own face because obviously nothing can get out ... out of the end.'

George always likes to show his expertise about firearms but again he is being deliberately obtuse. He knew exactly the inference that Snowden was making with his reference to a smooth barrel, because this is an essential component of a replica or a blank-firing gun that has been converted to fire real bullets. But Snowden didn't pick up on it because he knew where he was heading while George didn't.

'So since that time, when you used that firearm to shoot your blank weapon, blank ammunition, have you ever bought or possessed any other firearm ammunition?'

'No, sir.'

'Did you kill Jill Dando?'

'No, sir.'

'She was killed by somebody who was in Fulham on 26 April 1999; she was killed by someone who had possession of a smooth-barrelled, semi-automatic pistol similar to the type of gun that you've bought in the past; the cartridge left at the scene of the murder of Jill Dando has been examined and it has firearms residue left behind in it, in the cartridge.' Snowden's interviewing technique was to pause in the build-up to summarise where they were. 'Do you understand what I'm saying to you, Mr George?'

'I hear what you're saying, sir.'

'Do you understand it?' Snowden asked.

'I understand and hear what you're saying, in so far as you're telling me, sir.'

George's simpleton image was belied by his intuition here that he knew something was in the wings. This is not the reply of an urban idiot.

Snowden: 'The person who killed Miss Dando was seen leaving the area. He was wearing a dark, three-quarter-length coat. You have stated in interview that on that day you may have been wearing a three-quarter-length coat. Was that you leaving the scene of the crime, Mr George?'

'Or casual appearance,' George reminded him; he was enjoying the cut and thrust.

But Snowden's fuse was burning down to the charge. 'Exactly. Was that you leaving the scene of the crime, Mr George?'

'No, sir.'

'The police took your three-quarter-length coat from your flat at the time of the search.'

'Yes, sir.'

'A firearm expert, firearms laboratory has also examined that coat. Did you kill Jill Dando, Mr George?'

Snowden had George on the end of the line but George didn't yet know what line it was or what strain it would bear. But the timing of this 'Did you kill Dando?' refrain was perfect. He drops it in at the right time in the right place with the minimum of effort.

'No, sir.'

Snowden's fuse burns down to the bombshell. 'The inside pocket of your coat has been found to have a trace of percussion primer discharge residue. Did you kill Jill Dando, Mr George?'

Again, the timing is perfect. I felt electrified as I listened, even though I knew what was coming.

George must have bricked at this point but he didn't flinch. 'No, sir.' But he didn't ask about the primer discharge particle. Etienne did, though. Oxborough had deliberately and rightly not told her what they had on George.

Her voice rose in anger as she leant across to Snowden. 'I did ask you if any forensic analysis had come back and you didn't indicate to me anything about any firearms residue or any other type of residue being found.' Many solicitors would have terminated the interview at this point.

'Thank you.' Snowden dismissed her before locking back on to George. 'How do you explain the firearms residue in your coat pocket, Mr George? The coat pocket, the three-quarter-length coat that you may have been wearing on the day that Jill Dando was killed. How do you explain it?'

George replied genuinely confused. 'I can't explain it. I have no knowledge about it being there.'

As I explained in the previous chapter, I don't believe he did because he destroyed both the clothing that he had been wearing when he shot Jill Dando and what he changed into to visit HAFAD.

Snowden: 'Of course you haven't. But how did it get there, Mr George?'

'I have no idea, sir.'

Snowden: 'Isn't it possible that it got there because you were at the scene of the crime and you were the person that shot Miss Dando? Wouldn't that explain how it got there? It's consistent with the firearms residue found in the cartridge at the scene of the crime ... could you explain that to me?' Snowden's bombshell now released its antipersonnel bomblets.

George faltered a bit. 'I cannot explain that, sir.'

Snowden cranked up his case. He spoke confidently and without hesitation as he summarised where they were at now. 'We've already established that you're the person that wears the coat. Nobody else wears the coat. We've already established it's over ten years since you fired a firearm of any type; more than ten years. Somehow, you have got firearms residue in the inside pocket of the three-quarter-length coat, the dark coat, that you may have been wearing on 26 April 1999, and you're in a position at this point to give me an explanation as to how that firearms residue at the scene of the crime, how that got into an item of clothing that you were wearing.'

'I do not know, sir.' George composed himself and got back into his mantra of denial.

Etienne finally intervened, anger making her voice quiver. 'When was that forensic analysis, when did that come to your attention?'

'I'm just, can I ...' Snowden procrastinated. He wanted to keep locked on to George but he had to deal with Etienne. He knew that he could not just plough on regardless as that could well render the whole interview inadmissible as evidence.

Etienne: 'You haven't specifically answered ...'

Snowden interrupted her. 'Can I finish the question please, I need to ask ...'

'But it's an important point,' Etienne said. It sure was, but this was not a debating society; this was a skilled interrogator discrediting her client on a murder rap.

Snowden placated her. 'You didn't specifically ask...'

Etienne almost shouted, 'I specifically asked about primary residue.'

Snowden attempted to divert her. 'You specifically asked

about certain items.'

Etienne clarified. 'Of any forensic evidence ... '

Eric Sword suddenly came in to relieve Snowden. 'If you'll let ... something's been introduced, if you'll let your client answer the question.'

Snowden backed up Sword's attempt to shut Etienne up. 'Please.' His voice was at its most authoritative.

Etienne simmered back into silence, while Snowden turned on George again. 'Do you want to answer the question?'

Meanwhile, George who had been silently watching the exchange decided to come out of character and be real. The worst was over. He wasn't going to cave in. 'I just have. Several times, sir.'

Snowden was not into acknowledging George's wit under fire. 'You cannot explain how it got there?'

George stonewalled. 'I cannot explain at all.'

Etienne finally realised that it was her duty to stop this. She intervened stridently, 'This is evidence of which I'm not aware and I feel that I need to consult with my client. You did not make this evidence available to us prior to the interview and I feel that I need to consult with my client.'

Snowden knew that he had to comply as any further exchanges would be struck out by any trial judge and, as he had already done the damage, he admitted with grace with a view to how it will sound in court, 'I totally understand your point of view and I believe that that is the correct course of action at this point. You will now be given the opportunity to consult with your solicitor.'

Sword, though, decided to push it further, cutting out Etienne and going directly to George. 'That's if you wish to do so?' he asked him.

This encouraged Snowden, who also decided to give it

another shot, too. He also ignored Etienne. 'Do you wish to consult with your solicitor?'

George looked nonplussed. 'As requested, yes.'

Snowden then terminated the interview.

Etienne then made representations to the custody sergeant about being ambushed with evidence that she clearly thought should have been disclosed. In law, she was wrong about this. The police are under no legal obligation to give full disclosure but they must not lie about it if the solicitor advising the suspect asks them specifically whether they have disclosed everything they are going to put to the accused. Whether or not she was lied to is academic. Certainly, Mansfield never ran this at trial nor did he even make an application for the interview evidence to be struck out. Moreover, when he cross-examined Snowden as to why the finding of the particle was not disclosed to the suspect via his solicitor, Snowden replied confidently that he did not want to give George the chance to construct an innocent explanation.

The way the 'interview' game in the police station works is that the solicitor wants to protect the client from answering questions to which he has no convincing answer. The police, on the other hand, want to entrap the suspect by his own incriminating admissions or to lock him into an account that will prevent him from constructing a best-case scenario once all the evidence is known to him. Their default position is that they also want to make the suspect look bad: to show him as evasive, a liar, someone whom ordinary people would consider as likely to commit the crime of which he being accused. It is a subtle strategy that many criminal solicitors don't understand.

The problem is that, in most cases, the suspect has to play ball for at least part of the game. The Damocles sword hanging over him, since 1994, is that if he refuses to answer questions — gives a 'no comment interview' — the trial judge can direct that the jury can draw 'adverse inferences' from his silence. Thus, the solicitor is on notice to judge the correct moment to advise the client to refuse to answer further questions, so that he will not suffer the adverse inferences ruling in court.

Certainly, George with his epilepsy, medical history and low IQ could have been safely advised to give a 'no comment' interview long before he actually did. The proof of this particular pudding came at trial when Mansfield successfully argued before Justice Gage that no adverse inferences should be drawn from George not going into the witness box and submitting to cross-examination. The legal principles here are the same as those governing a refusal to answer questions in the police station.

Nevertheless, at his own insistence, George gave eight hours of interviews that were to prove extremely damaging at trial. They showed him to be a liar, sinister, shifty, much cleverer than he acted and a devious teaser of the police. During one prolonged exchange in which he deliberately wound up Snowden, Bob the Builder looked away from the TV screen in front of the jury to stare long, hard and venomously at George. Other jurors reacted similarly but not as blatantly as Bob.

This was during the third interview on 27 May when Snowden tried to establish when George had last fired a gun.

George: 'Replica or ...'

Snowden: 'Just when was the last time you fired a gun, Mr George?'

George responded evasively and screwed up his face as if he was being quizzed about the meaning of life. 'Are you talking replica weapons or ...'

Snowden snapped, '*Any* gun.'

George replied reluctantly, 'Well, that blank-firing, you know, that blank-firing time.'

Snowden was exasperated. 'Can you answer my question, please? When was the last time you fired a weapon, fired a gun, whether it was a blank-firing gun, a starting pistol, a real gun or any other gun?'

George replied vaguely as if digging deep into his memory banks. 'Well, at the time of that when we were in the flat with David Dobbins.' He had knocked on his young mate David Dobbins's door in 1986 wearing a gas mask and holding a blank-firing semi-automatic. When Dobbins opened it, George terrorised him by staging a mock assassination. Later, Dobbins and some other teenagers broke into George's flat and stole these replica guns. Dobbins gave evidence at the trial about these incidents from 15 years ago. He was a yobby young man wearing a suit with cropped hair and an earring; he spoke crisply and openly. He told friends that he could not see how his evidence could conceivably influence a jury as it had nothing to do with Jill Dando. After George was convicted, Dobbins began to blame himself for contributing to George's downfall and in August 2001, when the miscarriage of justice bandwagon was rolling, he hanged himself.

Snowden continued with his line of questioning about Dobbins's mock assassination incident. 'That was the last time you fired a gun of any type?'

George: 'Yes, sir.'

Snowden: 'And when was that?'

George evasively again. 'It was the replica weapon. That was at least ... it was more than ... err ... more than two years past.'

'I really need you to try again and be a little bit more specific than that,' Snowden ordered.

George refused to play ball. 'Well, other than that I would

have to say I don't recall exactly.'

Snowden: 'Again, can you tell me which year that was? Was it last year, Mr George? Did you fire any gun last year whether it be a blank firer, starting pistol or real gun?'

George thought long and hard. 'No, sir.'

'Did you do that the year before in 1998?'

'No, sir,' after more thought.

'1997?'

'No, sir?'

As the years tolled off, the process of checking the memory took longer.

'1996?'

'No, sir.'

'Did you do it in 1995?'

'No, sir.'

'Did you do it in 1994?'

'No, sir.'

'1993?' There were stirrings in the press ranks. We were back watching *Carry On Up the Old Bailey*. But how long could the joke be sustained?

'No, sir.'

'1992?'

'No, sir.'

'1991?'

'No, sir.'

'That's ten years, and you haven't fired a gun of any type in the last ten years?' Snowden recapped. But there was a method in Snowden playing the straight man to George's tease. The Cecil Gee coat in which the particle had been found had been bought in 1989.

'No, sir.'

'Did you fire a gun of any type in 1989?'

For all that it mattered, George did not preclude 1989. 'I don't recall, sir.'

Yet in another interview when Snowden asked him when he worked at the BBC as a messenger, he replied instantly, 'From May to September 1976.' Snowden picked up on it and commented sarcastically on his ability to remember clearly the events of 1976 but not if he fired a gun in 1998.

However, his evasiveness, procrastination, winding up and blatant lying over the guns — when he fired them, his membership of a gun club and the Territorial Army, his denial that he was the masked man holding a gun in the two photos — was to incur the wrath of the jury. He could only have got away with this if there was no other evidence before the jury.

At one stage in the interviews, Snowden tried to get George to speak about his membership and what name he used in the early 1980s at a gun club. George retreated behind his bad memory about why he was not accepted as a full member. 'I don't recollect that and, if it still exists, then there shouldn't be a problem in ascertaining that. I have no objections.'

Snowden commented, 'Well, if you can't remember which name you used, we don't know who to ask for, do we?'

George replied, 'It's not necessarily the case. You could ask under ... is a person under these names.' Snowden asked him what names he uses and George replied, 'All from the start?'

Snowden said, 'Yes please.'

George reeled most of them off: 'Barry Michael George, Steve Majors, Thomas Palmer, Barry Bulsara, Barry Michael George again.' He missed out Paul Gadd, which was adopted from 'My Gang' anthem singer-cum-paedophile Gary Glitter. His real name is Gadd, which is the name George used when he was convicted of impersonating a police officer and sexual assault. The attempted rape charge — it was rape but he plea-bargained it down by not contesting the charge — was under the name of Majors, derived from the indestructible, bionic Lee Majors, star of the TV series *The Six Million Dollar Man* and later *The Stuntman*.

Snowden then asked him if there was a reason for all these false identities and added, 'Do you tell lies, Mr George?'

George replied cagily, 'No, sir.'

Snowden pushed it further. 'Are you Freddie Mercury's cousin?'

George accepted that he wasn't and Snowden continued, 'Have you told people you were Freddie Mercury's cousin?'

George answered, 'I have done, sir.'

Snowden homed in, 'Is that a lie, Mr George?'

'Yes, sir.'

'Do you tell lies, Mr George?'

George backtracked, 'No. Exaggeration but not a lie, sir.'

On another occasion, this time in the context of the condolence notes for Dando that were found in his flat, Snowden asked him if he had claimed to be Freddie Mercury's cousin.

George qualified, 'In the statement, yes, that's correct.'

A slightly puzzled Snowden asked, 'Is it correct that you are his cousin?'

George replied cryptically, 'No, not in any sense of the word or meaning.' It was obvious that in his own fantasy world he did believe himself to be the cousin of Freddie Mercury.

Although the video of the interviews was shot from a static position and there were no zooms into George, what the video shows even more than the transcripts alone is that he is emotionally dyslexic. What he says is dislocated from the emotions that he is expressing through the sound of his voice, facial expressions and body language. His long-time friend Robert Charig repeated to me again and again that George 'can't read social reality very well ... this is why he misreads the cues so often, especially with women'. The other side of this coin, of course, is that he can't contribute to social reality very well either. Unless you know him and make allowances for his epilepsy and having been born with a cleft palate, he comes over as creepy, odd and sinister.

His vocabulary is also disturbing. Some commentators on the case had compared it to a kind of police-speak — 'I proceeded ... I could have ascertained ... That was the aftermath of what had happened ... Like I formerly expressed to you ... But they had at some point engaged with me in dialogue ... matters pertaining to me and my lifestyle ... the driver in it was looking very suspicious to my assessment of the situation ... I have told you the absolute correct truth ... I'm just trying to clarify this.' But there is more to his odd vocabulary and stilted, muddled syntax than is conveyed by the description 'police-speak'.

'Clarify' is one of George's favourite terms, and for good reason, because he is often stranded in the dislocation between what he says and what he means, and between his interpretation of social reality and the actual reality as most of us define it. Thus he is in a constant state of clarification that doesn't quite make it. This leaves him confused, misunderstood, unappreciated and, beneath his ersatz politeness and co-operativeness, angry. In the interviews, his anger occasionally flickers but mostly it is suppressed beneath his transparently false deference and eagerness to help.

Nonetheless, as with his speech, he has developed coping strategies for handling his social inadequacies, one of which is to pretend to be as stupid as people often wrongly assume he is. Playing the urban idiot but breaking out of it every now and again puts people off balance, giving him an edge. He often combines this with his professional hypochondria; many of the interviews show him clutching his side to nurse his scoliosis, a 'bad back' ailment that was taken more seriously by forensic psychologists than ordinary doctors. Amongst all this, he maintained his ground on not knowing or being able to recognise who Jill Dando was before she was murdered.

At one stage, he told Snowden, 'I-I-I ... up until her death ... did not know who Jill Dando was and that's the truth of the matter, sir.' George always pronounced her surname with equal stress on the second syllable. Dan-do. This is how the word would be pronounced in Japanese. He was married to a Japanese woman in 1991 and lived with her for six months. He likes to pepper his speech with Japanese phrases and words. Indeed, the word '*dando*' in Japanese means 'the way of obtaining rank' or 'the way of the bullet' or even 'the way of the man'. As it is written non-phonetically, Japanese has even more multiple meanings than English. Each one of the Japanese meanings of Dando would have been meaningful for George. But Oxborough were unaware of this when George was interviewed, or indeed when he was tried.

Snowden put it to him that he would have been able to recognise her. George iterated his claim, 'I actually did not know who she was and would not have been able to recognise her.'

Snowden then asked, 'Do you have an interest in television presenters.'

'Not particularly.' Although he'd not had any photos of Dando, there were a number of stills found in his undeveloped films of TV presenters of the early '90s, like Anthea Turner, Sue Richardson, Kathryn Holloway and Emma Freud.

Having attempted to show that George knew of Dando before her murder, Snowden turned to the condolence notes as it would be difficult, if he hadn't killed her, to equate George's ignorance of Dando with his grief-stricken behaviour after her murder.

Snowden asked him had he gone to Gowan Avenue following Dando's death.

'I don't recollect having done so now, but I ... err ... I need ... Yes, I have, my apologies. That was the aftermath of what had happened and like anyone, any other citizen, I basically, just, commemorative, you know, good will, you know, paying respects and that was it and I didn't do that solely, just on my own, you know, my own at expressing, you know, concern and, you know, remorse of what we had heard had, had happened as a community thing. But mainly on behalf of various people in the local community and that was expressed with genuine, you know ... express the loss of hearing about the lady but beyond that, you know, before that I didn't ... did not and have not heard of or knew about Jill Dando and that's even though I had way back, a few, quite a few years back, had worked at the British Broadcasting Corporation as a messenger.'

This shambling, incoherent recall of his so-called 'remorse' was superficially sincere but was utterly unconvincing. At another prompt from Snowden, he rambled off aimlessly again: 'I went on behalf of the community. I am a Born-Again Christian. Obviously, I wanted to do some sort of gesture of regret for what we have heard ... We had heard what had happened and we wanted to do something on behalf of the community to pay respects towards the situation of Jill Dando and obviously the gentleman friend of Jill Dando ... to express regret for her loss and on behalf of Fulham Baptist Church where I occasionally go.'

When he was first shown these forgotten condolence notes, he took a long time reading them and said without prompting, 'After the ... you know, took place ...' He avoided saying 'murder' but it was quite emotional for him seeing them for the first time for a year.

Snowden read out one of them — mangled syntax and all — to George: 'I found it difficult to relate openly until now. I am disturbed by the death of Jill Dando. Although I did not know Jill Dando personally, my cousin Freddie Mercury was interviewed by her back in 1986. I was present with him, so for this reason I feel it poignant to express together the situation of Jill's death and my coming to Christ. From Kensington Temple and Fulham Baptist Church and being a member of I feel for this is the time that the flowers that I have sent are on behalf of Fulham Baptist Church and Fulham Community in the absence of John's knowledge and our thoughts and prayers should be with Alan and Jill Dando's friends and family. Let us say a prayer.'

When Snowden read, 'I was present with him,' George became tearful.

The interview then turned to the flowers that he had given to the police manning the cordon and whether they had a condolence note. George said they did have a note, which he described as containing roughly the words '... basically I reiterated that myself and Freddie Mercury and the family or whatever basically regret the loss of Jill Dando as from the community point of view.'

When Snowden queried what George meant by 'sent' her flowers, he gave a sinister laugh and said, 'I meant sent ...' then he qualified what he presumably thought could have been interpreted as he sent her to her death, 'the flowers that I took.'

Anyway, just before midnight, when the last interview conducted by Snowden was resumed, Etienne read a pre-prepared statement:

... In the light of the evidence revealed in the last interview that firearms residue, after forensic examination, has been found in a three-quarter-length Cecil Gee coat pocket of my client which was seized from his premises in a search on 17 and 18 April 2000 and that the residue found was consistent with firearms residue found at the scene of the crime, I have made representations to the custody sergeant that there was significant, sufficient evidence to proceed to charge. My representations have been noted on the custody record by Sergeant Brown. In the circumstances, my client has decided to exercise the right to silence. Please respect that decision ...

The disclosure of the particle was an unexpected shock to George as he had taken care when planning and executing the killing to ensure that, ballistically, he was clean. The particle was a mistake, so he changed his game plan. He shut up.

In hindsight, George's biggest problem was that he did not understand how our criminal justice system works. He was familiar with it as he had three convictions and had been in prison for attempted rape but, like a lot of criminals, he believed all the guff about the accused enjoying the presumption of innocence, it being for the Crown to prove its case beyond a reasonable doubt, that the accused must be given the benefit of the doubt and so on. But as any trial lawyer will tell you, in practice the show does not work like that. Once there is *prima facie* evidence — in George's case, the particle or the fibre — then it is for a jury to decide, not a judge. And in such circumstances, juries can convict on no more than gut feel and sometimes they do just that, especially if they believe that the accused is a sinister liar. Juries just do not give the Georges of this world the benefit of the doubt.

Although Snowden and Sword concurred with Etienne's request to respect her client's right to silence, the following day, Sunday, Campbell decided to have a crack at George himself. Oxborough had secured another 24 hours' extension of custody from a local magistrate, which meant that they had now had the full 96 hours that the law allows the police to hold a suspect in police custody. George, however, gave two 'no comment' interviews and, later that day, after Campbell had conferred with the Crown Prosecution Service, he was charged with the murder of Jill Dando. For the record, he was arrested at 6.30am on 25 May and charged at 6.43pm on 28 May.

10

punch ko's itself

The media blitz that followed Barry George's arrest hardly had James and me cheering from the sidelines. In fact, our backs were to the wall as both our phones were melting as colleagues rang up for our reaction and what we now thought of our Richard Hughes theory. Journalists have memories like elephants for their colleagues' howlers. Crime author and journo Wensley Clarkson gleefully rang me soon after the arrest. Wensley has a fine line in gloating sympathy.

'Well, you and James must feel like falling on your pens,' he said. 'For the last year, you been pointing the finger at the neighbour ... Whatsisname?' As if he didn't know, but I told him hoping, forlornly, that he would show a bit of restraint. 'That's it, Richard Hughes. Now what are you going to do — issue him an apology? He could sue you and *Punch* for libel!

I commented flatly, 'Well, maybe George is a patsy. Who knows?'

'A patsy? The whole of Fleet Street say the cops are full on that they have got the right man. But you are telling me they would set someone up for something like this?'

Stephen Hawking would have problems getting his wheelchair round the games journalists play. 'Of course ...' he added with all the sincerity of a Dixon's salesman, 'you could just be right and the cops wrong.'

It was his 'just' that made me realise I had to invoke the right to silence; I think I asked him how his haemorrhoids were before switching to 'no comment' mode. It was definitely time to go under the duvet.

Unfortunately, *Punch* could not even join the George media feeding frenzy. The tabloids were running on it like the guy had already been convicted, but it would have to stop by the time he was remanded in custody and our next edition was on the news-stands. However, as the prejudicial coverage continued throughout the time George was being questioned, I got a neat take on it that would allow us to write something. I said to James, 'All this is blatantly flouting the rules on contempt. I'll do a piece on it.'

He replied, 'OK, just as long you don't mention Richard Hughes.'

Whatever the deficiencies of our criminal justice system, we do uphold the principle of a right to a fair trial, one cornerstone of which is that the accused is judged by what the draft treaty on human rights for the European Union calls 'an independent and impartial tribunal'. In an adversarial system of justice, which relies upon trial by judge and jury, a necessary condition of an impartial tribunal is that jurors are not prejudiced by pre-trial publicity. In

America, where freedom of expression is held in higher regard than in this country, prejudice caused by pre-trial publicity is countered by giving the accused's lawyers the right to cross-examine potential jurors to proof whether or not they will judge the case solely on the evidence.

In this country, our approach the same end is to restrict what the media can discuss about the case. The legislation that governs this is the Contempt of Court Act 1981, which essentially orders that when a suspect is arrested or charged, the media may not publish details of the evidence or the accused that 'create a substantial risk of serious impediment or prejudice' to a fair trial. In practice, these provisions are only important where there is intense public interest such as the arrest of Barry George or that self-appointed experimental euthenasist Dr Harold Shipman.

In respect of Shipman, for example, the British Medical Association put out a press release before he was convicted saying that he deserved to be sent down for ever. The trial judge regarded it to be very serious and reported it to the Attorney General's office but, after looking at it, they did not prosecute.

When Barry George was arrested, the red tops and the blue ones also reported all manner of prejudicial details about him, but what compounded the contempt was that they upheld the profile that Campbell had presented on *Crimewatch* a month before. The main culprit was the *Sun* in its coverage the day after George was arrested. The front-page headline screamed JILL COPS QUESTION FREDDIE MERCURY ODDBALL, while the subtitle was 'Loner Held in Dawn Raid'.

The story explained that George was a 'loner with a bizarre obsession for rock singer Freddie Mercury', had changed his name by deed poll to Bulsara and falsely claimed to be his cousin. It also reported that 'the suspect was known as the local weirdo' and was 'very creepy'. The source for the last quote said she heard him having an argument at a polling station four years previously and 'he hit the roof' when he was told that he could not vote because of some registration irregularity. He also fantasised about going to university to study music 'but the fact is, he couldn't play a note'. Another source said he was a 'fantasist' and he boned up on medical symptoms to dupe doctors into treating his phoney illnesses.

The *Daily Mirror* was more balanced than the *Sun*, but nevertheless it managed to give George's height, which although they got it wrong was nevertheless in breach of Scotland Yard's guidelines. As identification was an issue, they had specified that no photographs, sketches or physical descriptions of George could be published. The newspaper also quoted a neighbour of George's who refused to be named, saying, 'Barry told me he used to be in the SAS.' Another said, 'He was unemployed but told me he was training to be a stuntman.' George was also 'a scruffy loner'.

Although the *Mirror* and some of the other newspapers were less blatant than the *Sun*, the problem was what media lawyers call the 'jigsaw effect'. While one report may sail close to the wind, in combination with others who do the same the overall picture that emerges is that of a guilty man. So contempt of one newspaper may well involve its report being seen in the context of what else is reported. Although to the layman this might seem to be a contempt and libel minefield, the lawyers who legal articles do it on automatic pilot. They known exactly where the story crosses the line, and the reason that newspapers do is not the incompetence of lawyers or ignorance of the law, but commercial pressures from editors. Juicy stories like the arrest of a Barry George sell newspapers.

According to Campbell on *Crimewatch* and in other

interviews, the main suspect was a psychotic loner, in his thirties or early forties, who was likely to be unmarried, living alone, obsessive, with quirky habits, an unhealthy interest in celebrities ... this was how the press ran Campbell's thinking on the case in April, a year on from the murder. Of course, his priming of the press then was a perfectly legitimate investigative technique; Campbell's job was to catch the culprit and he was using the media to engage the general public in that task. However, it certainly wasn't legitimate to brief the press that George's arrest was a 'breakthrough' in the investigation and 'highly significant'. This was blatant code for saying that this is our man. That aside, what the press printed on George before he was remanded in custody was clearly in contempt.

Predictably, the Attorney General's office did not seem concerned about this at all and when I spoke to the official who had dealt with the Shipman case about the reporting on the George arrest, he said, 'We have not had any complaints about the Bulsara [George] case and we are quite happy with the reporting on it. We obviously looked at it with interest — like everyone else — but it was not referred to us and it was not regarded as particularly out of the ordinary.'

Of course, laws have to be enforced by institutions that are run by personnel and, if the personnel say the law has not been broken even when it has, then that is the end of it. This is the legal version of Humpty Dumpty semantics where 'When I use a word it means just what I choose it to mean — neither more nor less.'

These were precisely the kind of people who sued James Steen later on in the same year for contempt over using ex–MI5 officer Derek Shayler's inside information on how bungling by security services resulted in the massive Bishopsgate bomb that devastated the City in 1993. James submitted the article to the

Attorney General's office, who found much to object to and wrote a letter to that effect. James amended the article to comply with what he thought was important, then published it in the 24 July 2000 edition of *Punch* with the Attorney General's prissy letter on the cover. The cover blurb read 'Whistle-blower David Shayler tells the story MI5 does not want you to read.' The Attorney General sued and Justice Silber found James and me guilty of contempt, although, thankfully, in early 2001 the High Court saw that Justice Silber had misapplied the laws of contempt and they quashed the finding.

I attended the trial and the appeal; at the latter, the panel of High Court judges was headed by Lord Justice Phillips, the Master of the Rolls. The panel's attitude towards the Attorney General's counsel, Mr Crowe, was clearly itself contemptuous of the motives behind the prosecution of *Punch*.

My *Punch* article on the widespread contempt in the tabloid's reporting of Barry George's arrest was published in the 14 June issue; I didn't know then that Oxborough had been on George's case well before the *Crimewatch* programme some four weeks before. If I'd known that, I would have pointed out that Campbell was doing a bit of pre-trial jury conditioning by using the media, something I touched on in the previous chapter. As for the denial by the Attorney General's office that there were no breaches of the Contempt of Court Act in the reporting of George's arrest case, this literally was beneath contempt.

Soon after my article appeared, *Punch*'s prison correspondent Noel 'Razor' Smith sent me a piece on George that not even we could publish but would have gone teetotal to do so. Razor is an egregious, 37-year-old 'sarf' Londoner who was serving life imprisonment for bank robberies, having fallen foul of the two-strikes-and-you're-out legislation introduced by Tory Home

Secretary Michael Howard. He was in Belmarsh Prison when George was remanded. Aside from robbing banks, Razor is also a fine writer with a racy Damon Runyon style. Unfortunately, he likes money too much to settle for the pittance that most writers earn. His best work has been done from prison where he sends out articles that occasionally get an airing in the social conscience nationals like the *Guardian*. *Punch* also published his articles, including one brilliant piece on Jonathan Aitken's reception into Belmarsh Prison.

In June 2000, the bullish Razor bluffed his way into the prison hospital ward where Barry George was being held and conducted the first ever interview of Jill Dando's murderer. His copy makes fascinating reading; in fact, before the trial, I sent it to Mike Mansfield just in case he thought it might help the defence. Razor wrote:

> *Barry George is not your typical murderer. In fact, he looks and acts no different from the other 300 or so from the stage army of inadequates that fill up Belmarsh on a daily basis. In softer times, they would be care-in-community patients serving out suspended sentences for breaking windows, shoplifting or being a public nuisance. He does not strut around or revel in what might be construed as the role of a celebrity killer. He doesn't speak much but, when he does, his soft-spoken, polite London accent gives him a slightly feminine air. He is around 5' 11" and 12-ish stone, with less meat on him than a butcher's pencil; he has olive skin, brown hair and eyes. His short goatee beard that he habitually strokes as he speaks to you makes him appear distinctly like a New Age green rather a stone killer. His eyes look everywhere, except at the person he is addressing.*

He is held in Belmarsh Hospital or what is now called, in prison PR-speak, 'The Health-Care Centre'. He was held in Ward 2 with five other manic depressives or paranoid schizophrenics. George was in bed 4. When I spoke to him, he was reading a three-day-old Sun *that featured his case on the front page.*

After an opening preamble, I asked him what he was in for. He looked mildly annoyed at being drawn from his newspaper. After thinking for a moment, he replied, 'I don't know.'

I paused, then said bluntly, 'What do you mean, you don't know? You must have been charged with something.'

He blinked rapidly as though on the edge of tears. 'The police say I done a killing,' he replied quietly. The Sun *fell from his hands on to the bed.*

'And did you?' I asked harshly.

He thought for such a long time that I didn't think he was going to reply. Finally, he answered, stroking his goatee: 'No. I don't think so.'

I waited expectantly but he didn't elaborate. I tried a different tack. 'That's you in the paper, innit? Charged with the Jill Dando murder?'

His gaze shifted from somewhere over my left shoulder down to the newspaper on the bed. 'Yeah,' he answered. Tears brimmed in his eyes.

I backed off. 'What medication have they got you on?' I asked

'Memoril, I think,' he replied. Later, I found out that Memoril is prescribed for schizophrenics. The drug might have been responsible for him being so listless and ponderous.

I moved the subject on to something less upsetting. I

*asked him whether or not he was really related to Freddie
Mercury. He did elaborate this time. 'I never said I was
related to Freddie, I just used to like his music. Anyway, I
have got over him now. I like Phil Collins.'*

*To make a joke, I asked if he would change his name
one day to Barry Collins. He smiled as if intrigued with the
idea.*

*I then asked if he liked guns. He replied slightly
puzzled. 'What, Guns 'n' Roses?'*

*I shook my head. 'Nahh. Guns. Bang, bang, you're
dead.'*

*He shook his head in slo-mo. 'The police asked me
about guns. They think I did a killing.' He seemed reluctant
to use the term 'murder' but we were back to where we
started.*

*I asked him what he thought about the police and being
held so long for questioning. He shrugged, 'I didn't like it.
They shouted at me sometimes, but the food was nice.'*

I asked if they hit him.

*'No.' He paused while he shook his head. 'But they
had the handcuffs on real tight. Look.' He showed me his
wrists, which were still slightly reddened. 'They kept asking
me questions. The same ones all the time. And I couldn't
sleep because of all the noise in there.'*

*I had been writing down his replies and suddenly he
looked at my notebook and asked, 'Is that a statement?'*

*I shook my head reassuringly and assured him that it
was just notes for a book I was writing. He looked worried.*

*'I won't have to sign, will I?' He didn't take any notice
of my emphatically shaking head. 'Cos my solicitor says not
to sign anything.' He came over tired. He said, staring into*

space, 'I don't want to talk any more.'

He lay back on his bed with the Sun on his chest. Within a couple of minutes he was asleep.

Perhaps George is a master criminal pulling the wool over everyone's eyes except the police. If so, he is also a brilliant actor and the police are rather more insightful than in my humble experience they normally are. Still, they may have discovered the smoking gun. The trial will tell. My overall impression was that he is very child-like and open to suggestion. At the time of the interview, George was not a Cat A prisoner but that changed when he moved out of the hospital.

Razor's interview shows some classic George teases as he plays the urban idiot with just enough out-of-character cameos to show him sending up Razor. The claim, for example, that he is off Queen music and is into Phil Collins. Razor, nor I for that matter, would not know that you can't go from Freddie Mercury to Phil Collins; perhaps the other way round but not by the route that George says. He is a music buff and he is putting Razor to the test. Then there is his clever little spin on Guns 'n' Roses. George is obsessed with guns but he is smart enough to play the question along the lines the conversation is already on. Of course, Razor would never have known, but would certainly have appreciated that Gun 'n' Roses sang 'Bohemian Rhapsody', George's own anthem, at the Queen tribute concert in 1992. Then, after milking Razor for a bit of sympathy, he withdraws and cuts out. George 10 – Razor 0.

Reading it now, I am rather glad that the laws of contempt prevented us from publishing it as George clearly pulled the wool over Razor's eyes and James and I would have got more egg on our faces. At the time, though, I bought Razor's conclusions; he is no fool and it never even occurred to me that he could misread George so comprehensively. The picture he painted did not fit the gunman and I trusted the painter. Yet, Razor missed George completely just as a lot of people do. He outwits more people than see through him.

The piece by Razor was spiked but little did I know that my 14 June article would also be the last one that I would write for Punch on the case. Indeed, by the end of the year James and I would both resign over the way Al Fayed let some of his recent hirelings interfere with the loss-making magazine. He had hired Max Clifford the sleaze king in 1999 to promote Fulham football club, then took on Phil Hall after he'd been dumped by Murdoch as editor of the *News of World*. Hall didn't like James and Clifford loathes me.

A few months before, I had suckered him into a TV interview in July of that year for a documentary on Benjamin Pell, which Channel 4 had commissioned. Benjie the Binman was already famous for plundering the rubbish of showbiz solicitors and agents, then selling confidential and newsworthy information to newspapers. Clifford had brokered some Pell stories but when our TV crew arrived at his New Bond Street office he did not know that Pell had briefed us with affidavits, contracts and tape recordings detailing Clifford's wheeling and dealing. *The Daily Mirror* bought one Pell scoop about Elton John for £20,000 but Clifford gave Pell much less. He had also given evidence in the High Court when Elton John's manager sued the *Daily Mirror*. Clifford was bang to rights on both counts and when he could not talk his way out of it he blew his top on camera. It made great TV but hardly endeared me to Clifford. He is a man who never forgets a slight and tries to return it with the same kind of interest that he likes to make middling between his clients and the newspapers that publish their stories.

Although Clifford bent Al Fayed's ear about me, while James was editor I was impregnable from him as Al Fayed trusted James and respected his judgement. However, towards the end of the year, Rupert Murdoch sacked his then *News of the World* editor Phil Hall and Clifford recommended him to Al Fayed as a media consultant. Al Fayed hired Hall.

Hall began to suggest ways of how the loss-making *Punch* could be made profitable. Gradually, Al Fayed gave him editorial influence over James, which gained an added impetus when Justice Silber found against James and *Punch* in the aforementioned contempt claim brought by the Attorney General. In November 2000, James resigned over the way Hall was interfering in the running of the magazine and I followed him.

I published an article in the *Press Gazette* in November 2000 detailing the motives of Hall and Clifford. I also predicted that Al Fayed would soon regret delegating them the power. I already knew that Benjamin Pell had the griff on how Al Fayed had obtained through Macnamara details of how he was to be cross-examined in the High Court in his successful libel battle with Neil Hamilton in December 1999. Pell gave me tape-recordings of how the deal was struck and I handed these over to Hamilton's lawyers for his appeal against Al Fayed's victory.

Shepherded in and out of the High Court by Clifford, Al Fayed had to give evidence again. This time he was humiliated, ridiculed and exposed by counsel in front of an appeal panel headed by the Master of the Rolls, Lord Justice Phillips. Al Fayed was stripped of all dignity; he was reduced to a pathetic old man who couldn't even lie without being found out. It was cold revenge, which proverbially is the best way the dish is eaten. But I did not enjoy it; he had subsidised a great little magazine that I had been privileged to work on for three years. After he left the witness box, he sat at the front of the court, then turned and stared at me more in bewilderment than hatred. I don't think he understood what Clifford and Hall had done in his name and he felt that I had betrayed him.

Thankfully, I got the best of both worlds as my intervention did not help Neil Hamilton either. In Lord Justice Phillips's judgment, Fayed was defined as being so discredited at the original libel trial that even if this further abuse of due process had been before the jury, they would still not have found for Hamilton. Macnamara was heavily criticised — he had taken care to be out of the country while the appeal was heard — but it came out, too, that Al Fayed had pensioned him off. The handshake was rumoured to be half a million.

Benjamin Pell was beside himself with delight at causing all this trouble; he prefers causing havoc to making money. The trouble is, he is infectious. Too much exposure to him and you catch Pell fever. The symptoms included an agitated arm-waving, spluttering manner; speaking at twice the normal rate, twice as loud, at much higher pitch; a Talmudic passion for logic-chopping; insomnia; workaholicism; and much more besides. It is as though the only way Pell keeps sane is to drive everyone around him mad. It is extremely debilitating for everyone except its progenitor.

Benjamin decided that the way to restore my sanity and redeem his 'human dung beetle' public image was for me to write a book on his exploits. I agreed, as I did not want to go back to journalism. However, the Dando trial was slotted in for February and I had the feeling of unfinished business there. About the time that I resigned from *Punch*, George was committed for trial. I did not go to the hearing but I spoke to a few journalists who did and the general take on the evidence was that it was weak, and unless

Oxborough pulled something else out of the bag, George might walk. Mansfield was already on his case and doing an impressive job.

My publisher, John Blake, had wanted a book on the murder well before George was arrested, but I had shilly-shallied, always thinking that an arrest was imminent. Having followed the case for so long, it seemed crazy not to chronicle the dénouement. I felt spoilt for choice but, much to the chagrin of Benjamin, Dando seemed the one I should go for first. The trial was bound to be a humdinger and George could turn out to be a patsy ... and the thought did occur to me that I hadn't spoken to Richard Hughes for a while.

11

benjamin pell cranks up

The pre-trial was arraigned for Monday, 26 February 2001. On the Thursday before, Campbell rang *Punch* asking to speak to James Steen. He was put on to the new editor, Richard Brass, who explained that James had long resigned and was now working at the *Daily Mirror*. Campbell dithered a bit, then said, 'Well, I would appreciate if you could ask him to call me, but I would also appreciate it if you do not say anything to McVicar or tell him that I called.' Brass explained to him that I had gone from *Punch*, too, but did not commit himself to not talking to me about what he thought was an odd request.

Campbell did not tell Brass what it was about, but he left a number to pass on to James. Brass told James who then spoke to me; in turn, I rang up *Punch* to speak to Richard Brass to check whether he had missed anything out in what he told James. There wasn't any more, but it was obvious why Campbell was sniffing around. He knew I had some contacts in Belmarsh Prison and he almost certainly wanted to know if I had picked up anything incriminating about George on the prison grapevine. I had already come to terms with Campbell's prissy game of treating me as the man I was 30 years ago, rather than what I am now, so I wasn't concerned at the odd way he had revealed his hand. James rang him and left a message but, by then, Campbell had presumably lost interest in what was only a passing enquiry and he never returned James's call.

I knew that Campbell felt betrayed by my use of Detective Constable D, but he should have been confident that, if I or James had anything that was pertinent to his enquiries, we would have informed him, as we had over Richard Hughes. What little had come back about George was not obviously incriminating and, anyway, I couldn't judge the relevance of it because I didn't know any more than the bare bones of the case against George. I had not attended the committal and, as reporting restrictions had not been lifted, it had not been publicised. Moreover, I was still taken in by Razor's interview, as I trusted his judgement on prison and crime. That was his beat and he patrolled it well.

Moreover, what had been conveyed to me from other prison sources also implied that George could be innocent. These supported his own assertion — that he had brought the prosecution on himself to become rich and famous. He talked to other cons in the third person as if he was an expert on the killing and how the killer would have done this or that. 'He would not have done this because ...' was how it was conveyed to me. At the time it was filtering back, it had no significance as I didn't know what George was like. All I knew was that he had been in the Army and was familiar with firearms. The one thing he always insisted on to other cons was that the killer was clearly clued-up on ballistics because of the adapted gun and the professional nature of the shooting. This meant that the gunman would know about contamination from firearms residue and he would have disposed of the clothing in which he had committed the murder as he could never predict when he might be pulled in by the police. He would certainly never have brought contaminated clothing home.

What George was doing in these conversations could be taken two ways, and the way I had interpreted it originally was wrong — which was that the particle must have been planted because if he was the gunman he was too experienced with firearms to make such a fundamental mistake. At the time, I was buying Razor's take on George, which was also reinforced by reports from the committal that the evidence against George was flimsy. Later, after I had tuned into his head and spoken to his only long-term friend, Robert Charig, my interpretation changed. Charig told me that this is how George likes to mystify himself; that he would talk of himself in the third person. Once you factor in what George is like with his chameleon act and integrate it with Charig's comments, you then realise that what he was actually saying is that he did it, but is far too smart to take contaminated clothing back to his flat. But this is an interpretation based on assumptions about George's character; it carries no weight as evidence. So when Campbell called *Punch*, even if I had written out and passed on what I knew, he could not have used it to bolster his case against George.

February rolled round warmly out of the winter. The weather was even better than the global warming soothsayers were telling us we could expect. On the Sunday before the pre-trial opened, I assembled my notebooks, pens and press pass, boned up on my shorthand, prised out any shards buried in the cycle tyres of my Klein road bike and fussed over Clem. He was rarely left alone and going to court would mean leaving him in the flat from 9.30am to 5.00pm for an estimated eight weeks. This was no way to treat an honorary human being. At this time, I was friendly with a Norwegian woman — I still have the bore holes to prove it — but she did not like dogs, not even Clem, so it was pointless appealing to her to help out. He would have to stay in the flat looking plaintively from the balcony in the direction that I left, but even for a good dog like Clem there had to be some rain some time.

Benjamin was flapping around me — albeit on the telephone — going on and on about what evidence there was against Barry George and whether I thought he was guilty. It started on Saturday evening — as he is Orthodox, he goes under for the Sabbath but, come sundown, blitzes the phone. Since I didn't know what there was against George, I said we would find out on Monday. Then I said, as if from memory and not from my Sherlock Holmes 'quotes' database that I had just accessed in my computer, 'It is a capital mistake to theorise before one has data. Insensibly one begins to twist facts to suit theories, instead of theories to suit facts.'

He liked the quote but not my application of it. 'What Sherlock Homes story is that from?' But he didn't wait for me to answer. 'Facts before theory! It's a pity you didn't do that with Richard Hughes, isn't it?' I explained that I had never said there was any evidence against Richard Hughes except his own suspicious behaviour and words. Thankfully, as it turned out, I never mentioned the TV celebrity lookalike take that Hughes had made on the gunman and Benjamin had not read those articles on the murder that mentioned it.

On Monday morning, there was a reprieve for Clem as the

opening was put back until the afternoon. At 1.30pm, I cycled up from Battersea with my jeans tucked in my socks and a leather knapsack containing all my gear on my back. It took 14 minutes, but I knew that once I had refined the route and got all the cheats worked out, I'd pull it back to 12 minutes. I am the sort of cyclist about whom 'disgusted' of Tunbridge Wells writes letters to the *Times*. Pavements, traffic lights, one-way streets all get used the way they are not supposed to be; even I flinch at the outrage of it sometimes. When I cycled down to the Old Bailey, it was 1.45pm, a quarter-of-an-hour or so before most of the courts begin sitting for the afternoon. Benjamin was already waiting for me opposite the tradesmen's entrance to the Central Criminal Court. This is where the press, lawyers, jurors, bailed defendants, police and court officials pile in to be vetted for their *bona fides*, then they step into a plastic capsule that is a bit like a decompression chamber in some cheap, space-age TV series, before they and their luggage are screened by metal detectors for any banned devices such as cameras, tape recorders, guns and bombs.

As I chained my Klein to a post opposite my entrance, we made our arrangements to talk later. I am always a bit neurotic about leaving the Klein unattended as the professional bike thieves tour London in vans equipped to handle any of the commercial locks that cyclists use. But right outside the Central Criminal Court with CCTV cameras everywhere was insurance enough, I reckoned. As Benjamin didn't have a press pass, he was going to have to go to the public entrance in Newgate Street where the spectators line up for a seat in the public gallery of Number One Court. We went our separate ways.

I went through the swing doors and approached the glass-screened counter with its notice 'Passes to be shown'. I fished out my *Punch* press card and presented it to the bobby on the other side of the screen. 'Barry George case in Court Number One,' I said ingratiatingly.

He took one look at it and shook his head. 'That's no good. I can't let you in on that.'

'But I'm a journalist,' I said. 'Why not?'

'Because you need accreditation. Here.' He pointed at another notice, which detailed the rigmarole for accreditation. I had to have my editor fax in a request for me to attend the trial with my name, the name of the case and the date on the publication's headed notepaper. I retreated thinking I'd join Benjamin in the public gallery. I went round to Newgate Street and went to buzz the bell for entry, then stopped as I saw among the usual prohibited items were a bag and a mobile phone. I had both; I began my 'This is England' routine, which involves exasperated sighing, much shaking of head and glum, resigned grimaces. I knew that on the other side of the door would be overweight minions in undersized uniforms whose day would be made by saying, 'No, you are not allowed ...' no matter what, the pleasure they get from declaring these prohibitions being the trade-off for their low wages.

Nonetheless, I rang in the hope that there might be facilities for leaving the offending items, despite knowing in my heart there wouldn't be. Masters of the This-is-England routine are far too experienced to let anything sensible thwart their jollies.

The door opened. As the man opened it and saw me holding my knapsack, he could barely contain his delight. 'You can't come in with a bag, sir.'

'Well, can I leave it somewhere?' I asked. 'A locker perhaps, while I attend the Barry George case?' I then made the mistake of adding, 'I'm a journalist but I won't have accreditation until tomorrow.'

You play into their hands when you do special pleading with

a This-is-England hand. The moment I said it, I saw I'd really made his Monday, which, as the Fatman used to sing, is the 'start-to-work' most-hated day of the week. I watched the cerebral orgasm spasm out from his brain and spread across his face.

'Ohhh no, sir, we don't have lockers. You might leave a bomb in there. How would we know? Ohh no, sir.' It was poetry to him as his delivery showed.

I just looked at him blankly, thinking that he and all his kind should have their genitals bathed in sulphuric acid. Concentrated. But there was more to come. 'But what you can do, sir, is put it with the landlord of the host-el-ry on the corner.' He pointed to the pub.

The relish with which he said hostelry should have alerted me but I needed hope, which is always when you snatch at its lies. I nodded my gratitude.

'He'll be happy to oblige,' he added. As I turned to leave, thinking that it could have been worse, he delivered the punchline: 'He does charge, sir. Ten pounds per bag per day.'

I retreated. I needed the comfort of being able to go under the duvet. Today's This-is-England tide was flowing too strong for me. Defeated and demoralised, I trudged back to the Klein and cycled home to Battersea, obeying all the traffic laws and taking twice as long as I had done on the reverse trip in the morning. After Clem had wiggle-waggled all around me and I had hit the black coffee, I rang round for accreditation. Eventually, Michael Pilgrim, then of the *Daily Express*, and Boris Johnson of *The Spectator* obliged. Both said they would do it in the morning. I took Clem for a run and waited for Benjamin to call.

He did at about 4.30pm. 'Where were you? Why didn't you tell me … it doesn't matter. Guess what they have done. They confiscated my notes, that's what.' The normally treble voice went

187

falsetto — castrati, why bother being snipped, just catch Pell fever. 'It's outrageous ... my notes. I always take notes, you know that ... Who do they think they are?'

I didn't tell him; anyway, he was happier running on his moral outrage. It was another atrocity story from the annals of 'This is England'.

It transpired that Benjamin had been rather more resourceful than I in circumventing the bag prohibition, not by paying the bag tax but by hiding his behind a nearby advertising hoarding. As he always puts his stuff in a plastic bag, he had the advantage of it not attracting attention from some passing tramp. However, after he returned and was admitted to the court and saw that I was not on the press benches, he began taking notes of the proceedings. Mansfield was pouring scorn on the Crown's case, 'A particle here, a fibre there and an identification that is questionable ...'

The minions, though, were also watching Pell's note-taking.

When he left, after the case had been adjourned until the following day, he was stopped by a female usher — overweight and in an undersized uniform — and his notes were confiscated. She then called for a security officer who made a grand entrance overreaching his authority, 'You are not allowed to take notes in court. Only journalists and lawyers are allowed to take notes in court.'

Benjamin replied serenely, 'I am a journalist and I am a qualified lawyer, so can I have my notes back, please?' He held his hand out.

Jobsworthy looked at Benjamin's grimy, bin-rummaging hand and said, 'Well, that's what you say, but I 'appen to know that you are a well-known public nuisance. You're Benjie the Binman. We know who you are. What you're doing 'ere may well be in contempt of court.'

Benjamin swore that it came out as 'contemptibles of court'.

'Others will 'ave to decide that. But I can tell you,' which he proceeded to do with a wagging index finger, 'that you are not 'aving these notes back and you are not going to be allowed back in the public gallery while the Barry George trial is in session. That is an order. Do you understand?'

'Only too well. And tomorrow so will every newspaper in the country,' Benjamin sputtered in fury. One of Benjamin's favourite authors is Kafka even if, generally, it is he who turns situations Kafkaesque. But 'This is England' beats *The Trial* in spades.

That evening, Benjamin composed a letter to the trial judge, Justice Gage, pointing out he was a qualified lawyer, worked in the media and was attending the trial in that capacity. He also wrote on Jobsworthy's 'contemptibles of court' point, 'Your Lordship's direction to the press benches at 4.10pm was written verbatim by me as I appreciated how important it was for me to take heed of it when I returned home.'

Justice Gage had warned the press of the dangers of reporting *sub judice* hearings.

He rang me after he had composed the letter and e-mailed it to me. I said it was fine. But I then asked him about the court proceedings and he took me through some of what I had missed.

'There's no evidence. You're right, Mansfield is brilliant. I'm telling you, this guy could be found not guilty. The police did not do their job. They had Barry George in their computer files from the day of the murder and did nothing about it. I tell you I am hooked. This could be the trial of the century ...'

I could feel the landslide under my carefully constructed edifice of 'Barry George didn't do it, so Richard Hughes could still be a candidate'. I couldn't face holding my hands up to Benjamin, who I knew would turn my landslide into a Richter 10 earthquake.

That night, Benjamin delivered his letter to Justice Gage by hand to the Old Bailey while doing his rounds plundering the rubbish bags of offices as diverse as Took's Court where Mansfield practises and the Lottery Commission where licensed Monopoly plunders the plebs.

On Tuesday morning, we both again made our way to the CCC. Benjamin's letter had made sense prevail and, after receipt of a charming letter from Justice Gage assuring him that he could attend the trial and take notes, the previous day's notes were restored to Benjamin and an apology was conveyed by another minion on behalf of Jobsworthy. Meanwhile, neither of my faxes of accreditation had been received by the policemen manning the tradesmen's entrance. I used my mobile to chase up both the respective secretaries of Michael Pilgrim and Boris Johnson, then retired to a coffee bar opposite.

I was sipping and looking at my notes when in came a burly young man who was very nervy. He had a *Daily Mirror* that he kept opening and shutting while he waited to be served. He looked at me with a definite spark of recognition. He turned with his coffee towards me and more or less invited me to ask him to sit at my table, which I did. Charlie had just been acquitted of the rape of his wife. He'd been in Belmarsh for the last four months, so, naturally, I steered the conversation round to Barry George.

Charlie said, 'He don't really mix — thinks everyone is a copper. I'd see him on the exercise yard ... the guy you should talk to is George Willsford as he was with him more than anyone.' As an afterthought, he said, 'He has an SAS dagger tattooed on his biceps.'

When I asked which one, he had to think carefully.

'His right, I think. Yeah, his right. But he don't look like he could sort out mission imposs. He ain't SAS if you follow me. Like he limps a bit and lumbers round the yard. The guy who killed her must have been a bit lively ... ' He screwed up his face to indicate that he didn't think George was capable of pulling it off physically, never mind mentally.

Then a barrister without his robes but still wearing his neck frillies — snaps — came in looking flushed and triumphant followed by the customary pin-striped solicitor. Both Charlie and I looked at them. The barrister said to his companion, 'That was easy. Mansfield's not as sharp as he likes to think.'

My ears obviously pricked up.

I just butted in on their conversation. 'Sorry, but I am covering the Barry George case. What's happened?'

They didn't mind. On the contrary, the barrister beamed. 'We applied to have the ban on publication of photographs of the accused lifted. Justice Gage ruled in our favour.'

Whose favour, I asked.

He paused slightly before answering, 'The Mail Group, Associated Newspapers.'

I thanked him and he went to the counter. Later that day, I found out that the barrister's name was Adam Wolanski.

Meanwhile, Pilgrim's secretary rang me and said that she had faxed my accreditation to the Old Bailey. Around midday, I slunk into the tradesmen's entrance expecting to be shown the door like a cur that had crapped on the kitchen floor. But no. I had met the criteria.

'Yes, it's arrived ... When you come round here, we'll give it you as your pass...'

In fact, the policemen manning the entrance gate turned out to be OK and not at all like the court ushers and officials that

Benjamin had his run in with on Monday. As I walked up the three
flights of stairs that take you to the original part of the Old Bailey
where Number One Court is located, I felt slightly uneasy.
Although I had been writing about crime for 20 years, I had kept
away from Number One Court. It stirred up bad memories. In
1966, Justice Hinchcliffe sentenced me to '15 years to run
consecutive with the 8 years you are already serving, making 23
years in all'. It was for firing upon a pursuing police car after an
aborted armed robbery in Deptford. I was an escapee from
Parkhurst Prison, having served only two of my eight years.

Before he finished his sentencing remarks, I reeled away to
go down to the holding cage below the dock thinking my life
over unless I escaped again. One of my co-defendants, Freddie
Davies, was already there nursing his 12 years. He could only
think about his own sentence. 'I am dead. I'll never finish it ...'
He remembered that I had virtually double what he faced. He
was caught up in his own disaster, then realised that he was
bewailing it to someone whose predicament was worse than his.
To retrieve his lapse, he said something that at the time was
absurd but which later I came to value. He said, 'You'll be OK,
John; you're fit; you'll come out the same as you came in.' He
didn't; he died in prison of cancer. I came through it certainly
older but otherwise physically untouched, mainly because I
worked out daily. Rigorous, high-intensity exercise has been my
only religion ever since that moment in the cage under Number
One Court.

Most convicts think they are over-sentenced; I certainly did.
Justice Hinchcliffe's actions also gave me cause to rationalise away
my own culpability. He sent me down with a cold vindictiveness
that was edged in a remark I had made to him when I was in the
witness box. He intervened during cross-examination to repeat a

question that I had already brushed off when the prosecution put it to me. It wasn't really relevant to the charge. It was about the origin of a car that I had been using while I was on the run from prison. I had no intention of detailing where it came from and I replied with an exasperated impatience, 'Look, I have ...'

That was as far as I got. Hinchcliffe exploded, 'Don't you look me ...' He was a passable Judge Jeffries: grossly overweight, quick to anger and spectacularly good at showing it. He glared at me in fury, his face beetle-red with the rolls of fat under his chin quivering; I knew I was in the middle of the cross-hairs. It came out of nothing and I had no means of knowing why he was so irrationally incensed, but for sure I knew he was. I also knew I was going to get it in the neck if I was found guilty; when I was, it was no surprise that he gave me the treatment.

I often lecture about the criminal justice system. I am an anti-leftie. I argue that just desserts, humane retribution, is the best tool that society has for dealing with crime. Not perfect; just the best available. I also argue that it is in society's interests never to give the criminal cause to shake off responsibility for his own actions. The worst, of course, is when society stoops to the level of the criminal to exact revenge. However, in his own way, Justice Hinchcliffe also worked against the grain of society's interests. He gave me that extra bit of resolution to escape and I did.

In the early '90s, however, after I had been out long enough only to remember those days as another time, I became friendly with a highly-educated Swedish journalist who worked for the *Independent* as its political editor. She had been married to Hinchcliffe's grandson and he often told her how, when he was around his grandfather, the old boy would boast about how he had sent me down. He would say that I had threatened to kill him when he sentenced me but here he was still alive. Anneka is a hard-nosed hack who has a feel for stories that don't stand up. Even at a time when she didn't know me — just of me — she couldn't credit her husband's story about his grandfather. It was something that had become an issue between them and it nagged at her. I never found out why, but she had a querulous mind and when I met her she took me over it a number of times from different angles.

It was a memory I was reluctant to recall. To put an end to it, I said in pretty much the exasperated tone that had set off Justice Hinchcliffe that if I had made the threat it would be in the clippings — the archived press reports of the trial. I told her to stop the cross-examination and look them up when she was next in the office. She thought about it, then said that she didn't need to look. One thing replaces another. After that, if I was pushed into talking about those events, I noticed that I stopped whining about being over-sentenced and just used the anecdote of Hinchcliffe lying to his family.

When I walked into Number One Court for the first time in 35 years, Mansfield was in full flow, 'They have no case ...' He was running his 'no case' to answer application. Some 20 years ago, I used to play football with him over Clapham Common in a lawyers versus anyone-who-turns-up kickabout. He has put on weight but the gravitas more than compensates. He looks like an old lion who is going to be king of the pride until he dies. I saw Benjamin up in the gods to my right frantically taking notes. Justice Gage, who monitors any movement in his court, looked as perky as a scrawny chicken given the run of the yard. I sat on the benches behind the dock, so I couldn't see much of Barry George other than as a crouched-over blob sitting in the dock wearing a blue-ribbed sweater.

I got out my notebook ... my first entry, which I am looking at now as I type, is 'MM: Timing is critical in this case ...' [Mike Mansfield]. Little at that stage was I to know how critical it was or that I would call this book *Dead on Time*. There was more of the same lampooning by Mansfield of the Crown's case. He covered virtually all aspects of the case including the *Sun's* original coverage — 'The *Sun* has gone to town' — the mistakes by Oxborough in not following up the calls from HAFAD naming George. Everything that could be thrown in to show either that George could not get a fair trial or the evidence was not good enough to try him was thrown in and with some more. The word from the other journos was that the pre-trial would go on for about a week, then the jury would be sworn in and the trial itself would last about six weeks.

At 1.00pm when the court recessed until 2.05pm, George turned towards the back of the court to go down the way I had gone with my 23-year sentence in 1966. He was wearing a yellow tie and clutching a Bible in his right hand. At the time, these were just facts that had no significance beyond what they meant if attached to a description of a complete stranger. But through his goatee and moustache, I could see under an unruly mop of black hair the plumped cheeks and wide-faced features of the TV celebrity.

Unlike his lookalike, whose face always looks ready to break into a smile, George's face looks disposed to scowl. His body is pear-shaped with narrow shoulders and broad hips. He had obviously put weight on in prison and lost his olive complexion that so many witnesses remembered him by. He reminded me of the sort of man you see begging down the West End. Not down on his luck, just on the make; not dangerous but a low-lifer who will take you if you give him a chance. Nevertheless, I could no longer hold on to my hope that he might be a patsy.

I walked out of the court and left the building to meet Benjamin. Adjoining the Old Bailey, in Holborn Viaduct there are some poncy coffee shops and a greasy spoon. Even though, as an orthodox Jew, he would only have an orange juice at lunch, Benjamin always insisted on the greasy spoon because 'it's cheaper, more honest'. He sat at a round Formica table busily spreading his notes from the morning around him. I knew as I bought my coffee and his juice that I would have to come clean about seeing the TV celebrity lookalike in the features of Barry George. He was so impressed with Mansfield that he was already seeing acquittal; whereas I now knew that George was morally guilty, which on the whole tends to be an advantage for the prosection. Intellectually, I suppose, I was hanging on by my mental fingertips to the idea that he might be legally not guilty. If I had been as familiar with the lyrics of 'Bohemian Rhapsody' then as I later became, I'd have hummed, '*Caught in a landslide ... No escape from reality ... Open your eyes ...*'

As soon as I went to sit down, Benjamin was at me. 'Wasn't he brilliant ...'

I let him run on, reading out bits of what Mansfield had said that morning. Much of it, of course, I had not witnessed.

Then I said, 'I know all that ... but I think he is guilty.' I said 'think', not 'know'.

He blinked and stared myopically at me through the milk-bottle lenses. 'What do you mean, guilty? How do you know?'

'Well, I don't know because there is still the possibility of Richard Hughes.' As I said it, I realised it was ridiculous. I came clean. 'You know when I asked you last night what he looked like ...'

As he often does, Benjamin interrupted me and summarised what I was going to say. 'You rang and asked me what he looked like and I said "Phil Jupitus, ____ [the TV celebrity], Chris Moyles." Yes, so what?'

'Well,' I replied, 'Richard Hughes always said that his first impression of the gunman was that he looked like ____.'

However, we had to dash back for the afternoon session in which Mansfield took Campbell apart in his efforts to show that such was the blunder in not arresting George at the time he was being reported by HAFAD and others, that his right to a speedy resolution of the charge had been denied.

In the lead up to ridiculing Campbell's convoluted computer system in which these reports were filed, Mansfield asked, 'Do you agree that what you are describing was a failure to go through information.'

'Absolutely. And that's what I have written to myself,' Campbell nodded, looking down at his memos.

Mansfield knew that Campbell was playing Humpty Dumpty semantics. 'I do not want any ambiguity here, Mr Campbell. There was a failure.'

Campbell replied calmly, 'My idea of failure is not the same as yours, Mr Mansfield.'

Mansfield commented, 'Look, one's trying to be realistic here ...'

In my notes I scribbled, 'Realistic! Only because you're trying to knock Oxborough for six because they bungled on Stephen Lawrence.' Mansfield had run big with the whole Lawrence inquiry. Lawrence's murder had hardly been investigated, whereas Dando's had the whole Met on the case.

By the time I left the Old Bailey, the *Evening Standard* was splashing on George with a full-page mug-shot looking distinctly baleful. The large-font headline read FIRST PICTURE: MAN POLICE SAY SHOT JILL DANDO. It was loaded with intimations that he was her murderer. As he walked home, Gage must have shuddered, then winced as he thought about what tomorrow would bring when Mansfield charged in on his high horse. Cycling back, I occasionally saw passers-by reading it.

Clem started barking at me from the balcony as I came up to the front of my block of flats. I rushed upstairs shouldering the Klein. He was all over me, then he scampered out on to the landing anticipating his walk. I hustled him back in, went to the loo, changed into my running gear and took him over Battersea Park. I located a small log for him and he ran with that in his jaws; it made peeing awkward as he got it in the way of whatever bush or tree he stopped at. Sometimes he'd drop it, crouching eagerly in front of it while he waited for me to throw it.

When we reached Albert Bridge, he went through the railings and down to the water's edge of the Thames; it was high tide. He dropped his stick and jumped in, looking back at me to chuck it for him. I clambered over and gave him his allotted three swims. The farther out the better. Then I ran with him to the track on the other side of the park. While I had a quick workout in the gym, he hung around outside trying to lure people coming in and out to throw his stick.

That night, Benjamin rang after 1.00am. He had just bought the first editions. 'They have gone even further than the *Standard*. The *Sun* and the *Mail* ... you wait 'til you see them. They have got him doing karate, in combat gear ... You won't believe it ... Mansfield will have a field day. Some of it is so prejudicial. Unbelievable.' He rattled on like this until I'd had enough. Benjamin doesn't sleep but, like all normal people, I do.

The morning session started late at 11.30am, but it was worth waiting for. Mansfield seemed to take ages to rise. It wasn't just his face that said 'I told you so', but every moving part of his body. He is such a showman.

'M'lud, there are a few matters that have occurred overnight. The press ... It has had a devastating effect on the defendant; he feels personally destroyed by the publicity. He fears very much that he won't get a fair trial ... The *Evening Standard* printed a picture. It wasn't even a story. It was an excuse to publish a photograph ...'

On the *Sun*, he stated, 'The impression is the villain is on one side and on the other side is the victim with the headline: DID HE KILL JILL? Whoever reads this gets the impression that the defendant is the murderer. It's all innuendo. This case has an aura of guilt stamped all over it.'

Justice Gage looked nonplussed. He was acting as if he had not expected this to happen in the wake of his lifting the ban. He turned to Pownall, 'Does the Crown endorse this?'

Pownall said they didn't. 'My concern is for a fair trial ...'

In my notes I wrote 'conviction'. At that stage, I could not believe that Gage did not know what he was doing. No High Court judge could be that naïve. To me, his lifting the photograph ban was the hallmark of a 'bring home the verdict' judge. Yet, I was wrong and later came to eat my words. Time and time again, Justice Gage showed himself to be a constitutional judge who followed the letter of the law — not what he thought it should be or what would get George convicted.

Pownall replied po-faced to Gage's comment, 'If there has been excessive reporting, I would contend that once the trial starts, the press would stick to what's been said in open court before the jury. We concede that it is regrettable that it had an effect on the defendant at a very important time for him. But there is no prejudice and he can have a fair trial.'

Gage warned the press, 'I very much hope that nothing like this will be repeated again.'

Mansfield resumed his application that his client had been

denied a speedy resolution of the charge against him but there was much to-ing and fro-ing between George and Etienne and Mansfield. It seemed that, for a while, George wanted to sack Mansfield as he blamed him for not stopping Gage lifting the ban on photographs. Meanwhile, he was employing his formidable skills as a hypochondriac to present a range of symptoms to a stream of physical and psychological medics. Qualified medics could not cope with George. The only one during the trail who did was Matron. She is an Old Bailey institution about whom even Gage spoke in reverential tones. A steely, no-nonsense Scotswoman with a bustling air and a starched uniform, Matron always seemed to work wonders with George. The standing joke was that her standard panacea for every ailment was a firmly and deeply administered suppository.

Meanwhile, Benjamin did a design editor's analysis of the layout that the *Sun* used in publishing its story. On the front page, as Mansfield had argued, was Dando opposite George — Victim v Villain. However, the series of snaps across the middle pages used a different technique. Across the top of the page were printed a series of photographs of George that showed how he had changed his appearance. They were in chronological order, except for one, which was captioned 'Posing in combat jacket with Paras at Red Devil display'. This one was positioned so that it exploited how the reader's eye works as he reads the text. The 'combat' photograph was to the right of the text, which is where the eye is drawn as it comes to the end of a line. It is a subliminal device that any layout expert can understand but Mansfield missed in his submission to Gage that the tabloid's coverage of the opening of the case was deliberately designed to maximise prejudice.

Rather pleased with himself, Benjamin rang up Etienne's office, told them about this and faxed them his layout analysis.

That night, Mansfield stopped putting his rubbish out at Took's Court.

The next day saw more of the same. There was also a long session in chambers to discuss the implications of George's many medical conditions. Eventually, by the Thursday afternoon, Mansfield was claiming that medical problems with the defendant meant that he was forced to ask for a long adjournment. A grim-faced Gage was obviously going to have to grant it and he did — the restart of the pre-trial was scheduled for 23 April. It was almost certainly over the prejudicial reporting but that was not conceded by Gage. Instead, it was granted on medical grounds. He also dismissed Mansfield's application that, because of police failures to act on the HAFAD reports, George had been denied in law a speedy resolution of the charge. He then turned to the matter of the 'lurid press' reporting. He said, 'I know this is shutting the stable door after the horse has bolted, but I would like only one photo to be used. This should be agreed by both sides.' There was some mutual conferring between Mansfield and Pownall and both indicated that that was mutually acceptable.

The photograph that was chosen and agreed upon by Etienne was one that the police offered her. It shows a clean-shaven George in a track suit walking along a pavement while he was under surveillance. He appears quite normal, even pleasant, certainly nothing like any of those that appeared in the press after Gage lifted the ban. Yet among the latter, the only recent ones were the mug-shot or the one in which he was in handcuffs — the others were all early photographs. But in neither the mug-shot or the handcuffs one, nor the early ones, is there any resemblance to the TV celebrity lookalike. In the one that Etienne agreed upon he looks like his twin brother! I fancied that the officer behind this particular sting was Oxborough's ducker and diver, Horrocks.

Benjamin rang me again with early editions to tell me the news. He also said, 'Well, now we have seven weeks, you can write my book.'

I replied, 'Naturally.' Then I said goodnight and went to sleep.

12

carry on up the old bailey

Some of the hacks attending the trial saw me as a bit of a novelty. Like those correspondents who spend their working lives telling us what the Windsors are doing, crime and court reporting tends to be a specialist branch of journalism. I wasn't part of the Old Bailey beat and, of course, they knew my history. Thirty years ago, they would have been writing me up — 'Ex-Public Enemy Number One John McVicar was led from the dock a broken man facing the next 20 years of his life in a top-security jail ...' Naturally, some of them were uneasy at my joining the club but, generally, they displayed a live-and-let-live attitude towards me.

Steve Bird from the *Times* is a genial young guy who is brighter than most on the Old Bailey beat and looked at me busily writing notes during the earlier hearing and asked, 'How's your shorthand?'

I moved my head from side to side like a hypnotising mongoose. 'Well, pidgin. But I'm brushing up on it.' He laughed; all hacks know the slog required to master it. I could see from his open notebook that his was pretty good. All mysterious squiggles, strokes and dots; no abbreviated longhand. I hated him.

Shorthand used to be an essential skill of any journalist or reporter but the ubiquitous tape recorder has largely replaced it. In terms of accuracy, the second course is better, as in transcribing a recording one picks up all the buried or subliminal nuances that are lost if you are absorbed in capturing a contemporaneous record. I also touch-type very quickly, so transcribing from a recording is easier for me than most journalists; overall, though, shorthand is more efficient. For a court reporter, it is also essential as recording equipment is not allowed in our courts and court transcription is prohibitively expensive — typically £800 per day's proceedings. Like all hacks who don't have shorthand, I get by with my own idiosyncratic abbreviated longhand but it was always a poor relation to Benjamin's.

We would sit in the greasy spoon and compare notes or later over the telephone, and always his record proved more accurate and comprehensive than mine. But Benjamin is no shrinking violet when it comes to something that he is better at than you. He did like to rub my nose in how much better his notes were than mine. He is the classic school nerdy swot who lets the dashing rugby captain crib his essays but plays hard to get sometimes. 'What do your notes say?' would often be a rejoinder to some question of mine about what, for instance, Mansfield had argued that afternoon; then after listening a bit to my faltering, deciphered rendition of what I had written down, he would snap, 'No. He didn't say that ...' Then he would proceed to tell me what Mansfield had actually said. I didn't like it.

carry on up the old bailey

During the seven-week break in the pre-trial hearing, I decided to learn shorthand, thereby killing three birds with one stone: it would give me a legitimate excuse not to do Benjamin's book; I would be liberated from my dependency on his George trial notes; finally, any hack in court who looked over at my notebook would not see the mark of a cub reporter — longhand — but the touchstone of a seasoned hack, shorthand. This was too good a vision to pass on, so for the next seven weeks I was utterly absorbed in a Pitman 2000 Shorthand Course. This was also a perfect allegory of my working methods. When faced with a daunting task, rather than getting on with the job with tools at hand, I invariably become absorbed in polishing the tools.

Nevertheless, it was an enjoyable seven weeks. And on Monday, 23 April, when it was back to court again, I felt the batteries were fully charged. I was a new man. Defaulting on his book had also driven Benjamin crazy and now, having finally passed my crime reporter's rite of passage, I was the genuine article. I walked Clem early and took the 9.30am bike ride up to the Old Bailey. I also found a new game. I was training well over Battersea Track and I'd had the Klein serviced, so I was like one of these oldie veterans who can cut 2 hours 35 minutes for a marathon. On my way in, I would wind in some young mountain biker, then sit in his slipstream, dogging him into burning himself out before kicking past him. The only elixir of age is to break the spirit of the young. The trouble is, although I would arrive on a high of victory, it would take about 15 minutes before the sweat stopped popping out of my head and coursing down my face.

Not much had changed. George was malingering with a vengeance; he rarely appeared in the dock and the court hardly sat. The only good news was that Mansfield had another publication to complain about, *Hello!*, which was now edited by Phil Hall, my old enemy from *Punch*. He had parted company with Clifford and left Al Fayed's employment only to be offered the *Hello!* editorship. The 13 March edition of the magazine had published the handcuffs photo in a feature on Dando's murder. Gage already had a copy of the offending article but Mansfield took him through the gravamen: '... tends to suggest that the person who has been arrested is responsible'. What compounded the offence, in Mansfield's eye, was that it was the sort of 'magazine that ends up on dentists' tables where it will be read casually and can rekindle memories of previous publications'. As with everything, Mansfield milked every angle of prejudice that could be created by reading this edition of *Hello!*.

Gage was not amused by the flouting of his February order and told Mansfield that he regarded this as a serious example of contempt and would be reporting the magazine to the offices of the Attorney General.

The next day was virtually the same, except we did not have any Phil Hall contemptibles to warm the cockles of me heart. Mansfield continued with his abuse of due process arguments, but very soon George was slummocking over on his chair as he suffered *petit mal* epileptic fits and all manner of other convulsion symptoms. Like everything he does, George over-egged his act. He staggered in and out of the dock like he was blind and senile, he blinked and grimaced as if he had come out of the darkness into the blazing sunlight. It didn't look very convincing, an inference that the knowing smirks of the dock warders only reinforced. Nonetheless, it was established that however much he exaggerates his symptoms or fakes them, George has — and has had since childhood — *petit mal* epilepsy. Even when it was accepted that many of the symptoms he was manifesting were of psychological origin, some ingenious medic decided that this was also an illness.

George was suffering from 'somatization'. This is a psychological illness by which the patient converts stress into medical symptoms; in George's case, for example, 'mild scoliosis' as he called it. Scoliosis is the abnormal curvature of the spine. Much of the later police interviews he spent clutching his right side with his left hand to relieve his mild scoliosis. This condition has replaced a slipped disc as Article 1 in the Malingerer's Charter.

There was also his irritable bowel syndrome. I remember thinking to myself that perhaps there are scoliosis or irritable bowel germs in the air that, like that homing pigeon particle destined for his pocket, had had written into their genetic code instructions to infect George. The situation cried out for Matron to do what was necessary to make him take his medicine.

Gage, though, seemed on the run with his court turning into a hospital ward and while he showed his irritation, he never cracked the whip. Indeed, he eventually acceded to Mansfield's requests that, to make allowances for George's illnesses and histrionic embellishments of his symptoms, the court recess for ten minutes every hour. Pownall was ignored when he rose to mutter darkly and incredulously about how there had been no *petit mal* attacks in Belmarsh Prison.

After this concession another one followed: a clinical psychologist with expertise in epilepsy was given permission to sit alongside George in the dock. Dr. Young was given that job much to the suppressed but detectable chagrin of the Horrocks camp who were sitting behind counsel for the Crown. Horrocks has a mobile expressive face and is a bit of a card. He generally sat on the benches behind Pownall where the jury could see his expressions as he reacted to the evidence. He was never called to give evidence but he was one of the most effective bit players in the show. His face as he watched George bonding with Young in the dock is an abiding trial memory that I savour with relish.

Dr Susanne Young is attractive, albeit 37–ish and BLONDE. She isn't a Dando lookalike but she has a concerned, caring look under the blonde hair and she was the right age — one didn't need to be a Horrocks to smell a rat here. Someone selected her for the role of nursing George in the dock! And if you are of the persuasion that very little happens in court by accident, then you might think that this was Mansfield's getback over the way Horrocks had outfoxed Etienne over the photo.

Nicholas Witchell had taken to making the occasional caustic asides on the press benches: 'Barry couldn't have done his scoliosis much good running down Gowan Avenue.' Somehow in becoming a figure of fun, George had become Barry. Ingrid Kelly, the *Tonight with Trevor McDonald* producer, — often called him 'Barmy Barry' or a 'Muppet'. Later on, when Benjamin started to feed me his Ninjutsu research, I used to retort to her muppet line, 'He may be a Muppet, but he's a Ninja Muppet.' It was *Carry On Up the Old Bailey* time.

It was all part of the show, of course, but as I cycled back that Tuesday I did wonder if George would even be tried. If he managed to persuade the medical experts that he was not sufficiently aware of what was going on around him and could not instruct counsel, then all the courts could do was try to establish in his absence whether or not he was responsible for the murder. He could not be found guilty or, for that matter, not guilty.

I ran Clem that evening with my mind on what this would do to my book. He now had his own small log that I kept in the courtyard to the flats. It was raining and chilly but he headed merrily for Albert Bridge for his usual swim. He went in once and returned. I threw it out again and it was slightly farther than I felt comfortable with, but always I reassured myself with the knowledge that if he got in trouble in the current I could rescue him. This time he was in trouble and I was encouraging him from the bank but the tide he was swimming against was too strong for him to reach the steps. I began to get alarmed but I knew I would have time to get to him if things went wrong. Then I could shepherd him in my arms downstream and find somewhere to cling to on the steep concrete bank until someone found a rope and hauled us up. I had done it before, as the only place you can clamber up along that stretch is the steps by Albert Bridge.

He kept looking up to me as he battled against the tide. Then he lost his stick and tried to retrieve it but couldn't; he went back to swimming against the flow. He still kept looking up at me with utter trust in his eyes. I should have known, but I didn't understand. I thought I would have time. I should have gone in then, but I looked away to see if I could summon help before I plunged. Just a glance. When I looked back he was on his side just under the surface floating downstream. There had been no struggle or gasping for breath. He had just gone. A part of me knew he was dead, but I had to give him every chance. He had come to me from my mother and had been a daily part of my life for seven years.

I jumped in and within a couple of strokes I had him. I had timed it so well that I suddenly hoped I would be able to revive him. I grabbed him and pulled him up. His body was like a rag doll and his head lolled over. I shouted, 'Clem, Clem.' Then I went under and I had to resurface to do it again. I shook and shook him, not believing what I could see, feel and knew. I remember sobbing, 'Please live.'

I knew he was dead and I became aware of the danger to myself. My clothing and training shoes had become waterlogged and were dragging me down. I tried to swim with him back against the tide to the steps but I had to let him go.

I watched his body drift downstream. For a few seconds, I just looked. He had been so precious to me that I wanted to save his body and bury him but I knew I had to save myself. I was so demoralised that I couldn't think properly and, instead of swimming downstream, I tried swimming against the currents to get back to the steps. It was also becoming quite cold. I considered trying to pull off my heavy long-sleeved training sweater but I knew it could get snarled up around my neck.

I had to stop swimming because I felt myself getting tired and slightly dreamy. I floated on my back just going with the currents. I started shouting for help. I remember thinking this is how you drown; it is so easy. Then a woman poked her head over the bank above me. I could see she had a mobile phone in her hand. 'I'll ring the police ...'

I asked her to get a boat. Maybe four or five minutes, certainly far quicker than I expected, a police launch swung over to me. Two of them leaned over and hauled me up. I thanked them and told them what had happened. But I just wanted to be on my own. I could hardly look them in the eyes. I still couldn't comprehend what had happened. Again and again, I said virtually to myself. 'It happened so quickly. He just went under ...'

One of them said to me, 'Quite often, the owner dies and we find the dog has survived.'

I shook my head, 'No, I held him. He's dead.'

Another one said, 'Where is his body, then?'

I said it had drifted off but I picked up a note of scepticism in his voice and it occurred to me that he probably thought I was a jumper who had lost his nerve. It didn't matter. I asked them to land me near the steps. They kept saying they felt it was better if they took me to hospital. I insisted. But they couldn't get near enough to the steps without risking damaging the rudder; instead, they got me near a ladder past the bridge, which I could clamber up and get on to the towpath. Before I did, they took my particulars and I thanked them.

I ran home with the rain washing down my tears. The recklessness with which I had put him into danger, then not acted soon enough, haunted me. When I got back, even before I took off my waterlogged clothing, I rang some friends who were as upset as me. Clem was everyone's favourite — even Benjamin, who would rather eat a bacon sandwich than stroke a dog, loved Clem. I got more condolence cards for Clem than will commemorate me when I die. The sweetest remark was made by Charlie, James Steen's three-year-old son, who, when James told him, said, 'Clem's gone to heaven.'

Clem loved people, was always ready to play and was such a character.

The following morning, I just did the same as I had been doing ... cycled up to the Old Bailey, but it was a sad journey. I was already dreading the return, knowing that there would no joyful Clem to greet me, just the memory of my irresponsibility.

I was wrecked and thought I looked it, but I didn't know if it showed. I didn't mention what had happened to anyone and I tried to act normally.

Again, the court was not sitting; this time it was not only George but also the Lord Mayor's Day. A bunch of elderly worthies in fancy-dress parading through the Old Bailey — I avoided it like the plague. Three days of non-action had decimated the hacks and, instead of the 50 or so journalists there at the opening, now there were only about ten. Among the die-hards was a hardcore of three book writers, including me, and two TV female journalists both working on reconstructions, plus one or two others like Nicholas Witchell, Dando's BBC colleague, and Martin Brunt of Sky. I have already mentioned Ingrid Kelly, the producer on *Tonight with Trevor McDonald*, whom I sat next to for a lot of the trial. Irish–Italian, 38, with a mean speed in shorthand, hearing like a bat, a punky dresser and a take-it-leave-it cockney accent. She can be very warm and charming but, if the mood takes her, which it often does, she has a mean line in sarky put-downs.

This particular morning, I was standing just outside Number One Court with the other two book writers and Ingrid came up. She had just been chatting with the Crown lead, Pownall. I was just listening that day, but she began telling us what he had told her about the delays, then she said, 'Ahh, Orlando is very sad at the moment. His wife has been getting on to him over letting the dog in the bedroom but the poor thing is dying. He is such a kind man.' I felt worse than George was acting, and I desperately wanted to pour my heart out to Ingrid but said nothing.

Gradually, a formula was devised by which Mansfield could make applications and submissions with or without George in the dock. And he ran the whole gamut of the evidence. Gage was right down the middle, and where the issue was too close to call he gave it to the defence. Even when everything he knew was bearing down on him not to, he acted constitutionally. A good man and a noble judge.

The peculiar dimensions of George's mind were also highlighted by the way that George instructed Mansfield to cross-examine Griffin in the trial. The postman gave evidence that this request for his phone had been made at the Fulham Palace Road end of Gowan Avenue. George decided that he wanted to be at the top of Gowan Avenue, the Munster Road part, presumably because that is where the café was. A reluctant Mansfield had to put this to

Griffin, who assured him that it was at the Fulham Palace Road end. Mansfield did not press the matter as he knew that it mattered not a whit at what end of Gowan Avenue it happened — neither version went to George's guilt or innocence. What did matter was that he was having to put to a witness something that, by the way he rejected it with absolute certainty, was self-evidently untrue. This diluted the impact of when it was necessary to suggest to a witness — because his evidence did go to George's guilt — that he was mistaken. The reason Mansfield could not dissuade George on this instruction to challenge Griffin — and there were others that harmed the defence over arbitrary issues — was that George thought that, as he had redefined Griffin's reality once, he could do it again. When he approached him six weeks after the murder, Griffin had not recognised him; he felt confident he could do it again in court. Once George is running on his own fixed lines, he becomes impervious to reason, obdurate and rigid in his thinking.

There were three other significant events before the trial actually started on Friday, 4 May. The most dramatic — and it also was emblematic of George's mind — occurred virtually to the minute on the second anniversary of Jill Dando's murder. There is a grandfather clock just under the public gallery, which was above and to the right of where George sat in the dock. Right on 11.33am, he began shaking and blinking. By now, some of the press were on to George, and Nicholas Witchell, who was on the end of the front press bench next to the dock, sighed, looked up to heaven and muttered, 'Time for another wobbly.' After a few minutes of that, George staggered out in a lather, holding on to chair tops and so on. Gage adjourned; Matron made her first appearance. We, on the press bench, were laughing and shaking our heads in astonishment at George's timing. Horrocks was rolling his eyes. The sheer audacity of George bringing proceedings to a halt when he knew that everyone present would make the link just took the biscuit. Of course, he would never have done this in front of the jury, but it was safe, he thought, to do one of his characteristic teases for the press. Again and again, the show turned *Carry On Up the Old Bailey*. The second incident was over Dr Young and the third, the swearing in of the jury.

On Tuesday, 1 May, Pownall raised the issue of whether Dr Young should be allowed to stay alongside George during the trial. Dr Young is a qualified clinical neuro-psychologist who has trained in epilepsy, and had been drafted in by the defence as a medical watchdog. She provided evidence as an expert witness as to George's state of mind, as well as offering him her personal attention — until the Crown objected. By now, she was fully bonded with George and would hold on to his arm whenever she spotted the signs of seizure. He would bat his eyes a bit and rock slightly and she would be solicitously tending him as though he had just been pulled out of the World Trade Center rubble. She was also occasionally administering pills that he swallowed with his elaborately choreographed 'cup of water' dance. Young would attract the eye of Katie, the court usher, who would pour some water into a plastic cup; she would then approach the dock and put the cup next to the dock warder; he would push it along the top of the dock towards Young who would then hand it to George. He would now take his pill and sip water like he had just been rescued after a month in the Sahara. George loves getting people dancing to his tune. It was noticeable, though, that George is ambidextrous — he was unerring in taking cup to lip with his left hand. So while he is right-handed, he clearly could have held the gun in his left hand when he shot Dando. As Mansfield was later to suggest to the jury, the position she was in and the way she was forced on to the ground pointed to a left-handed gunman.

Whether Young could stay in the dock was not to be decided until after the jury were sworn in at 10.30am the next day. There were about 80 potential jurors called into Number One Court; they displaced us from our benches and we had to stand by the court entrances as the selection process unwound. Eventually, after various jurors were excused on grounds such as holidays booked or the need to be at the bedside of their dying mother and so on, seven women and five men were selected and sworn in, mostly on the Bible.

Benjamin and I and some of the press gave them nicknames — Bob the Builder was Witchell's sobriquet for a typical pencil-behind-the-ear, beer-bellied guy in his early 50s who sat only about six feet from the place I had staked out for myself on the press benches. In fact, Bob was actually a William, but Bob he stayed. There was Gnat; the Manager (because he looked English middle-management); the Engineer (he read the *Guardian*, which is the social engineer's paper); Maori (because she looked like one); Indian (because she was Indian); the Housewife; the Goer; Wild Child; and SS Commandants 1 and 2.

Like any jury, they were a motley crew. The most professional-looking was the Indian. Mainly they came from North and East London, which proved lucky for me as I managed to get a feed, through an intermediary, on their thinking. However, what gave us a running commentary on their views was the continual to-ing and fro-ing from jury room to jury box that went on throughout the trial. There was the hourly ten-minute break for Dr Young to meditate with George; then Mansfield was ever-ready to raise some point with Gage in the absence of the jury. Particularly as they were leaving, jurors would talk to each other about whatever was contentious. When they were animated, their body language, expressions and general demeanour spoke volumes.

The day before the trial started, Pownall came back again to Young's presence in the dock. 'I do not question the integrity of Dr Young or her genuine and proven desire to help the defendant. Occasionally she comforts him by touching his arm or leg. This can encourage or create a false impression ...' What he didn't say was she is a blonde female about the same age as Dando. Opposing him, Mansfield played up how Young had tuned into George's psyche and was doing sterling work downstairs with the meditation sessions, i.e. if she doesn't stay in the dock we might have more wobblies. A compromise was reached. Dr Young went from the dock to the benches behind the defence team where she could rush over to the dock with the smelling salts and lace hankie if George had an attack, while next to George would sit a mental health social worker.

The next day, Verona Reece, 29, black, was installed next to George; she was female but did not look anything like Dando nor did she have the professional mien of Etienne. Nevertheless, George soon got as pally with her as he had with Young — despite his coarse, surly looks and his failure in relationships, he seems able to engage the sympathy of women who enter his life in a professional capacity. Etienne also mothered him a bit and he clearly had a much better relationship with her than he did with Mansfield.

In the corridor outside Number One Court, after Gage made his ruling, I bumped into Jim Sword and I expressed relief at getting Young out of the dock. He replied, 'Yeah, I know. We are finally getting there.' Meaning conviction. Sword looked quite grim-faced but he always does. Benjamin and I had proofed George's moral guilt to our own satisfaction, so I was not shy about conveying my wish that he also be found legally guilty. I certainly showed Sword whose side I was on. While Campbell had blackballed me, I was still keen to try to build some kind of bridge with other members of the squad. The book needed a guilty verdict first, but clearly some input from Oxborough would not come amiss.

On the Thursday, Gage told the jury that the defendant might suffer *petit mal* epileptic attacks during the trial and may leave the dock from time to time. The woman next to him, he explained, was there to provide assistance if George needed it. As always, despite it invariably being thwarted, Gage pushed punctuality.

'Members of the jury, I trust you will all be ready to start promptly, and I stress promptly, at 10.00am tomorrow.' It was wishful thinking; occasionally, Gage would carpet the dock warders for bringing George in late but, generally, he had to submit to forces that no judge could counter. The interminable delays stretched the trial to twice its expected length.

After the jury had left for the day, there were some applications on behalf of ITV and the BBC for the sketchers to draw George. They are all women and earn a fortune doing these drawings that all newspapers and TV reports carry of court proceedings. Mansfield had had enough of the media demonising George and he enjoined upon Gage the danger of letting them draw George's face. Gage agreed and, such was his fear of another prejudice-fest, he ordered that the sketchers would have to submit all their drawings to Mansfield for his approval. Every day, they used to line up before him like kids outside the headmaster's study to show that they had done their homework according to the brief. There was much grumbling about this indignity, much to the delight of us underpaid wordsmiths.

Meanwhile, I had discovered that even with seven weeks of Pitman's under my belt, Benjamin was still far more accurate than me. When he saw my shorthand and realised how I'd been spending the seven-week break, he took a great delight during our greasy spoon sessions in demonstrating that his notes were still far superior to mine.

Once he made an oblique comment on his facility. 'This was what happened to me at law school. I had to have the best notes, so I learned how to take down every word at lectures. But when I came to take my exams, I knew so much I couldn't answer anything without writing everything. In one exam, it paralysed me and I did not write one word. Don't you think that's sad?'

I didn't say anything, but I didn't think it was sad at all. Serves the little swot right.

13

the crown comes in high

On 4 May, Pownall came in 'high', as it's known among trial lawyers. He used his opening speech to talk up rather than downplay all the evidence, then let it build up as the case developed. This meant that his case only had one way to go — down. Especially since Mansfield was assembling his siege machine to demolish the walls of the Crown's citadel. Nevertheless, that is how Pownall opened and, in some respects, this was one of his best personal performances at the trial. He wasn't to peak again until he made his closing speech when, with his case burnt out, he rose up phoenix-like from the ashes with an impassioned, cogent plea to convict.

He began cleverly in that he set the murder scene in staccato pity phrases. 'The pathologist found two gunshot wounds, an entry wound and an exit wound. The bullet entry was located behind the left ear. The exit wound lay above the right ear ... There was a small bruise on Miss Dando's right forearm that could have been caused when it was grasped by her assailant. There were no characteristic defence injuries.'

Pownall was then 48, tall, with black hair that is thinning and beginning to lose its lustre. His bearing is *noblesse oblige* public school and he looks like a John Buchan hero; even his classic pin-striped suits have turn-ups. He's a jolly good chap. He chose to interlace the evidence he proposed to call in the telling of the story of Dando's death, her forthcoming marriage to Farthing, then the arrest of George and how Oxborough made their case. He didn't do much summarising of what he was going to say or even what he had said. He held the jury with his measured, earnest tones as he took them through the different features of the evidence against George.

He conceded that there was no motive but said, 'it was not for the Crown to prove motive ... Whether he [George] harboured a hidden grudge against her, believing her to have wronged him or figures he idolised such as Freddie Mercury, is impossible to gauge with any degree of certainty. The only apparent connection between Miss Dando and Freddie Mercury is that the deceased, along with other celebrities, appeared on a film produced for Comic Relief in 1993, when she and others mimed a Queen song.' He didn't tell the jury that the song was 'Bohemian Rhapsody' and a measure of his interest in this connection is that in his notes he misspelt Mercury's first name as 'Freddy'.

He made an early introduction of George, detailing his background and connection to guns, then he introduced one of the main planks of his evidence — those witnesses who saw George or someone who fitted his description hanging around

Gowan Avenue that morning. One, Helen Scott, actually saw him the evening before at the Fulham Palace Road end playing with the pedestrian crossing lights; but the Crown misinterpreted what he was doing. They suggested that he had begun his murder watch then and had started fiddling with the pedestrian crossing button to draw away any suspicion that this woman might be harbouring. In fact, this is what attracted her attention and made her suspicious, as there was no traffic coming along that would warrant him using the pedestrian lights. The Crown's interpretation of his behaviour was untenable on its own terms because, if Dando had driven past in her car, George could never have covered the distance to catch her going into number 29.

The muddle that Oxborough had created with their system had transferred itself to the Crown. Once you grasp that George turned left as he left number 29 because he was going towards his drop near HAFAD, then it is obvious what he was doing the night before the kill. He was testing how long it would take to cross Fulham Palace Road if traffic forced him to use the pedestrian crossing.

The Crown's worst mistake — over the HAFAD timings — was difficult to spot during Pownall's opening speech. He covered the statements of the four HAFAD witnesses and the different timings that they gave to George's arrival on 26 April; despite their contradictory accounts, the consensus seemed to be that he arrived around noon, which would give him an alibi. However, this would not be clarified until they gave evidence.

Then Pownall said, 'The Crown's case is that he returned home after the shooting and changed his clothes. Why? At different stages during the course of that morning, he was wearing the clothing described by him in his witness statement. He then went to HAFAD in the hope that they would provide him with a sanctuary and an alibi. Of sorts.'

Without being sure exactly why, I knew that this was nonsense. On my first recce of the crime scene some two years before, I had picked up the turning left problem, but obviously George had done that because he was going to HAFAD. As his clothes were noticeably different, it followed that he had changed between crossing Fulham Palace Road and arriving at HAFAD. But where was his 'drop', the place where he had planted his change probably the night before, then went there immediately after the killing to change. It would be somewhere where he could change without being seen and the clothing and the gun would be safe until he picked them up that evening or the next day. I was already filing a 'to do' in my head — search for the drop.

Mansfield would not have known about the Crown's version that George went home after the kill until he received an outline of Pownall's opening a few days before the trial started. Of course, the defence were aware of the HAFAD timings long before that, probably around the time of the committal in October 2000 when the HAFAD's statements were served on Etienne. Once they saw these statements, the defence could see that the Crown's case would be that George arrived at HAFAD around midday, which would fit in with the murder as long as he stopped to change clothes along the way. That is, he did not go home to change but did it en route from Gowan Avenue to Gresswell Street. In other words, he had a 'drop' where he had planted his yellow top and jeans, then, after changing, he went on to HAFAD. Later that day, he would have retrieved the Barbour-type jacket that he was wearing when he committed the murder and disposed of it. This was the only scenario for the Crown that made sense, once it was accepted that George was at HAFAD at noon.

In his original statement to Gallagher, George had said he left Crookham Road for HAFAD at 12.15–12.30pm, but it was clearly better for the defence if he arrived there before the murder. In January, then, the defence filed an alibi in which George changed the time he left Crookham Road from 12.30-ish to 10.30–10.45am. But once Pownall disclosed that the Crown's case was that, after the killing, George went home to change his clothes, the notice of alibi and its change of timing was redundant. By saying that George went home after the killing, changed, then went to HAFAD for noon, the Crown gave him a watertight alibi.

Identifying who was responsible for this monumental blunder by the Crown is a bit like trying to discover who made the decision to take the Crombie overcoat to the photographic studio. Of course, under the joint enterprise rule, they are all guilty because, whoever took the decision, the others all missed its import. Mansfield didn't, of course; in February, he was up to speed on all aspects of the case. I would like to have been inside his head when he first read Pownall's opening speech.

It took Benjamin and me a few days' scrutiny of Pownall's opening speech to twig the bombshell that the Crown had planted under its own case. But we still had to wait for the HAFAD witnesses to give evidence to see how explosive it would turn out to be.

Pownall trundled through George's return to HAFAD two days later, then he outlined the snippets of conversation that he had had with various women in which he mentioned the murder of Jill Dando or seeing a Range Rover. Others were from years back, that showed him knowing of Dando before the murder. If you were really scraping the bottom of the barrel, then these could be considered some kind of corroboration. There were also the gun connections in the 1980s. Plus all the books, periodicals and newspapers found at George's address, some of which had articles about Dando in them — how could they not? As Mansfield wearily pointed out to a detective who came up with some statistical nonsense about the incidence of Dando references, there were many more about Manchester United. The books that could have opened up George's *modus operandi* — his DIY manuals for assassination; the Ninjutsu ones and *Secret Hiding Places* — were mentioned by Pownall as being found in George's flat but they were not made court exhibits or flagged to the jury as having any significance.

Pownall ran hot on the particle — 'This aspect of the case, it is submitted, provides compelling evidence of his guilt ...' — but we know what happened to that. Same with the fibre. Finally, he dealt with the interviews, which really did no more than show George to be a liar. The Crown had not seen that it was the way that George lied, rather than what he lied about, which was important.

Nonetheless, until the implications of HAFAD were clarified, the overall effect of Pownall's opening was that there was a lot of evidence that together pointed conclusively to George's guilt. Perhaps the biggest problem with it was how the fundamentals of the Crown's case were mixed up with far too many bottom-of-the-barrel-scrapings. The jumble of detail was confusing even to journos who had heard much of it trailed and scrutinised during the pre-trial.

Pownall told the jury, 'Theories and speculation are no substitute for evidence.' And so the evidence all had to be established and presented in court, but it did go on and on. It was almost as if the CPS thought that because the investigation had proved so expensive and exhaustive, so also should the Crown's case. Witnesses came and went — Dando's brother; Farthing, even though he attended the trial, did not give evidence but a statement from him was read out; a pathologist; policemen arriving at the scene of the crime; detectives on discovering evidence; more pathologists; ballistic experts; the three women who found the body; witnesses in Gowan Avenue; HAFAD ...

The first real block of evidence that was to shift the mood of the jury towards conviction was the women who identified him hanging around in Gowan Avenue before the murder. There were four of them: Susan Mayes; Terry Normanton; and the de Rosnays, Stella and Charlotte. Only Mayes made a 'positive' identification on the identification parade and she was just as sure and emphatic in court — 'I saw the defendant'. Mayes was an impressive witness. Dark, natural, neatly-groomed hair, 40, attractive but with pinched features, well-dressed, organised, educated, thoughtful, but also fair-minded ... she handled Mansfield with aplomb because she could tell the truth and did tell the truth.

Mansfield's great strength with witnesses is that he masters his brief and assumes that anyone testifying to anything damaging about his client is probably lying and is, at best, mistaken. And, in various ways, a lot of witnesses do lie or are at least economical with the truth. They edge the truth; they pick winners; they invent things. Mansfield takes these witnesses to the cleaners but where a witness is just telling the truth without embellishment and to the best of their abilities, his approach often puts their truth in relief. It was so with Mayes.

Once, in answer to a suggestion that she didn't know the man, she glanced at George and answered calmly, 'I am looking at him now.' Mansfield becomes ostrich-like when a witness tells him an unpalatable but indisputable truth. It just doesn't register with him; he ignores it completely.

Mayes saw George hanging around Gowan Avenue at 7.00am and acting oddly when she looked at him. He began wiping the windscreen of a double-parked red car with his bare hand even though it was raining. She 'was very sure' it was George.

'When I first saw him, he was just standing there looking at the houses on his left. He then looked at houses on the other side ... There was no one else in the street. I had him in my view about a minute. I paid attention to him because I wondered what he was doing ... As I drew alongside him, he looked down to the ground as if he did not want me to see him. He then started cleaning the windscreen. I looked back a few seconds later and he had stopped. He looked Mediterranean, slightly olive-skinned with black, layered, shoulder-length hair.'

From a number of sources, we know that George's hair at the time was relatively short, so it follows from Mayes's evidence that George was wearing a wig during much of his murder watch. She paid a great deal of attention to George and picked him out over a year later. This was an observant, accurate witness.

Upfill-Brown, the man opposite Richard Hughes and who came out at the same time, also saw the gunman and paid a lot of attention to him. He said at the time that the movement of the man's hair made him think that it was a wig. Again, the length he described supported that. Yet, in the process of the evidence going from Oxborough to the CPS and on to Pownall, this was lost. The jury was told that George was not disguised. Again and again the jury had to hack through the thicket of confusion sown by the Crown's case.

Terry Normanton was going to her embroidery class just before 10.00am on the day of the murder. She saw George hanging around 29 Gowan Avenue. She did not make a positive identification but she did say that, without the goatee and moustache, she would have picked out Number 2. Normanton, 58, a diminutive, autistic woman, with her tightly-bound hair and peculiar, unsteady gait, came over as strange. Her voice, though, was very clear and she was precise about what she had seen. She wobbled a bit under Mansfield's gentle probing but the underlying unity between her description and the other woman who saw George left little room for doubt that he was hanging around Gowan Avenue that morning.

What little doubt there was would have been removed entirely had not Mansfield demolished Charlotte de Rosnay's partial identification of George, which, in turn, removed the corroboration of her mother-in-law's identification.

Charlotte, along with her mother-in-law, Stella, had seen George cross Gowan Avenue outside their house, number 55, around two hours before the killing. They were looking out of a bedroom window and focused on George because he looked like a downmarket version of Alexis de Rosnay, Charlotte's husband and Stella's son. Alexis worked for merchant banker JP Morgan and was hardly pleased with his wife and mother's comparison.

Everything about Charlotte was expensive, including the hip-grinding way she sashayed into court. Her languid features and rolling, shimmering locks were reminiscent of 1950s film star Veronica Lake. I don't know how many woman-hours had gone into honing her runway catwalk, but such was its effect on the male congregation I am sure that Mansfield could have made it into an irrefutable defence for any man charged with indecently assaulting her. She gave evidence twice; once in the pre-trial and before the jury. On both occasions when she made her entrance, the press benches were packed with panting hacks and tut-tutting hackettes, none of whom could quite get their heads round this dreamy, Harvey Nichols-ish vision.

Pownall took her through her evidence and how she had asked to see Number 8 again. Then he reminded her that, next, she asked to see Number 2 again. He asked her what her impression was of Number 2.

Charlotte replied, 'I could recognise the shape of his face, but due to the fact that his face was concealed with a moustache and a beard, it made it very difficult to be sure.'

Pownall quickly moved in on what he was angling for. 'Were they then — having viewed the sequence for the third time — were they equal contenders?'

She said that they weren't.

Pownall continued, 'Which of the two, if at all, was a predominant contender?'

She took the cue. 'Two,' she said emphatically.

Mansfield got to his feet too late to prevent it; he said to Gage, 'My Lord, there is a matter which I am very concerned about ...'

After argument about this, the jury filed back in and Mansfield went to work on Charlotte. He asked her how she was first approached by the police. He said, 'Did the officer come to your house in uniform?'

She stood in the witness box with her right arm resting on the side, utterly unaware that her clenched fist was acting like a barometer of the stress she was under. The greater the pressure, the whiter the knuckles. She replied to Mansfield, 'At the beginning, it was two officers in uniform.'

Mansfield leaned over his lectern, his beady eyes locking on to her; he asked, 'Were you keeping abreast of what was going on?' The fist tightened and the knuckles whitened.

She replied, 'Through the newspapers.'

Mansfield asked, 'No other way?' Under her foundation cream, the colour drained from the collagen-enhanced face. Her fist clenched even tighter. It was cruel, but nevertheless marvellous theatre.

'Yes.' The terse affirmation meant that it was just newspapers.

Mansfield crooned, 'Are you sure?'

'Yes.'

Mansfield then asked innocuously, but the emphasis gave the game away, 'The next formal date was October 2000 at the ID parade. How had you been keeping up to date?'

'I knew he'd been arrested.' She must have felt Mansfield reeling her in.

'Who?'

'Barry George.'

Mansfield again hammed up his question. 'How were you were kept informed of the affair?'

'It was in all the newspapers.'

Mansfield continued, 'Any other way?' If Mansfield could have had one prop, it would have been a truncheon.

'No, I was not.' Her face looked frozen.

'No discussions with anyone else?' She was being pulled closer to the bank.

'No.'

'Are you sure?' he asked again, this time more sardonically than before. But his visible contempt was all his own; it was not simulated to serve the cause of his client. Mansfield has no time for the likes of Charlotte de Rosnay; she did not belong to any society to which he would give the nod.

'Definitely,' Charlotte answered, but she didn't sound sure or look it. She waited to be scooped up by Mansfield's hand-net.

She had no place to go except where Mansfield decided. He asked, 'I want you to be extremely careful about your recollection. You now know that the person you preferred is the defendant, don't you?'

'Yes.' Her voice was very still.

'Did you know that the person you preferred had also been preferred by Susan Mayes and Stella, your mother-in-law?' Mansfield asked.

After the identification parade on 5 October 2000, Stella and Charlotte had travelled back with Susan Mayes who told them that she had picked out Number 2.

'No,' Charlotte answered truthfully.

Mansfield now came to the crunch. 'I would like you to separate out when you first discovered that other people who attended the identification parade with you on 5 October had identified Number 2. I suggest that the person you glimpsed ... you would describe it as a glimpse?'

Here, Mansfield was securing his fall-back position.

Charlotte caved in. 'Yes.'

Mansfield attempted the same ploy with her mother-in-law, Stella. A cultivated, slim, haughty Frenchwoman, Stella was very precise in correcting Mansfield. 'I got more than a glimpse; I got ten seconds, which to me is more than a glimpse. I realise in hindsight it was more than a glimpse. It was a look.' Stella handled Mansfield well, but she is made of much sterner stuff than her daughter-in-law.

They both saw the same man for the same period, but Charlotte acquiesced at Mansfield's suggestion that it was just a glimpse. He now expanded on the bridgehead he had established in her mind. He dropped his voice to a soft, intimate, enticing tone, 'That person was not at the parade, was he?'

Charlotte equivocated, 'It was difficult to tell because of the facial hair.'

It was resistance of a kind. But Mansfield was not going to let her stay in the holding net. She had to choose either the bank or going back into the pool. He rushed his question slightly. 'I appreciate that bit, but I am trying to do this as carefully as possible. I repeat — the man you glimpsed was not on the parade, was he?' His voice fell away seductively.

Charlotte still held out. 'I wasn't sure.'

Mansfield, though, knew her resistance was token. 'It's more than you weren't sure. He wasn't there at the parade on the 5 October?' His voice was harsh, his inflexion making the question.

Charlotte stared at Mansfield ... for seven eternal seconds. The court room resounded to the proverbial pin-dropping, before she answered, 'I said no.'

Mansfield had her. 'We know what you then said on the parade because we have seen it twice. That was your state of mind?'

She capitulated. 'Yes.'

Mansfield turned away as if she no longer existed — which she didn't to him — and said to Gage, 'I have no further questions.'

He sat down like a poker player sweeping in his winning pot. It was great theatre but, while it was cruel, of course Mansfield was merely doing his job. Charlotte sashayed out of the courtroom as suggestively as she had came in but no longer a vision, just a spectacle. Whenever I think of the testimony of the two de Rosnays, I wonder what Stella actually thinks of her daughter-in-law.

The Gowan Avenue women put George in the street that morning. Stella said on the parade, 'My gut feeling was it was

Number 2,' (George) and she stood by that in the witness box. There was, therefore, an 'underlying unity' in her, Mayes's and Normanton's descriptions. George was also an oddball with an experience and interest in firearms. He had lied and lied in the interviews.

The only other evidence that counted in the jury room was HAFAD. The four women all gave evidence and the only one whose testimony stood up to objective scrutiny was a woman named Susan Bicknell. She underpinned the alibi that the Crown had given George. The trouble was, Bicknell came over as somewhat odder than Barry George. Nevertheless, her weird appearance and even weirder way of giving evidence made it easy to dismiss her evidence once the gut feel that George was guilty was in the ascendant.

The other three HAFAD women — Rosario Torres, Leslie Symes and Elaine Hutton — all gave a variety of timings of when George had arrived at HAFAD on 26 April. Hutton and Symes came over as contradictory, while Torres appeared confused. Bicknell, while also genuine, was pure *Carry On Up the Old Bailey*. She weighs about 20 stone, is an uncertain forty-something, gabbles faster than Benjamin and has a mind that has only one mode — chaotic. It proved as impossible to stop her talking as it was for her to keep her evidence to the point.

George arrived after the murder without an appointment — even though he knew from his previous two visits that he needed one. His agenda, of course, was not to discuss his problems but to present himself in clothing and a manner that would be utterly incongruous with the gunman who had just murdered Jill Dando. Bicknell was given the task of turning away this interloper by making an appointment to deal with his problems at a later date.

Bicknell began her evidence, 'I had to sit down as my back

was hurting so much. I cannot stand up for longer than five minutes. Actually, I had a horse-riding accident in, I think, 1999. I suffered a number of back injuries and I went to three or four doctors who were really able to help me. I have tremendous problems with my neck ...'

The indefatigably polite Gage tried to get back to the point. 'So you would know then about Mr George's medical matters?'

Bicknell, 'Yes, I would understand about his medical problems ...'

As she went off again, Pownall winced. He was clearly allergic to the Bicknells of this world. 'Forgive me for interrupting. If it is necessary to go into details, we can, if it is necessary.' Firmness is a poor substitute for a psychiatric ward, a strait-jacket and enough diazepam to tranquillise an elephant.

Bicknell blathered on, 'I had to sit down as my back was hurting so much. I cannot stand up for more than five minutes ... I couldn't see him properly. The light in the hallway was not very good at the time and I was wearing my photo-magnetic lenses at the time so it was difficult to see him ... My husband drove me from Twickenham as it was my first day. And it is a journey of 40 miles and that's why I left home at 7.30 in the morning ...'

Pownall interrupted her to ask for the impossible. 'Can you try to remember without going into all the details?'

'I'm really sorry but I actually knew Jill Dando. I actually met her in about 1994 and this is all extremely upsetting for me. If you want me to bring in some paper to show that I did, I can bring them in tomorrow ...'

It went on and on. Pownall began to wilt as his reaction to Bicknell closed down his faculties. He let her gabble on, then at one point as she paused for breath, interjected, 'What time was it?' This was referring to when George had arrived that morning.

Bicknell replied, 'In my concern to get work on time that day, I forgot my watch. The clock said 11.50am. I cannot speak for the accuracy of the clock but the clock was never more than five minutes out in my time there.'

It was the only coherent answer she gave and she never budged from this timing or its basis. Moreover, she was the only one of the four who had not changed her timings as the import of the reward money for the murderer worked its way through the office. A rational appraisal of her evidence left her timings set in stone; but she, along with everything she said, could be dismissed as part of what one witness who runs an army surplus store called the 'nutter factor'. He had originally stocked replicas and disabled guns but discontinued the line because of all the gun-nuts who used to come into the shop and play with the guns for hours but never buy one.

Bicknell manifestly was not lying, but anyone running on a gut feel that George was guilty could easily bypass her evidence by dismissing her, clearly unfairly, as a nutter. After all, what counts inside 'the black box' is what jurors decide to believe, not what arguably and rationally they should believe.

While Benjamin and I thought that HAFAD went to George's certain acquittal, the witness that went to our understanding of why George had murdered Dando was Ramesh Paul. He was the London Traffic Cars controller who saw through George both at the time he had arrived after leaving HAFAD on 26 April, and also when he returned two days later. Although his evidence played no part in convicting George, it tripped Benjamin into making the Freddie Mercury connection.

Benjamin was partly drawn to the case by the Freddie Mercury connection. He, like George is a Queen and Freddie Mercury nut. George had adopted Freddie's real surname and everyone knew that he played his records day and night; his flat was a shrine to Queen music and he copycatted clothing of Freddie's. Later, Benjamin drew some of the parallels between him and George, which he claimed (and I agree with him) gave him an insight into his mind. They had had disturbed childhoods; both had personality disorders that they can switch on and off at will, certainly sufficiently easily to outwit cops and psychiatrists; both were treated as pariahs by conventional society; both suffered an acute sense of grievance at the way society dismissed them; both enjoyed tricking and teasing those who rejected or discriminated against them; both were desperate for fame and recognition of what they believed were their unique talents; both were chronically untidy but retained their own order among their seemingly disordered living quarters; both were obsessive collectors ...

Ramesh Paul reminded me of those sharp, professional Indians who sell computers down Tottenham Court Road. Short, a little overweight but right on the ball. Professional witnesses like policemen or scientists have a court air, but most lay-people are either overawed by the occasion or adopt a stilted formal attitude that they believe is right for the venue. Paul came into the witness box oozing confidence and in it was relaxed, natural and completely at home. Most of all, his testimony was crisp and connected. Everyone warmed to him, including Gage but especially the jury. When Gage recessed for lunch and said that he might want to have lunch in the canteen, Paul asked, 'Will I get a free lunch, Mr Judge?'

Gage replied, 'You would have to find someone of much greater authority than I to grant you that.'

On 26 April, Paul told Pownall that George came into London Traffic Cars at 'about one o'clock ... He said he had no money but he wanted to go to Rickett Street. He appeared in a hurry to go somewhere but had no money to go there. I laughed. The ride is four quid and for the drivers four quid is like four hundred quid ...' Paul laughed at the audacity of the asking. He continued, 'He did not sit down. He was up and down looking at the door, looking out of the windows. He did that a few times ... He was there quite a long time — 15 minutes. I wouldn't say it was less than 15 minutes.' The phone then rang with a call to collect a package from Rickett Street. 'I told him, "You're in luck, there is a car going that way and you can have a free ride." It was about 1.15.'

The driver reported back to Paul that George was very 'agitated' on the journey. When he heard that Dando had been murdered just around the corner from the minicab office an hour-and-a-half before George came in, he reported this unusual customer to Oxborough.

Two days later, around midday, George came into the office again and he approached the counter, which was screened off by a glass-and-wood partition. 'There is only one gap in the glass and he was speaking to me through that gap while I was on the phone. Gibberish. He was asking me stupid questions, totally stupid questions that I didn't answer ... Instead, I told him to shut up. He was looking at me but I think he was in a world of his own. He asked me if I will remember him, what he looked like, what he was wearing. He kept asking these questions — the colour of his trousers, what he was wearing. I told him I could not see him from the waist down but I could remember him for the next ten years because he brought it all up.

'On the day he came in the second time, he was wearing a red T-shirt. But on the day Jill Dando was murdered, he was wearing a yellow shirt. When he asked me if I remembered what he was wearing that day I said, "No, I can't."

'Afterwards, he said, "Look up to the sky, what do you see?"

'I said, "Blue."

'He said, "No." He kept going on about it. "What colour is the sun?"

'I said, "Orange. Red."

'He said, "No."

'There were gaps in the conversation because I was busy. He told me to look up again. I said "Yellow" just by the off chance. I was going through all the brightest colours. He said, "Yes, that's it."

'When I said, "Yellow," he looked happy. When I remembered, he had wanted to shake my hand he looked so happy. But he couldn't through the glass slat.'

Paul occasionally looked directly at George in the dock with a contemptuous expression on his face as he recalled these encounters. Everything about Paul's account and demeanour suggested that he knew George was up to something when he came in the second time. However, he didn't know what George's game was, nor did Pownall have any reason to explore it. Curiously enough, it was Mansfield in cross-examination who pushed Paul into a stronger articulation of his suspicions. He put it to Paul that George had been muttering that he did not want to be blamed for Dando's death, but that he had not mentioned colours during the conversation.

Paul looked at Mansfield as if he was crazy. He replied emphatically, 'He was indicating colours ... I still remember him because he was acting strangely. I do remember because he said, "Look up to the sky."'

Paul was another witness who spoke such unabashed truth that the effect of Mansfield's cross-examination was not to qualify it but to put it in relief. Paul commented, 'He practically shoved it down my throat. He wanted me to remember him — what he looked like, what he was wearing. Why? Only he knows why.' Then he looked contemptuously at George. 'He is there ...' The unspoken words 'ask him' hung there for the court to hear. There was clearly a hidden agenda in George's behaviour, but at that moment I was as ignorant about it as the Crown was.

Paul also picked up the other big clue to this hidden agenda. He noticed and knew that on his second visit to Traffic Cars, George spoke in a false accent with a purpose. 'He spoke in English but with a foreign accent behind it. It was like some of the Arabs, the Arab drivers. That is why I thought he was not English. It was to make me believe he was a foreigner. The impression I got was that he was a nutter, but he isn't a mental case ...' He looked scathingly at George as he said it. 'He can speak if he wants to, but it was put on. I knew he was a Fulhamite ... someone who has lived in Fulham all his life.'

Another pointer to the hidden agenda was Mansfield putting it to Paul that George never mentioned the colours of the clothes he was wearing. This had no import in the Crown's case, yet Ramesh Paul put it in his statement soon after the murder. There was certainly no possible reason why he would make it up. Mansfield had no reason either to put the question unless he had been instructed to do so by George. And only George knew the import of yellow ... well, apart from Benjamin.

Ramesh Paul left the witness box at 2.35pm on 15 May 2001. Normally, I hightailed it home after the afternoon session, but at the next hourly break in proceedings, Benjamin signalled to me with a sipping tea sign that he wanted me to see him in the greasy spoon. I wandered round at 4.15pm. As we walked in, I could see that he was agitated and shaking, which meant that I would have to listen to his latest fixation while shielding my coffee from the spluttering saliva. He kept it under wraps until we sat down, then he let rip.

'I know why he did it. You'll never believe it. It's spooky, weird. When Ramesh Paul was giving evidence, the hair at the back of my neck was standing up. You will never understand, but it is all to do with Freddie Mercury. It has to be because he used the lyrics. I have thought about it all afternoon. It can't be a coincidence. Even the accent.'

I just wanted to drink my black, unsweetened, unsaliva'd coffee. But, like Pownall with Bicknell, there was no stopping the torrent, I just did the verbal equivalent of battening down the hatches and waiting until the storm had passed. All the different points that Paul's evidence made came out in a jumble: the 'Look up to the sky' dialogue with Paul; the wearing of yellow; imitating Freddie Mercury's accent as Paul described George's that day; how the condolence notes were George's equivalent of a suicide note; killing her must have been all mixed up with 1986, the year of the apocryphal Dando/Mercury interview; it could be to do with how he felt Dando's friend Cliff Richard had humiliated Mercury over the musical *Time* …

I didn't argue or really listen much. Benjamin's mind works in a kind of pointillistic way. It jumps around making points that often don't cohere into a picture until most of the dots are in place. But I was too tired that day to follow the building up of the picture and it was all too far out anyway.

However, over the next couple of days, he made me listen properly, then pushed me into being the devil's advocate. I found I couldn't knock down his theory. So as Sherlock says, 'We must fall back upon the old axiom that when all other contingencies fail, whatever remains, however improbable, must be the truth.' I accepted the Freddie Mercury thesis.

Paul had sussed George but he couldn't fill in the details as he wasn't a Queen freak like George and Benjamin. Benjamin and I knew that George was guilty — the puzzle was why he had killed her and we had a few problems with how. Yellow and the verbal dance George played with Paul over identifying the colour provided the key to solving some of these questions. 'Look up to the sky' is a line from 'Bohemian Rhapsody':

> No escape from reality
> Open your eyes
> Look up to the skies and see
> I'm just a poor boy, I need no sympathy

> [From 'Bohemian Rhapsody',
> words and music by Freddie Mercury]

Most people would say 'look up at the sky', which was exactly how a number of hacks who reported this exchange did in their articles the next day. Mine and Benjamin's notes are emphatic — 'to the sky'. Yellow was not merely Freddie Mercury's favourite colour; he was obsessed with it. George obviously changed into yellow for two reasons: in homage to Mercury, but also because it was so distinct from the dark-brown Barbour that the gunman wore.

The accent that George put on was also an embellishment in homage to Mercury. Paul had said that he spoke like 'my Arab drivers', which is pretty close to how Freddie spoke. Mercury was of Indian extraction and was brought up in Zanzibar, but spent a lot of time in Munich. George used to imitate it as he did everything about Freddie Mercury. Presumably, George pulled his Freddie-speak on his second visit because he was jubilant at how everything was working to plan.

It was now as plain as a pikestaff to Benjamin and me how George had planned the murder. After the kill, he walked down Gowan Avenue towards his drop, where he had previously planted both his change of clothes and his props for engaging the HAFAD women — his letter of complaint about his housing, cancer and irritable bowel problems. After changing, he went to HAFAD, then to Traffic Cars but, as with everything else he did, George went over the top. He over-egged his act. He was making too sure they remembered him, which he compounded two days later by pulling the same number.

14

horrocks knows his lyrics

By the time the Freddie Mercury thesis had worked its way through my head, Pownall's 'high' opening had sunk lower than the threshold needed by a jury to convict. Neither Benjamin nor I felt comfortable seeing a cold-blooded, calculating murderer walk. Moreover, the thought of him doing it again was rather pre-empted by the possibility that he might have done it before anyway. My discomfort was also aggravated by the prospect of writing a book that claimed the acquitted Barry George was actually guilty. Yet, I could not see how putting what we had before Oxborough could save the day unless Barry George went into the witness box. It was too late for the Crown to switch horses with new evidence that had actually been under their nose from the day of the murder. We took this particular hot potato to my publisher, John Blake.

John heard us out, then said seriously, 'You can't keep this back. You have to give it to the cops. If he is acquitted and you write this up — forget libel for a moment — then every reviewer would pounce on you and say you helped it happen. You have to tell them.' In some ways, he merely clarified what I already knew. We couldn't sit on it, but I left it to him to contact Campbell. I thought that Campbell would not be able to respond if it came from me but coming from John Blake he would probably have to listen. Which he did.

He instructed Horrocks to ring me and we set up a meet. Again, I was providing information to Oxborough but, by the time the meeting was scheduled, it looked almost certain that George would not go into the witness box, which meant that the Freddie Mercury stuff could not be adduced. Even if he did give evidence, sneaking it during cross-examination with Mansfield riding shotgun would be like gun-running for the Taliban.

Between the Ramesh Paul breakthrough and seeing Horrocks, Benjamin began checking out the books that the police had discovered in George's flat. Once I put together my caballistic theory based on magical thinking, the next obvious thing to do was search for other ideas or philosophies that may have influenced George. Oxborough had found two Ninjutsu books — *Ninja, the Invisible Assassins* and *Ninjutsu — History and Tradition*. The Ninjutsu websites showed that one of the blurbs to the former included a section on 'how to commit the perfect murder'. There were also other books, a couple of which were titled *Construction of Secret Hiding Places* and *Ambush and Counter Ambush*. It all appeared to be a DIY course in murder but Oxborough had not even read these books, which meant that any significance they contained would have been missed. Benjamin ordered them over the Internet, but they had not arrived in time for our meeting with

Horrocks. Once they did, of course, everything fell into place and I don't think even Horrocks would have had the gall to rebuff us. Although, on second thoughts, I am not so sure ...

Horrocks arranged to see us in the offices above the Old Bailey on the afternoon of 4 June 2001. Benjamin insisted on being present. He said to me, 'I am sick and tired of being dismissed as Benjie the Binman who nicks stories from rubbish bags. I have to be taken seriously. This is my idea, not yours. I solved this murder not you. If you go by yourself, you would get all the credit and I am not having that ...'

Once Benjamin sees fame beckoning, he becomes unmanageable. I had to agree, although I knew it would turn into a disaster. I warned and warned him that he had to keep himself under control and not run amok whenever anyone challenged his ideas; he swore that he would be on his best behaviour.

I met up with Jim Sword inside the Old Bailey before we walked up to the office section above the courts to meet Horrocks. As he led me into the designated office, I sprung Benjamin on him saying that I wanted my 'colleague Pell' present. Sword didn't question it, as he didn't know who I was referring to; he went down to the tradesmen's entrance to collect Benjamin and take him through security. I avoided eye contact with him as he brought Benjamin into the room. We all sat down; both detectives were showing by their body language that while they had to examine every avenue, they suspected this to be another dead end. Sword's face was set like a tombstone.

Benjamin immediately began fishing out pieces of clipped foolscap from a couple of black bin bags and arranged them on the desk between us; there were lots of passages highlighted by a green marker pen. Benjamin had prepared all the evidence to uphold his thesis. They both watched him like he was a real dung beetle that they wanted to stamp on before he got too busy.

What I had already predicted to Benjamin before the meeting now looked as set in stone as Sword's face. However convincing our case, Oxborough wasn't going to embrace a theory from the likes of us — a theory which would demonstrate that for two years they had missed what was under their noses. They would know, too, that it could not be called in evidence at this stage of the trial. We were never going to be given a straight run. I felt slightly disengaged, like I had a god's-eye view above the four of us. Benjamin looked as crazy as Bicknell and George put together, compulsively shuffling and laying out his print-outs of Queen lyrics and transcripts of the trial.

I had composed a written outline of what we had to tell them, obviously with more than an eye on what could be great material for my book. I was also mindful of how detectives like to dictate the shape of meetings and this way I could set the agenda. I handed Horrocks and Sword copies of what I had prepared. After some initial demurring from Horrocks, who clearly knew my game, they both began reading diligently.

The essential parts were as follows (which, as it summarises only what we knew then, the reader may want to skim):

> As we approach the closing of the Crown's case, it no longer looks certain that Barry George will receive the life imprisonment that he rightly deserves. As a consequence, Pell, my publisher, John Blake, and I have concluded that we have to place before you what we believe fills in some of the gaps in the Crown's case. We are mindful that such evidence as we are able to provide can only be adduced during cross-examination of Barry George and we bear that in mind in our presentation of it.

In the Crown's opening address, Pownall stated, 'Many theories were advanced about the identity and the motives of the killer ... Gauging the precise level of the defendant's interest in Miss Dando before her death is inevitably difficult. Whether he harboured a hidden grudge against her, believing her to have wronged him or figures he idolised such as Freddie Mercury, is impossible to determine with any degree of certainty. The only apparent connection between Miss Dando and Freddie Mercury is that the deceased, along with other celebrities, appeared on a film produced for Comic Relief in 1993 when she and others mimed a Queen song ...

Implicit to the Crown's case is the assumption that Barry George in some way held a grudge against Dando that led to him becoming obsessed with her before stalking and murdering her. Yet, as Gage held in the pre-trial hearing, there is no evidence of any obsession or stalking. Indeed, on the surface, the kill bears the cold hallmark of a contract killing done for money ... Yet, it was committed by Barry George and while, in Pownall's words, 'gauging the level of the defendant's interest in Miss Dando before her death' is difficult, we believe that interest is staring Oxborough in the face.

The key to understanding the nature of Barry George's interest in Dando lies in the signature of the murder. This interest had nothing to do with a fixation or obsession with Jill Dando, but was all about Barry George's enduring identification with and fixation on Freddie Mercury. We think that there is very strong evidence for concluding that Dando was almost a sacrificial victim, killed in delusional homage to Freddie Mercury. The signature to the murder and, consequently, the key to open the door on Barry George's motive are written in the lyrics of Queen songs.

This kind of criminal motivation — rooted in a kind of rock-song cabbalism — is rare but not unknown. Charlie Manson in the 1960s believed that the devil and/or God was talking to him through the lyrics of Helter-Skelter and he used these messages to orchestrate the murders of Sharon Tate and LaBianca; two US teenagers — The Trench Coat Mafia — who went on a killing spree in Columbine High School, six days before Barry George murdered Dando, were inspired by dark, heavy industrial bands like KMFDM and Rammstein and Marilyn Manson (no relation to Charlie); and last week, Luke Bass, 19, who modelled his looks on Eminem, pleaded guilty to an especially brutal attack on his ex-girlfriend with a padlock and chain, which was inspired by the white rapper's hit single 'Stan'. Incidentally, Barry George almost certainly took heart from the Columbine attack. Finally, mention must be made of Timothy McVeigh who carried out the Oklahoma bombing. He said that he was singing 'Bohemian Rhapsody', the Queen anthem, to himself when he parked the truck containing the explosive. He claimed to be inspired by it.

We know that Barry George was obsessed with Freddie Mercury and his music and, as much as his limited resources allowed, modelled himself on the singer:

- *His home was a shrine to the singer with Queen posters and Freddie Mercury photographs everywhere, although the video made by the search team shows that this was removed between his being contacted by the police in February — they put six notes through his door — and a statement taken from him on 11 April. This dismantling of the shrine is a telling pointer to Barry George's wish to stop Oxborough delving into his Freddie Mercury obsession.*

- *Neighbours complained constantly about the way he played Queen music night and day at maximum volume.*

- *Barry George adopted the original surname of Freddie Mercury and, as we know, claimed to be his cousin.*

- *He wore a Superman T-shirt because in the mid-80s this was one of Freddie Mercury's favourite garments (Pownall missed the significance of this in his cross-examination of Sally Mason).*

- *Although he cleared out his flat of most of his Queen memorabilia, Barry George retained a sticker on top of his TV that asked 'Are you mad?', the latter word being one Freddie Mercury used a lot (cf. 'I'm going slightly Mad', the B-side of that single being 'The Hitman').*

- *He mimicked Freddie Mercury's peculiar accent (Indian / Zanzibar / German) and drew on his vocabulary.*

- *He loved yellow, which was Freddie Mercury's favourite colour.*

- *The business card found at Barry George's address carried the logo of a juggler, which is lifted from the album cover of* Innuendo.

- *He married a Japanese woman soon after 'La Japonaise' was released. Freddie Mercury collected Japanese antiques and at home often wore a kimono. Ironically, the only Japanese website to Queen, on which Barry George posted messages as Bulsara, is named 'Partners in Crime'!*
- *Just as Freddie Mercury did — 'I'm a chameleon' — Barry George liked to change his appearance and also, in his limited way, was a performer like his idol.*
- *He used to join the wake outside Freddie Mercury's home on the anniversary of his death. He also used to use the singer's address for mail and gave it to the police on a road traffic offence.*
- *Freddie Mercury loved flowers — especially yellow daffodils — and Barry George devoted part of the day after Dando's death buying her flowers and delivering them to the police who had cordoned off Gowan Avenue either side of number 29. They were almost certainly yellow ...*

Examples of the manner in which Barry George modelled himself on Freddie Mercury are countless and the idea, as claimed in the Crown's opening, that Barry George had similar obsessions with other idols, is just wrong and misleading. These were passing role models, but Freddie Mercury was his Oscar part, the rest were bit players. Barry

George lived his life as much as he could through his image of Freddie Mercury.

The Room 408 note found in Barry George's flat is clearly a reference to his one-time intention (never carried out) to contact Rachel White at BBC's Radio 4 who was then producing a documentary on people whose lives had been powerfully affected by some song. Barry George's choice was almost certainly 'Bohemian Rhapsody'. Although, post-26 April 1999, perhaps he would have picked 'April Lady' as a more fitting example.

Before going to Barry George's motive for murdering Dando, I want to deal with the signature aspects of the kill that have connections with either Queen lyrics or Freddie Mercury. There is nothing conclusive in any single one of them, but taken together they point to the killer deliberately drawing on both songs and Freddie Mercury in his modus operandi.

The evidence of the minicab controller, Ramesh Paul, was decisive in Benjamin Pell making the connection between Freddie Mercury and the murder. He turned up at about 12.55pm on the day of the murder, after leaving HAFAD and talking to an American woman in the street about the police helicopters circling overhead. Barry George claimed to have no money on him and hung around for a free ride, which bizarrely and unpredictably he got. Two days later — on the 28th — he returned both to HAFAD and the minicab office in that order. Paul was an honest witness, though, and he sussed that Barry George was 'no nutter' as there was a method to his madness; he also spotted that Barry George's accent was phoney. He knew that this obvious 'Fulhamite' was putting on the way he was talking.

What Paul could not work out was that this was Barry George's version of Freddie Mercury-speak. Rather than trying to create an alibi, this was him setting up an incongruous image that was utterly incompatible with the likely demeanour of someone who had just committed murder.

Paul also saw through the artificiality of the way Barry George cued Paul to remember the colour of the clothing he wore on 26 April. He said, 'Look up to the sky …' When Paul responded 'Blue', Barry George replied that that wasn't the colour. And he asked twice more until Paul answered, 'Yellow.'

The lyric of 'Bohemian Rhapsody':

Open your eyes
Look up to the skies and see
I'm just a poor boy, I need no sympathy
[From 'Bohemian Rhapsody',
words and music by Freddie Mercury]

What gives this added weight is that 'Look up to the sky' is not colloquial. Most people would say 'at the sky' and, indeed, some of the hacks instinctively wrote that down, but both myself and Pell have 'to' in our notes.

After Barry George had extracted the answer he wanted, Paul said he looked 'happy'. Presumably, this demonstrated that the plan was right and that he was on-message with Freddie Mercury's wishes as communicated through the lyrics. Paul's 'yellow' might even have been a sign to him that Freddie Mercury was pleased.

Yellow was Freddie Mercury's favourite colour and the colour of the tunic that he wore at the last Queen concert in

1986. The yellow tunic has become as much a trademark of Freddie Mercury as the white Vegas suit of Elvis Presley. Freddie Mercury impersonators and Queen tribute bands invariably use it.

Doubtless, Barry George changed into a yellow top — which, incidentally, was destroyed soon after the kill — not only as a distinctive colour that people whom he deliberately set out to meet would remember, but also to pay symbolic homage to his hero in the sky. Certainly in the CCTV shots of Barry George — the back shot is too blurred to allow him to be identified — walking along by Fulham Football Ground, he is wearing a yellow blouson or long-sleeved shirt. The only yellow garments found at his flat, though, were short-sleeved T-shirts.

In the Crown's opening, the bullet that killed Dando is described as 'yellow' but, according to one detective, it is an ordinary brass-coloured bullet that was loosely but nonetheless presciently described as yellow. As we know, yellow is significant and it was the colour of the tie that Barry George wore for the first two days of the pre-trial hearing.

It bears remembering when thinking about this disordered loser, that while he is not the proverbial rocket scientist he is a lot more intelligent, devious and slyly funny than he appears and acts. A startling example of this was when he had one of his petit mal epileptic fits in the dock during the pre-trial hearing precisely on the time and date of the two-year anniversary of the murder. He is revelling in being in the legal limelight; he enjoys tantalising the police and journalists with his guilt.

The kill itself had some of the ritualistic overtones that we see in Barry George's use of yellow and 'Bohemian

Rhapsody'. She was killed with a bullet just above the left ear fired horizontally when her head was 20cm above her porch of 29 Gowan Avenue. Whether Barry George pushed Dando on to the floor or ordered her there at gunpoint is not important, but doing so clearly made her execution much more difficult for Barry George. The point about getting her on to the floor is significant as, generally, people who are surprised by a gunman are reluctant to get on the floor as it makes one far more vulnerable than staying upright. He would have had to order her down under threat, which would have taken time, when seconds were crucial to him not being spotted or caught in the act.

He could have 'put a gun against his [her] head' while she was standing to stay true to the lyric, but it looks as if he further refined his ritual sacrifice by copying the original sleeve of the 'Bohemian Rhapsody' single, which pictures the band sitting on the floor. This is a famous cover that is notorious for its power of making Queen fans argue as to what it means. Unless one is a fan, it is difficult to appreciate how fanatical they are about the band and how fascinated they are with deciphering the meaning of the lyrics. Even ten years on from the death of Freddie Mercury, the dedicated Queen websites demonstrate this.

I have good reason to say that Barry George did not return to Crookham Road after the kill, but used a drop for changing into the yellow top that we see on the CCTV footage at 12.44pm. He definitely used a wig on the kill, which, given the original search orders, presumably Oxborough once suspected. However, even the wig may have had a ritualistic dimension that went beyond disguise. Freddie Mercury never performed in concert after 1986, but he did make videos when he would disguise himself to cover up the ravages of AIDS. On his last video — 'I'm Going Slightly Mad' with the B-side 'The Hitman' with its evocative couplet 'I'm a head-shredder/That's better' — he wore thick padding to hide his emaciated body and a three-quarter-length black coat. He also wore a 'wild-haired' wig, which Upfill-Brown also spotted on Barry George.

One can obviously take this a lot further, but even for the purposes of cross-examination it is already beginning to take on a slightly TV-whodunit air. Of course, we are journalists and our standard of proof is lighter than Oxborough's; we also enjoy, in these days of tape recorders and no verbal, a lot more literary licence. Nevertheless, I want to emphasise that Queen and Freddie Mercury were an epochal rock 'n' roll band. They entered the sensibilities of their fans to an unparalleled degree and Freddie Mercury was worshipped by Queen followers with an almost religious-like fervour. 'Bohemian Rhapsody', however, was always held to have a 'dark side'. A member of the band once spoke of 'the yellow door that leads to the fantasy and monster world' that is lurking in the lyrics of the song.

Consequently, Queen attracted more than its share of nutters. I haven't seen any of the medical reports on Barry George, but I suspect that his personality disorder borders on a mixture of the underdeveloped schizoid/obsessive-compulsive side. Whatever his true condition, he clearly was drawn into the dark side of Queen cabbalism. As far as I can gather, he harbours no guilt or even doubt about his crime — presumably because it was necessary for the integrity of Freddie Mercury's soul or memory or whatever. In his own mind, I suspect, he genuinely felt sorrow for Dando's death but, as any appointed executioner, saw it as an order from powers whom he had to obey.

His motives for selecting Jill Dando rather than someone else are more opaque than the transparent symbolism of his modus operandi *that is patently derived from Queen and Freddie Mercury. Except in Barry George's head, Dando does not lead directly or clearly to Freddie Mercury but there are two such paths that presumably had significance to Barry George — Breakfast TV and Cliff Richard. We haven't yet seen the 1993 Comic Relief CD in which Dando mimes to 'Bohemian Rhapsody', but Barry George was already expressing dislike of the BBC before then and he did not couple it to Dando. It beggars belief that if Dando, either through her newsreading on Breakfast TV or miming to 'Bohemian Rhapsody' had offended Barry George, he would not have expressed it. If he had done so, those who heard it would have contacted the police after her murder. What evidence we have goes to showing that his expressed dislike of the BBC and his attitude towards Dando ran not on the same track, but on entirely different ones.*

That is the pre-kill sum of it. No animosity to Dando long after what the Crown suggests triggered it and long before he murdered her. And given the publicity that her murder provoked, coupled with the reward for information, and the way in which Barry George always left an indelible calling card in the memory of those he spoke to (one of his many fantasies such as Freddie Mercury or the TA or the SAS), we would have heard about it. On the evidence, there was no obsession or even dislike of Dando in the years before her murder. His hostility was directed at the BBC.

Indeed, there was no hostility directed at Dando after he

murdered Jill Dando. Quite the contrary, in fact, because Barry George went into a mourning tailspin. He bought flowers for the impromptu floral shrine that was laid around 29 Gowan Avenue. In that week, he visits his local housing department and suggests they commission a memorial to Jill Dando; he solicits condolence cards from a number of local shops but does not lay them at the shrine.

The day following the murder, there are no sightings or reports but on the 28th Barry George visits both HAFAD, where he creates a hullabaloo, and Traffic Cars straight afterwards. In both places, he goes on about being suspected for the Jill Dando murder as he fits the E-fit, which had not yet been issued.

The condolence cards were written over the next few days and Barry George's message on them is standard. 'Although I did not know Jill Dando personally, my cousin Freddie Mercury was interviewed by her back in 1986. I was present with him so for this reason I feel it poignant to bring together the situation of Jill's death and my coming to Christ.'

He also mentioned this to one of the women at HAFAD — that the reason he missed his appointment on 27 April was he was laying flowers to Jill Dando on behalf of his church.

The 1986 interview is apocryphal. Freddie Mercury rarely gave interviews as he had a healthy dislike of hacks and he did not give one to Jill Dando in 1986 or any other time. But 1986 is a highly charged year to Barry George both personally and in relation to his fanship of Freddie Mercury. His sister Susan suffocated after swallowing her tongue during an epileptic fit. She was two months pregnant.

Barry George's pipedream of a business career in the music industry never got beyond advertising in a Billboard publication and printing out business cards. The Billboard ad is in a trade magazine and Barry George lists himself as Managing Director under the name Paul Gadd — Gary Glitter's real name; his company director and sales manager is listed as Don Arden – 'the Al Capone of the pop world'. In fact, Arden himself was in big legal and financial trouble in 1986. This was also the year that Queen performed their last concert. Most important of all, it was the year that Freddie Mercury was humiliated by the selection of Cliff Richard as the lead in the musical Time.

Time, *which was written by Freddie Mercury's friend Dave Clark, is a song that was first recorded by Freddie Mercury, but Cliff Richard, not Freddie Mercury, got the lead in the theatrical version. Freddie Mercury had always wanted to star in a musical and this humiliation — rumours were already circulating that the backers went for Cliff because Freddie was HIV+ — incensed Queen fans. Cliff's image was no less Jesus-creepy then than it is now. He did not know Dando then and their later association does not really surface in the press until the late 1990s. Indeed, she spends the New Year of 1999 with him, which was widely publicised as by then she had become a tabloid celebrity and there was also a lot of publicity about her impending marriage to Farthing.*

It is speculation, but presumably two fault lines in Barry George's head collapsed into seeing Dando as responsible for despoiling Freddie Mercury's memory: first, his dislike of the BBC and his unhealthy interest in TV news presenters generally. What may also have come into this is Bob Wheaten, who produced Breakfast Time *in 1991 and, at that time, was cohabiting with Dando. Second, she came out in the press as the best friend of Cliff Richard who had humiliated Freddie Mercury in 1986 by grabbing the lead in the theatrical version of* Time. *She also lived locally, which made it possible for Barry George to target her.*

This could have been reinforced by a cabbalistic reading of dates, Queen song titles and lyrics. Barry George was just 39 when he murdered Jill Dando, which was Freddie Mercury's age in 1986 when Cliff Richard took the lead in Time *and Jill Dando conducted the apocryphal interview. Queen recorded a song titled '39', which is the first track on the album* A Night at the Opera *and is followed by 'Bohemian Rhapsody', then 'Death on Two Legs'. This is the sort of music that Barry George listened to day and night and the lyrics of which turned into, as they do with a lot of die-hard fans, canonical texts.*

Now this might all seem bizarre, weird and speculative but it always was that kind of murder with no conventional or even outlandish theories making sense. Even with Barry George's arrest, given his denial of any involvement, we are forced into conjecture and speculation to make sense of it. However, as Barry George approached his thirty-ninth birthday, he clearly began to prepare for his rite of passage to infamy. He girded his loins by ordering SAS clothing in the first week of April and presumably began studying How to Commit the Perfect Murder *(Ninja) — which is the one where you are charged but acquitted — in the Ninja book found at his flat.*

There are also the lyrics of 'April Lady':

It's been good to have you around
Goodbye April lady

[From 'April Lady',
words and music by Brian May and Tim Staffell]

After the kill, Barry George incorporates Jill Dando into two aspects of his running fantasy about Freddie Mercury: the 1986 interview and his own coming to Jesus. These are somehow connected, although without his co-operation one can only guess at what it all meant to him. Perhaps he saw them both united in a backdated 1986 afterlife or something?

But there are never any vindictive references to Dando either side of the murder, yet he still murdered her. Her murder doesn't look personal and, from what little we know, the cabbalistic scenario best fits the facts. If he didn't hate her, neither was he obsessed with her, she presumably was selected for death by his own personal readings of the sacred texts, her association with Cliff Richard and the BBC.

Finally, there is Barry George's own claim to fellow prisoners that he brought the murder charge on himself. There is something odd about the way he pushes himself on various people soon after the murder. Certainly sufficient for a number of them to ring up Oxborough and report him as acting suspiciously. Yet, after this did not lead to any interest, he goes quiet but between being warned that the police wanted to talk to him and his actual questioning by Gallagher, he does two things: he strips his flat of Freddie Mercury memorabilia and he shuts up, hinting to others that he had a connection with the murder. However, once he thinks Oxborough cannot charge him, he begins teasing acquaintances with his possible guilt.

If Barry George wanted to gain notoriety for the murder,

presumably his golden scenario is that he is charged with Jill Dando's murder but acquitted. Thus, the possible discovery of new evidence can never jeopardise his legal innocence and he could traffic to his heart's content in his association with the crime.

Horrocks looked lugubriously at me at one stage and said, 'I am interested in one thing. Who told you that he didn't go home after the murder but used a drop?'

I said that I had to protect my sources and that telling him would not do Oxborough any good anyway. I explained that I had had a number of reports from inside the prison, but I emphasised that George always spoke in the third person, that he never admitted anything.

Later, he said to Benjamin as he walked us out, 'We looked everywhere for that drop. I wish I knew where it was.'

However, Horrocks was probably 'interested in one thing' — to get rid of Benjamin, me and our crackpot theory. Neither he nor Sword laughed in our faces or said that it had been a waste of time, but in the discussion after they had finished reading the briefing paper there was no acknowledgement that we brought anything new or relevant. As I knew exactly the way the wind was blowing, I decided to snatch some dignity from the meeting by nailing them on two clues that their investigation had missed, where the facts spoke for themselves and did not rely on a lyrics-based interpretation. I grabbed the floor in a rare conversational gap when Benjamin was trying to draw Horrocks into debating the significance of the lyrics.

I laid both on them with a vengeance. The first one was when I reminded Sword that at the time they searched 2b Crookham Road they found no Freddie Mercury memorabilia.

'That was because,' I said cockily, 'he had removed it in case Oxborough got too many clues into his motives. They were there when Gallagher first moved on him.'

Horrocks never gave anything away, but Sword shopped the business. He went rigid, staring into space as his face turned ashen. He remembered what they had missed. I kind of felt sorry for him; he is an OK guy who cared about taking George out of circulation, not out of justice for Dando or for his own career, but because it was right.

The other telling point was when I said to Horrocks that the other reason I knew George used a drop and destroyed all the clothing associated with the crime was because they had not recovered any long-sleeved yellow garments. I reminded him that they had CCTV footage of George walking along the east side of Fulham Football Ground around the time he visited HAFAD, which is only 50 metres away. The yellow garment is long-sleeved as described by the American woman whom he spoke to about helicopters just before the timing of the CCTV footage. But no long-sleeved yellow garments were found in his flat. I laid it on him like you do a trump card. Unlike Sword, Horrocks took it on the chin without registering that I had scored a hit. It was a Pyrrhic victory; I still had another chapter ...

Benjamin, though, was beginning to crank up as he realised that he was not going to be invited to do his Freddie Mercury party piece. He began to get agitated. 'Are you saying that this is all coincidence? Yellow. Look up at the sky. Coincidence? Did you even look at the lyrics?'

Horrocks replied avuncularly, 'Of course we did. You might not think it, but this was my music when I was young. We had people ringing up the first day about "Bohemian Rhapsody" ... "gun to the head" and that.'

Benjamin snapped, 'It's not "gun to the head", it's "Put a gun against his head ..."'

Horrocks rolled with the rebuke like anyone who is corrected by a pedant. Benjamin began shrieking in falsetto and rising, 'What do you mean you had people ringing up? Show me where I am wrong. Those condolence notes. Do you think that is another coincidence? There was never ...' He was on the countdown to blowing a head gasket.

'Benjamin, Benjamin,' I appealed to him. 'I'm trying to write a book. They have their job; I've got mine. They are entitled to their opinion.'

Benjamin replied, 'Not if it is wrong, they are not. They are wrong. You know they are wrong. Tell them they are wrong ...'

He was spluttering, waving his arms about and his eyes were darting around all over the place. I felt sad. He was ever the mad genius whose ideas were never listened to because of the way he looked, behaved and, like Barry George, over-egged whatever he had to say. However, when the meeting broke up, one thing occurred that was revealing and bore fruit. As we went to leave, Horrocks handed me back the briefs I had printed out for him and Sword. It was mean-spirited. Yet, I also knew that he was cutting off his nose to spite his face.

I was tempted to let him, but intuitively I knew it was important that he kept them. I pressed them on him, saying that I had the original in my computer. I even said he could throw them away if they were no good. Suddenly, I felt like I was back in the playground under the threat of an 'it touched you last' decree. I was determined not to take them back. Horrocks sucked the lemon; he had touched them last and had to hold to them. He muttered something about telling Campbell about our ideas.

After the meeting, Benjamin was extremely bitter. 'This is

the story of my life. I am right but nobody listens. It was just a waste of time. We go to all that trouble and they treat us like we are wasting their time. They know we are right ...'

Even before the meeting started, I had seen things through a colder eye. I told him that they were never going to come in on a theory from us, which they could not even use and which they could have worked out themselves.

Benjamin reflected, 'Campbell won't understand either. He won't let himself. No policeman would. You were right. They can't think abstractly; they don't appreciate ideas and George was driven by ideas.' Then he said, 'But if they give it to Pownall, he will understand. He is an intellectual like us. He will grasp it.' It seemed that Horrocks on the way out had told Benjamin that Pownall would see it, too. I had not heard that.

As the Crown case was moving to a close, I decided to take the bull by the horns. Most of the time, I was confident that we were right but there were moments when my natural cynicism made me wonder if I had come under Benjamin's spell. Sometimes his brilliance glistens like fool's gold. His free-wheeling, brainstorming style of analysis can carry you beyond what the facts sustain. His mind teeters on the edge of madness. It is as though his passion for rationality spills over into the irrational and he can take you with him. After his Freddie Mercury insight into the case, he began seeing connections between George's behaviour and Queen lyrics that carried the hallmark of his own magical thinking. As a reality check, I devised a kind of Freddie Mercury and Barry George litmus test.

Just as the Crown case was closing, I decided to wear an almost fluorescent short-sleeved yellow shirt, which sometimes I wear for cycling at night, for court. It picks up the light, so it makes me feel more secure about some drunken driver ploughing into me. I wore it under a navy-blue cotton blouson that I took off in court. Ingrid blinked disapprovingly, 'Are you trying to blind us, John? And, believe me, it is definitely not going to get you any phone numbers, if that's what you think.'

When George came up from the steps into the dock, I stood just in front of the side of the dock where, as he came level with the court, he would see me. Horrocks was watching me from the other side of court — he obviously knew what my game was — but I saw Pownall looking, too. George came up into the dock, then as he saw me he just stopped in his tracks. I eyeballed him, like I know what you're on, Barry. He never gave anything away — just looked straight at my shirt for maybe three or four seconds. It was a shorter version of the time when Charlotte de Rosnay stared at Mansfield. Then he turned and sat on his seat. Bingo. Benjamin got it, too. Another interesting bit for the book. But it got better ...

The next day, I was in the Old Bailey canteen and Barry's sister, Michelle Diskin, came up to me. I had already made contact with her soon after the trial started by throwing my book-writing cap in the ring. I just said that I was doing a book on the case and would like to talk to her. At the time, she said that she would bear in mind what I had said but, apart from a few nods and hellos, I had not said anything else to her. This time she said, 'Do you have a card or phone number. I am not saying anything will come of it, but Barry wants to know how you can be contacted.' Jackpot. I said that I would give her my details. I wanted to rush up to Horrocks and say, 'I told you so,' but resisted the impulse.

That evening I wrote her a letter:

john mcvicar

June 27, 2001
Dear Michelle,

As you know, I am writing a book on the murder and the trial and obviously I would like to talk to Barry about the latter. However, looking at it from his point of view, he must not only tell his story but also be paid for it.

When I spoke to you in the canteen last week, I reminded you of the feeding frenzy that the press will instigate after the acquittal. You replied that you know as you have been through it all before. As you spoke, I was reminded of a letter that Brian May wrote to some Daily Mail *hack last December. It was in reply to a request for an interview by some woman. He wrote of how he 'loathes and despises such scurrilous publications as the* Daily Mail *... scummy paparazzi ... parasites ...' And so it goes on.*

The Max Clifford school of sensationalist journalism is about as appetising as watching sharks at a kill. Yet, I also swim in the same waters and, naturally, I am tempted to want to use what I say to you to put myself in contention for taking my own bite. This is obvious.

I would like you to talk to my publisher, John Blake, who is an ex-journo and a dab hand at brokering big serialisation deals for his more sensational books. Blake is not a shark... but I would say that, wouldn't I? He also swims in the same water. Yet, the reality is that sharks have to be fed because they will not go away until the story is told. Your aim must be to feed them so that Barry's story is both told with integrity and at a price that is fair.

It has not gone unobserved how you have supported your brother and shouldered the opprobrium with bravery and dignity. My advice is that you encourage Barry to strike some kind of deal with a skilled media lawyer to broker the telling of his story. Mike Mansfield can advise you on that but David Price and Mark Stevens also spring to mind. If there is anything I can do to advise you, you can have it off the record but I am not a big player in this field and I don't need to remind you that I have my own vested interests, too.

Faithfully,
John McVicar

It was a crafty, grovelling, self-serving letter written in the context of George being acquitted and being in competition with the biggies in cheque-book journalism. I put in the Brian May reference because I thought it might earn me brownie points with Barry. Brian May had been a member of Queen and all the fans knew how he had come to loathe the tabloid media. I gave it to Michelle who carefully put it in her handbag but, apart from thanking me, did not say anything. Nothing came of it. Later, though, when the jury were deliberating, I saw her in a huddle with Mansfield's wife, Yvette Vanson, who makes TV documentaries. Vanson did a documentary on the Lawrence family, presumably on the basis of an introduction from Mansfield. It was not difficult to imagine the credits on the screen: 'Barry George — Not Guilty' by Mrs Mansfield.

15

pownall rises from the ashes

The Crown's case moved to a close on a high note for the defence. The particle had gone down in flames. Apart from the particle, the only other item of evidence that went directly to the scene of the crime was a microscopic fibre that had been found on Jill Dando's coat and which matched the material of a pair of George's trousers. However, the forensic scientist who did the analysis described the match between the two as 'weak' as the material was 'relatively common'. Yet, when he gave examples of what he meant by weak and relatively common, the court witnessed again a scientist talking from the standard of a scientific standard of proof and the Crown not clarifying the difference between that higher standard and the criminal one of beyond a reasonable doubt.

The Crown's fibre expert, Dr Geoffrey Rowe, gave two

examples of the commonality of the type of fibre found on Dando's coat and which matched George's trousers. 'I wouldn't be surprised,' he told the court, 'if I examined every garment in this room and didn't find a match, but it's still relatively common.' There were some sixty or so people in the court room!

Another example he gave was about the relative rarity of such fibres. 'About three or four in a hundred. Thus, a hundred garments chosen at random would be likely to throw up fibres of the kind used in Barry George's polyester trousers. I can't give actual figures, but it is not a rare event to find a random finding for such material.' Thus, if he took a hundred garments at random he would expect there to be three or four matches with the fibre.

For a criminal standard of proof, this was highly significant. OK, it is not DNA or fingerprint significant, but three or four out of a hundred is pretty close to beyond a reasonable doubt. Nonetheless, this evidence, which in my view was no less damning than the particle, was buried by Mansfield.

As was the case with the particle, the fibre expert, Mansfield's last witness for the defence, was far more impressive than the Crown's. Mark Webster had the jury rocking in the aisles as he outwitted Pownall. The Crown lead tried to re-establish that there was still some kind of match between the fibre and the trousers. He put it to Webster that the fibre did not exclude the defendant.

Webster replied, 'No.'

This 'no' was one of those negatives that could go either way. Webster knew it, too. He was roostering to upstage Pownall. At this point in the trial, it was all downhill to acquittal and Pownall was scrambling to stay on his feet, never mind push the Crown's case back up on top.

In a tentative question, Pownall attempted to clarify the 'no' his way. 'It is consistent with his trousers and the coat?'

pownall rises from the ashes

Webster was pre-prepared. 'I did not use the word consistent. The sun rises in the east and sets in the west — that is consistent with the sun going round the earth. But it is not the case.'

It went down well and floored Pownall, but Webster's sun line was delivered without fluff or hesitation. Perhaps he'd used it before ... who knows, but this was not the remark of an impartial expert trying to be, in the words of Dr Keeley, the scientist who discovered the particle, 'objective, critical and fair-minded'.

Then right at the end of Webster's cross-examination and the closing of the defence case, a plainly aggrieved Pownall attempted to weight the fibre evidence in the context of the particle, in that both go to the scene of the crime. However, Webster wasn't going to assist Pownall to let the evidential weight the particle and fibre each had independently add up to a sum greater than their parts. Certainly, common sense dictates that they should. After all, there was a firearm's particle in the Cecil Gee coat similar to the residue from the bullet and there was a fibre on Dando that matched a pair of George's trousers. If each go some way to guilt, surely put together they go even further? Well, they do in my book of coincidence, but not in Webster's.

He lectured Pownall with another vivid image. 'You must consider each piece of evidence in isolation. You cannot prop up evidence with other pieces of evidence. It is not in my opinion significant evidence. The fibre is not a rung on the evidential ladder upon which you can safely put your weight.'

Pownall slumped back on his bench. This was the last word from the final witness in the Crown's case. The court loved it, of course, including the jury; this was the theatrical side of the show. Their mood seemed to be openly for acquittal now. Sometimes, as they filed out during one of the breaks, it looked as if the Indian, the Maori and others were taunting Bob the Builder with what they regarded as his untenable position. He often looked flustered.

Pownall knew that George was guilty and he knew that he had lost the case ... well, he thought he knew. Perhaps he should have stepped back when Webster pulled this number. He should have just had a rethink, then asked Webster when his imagery had been scripted and with whom. The fibre joined the particle as evidence that was not properly weighted at the criminal standard of proof.

The defence case only lasted three days and contained little of interest except that George had called in an electrical engineer at 2.00am on the day he killed Dando! The engineer was there for two hours. This was the first Benjamin or I knew about the incident, which only reinforced our alibi of incongruity. This was George doing before the killing exactly what he did after it: presenting himself as utterly different in dress and demeanour from someone planning and committing a murder. I asked Horrocks about it and he told me that George had rung up the Electricity Board with a disaster scenario that had to be investigated but the fault turned out to be trivial. Even though he had read my analysis of George's number at HAFAD and Traffic Cars, Horrocks did not give this call-out any significance. Horrocks plays a mean hand.

When I told Benjamin, he just went ballistic. 'They have read what we said. They know he went to HAFAD; they know he needed an appointment; they know he created a scene so he would be remembered, he is wearing yellow; they know he next went to Traffic Cars where he never had any money; now we find they knew all along he got an electrician out at two o'clock in the morning on a wild goose chase. And none of that is significant! Everyone I tell it to thinks it's significant. Of course it's significant. And they are detectives ...'

He had a point. The jury were crying out for some explanation about these seemingly unconnected but bizarre actions of George's: the electrician, HAFAD, London Traffic Cars. All done around the killing but all done with the hidden agenda of maximising attention.

The closing speeches added little, but Pownall's showed that he had seen the analysis we had given Horrocks. He incorporated some of what I had written. I was amazed as it came out of the blue. He had not spoken to me throughout the trial nor acknowledged even by a glance that he had seen the briefing paper I had pressed on Horrocks. Given that no one else had mentioned it, I presumed either he had not seen it or had dismissed it like Oxborough. He spoke of there being 'a dark, complex side to some people's minds, which causes them to act in a dreadfully destructive way for no rational reason'. He noted, 'You might think it was obvious that the police had done their homework, but still he tried to play cat and mouse in the interviews.'

He stressed how George had constructed 'an alibi of behaviour', which, in the absence of the jury, Gage asked him to clarify as he had not mentioned it before. He told Gage, 'Just to be clear on the Crown's position. He went there [HAFAD] looking for sanctuary, where people could see him in a yellow shirt. On the 28th, he wanted people to identify him as wearing different clothing and also as someone behaving in a manner inconsistent with that of a killer.' This was indeed our alibi of incongruity. Pownall had discarded the position he had taken up during the trial that George had attempted to construct a time alibi. He also looked at George accusingly as he spoke of his arriving at Traffic Cars on the 28th and asking Ramesh Paul to look up at the sky. Indeed, he turned to stare at George when he said this and there was venom in his voice as he referred to George's 'yellow' game with Paul. Of course, the jury did not know what he was doing, but it was Pownall saying to George, 'I now know what you are about. I know why you murdered her.' Pownall was impassioned because he was clear — for the first time, the murder made sense.

After he had finished his closing speech, he came up to me in the corridor outside Number One; this was the first time he had spoken to me. He said, 'Thank you for that. I nearly broke out into song but I suspect my voice is not good enough.'

I laughed. As he walked off, he said, 'Look up at the sky ...'

'It's "Look up to the sky",' I replied, correcting him. He laughed and walked off as Ingrid Kelly came up to me.

'What was he saying?' Ingrid asked.

'He was just saying he felt like bursting into song,' I answered enigmatically.

She replied, 'Singing! He won't be singing when he hears the verdict.'

When he opened the defence, Mansfield said that the case against George hung 'by the merest of threads ... but by the end of the case, we say, it will have disappeared altogether.' By the time he delivered his closing speech, the Crown's case had not just disappeared, it did a 'George is not guilty' dance in front of the jury. He reminded the jury, 'Before you can convict, you have to be sure, satisfied that you are sure, each and every one of you. This isn't a game and it isn't some kind of sport which one's indulging in here. This is an important principle of English justice. So the principle sets the standard to convict very high in the hope and in the expectation that the innocent are not wrongly convicted ... Can you be sure, hand on heart, sure that this man pulled the trigger? If you come to the conclusion on the facts in this case, on the evidence in this case, that this defendant was in HAFAD at some time between 11 and 12 or may have been ... that he was or may have been ... very important that, if he was or may have been, we say quite bluntly and baldly — that is an end of this case. Like it or not, whatever feelings you may have, that is an end of it.

'Then there's the situation, which again, as we don't know how you're thinking ... you might in this case think, putting it colloquially, it's a bit smelly. Don't like it. Don't like it. Probably. Maybe. That's no good. We're not here to return a verdict of probably he did, possibly he did, maybe he did. Again, you have to be sure that extraneous feelings don't encourage you to step over the line of duty you have to perform and the risk of suspicion cannot be translated into guilt.'

It was a bravura performance that had even the prosecution team sitting back in open admiration. By the time he sat down, everyone, including Witchell and Horrocks, were accepting acquittal. The only person among the players who seemed not to buy in was Bob the Builder. At the end of the defence closing arguments he seemed more resolute than ever, while the rest of the jury appeared to have gate fever. Perhaps he had marshalled his obduracy reserves?

I think Gage accepted that George was legally not guilty, too. Towards the end of the trial, he had begun nodding at George instead of ignoring George's crass attempts to ingratiate himself with Gage by bowing to the bench before he sat down in the dock. Gage made a lot of uncharacteristic errors, as well, in his summing up. None of any consequence, but he appeared to be nervous as he read out his speech and, under the desk, his left hand kept tugging at the right-hand sleeve of the crimson robe. It was like a nervous tic. I just thought that this was the manifestation of the strain he was under. He knew that George was morally guilty but he was virtually going to have to direct the jury to acquit. On occasions, he became quite ratty with Pownall.

Gage carefully instructed the jury that they were not to draw any adverse inferences from George's decision not to go into the witness box and answer questions. There had been a 'trial within a trial' dog fight over this. The issue was whether or not George's epilepsy might make it too stressful for him to answer questions accurately or might even trigger an attack.

Dr Young, George's personal neuro-psychologist attended every day of the trial and personally dealt with George on a day-to-day basis. Dr Young is an inspiration to all who swear by the powers of meditation. It was only the meditation exercises that she did with George downstairs, while the court was in recess, that enabled him to cope with the rigours of the trial.

She also did some tests on George. One of her tests was to evaluate George's capacities for foresight and to plan ahead — this was her 'zoo' test. How would George cope with the task of planning a trip to the zoo?

Well, of course, we had another George miracle; he demonstrated to Dr Young's satisfaction that he could not plan a trip to the zoo, that he got hopelessly muddled over how he would find out where the zoo even was, never mind travel there and generally organise the trip. This is someone who, she heard in evidence, had travelled all over London, popping into Internet cafés along the way to log on doubtless to Freddie Mercury sites and play Ninja games. In fact, in the trial within a trial she merely trotted out her conclusions from the zoo test. We had to wait for a *Tonight with Trevor McDonald* feature, produced by Ingrid Kelly, that went out three days after the verdict to get all the glorious details.

Like much of the forensic evidence, so with the psychiatric

evidence: it was often partisan. Anyone who has done a postgraduate degree knows very well that if you are prepared to put in the time, you can obtain a doctorate. It is like if you run, you can run a marathon. What matters is the time you run the marathon in and the quality of the doctorate. Most marathon runners are fun-runners, and most PhDs are a joke.

The only two errors of any consequence that Gage made in his summing up went to the character of the man. He picked up one point that each leading counsel had missed and he incorporated them into his summary to the jury as if both had been adduced in the trial. The first was Mansfield not making the point about George going up to Griffin the postman six weeks after the murder. If Griffin had seen George in April, then six weeks later when George came up asking for his phone so he could ring the police, Griffin would have recognised him then as the man in Gowan Avenue. The second was Pownall's mistake of not realising how he could have used George mentioning to the Baptist policeman, Culenberg, that he'd seen a red car in Gowan Avenue on the day of the murder. This was the red car the windscreen of which Susan Mayes had described him wiping with his bare hands at 7.00am. George had thereby used a damning truth to construct a lie.

These mistakes could have been the trial barrister coming out in Gage, in that they were such obvious mistakes to him that later he incorporated them in his summing up, forgetting that these were points that had been missed, not made. I don't know, but I think it more likely that Gage did it deliberately, just gently pointing out to Pownall and Mansfield where they had missed an opening. Nonetheless, he did it in such a way that his summing-up remained even-handed; this to me is the man and I am sure I am right.

Perhaps I share some of Stella de Rosnay's disdain for the English but during the trial, Justice Gage — like Dr Keeley, Susan Mayes and, not least, Bob the Builder — made me feel that there are some among us with whom we should be proud to share the same land.

16

the verdict

In law, the verdict means the finding of a jury. The word verdict combines two syllables of Old French and Latin origin: *veird* meaning 'true'; *dict(um)* meaning 'saying'. Thus, verdict means 'true saying' — the jury speaks the truth.

Jurors, of course, are the silent, passive onlookers at a trial. They never speak in court except to swear the oath and, through the foreman, deliver the verdict or lack of one if they disagree. Yet, suddenly, when they are sent out to deliberate, the stage is theirs. They are now the show; everyone looks to them; everything hangs on their verdict. Yet, the process that produces that verdict occurs backstage; it happens in a black box where everything is unmonitored, unrecorded and unreported. Finally, they come out into the light to deliver their verdict and through their foreman they speak the truth when they say 'Guilty' or 'Not guilty'. That's all folks.

No reasons why they decided one way or another. They make mistakes; not everyone accepts it, especially defendants who have been found guilty, but in law and for the public record what they have decided is true is the truth.

Gage sent the Dando jury out on Wednesday morning. As always, he stressed that they must take their time. 'I do not want you to think that you are under any pressure of time.' The jury had already been told that they would be sequestered in a hotel at the end of every day of deliberation. This meant having access only to allowed, monitored telephone calls and none to newspapers or TV, and was likely to put pressure on them to come in before the weekend. Under the watchful eye of the jury bailiff, they filed out clutching their pens, files and notes. They were directed that they should only deliberate while in the jury room, which meant during the normal court hours of 10.00–1.00pm and 2.00–4.30 pm, but small groups still thrashed out the arguments during the lunch break and in the evening at the Kensington Palace Hotel. The first day, though, was spent organising the exhibits and their papers, developing a way of democratically debating the issues and, not least, electing a foreman.

There were already two camps; a minority of convictors and a majority of acquitters with a few drifters like Wild Child who, incidentally, made it very clear that she did not regard jury service as part of her constitutional obligations as a citizen. Her hairstyle was a pretty good guide to her mood. The waspish Ingrid used to interpret it for me. Tight back in a bun meant she was taking it seriously; ponytail was 'don't ask me, I'm just a teenager'; hanging loose was 'leave me out, I am still recovering from last night'. But she was a classic drifter. Drifters may have opinions but they don't stick on them.

In the meantime, the erstwhile players have to wait offstage. The investigating police officers and counsel have to stay in the building because they never know when there might be some question from the jury that requires their input. They are also paid to do so. It is slightly different for journalists as, to some extent, they are mostly only interested in just the verdict. They certainly want to be there for that, as they all aim to cull the reactions and the spontaneous comments of the interested parties. Staff journalists are paid, of course, so many of those had no problems just hanging around. Freelancers are slightly more tempted to cut out as waiting is wasted time, which can obviously be put to more profitable use.

Some wing it a bit and take a chance that the jury will not come in, perhaps on a particular morning, or they will go early in the afternoon as it looks like their deliberations will go over until the following day. You get some warning whenever the jury is coming back — whether it's a verdict, a question, a request for an exhibit or a direction — as it's announced over the tannoy, 'Parties for Barry George ...' But you can't really leave the building even if someone phones you by mobile, as you only have a few minutes grace.

I decided that I would stay for the lot. I was already a dedicated jury-watcher, so I hung in there, as did Benjamin. He was in the public gallery section, so we only had our lunchtime greasy spoon meets to compare how we were reading events.

I did the rounds on the background to the Old Bailey, journalist opinions, what Horrocks was thinking, even other cases. For example, the Jeffrey Archer case was on at that time and I ducked into Number Eight Court to watch Mary Archer playing her Miss Innocent role again. Mr Justice Potts shut up one of her rambling attempts to bamboozle the jury with some erudite twaddle: 'If you listen to the question, then answer, it will be a lot better. That's the way we do it here.' She was oblivious to the fact that the jury were openly laughing at her. It was entertaining. There were far more journalists watching her husband's trial than there were hanging on the George verdict.

While I was doing this, Benjamin studied some of George's Ninjutsu books that he had ordered through the Internet. Throughout all this, the word was 'not guilty'. The only person I spoke to who still predicted a guilty verdict was BBC radio journalist Danny Shaw. Horrocks, who, even as the Crown's case was nose-diving, was confidently claiming 'this is a convicting jury', now shook his head gloomily and said 'not guilty'. It seemed impossible for 12 reasonable people to get round the HAFAD alibi.

Thursday, 28 June gave us an interesting window on the jury as they asked for three exhibits: the original statement George had made to Gallagher, the videos of the women in Gowan Avenue that morning and the interviews George had given when arrested. The Crown supplied them with a video of the interviews, as well as the original statement taken by Gallagher but they watched the ID parades in court. We had already seen them once early on in the trial, but this time Gage invited the jury to sit closer to the TV screen and the jurors — including the Housewife, Gnat, the Indian and the Maori — all crowded down on to the press bench below the jury box. Right at the back, Bob the Builder and the Manager sat aloof from what was being proofed by the others. Bob barely looked at the screen — it seemed as if he had not changed his mind since having made it up during the playing of the Barry George interviews.

The early deliberations had produced a stand-off between the two convictors who stood on the IDs and dismissed the HAFAD alibi against the six or so acquitters who may have been unsure about the IDs but believed the alibi. The acquitters were plainly affected by Mayes, Normanton and Stella de Rosnay because, when you watched this evidence, rather than listened to Mansfield analyse it, you could see that they had seen George hanging around Gowan Avenue that morning. Nonetheless, there was a long way to go. The jury never came back with any more requests for exhibits or directions of any kind.

On Thursday evening, my phone was melting with Benjamin going on and on about what he had discovered in the Internet books on Ninjutsu and *Construction of Secret Hiding Places* that had arrived from America. I knew I was going to get the full treatment the following day, compete with print-outs, notes, waving arms and saliva'd coffee. I broke early for lunch as juries don't return verdicts at 12.45pm.

Benjamin was like Lenin inspiring the Bolsheviks to revolt — just as verbose and just as sure. The greasy spoon did not serve vodka, which was regrettable because as Benjamin started to lay his Ninjutsu theories on me, I not only knew I needed a few shots but also why Russians drink so much of it. It is a terrible thing having a know-all telling you what you should think. The gods gave Russians vodka to insulate them from the oppression of so many know-all leaders. I certainly needed it that afternoon.

All I wanted to do was watch the jury and wait for the verdict. I had embraced Freddie Mercury, listened to the songs, studied the lyrics; now I was supposed to take a course in Ninjutsu and the Baptists to understand what was inside George's head. I remember thinking, I just want to write a book about the murder, not explore every cell in this sicko's brain. But I didn't say it because that is exactly what Benjamin was trying to make me do.

'Don't you see,' Benjamin said, thrusting some book under my nose, 'Dan-do is an accursed monster who is a tool of Ashatar. A Ninja warrior must kill a Dan-do or suffer dishonour for eternity. The pronunciation he did in the interviews ... that is the way it is pronounced in Japanese. You kept going on about it at the time. Don't you remember?'

I nodded.

'Significant. Do you agree?'

I nodded glumly.

'And do you know what *dan-do* means in Japanese?'

I shook my head even more glumly.

'It means a way of obtaining rank,' he shrieked. 'He killed her because she was a monster and to obtain rank. That's why he did it.'

But I had already settled for it all being to do with Cliff Richard. I didn't mention this, but on the whole I preferred it being the fault of Cliff Richard and not the Ninjutsu monster. I have aversions. I don't like Cliff Richard or, for that matter, anyone who likes Cliff Richard.

But Benjamin had more, lots more. 'And Dando was getting married on the day of the Tabernacle, when Jesus Christ was born. It was 1999, which, under the Hebrew calendar that evangelical Christians follow, was the year 5760 since the world began. However, it was also the year of the beast! George was a born-again Baptist and she was marrying Farthing in a Roman Catholic Church on the day that Jesus Christ was born — he had to kill her. He had a book called *Construction of Secret Hiding Places*, which he studied to create his drop. It's all here. Don't you see ... You found his drop but in here is how he chose it. You must read it. It will blow your mind.'

I didn't want my mind blown unless it was with vodka. At one stage, I said, 'Benjamin, I believe in you, I believe in Freddie, I believe George killed Dando, but I can't believe everything because I'll end up believing in nothing.' I forget whom I was quoting but I was trying to say to him that if you analyse everything to the 'N'th degree, you end up disappearing up your own arse. After an hour of this, it was exactly where I felt I was. I wandered back to the Old Bailey praying — and I am an atheist — for the Sabbath to come early. Benjamin would be going under at sundown for 24 hours — sweet respite from the Benjamin Pell phenomenon.

But the weekend turned into a Japanese frenzy for me. I had interviewed Robert Charig, George's neighbour, a couple of times and much of what Benjamin had tripped into had been confirmed by him. He was really George's only long-term friend — they both practised martial arts together and, through his entrée as journalist, he got George into press gigs featuring rock stars. Oxborough had threatened to subpoena Charig to give evidence against George but, in the end, relented.

George went big on Japanese culture when he married Itsuko Toide in 1989, soon after Freddie Mercury's foray on record into Japanese music, which resulted in the release of the album *La Japonaise*. He met her outside a local language centre in Ealing, but neither spoke the other's language when they married.

Robert Charig recalls seeing them together at 2b Crookham Road. 'They used to spend all their time bowing and nodding to each other as if they were preparing for a bout of sumo wrestling, which is what the marriage turned into. I bet if she had known some English she wouldn't have moved in. Later on, Barry picked up a lot of Japanese phrases and he still peppers his speech with them.'

Itsuko tidied up George's unbelievably dirty, cluttered flat, installing raised platforms and Japanese screens. Yet for all the mess, George knew where everything was and, while he let her do it, he complained. She also installed a shrine to her own god — the Emperor. It was a small wooden cabinet that had two doors which opened up on to a number of small apartments containing sacred objects. In the middle was a picture of Emperor Hirohito in a business suit. This was an object of levity to George as his gods then were those of Ninjutsu, Queen and Freddie's Zoroastrianism.

Of course, this was pre-1992 and before the Freddie Mercury memorial concert when George became a born-again Baptist.

john mcvicar

Zoroastrianism is actually one of the world's oldest minority religions; its founder lived around 600BC. It's Manichean cosmology infused with Christianity and a vision of some final showdown between good and evil — Armageddon — still influences evangelical movements such as Baptism. The apocalyptic viewpoint promoted in the *Book of Revelations* gives victory to Satan and the Anti-Christ. Zoroastrianism underpins the themes played out in the film *Highlander*, which is one of the reasons that Freddie gave the movie his unstinting support.

Highlander, which was released in 1986, was George's favourite film; he knows every scene by heart and will sing unaccompanied such Queen songs on the soundtrack as 'Dead on Time'. Freddie himself was buried with full Zoroastrian honours in 1991. George purported to believe in it but he was never a member of the Zoroastrianist church. Nonetheless, it has strong affinities with Ninjutsu, especially with its emphasis on carved magical symbols.

After George's arrest, Campbell sensed that there was a Japanese connection to the murder of Dando and he looked to George's ex-wife Itsuko to provide the key that would unlock the reasons why he had murdered Dando. Once they had gone through all of George's possessions and gathered statements, it was painfully apparent that there was no evidence of him having stalked Dando or displaying any obsession with her.

When Itsuko was contacted by Oxborough, she insisted that while she was willing to talk to detectives about George, she would only do so to female police officers. Campbell, in keeping with his gut feel, wanted to conduct the interview; so he left for Japan in July 2000 with a policewoman thinking that Itsuko would acquiesce to his presence.

Her reasons for insisting on exclusively female detectives was to do with George's sexual abuse of her, which is why she left him after six months of turbulence and violence, including rape.

Campbell's breach of their agreement was seen by her as dishonourable and she refused to talk to Oxborough, even when Campbell back-pedalled and offered to meet her conditions of women only. Campbell's reported plea to her was far more prophetic than he even knows now: 'You may have knowledge of certain matters that no one else can answer.' Ironically, in response to Itsuko's comment that she did not believe George could have murdered Dando, Campbell retorted, 'She has spoken of his violent aggression and irrational behaviour, yet in the same breath she says he could not have done it. But how could she know?' In fact, she knew much more than she was aware she knew.

Female detectives, though, may well have picked up from her George's immersion in Ninjutsu, which, in turn, may have led to the unravelling of the real significance of the crimping on the cartridge of the Dando bullet.

Crimping occupied a lot of police and trial time. It is usually a mechanised process during which the cartridge is pinched on to the bullet by punching small indentations into it. If done manually, it is usually because the cartridge has been reused, which often leaves the assembly loose. If done mechanically, it is invariably associated with countries that were once in the Soviet bloc. The reason for this is that these countries were profligate in their use of ammunition and overheating could make the cartridges expand, thereby leading to jamming. Crimping obviates this.

The Remmington bullet that George used on Dando was manufactured in the USA where ammunition is not crimped. Neither was the Dando cartridge a reused one, but it had what everyone assumed to be six crimping marks on it. In fact, with the help of defence ballistic experts, Mansfield ingeniously integrated this into his Arkan hit scenario. Thus, the Serb deputed to carry out the assassination could have been supplied with Remmington ammunition and crimped it out of habit, not realising that it was redundant to do so. The Crown had no answer to this except to rubbish the whole Serb theory.

Long before the trial, Oxborough had gone the rounds on the purpose of the crimping, but had drawn a blank as no one stepped outside the crimping framework for an explanation. Yet, Oxborough had the answer under their nose — George's Ninjutsu books. Benjamin was spot on again.

After Benjamin alerted me to the way in which Japanese martial arts defined George, I tracked down at his insistence an authority on Ninjutsu, Ben Williams of Los Angeles, where he runs the Dojan Center. Amongst other Ninjutsu gear that Ben, who is a Master Ninja, sells on the Internet, is a *shuriken* — a set of 'six hardened steel spikes that come in a black canvas sleeve which straps to the forearm'. Six — the same number as the putative crimping marks. The obvious question to ask Ben Williams about this strange coincidence was whether the six marks on the cartridge were significant.

Williams is a journo's dream as, just on the basis of a telephone approach, he delivered the goods with all the build-up of tension of a Hitchcock thriller. Thus, when I asked him if the six crimping marks on the cartridge had any significance, he replied, 'Are you sure of the number?'

I replied that I was and, impatient for an answer, I repeated my question — is six significant?

He wanted more clarification. He asked, 'What sort of pattern were they in? Were they circular or in a straight line or were they in any other pattern?'

I could feel the sweat trickling down my armpits at his tension-building bit. I told him they were in a circle. His pause was perfectly paced for the dénouement.

'That is exactly the Ninjutsu symbol,' he answered. 'It's the circular shape of a chrysanthemum flower and that, for the Ninja warrior, is a scared symbol. The chrysanthemum is the Japanese Emperor's symbol of divine authority and, until it was banned by the Americans, was embossed on military hardware to endow it with magical killing powers. Your killer knew what he was doing.'

It was one of my most memorable eureka moments.

Unfortunately, Gallagher's six calling cards mirrored the six points George had put on the cartridge containing the bullet he fired into Dando's head. The cartridge embellishment was a typical tease of George's, but the symmetry of the cards confirmed that the secret powers approved. There are no coincidences, only meaning for a cabbalist. The number six has a mystical symbolism for evangelical Christians like George, but more importantly it is the sacred number of Ninjutsu.

In Christian mythology — George proudly espoused being a born-again Baptist — the six-pointed star is the Star of Bethlehem which points to the Advent of Christ. 'Immediately after the tribulation of those days ... shall appear the sign of the Son of Man in heaven ...' (Matt 24:29–30). The six-pointed star is the symbol of the perfect life, the perfect balance of the Christ-man. However, this symbol is even more potent in Ninjutsu culture, which for all his devotion to Freddie and Baptism, is the cornerstone of Barry George's weird pick 'n' mix belief system.

In terms of the evidence presented at trial, of course, anything that unpacked the way in which the murder had the signature of Ninjutsu or Mercury written all over it would have sunk George. The run he got at trial had a lot to do with the mysteries of this oh so surreal murder.

George might have been acquitted on Saturday. Some of the acquitters had started to think that he might be guilty but there was still enough doubt to produce a 10–2 majority by the close of deliberations. However, two things prevented that: first, the Housewife suffered a bereavement, so on Saturday morning she was stood down; second, Gage did not give them a majority ruling until Saturday afternoon. Thus, Gage's timing meant that the only majority verdict they could bring was 10–1, not 10–2 or 11–1, and there were two hardline convictors!

On that Saturday, I wandered about the Old Bailey, looking at the building, the statues and plaques. There were only three courts sitting that day and it was very quiet. Dave, one of the old-time reporters, took me round and showed me the 'most important part of the building'. It is a marble plaque on the wall of the ground floor at the north end. It states:

> *Near this site William Penn and William Mead were tried in 1670 for preaching to an unlawful assembly in Grace Church Street. This tablet commemorates the courage and endurance of the jury. Thos Vere and Edward Bushell and ten others refused to give a verdict against them, although locked up without food for two nights and were fined for their final verdict of Not Guilty.*
>
> *The case of these Jurymen was reviewed on a Writ of Habeas Corpus and Chief Justice Vaughn delivered the opinion of the Court which established The Right of Jurors to give their Verdict according to their Convictions.*

William Penn left England for America and he gave his name to the state of Pennsylvania. I thought about what I would like to see engraved on a plaque in the Old Bailey and it was Dr Robin Keeley's words on 5 June 2000, when he was being taken through his discovery of the particle by Pownall: 'It is my job to be objective and critical of my own work. My job here is to be objective, critical and fair-minded.' He had been called by the Crown, but he favoured neither prosecution nor defence — only the truth.

After Gage's majority ruling, there was little time left, even though it was obvious that the Manager was bearing the brunt of the pressure from those who wanted to go home for Saturday night and Sunday morning. He looked haggard and brow-beaten, his shirt was damp with sweat and he was staring vacantly into space as Gage told them that they would have Sunday off. He seemed to be bearing the brunt of the acquitters' arguments, whereas Bob the Builder looked impervious to argument. He was quite jaunty and clearly prepared to go all the way. Wild Child, though, was visibly muttering to herself in fury at being compelled to stay in the hotel over the weekend. But the Maori and the Indian were also showing frustration at being held prisoner by the convictors. Nonetheless, the short money was still 'not guilty' and 'disagreement' was the only other runner.

On Monday, the mood outside the jury room was that there must be a verdict that day. It was obvious when the jury filed in that they were not going back to the hotel for another night. There was an excited buzz among the hacks and there was a lot of tense smoking and coffee drinking. I wandered along the corridor before lunchtime and caught Campbell's eye. He was sitting on a bench reading some papers. He looked quite coldly at me, then contemptuously went back to his task. I was startled as he had never openly expressed hostility towards me during the trial. Of course, I was still hoping that he might give me an edge because of the help that Benjamin and I had given Pownall. I realised then, of course, that there had been conflict between him and Pownall over the use of the material Benjamin and I had supplied Horrocks.

At 4.10pm, the tannoy called us into Number One Court. At first, no one was sure it was a verdict. The first I knew was when Dr

Young positioned herself by the dock ready to go in with the smelling salts if George collapsed. The Clerk of the Court asked Gnat (the foreman) for the verdict. He could hardly bring himself to say, 'Guilty.'

The court gasped collectively. Hardly anyone had seen it coming. It was 10–1 and Gnat was the sole dissenter. The other convictors had been turned by watching the interviews in the context of the identification evidence.

George took it on the chin without flinching. He had trained himself for this moment by remembering one of the inspiring passages from one of his favourite Ninjutsu books, *The Fifth Profession* by David Morrell: 'To act without thought — to respond instantaneously to instinct — insured victory over an enemy who had to plan before he struck. An extra advantage was that Zen Buddhism encouraged meditation, whereby one was purged of emotion and achieved a stillness at one's core. The samurai trained themselves to be neither fearful of death nor hopeful of victory and thus, entered into combat with a neutral attentiveness, indifferent to — but prepared for — the violent demands of each instant.'

Gage told him as he sent him down for life, 'Why you did it will never be known. It is probable you can give no rational explanation ...'

Once George was sentenced, there was pandemonium as all the hacks tore off to file copy. I immediately buttonholed Pownall outside the court. He looked dazed but was jubilant and expressing astonishment. 'I cannot believe it. The most I hoped for was a hung jury. I just cannot believe it. But thank you so much for your help.'

I played it down, saying that it was merely a literary interpretation. He replied, 'Maybe, but I'm sure you are right. Thank you.' Given Benjamin's contribution, it would have been more fitting if Pownall had thanked him.

★   ★   ★

The chilling irony of Jill Dando's murder is that the victim's and her killer's relationship to fame were two sides of the coin of celebrity-itis. She had become a celebrity not for being able to do something uniquely or extremely well, but through coming over as personal, engaging and genuine while fronting TV programmes no better or worse than numerous other TV presenters. But in her case it would not have mattered if it had been worse because, in the age of TV personalities and celebrity, Jill Dando embodied the highest English virtue — she was nice. And as she was nice and on TV, she was famous. But it was fame that had no substance. It was the fame that the gabbling plebs of *Big Brother* desperately want — fame for being famous; fame for its own sake, not for doing anything worthy.

Dando had never sought such fame but welcomed it when it was granted her. George, on the other hand, had always sought fame ... any kind, at any price. He wanted to be famous not for excelling in some field, but for anything that could put him in the public eye. It didn't matter what it was. Even jumping over buses on roller skates in a madcap stunt in which he broke his femur and ended up in Casualty rather than on the front page of the *Sun*.

This is the kind of fame sought by the ancient Greek, Herostratus, who, before he was put to death, explained why he had burnt down the Temple of Diana at Ephesus, 'Because it will make my name immortal.'

Everything George did he failed at — singing, BBC messenger, academia, record producer, the Army, the police, handgun shooting (he was rejected by his Kensington gun club), women ... and his only taste of fame was in lies and fantasy, until he executed Dando.

His quest for fame is the founding metaphor of George's mentality. Against this backdrop, 20 years of magical thinking cut fault lines in his head along which fantasies about Freddie Mercury, Ninjutsu and evangelical Baptism flowed freely, meeting looser and looser reality checks. Finally, these fault lines imploded on the decision to kill her — the accursed Dan-do, the 'nymph in yellow', the friend of Cliff Richard, the woman who besmirched her avowed Baptist faith and Middle England's sweetheart, the presenter of *Crimewatch*. It was far too intoxicating for George to resist.

In killing her, he finally succeeded, as well, in doing something that he had set out to do. This was in itself an immense source of satisfaction to him; he had followed the right path and providence had affirmed his madcap delusions. He had gunned Dando down with no more animosity than an Inca priest would feel towards the child whose heart he was ripping out as a sacrifice to the sun god.

The condolence notes he wrote just after the murder show that some nagging doubts surfaced, but these were banished when he read in the press that Dando had taken a phonecall while she was in Copes, the Fulham Palace Road fish shop, confirming that the tickets for *Mamma Mia!* were reserved. Farthing had ordered these for her as a treat; they were for the Abba revival musical then running at the Prince Edward theatre. For George, 'Mamma Mia' meant only 'Bohemian Rhapsody':

> *Mama mia, mama mia, mama mia let me go*
> *Beelzebub has a devil put aside for me, for me, for me*
>
> [From 'Bohemian Rhapsody',
> words and music by Freddie Mercury]

Providence had decreed that he execute her; fame, however, was 'in-waiting'. At first, he nourished his ego with the fact that only he knew the answer to the question on everyone's lips but, like his fantasies of fame, the pleasure from his secret began to pall. He had performed a miracle; he wanted recognition and applause for it.

A failed prosecution became his dream scenario. While awaiting trial, he often boasted to other convicts, 'I set out to get myself charged, so after I'm acquitted I will have books written about me that will make me rich and famous.' In another pearl of George wisdom, he said, 'The best perfect murder is not one you don't get arrested for; it is one you get charged with, but are acquitted.'

He knew that he would be immune from prosecution even if, after he was acquitted, he went public on how he had committed the crime. Although, if he had been, he probably would not have told all. As his friend Robert Charig reminded me, 'He desperately wants fame, but not infamy.' Nonetheless, he would have trafficked in it; that is all he had and he would have used it.

In the month when he turned 39 — the title of one of his favourite Queen tracks and Freddie's age in 1986 — he had executed the April lady:

> Goodbye, April lady
> It's been good to have you around
>
> [From 'April Lady',
> words and music by Brian May and Tim Staffell]

'To deliver the master stroke' (from the Freddie Mercury single 'The Fairy Fellers Master Stroke') was to be charged with her murder, then to be acquitted and claim his fame-in-waiting. Such a perfect murder would make even a Master Ninja gasp in admiration. What a master stroke!

He was not mindless of the risks involved, so it needed some finessing. George took some more precautions after his first encounter with DC Gallagher. As Gallagher had looked at the coat that he said he was wearing on 26 April 1999, he anticipated that the police would come back and search the place. George decided not to over-tempt fate and removed some of his Ninja books as well as much of his Queen memorabilia, including taking down his Freddie Mercury posters. This faded the two distinguishing signatures to the murder, but he left enough there for the police to work out if they were clever enough. By the same impulse in the police interviews, he also kept using the Japanese pronunciation of Dan-do. He was the Ninja Jerry who could tease Oxborough Tom with the truth and never get clawed by it.

For reasons that George could not anticipate and will probably never understand, he did get clawed — not by the truth, but by the intuition of a few jurors who were sure they knew more than they could prove. Yet, while the jury's unexpected verdict closed his chosen dream, ending it scripted another unanticipated but equally enticing one.

He is now 'a victim of a miscarriage of justice'. One book — the Cathcart one — has already raised doubts; others will follow from the usual specialists in the genre, such as Bob Woffinden and Paul Foot. And *Dead on Time* will not deflect them. After all, for 40 years, like pulling a rabbit out of a hat, these people conjured up James Hanratty's innocence and even when a DNA test on the semen he left on Valerie Storey's knickers proved his guilt, they demonstrated how that was flawed, too. For the miscarriage of justice *apparatchiks*, George is innocent ... period.

And George is taking to his martyrdom — he has attention, fame and, while he has no riches, he has sympathy instead. When Nick Ross wished George 'a long and fulfilling life' just after the verdict, he did not have an inkling how prophetic his unctuous wish would become. In George's own head, he is still ahead of the game. No one really knows his secrets.

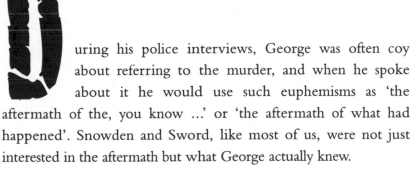

17

what george did know

uring his police interviews, George was often coy about referring to the murder, and when he spoke about it he would use such euphemisms as 'the aftermath of the, you know ...' or 'the aftermath of what had happened'. Snowden and Sword, like most of us, were not just interested in the aftermath but what George actually knew.

Barry Michael George was born in Hammersmith on 15 April 1960. His father was English, his mother Irish. He was baptised as a Roman Catholic but his weaning was troublesome as he was born with a cleft palate. This created more problems for him psychologically than his diagnosis in his teens of *petit mal* epilepsy. There were already two daughters and his father desperately wanted a son but the difficulties, especially with feeding, and the stigma of a boy with such an unsightly handicap led to him rejecting Barry.

Correctional operations to remedy the condition were successful, but he retained upper lip scarring and speech difficulties.

In early childhood, he was disruptive and attention seeking, which led to him being admitted to a special school for maladjusted children. When he was seven, his father left his mother. Barry was a social worker's prayer — a certified victim.

Barry's education was troublesome and he was sent to a state boarding school for children with special needs. Many of the fellow boarders were delinquent, but already he was expressing an intense ambition to be famous. He said to other children that when he left school he would become a rock singer; his first idol was Gary Glitter. Other pupils ridiculed him for his aspirations, for while he was always prepared to sing and play air guitar, his voice was ropy. Later, he adopted as one of his many pseudonyms Glitter's real name, Paul Gadd. At 15, he left school without any qualifications but, eventually, just after his sixteenth birthday, was taken on as a messenger boy by the BBC at White City on a six-month trial. He used the name Paul Gadd.

He only worked there for five months and was asked to leave because his performance was unsatisfactory. His timekeeping was haphazard and he often became confused when carrying out routine tasks. He was bitterly disappointed at not acquiring a permanent post as he saw his BBC niche as a stepping stone to stardom. The celebrities whom he saw and heard about were already being incorporated into his rich fantasy life of rock 'n' roll fame. Socially, he was outgoing and he was also sexually attracted to women. But they weren't to him; he was persistently rejected and was permanently frustrated at not being able to acquire a girlfriend.

After the BBC, he was never to take another regular job, although he did earn some sporadic income as a stuntman in his early 20s. His epilepsy enabled him to register as disabled, which gave him a much better benefit cushion than being just unemployed; he also quickly became a dab hand at what was known in those Thatcherite days as a 'welfare scrounger'.

Meanwhile, along with his fantasies of fame, he also took further flight from reality in the way he rationalised failure. Society discriminated against him unfairly because of his handicaps. He saw it as his right to redress the balance. His victim mentality was becoming strident and proactive.

At 20, he tried to join the police force — his father had been a Special Constable for a while — but he was rejected because of his epilepsy and lack of basic education. This humiliation and his disappointment led him to seek revenge on those who had rejected him and he mocked-up a crude police Warrant Card, utilising the letterhead of his rejection slip from the Metropolitan Police. He began using this to obtain lifts and impress strangers; invariably, he appointed himself a Detective Constable. He was living out his fantasies as best he could.

He began to follow women home, then approach them after he had found out where they lived and worked, trying to use his inside knowledge to impress them. He also boasted about his connections with the rock industry. He could not understand why these approaches obviously frightened women; but to find some sexual outlet, he began resorting to street walkers in the Shepherd's Bush area. He hardly drank, did not smoke or take drugs, could travel free, had subsidised accommodation and had his mother's support, so he could afford this occasional extravagance. But he resented paying for what he believed would be his right if women only saw him for what he really was.

Using the Warrant Card at one's woman's home, though, led to a complaint and his first arrest. He pleaded guilty at Kingston Magistrates' Court for impersonating a police officer and, after psychiatric reports, was fined £5. The offence was seen as having a prankish rather than a sinister element, which George played up to outside the court where he posed for photographs for a local newspaper. Despite his name Paul Gadd, he boasted to the reporter that he was related to Jeff Lynne who was then fronting the Electric Light Orchestra. His first brush with publicity proved intoxicating; he saw that fame could be claimed rather than earned.

He next publicity stunt was to mock up a karate trophy and take it along to a local newspaper where he asked to have his feat of winning the British Karate Championship publicised. He told the reporter who dealt with him that he practised eight hours a day but when he wasn't chopping through tiles he was a singer with Xanadu and a session musician with ELO. 'Xanadu' was a massive 1980 hit for ELO and the title of a fantasy movie released in July of the same year starring Cliff Richard and Olivia Newton-John. This futuristic roller-skating film inspired George to learn to skate; he eventually became skilled enough to perform stunts on skates. In 1983, he skated down a ramp at a local fair and jumped over four double-decker buses, fracturing his leg in the process, but the pain didn't matter as he appeared on regional TV and was profiled in the local press.

George's karate claim was to backfire on him when he was exposed by the local press as a fraud but he was not embarrassed and, indeed, revelled in the further publicity. He had long incorporated lying as his right to redress the unjust discrimination of society. It was around this time that he first began to incorporate martial arts into his fantasies. Again, he partially acted out the fantasy as he began to practise karate, which later turned into a fascination with Ninjutsu and Japanese culture.

In July 1980, George committed two sexual assaults, each time approaching woman whom he had followed, then forcibly kissing them as he fondled their breasts. He was convicted of one in 1981 and, luckily, acquitted of the other. On the guilty assault, medical evidence was called that related to his epilepsy and personality disorders, which doctors said led to his 'inappropriate behaviour'. He was eventually sentenced to three months, which was suspended.

He desperately wanted sex but no woman would accommodate him except when he paid. Women, like society, became part of the enemy from whom he was justified in taking whatever he could get away with; preying on women became his hobby.

Early the following year, he raped a woman but was not arrested until thirteen months later. In exchange for him pleading guilty to attempted rape, the Crown Prosecution Service dropped the rape charge. He was sentenced to 30 months plus the earlier three-month suspension.

A month or so before the rape, he was found in the grounds of Kensington Palace, then the home of Princess Di, in combat gear and with a knife and climbing rope wrapped around his waist. He was cautioned by the Park Police. They noted that he was 'a fanatic when it comes to military things'. He had joined the Territorial Army in December 1981 and his 'action-man' fantasies took a military twist that was to prove permanent. In 1982, with the Falklands War raging, he also joined a gun club. However, as with his aspirations to find a position with the Army and the police, he was turned down as a member.

In prison, during 1983–4, he learned that as a 'nonce' — sexual offender — he was held in contempt by any prisoner who was anybody. He identified with the hit-men gangsters and armed robbers but was humiliated at being dismissed by such types as 'a sex case'. Nevertheless, he used his knowledge of guns to cultivate an image of a man to be reckoned with; a man who could kill and, if necessary, would. When he came out, he resolved not to pursue sex by force and rarely did again.

With the help of a bright journalist from Chiswick whom he befriended, Robert Charig, he began to advertise himself as a stuntman in TV and film. He hardly got any work but, through Charig, he ligged his way into record launches and rock events. At one party, he found himself chatting up Mandy Smith, who was then presenting a breakfast TV show because she had been the child-bride of Bill Wyman. He even met Robert Taylor of Queen at one gig.

He became fascinated with Queen's music, and especially Freddie Mercury. He had already adopted other aliases such as SAS hero, Thomas Palmer, but Freddie became his alter ego. He wasn't gay, but Freddie was like him in so many other ways: sensitive, misunderstood, with a slight speech defect, discriminated against as a child, talented, enigmatic ... or so he thought. There was also the profundity of the lyrics, Freddie's incredible stage presence, the flouting of all conventions.

In 1986, the film *Highlander* came out, which combined many of the fantasies that he had nourished since adolescence. It was a mythology combining Japanese martial arts, supernaturalism, magic and Queen music. George watched it so many times he can talk someone through it line by line and song by song.

The opening words of *Highlander* intoned over the text said it all for George: 'From the dawn of time, we came moving silently down through the centuries, living many secret lives, struggling to reach the time of the Gathering when the few who remain will battle to the last. No one has ever known we were among you until now.'

Then cue to Freddie with all the operatic stops out singing 'Princes of the Universe'. This is the theme of the film, 'the six immortals' battling to the death for eternal sovereignty. All the fight scenes have Freddie singing 'Who Wants to Live Forever?' George was immersed in *Highlander* with its magic, secret powers, immortality, Ninjutsu, samurai, assassination as an art form and, best of all, murderous Queen music all the way through the film.

The six immortals live over different periods of history but always their destiny must be to kill the others in the only way possible — chop off their head with the magical sixth-century BC samurai sword. Thus another Queen song in the movie is 'Don't Lose Your Head':

> *If you make it to the top and you wanna stay alive*
> *Don't lose your head*

> [From 'Don't Lose Your Head',
> words and music by Roger Taylor]

Naturally, this injunction is important for all of us, but especially so for immortals, as unlike us, if they lose it, it forecloses on their option on eternity. But mortals like us don't need to be dispatched with the *Highlander* version of a stake through the heart. The best method for ordinary folks is defined by one of the six, Juan Ramirez, who tells another of his kind, 'Shoot him in the back of the head — that's the best way.' 'Dando' in Japanese can also mean 'the way of the bullet'.

George had to shoot Dando in the back of the head.

1986 was a landmark year for George, combining some of the highest and lowest spots of his life. *Highlander* was released; Freddie was outed as HIV+; his eldest sister swallowed her tongue during an epileptic fit and suffocated to death. His fanworship of Freddie Mercury became the most enduring theme in his life and, along with adopting Freddie's real name, Bulsara, he styled himself as his cousin. As his dreams of making it as stuntman waned, he also developed plans to start a career as a record producer, had cards printed and advertised in a trade magazine. It was another fantasy that he took some concrete steps to make real, but not enough to have any chance of success. This pattern marks all of George's ventures. He has what is an irrational or impractical ambition, then just does enough to give it the cursory trappings of reality. He was never a complete fantasist.

After Freddie was outed in the *News of the World*, he was never to perform live again. George fixated on the Freddie of 1986. The 39-year-old Freddie was also upstaged in that year by Cliff Richard who secured the lead in the musical *Time*; despite that, Freddie had made the song his own and was desperate to perform in a musical opera. What was especially embittering was that it was written by Dave Clark, Freddie's long-time friend. George instinctively made Freddie's woes his own. Freddie and Queen were now integral to his own customised other-worldly fantasies and they had as much substance for him as, say, a powerful supernatural belief system such as Christianity or Islam has to a believer. Finally, the single 'A Kind of Magic' was released in April 1986 and the album of the same name the following month — it became George's bible. Its theme of black and white magic, which also underpins 'Bohemian Rhapsody', is extremely close to Freddie's Zoroastrian religion. The same theme has affinities with Ninjutsu, as well. All of this imprinted itself on George's mind.

He drifted through into the late '80s, when he married Itsuko Toide, who came from a Japanese stronghold of Ninjutsu, the city of Sendai. Freddie had long been fascinated with Japanese culture and was a collector of its art. George began to learn Japanese and practised Ninjutsu with his friend Robert Charig. Again, these superficial trappings were to give his fantasy sufficient reality to pass muster in his own head. But increasingly, as his fantasy world became dominant in his thinking, he became more and more vulnerable to other-worldly influences. The marriage, predictably, was utterly unsustainable and he reverted to violence and rape; within six months, Itsuko had left him.

George attended the Freddie Mercury tribute concert on Easter Monday 1992; in the religious-like fervour of the occasion he became a born-again Baptist. Freddie was sacred and lived on in as real a sense as some religious adherents believe that their loved ones do in heaven. Ninjutsu fostered this with its surreal overlap between this world and other spiritual worlds. He read books like David Morrell's *The Fifth Profession* with its stories of samurai heroics and fantasies as if they were real history, not fiction. During Operation Desert Storm, he revived his SAS-style images of himself being the man in the balaclava who does the business; he filled out forms to rejoin the Territorials but characteristically didn't send them off. He had also linked up with some gun club members and sporadically pursued his enduring fascination with guns.

Increasingly as the 1990s unfolded, however, he became disillusioned with his lack of success in life, which the fantasies could no longer paper over. He began to feel disillusioned with the fame and attention fantasies that had sustained him since his teens. Reality was grinding its way into his fantasies. He had a new pursuit, however, which increasingly absorbed him — combing the worldwide web in Internet cafés for other Queen fans, Ninjutsu books and websites and apocalyptic Christianity.

Around this period, he also became aware of Jill Dando who lived round the corner from him in Gowan Avenue, only a few doors away from one of the local doctors with whom he registered in 1996. She presented *Crimewatch* and he occasionally saw her in the area, but she did not figure in his fantasies.

At the end of 1999, publicity about Jill Dando and her

impending marriage to Alan Farthing penetrated his consciousness; in particular, her friendship with Cliff Richard, the same pop singer who had, in George's twisted imagination, humiliated Freddie in 1986. She, like George, was also a Baptist, but was planning to marry in a local Roman Catholic Church! He also noted that her wedding day was set for 25 September, which was also the day of the traditional birthday of Christ under the old Hebrew calendar, the first day of the Tabernacle. The year 1999 was also significant: under the Hebrew calendar, 5760 — the year of the beast; moreover, the name of Dando was also a monster in Ninjutsu mythology, 'the accursed Dando'. Well, at least in the Ninjutsu games he played in the Internet cafés. He didn't plan to kill her, but the idea that she deserved to die came into his head. It preoccupied him; everything he thought pointed to her as someone who should be killed.

If God believed in her and He forgave her sacrilege over her wedding and friendship with Cliff Richard, she would enjoy eternity in the afterlife anyway. He began to believe that Freddie had told him that he should be the executioner as well; the lyrics of 'April Lady', '39', 'Bohemian Rhapsody', 'The Fairy Fellers Master Stroke' were signs from Freddie. George himself was 39 in April 1999, the same age as Freddie had been in 1986 when he was at his peak. It was also a way in which he could prove himself, show he was a true Ninjutsu warrior and earn the goodwill of the secret powers.

Even to him, it was all a jumble. He wasn't really sure what reason or message was critical but he came to be sure, dead sure, that she must die by his hand. There were too many things that told him he must kill her. Once the idea had formed, it enthralled him. He would kill her and he would also get away with it. And the outrage it would cause! The presenter of *Crimewatch* killed outside her house! He wondered why he had not thought of it before. It was just too inviting to resist. But how? He studied his Ninjutsu books. How to commit the perfect murder, to be invisible to your enemies, to ensure that they would not suspect you afterwards. He devised an elaborate plan.

In early April, he ordered an SAS jumper from an army surplus store. It made him feel like Thomas Palmer, one of his action-man heroes. He had a converted gun and ammunition that he had acquired after the dissolution of the gun clubs in the wake of Thomas 'Dunblane' Hamilton's slaughter of the innocents at an infants' school. The plan took him a long time to conceive and perfect. In disguise, he would kill her on foot, then cover his tracks by changing in a derelict park building that he knew well in Bishop's Park. He was painstaking about ensuring that there would be no ballistic evidence that would sink him at trial. Of course, he would be arrested and fame would be his after he was acquitted, but he had to do everything humanly possible first to earn the goodwill of the gods. Everything had to go after the kill: the gun, the clothing he had committed the murder in and the clothing he changed into afterwards. It was quite simple, but so cunning, and daring ... so pure Ninjutsu.

The key to covering his tracks was to wear a wig when he killed her, then to present himself immediately afterwards in both appearance and manner as utterly different from the gunman. The park was a place of trees like Sendai, 'the city of trees'. Around the back of the old offices in Bishop's Park, he had access to a small room where he could hide his change of clothing, then when he had killed her, he would exchange these and go on to a local advice centre where he would ensure that everyone would remember him. He decided to hide the gun separately from the clothes, just in case a tramp or someone found them. He dug a small hole in the ground near the park office. It was easy.

The hard bit was finding Dando. He began monitoring Gowan

Avenue but he never saw her car. Then suddenly it began appearing regularly early in the week up to 26 April. She actually stayed there on the Monday night before he got her and she was there on Saturday. He decided that the time to spring her was on Monday morning as she left for work. He called out an electrician early that Monday morning — Bob Mosley — whom he kept talking to as if he was merely a normal guy who was worried about a fault in his mains. After Mosley had left at 4.00am, George prepared himself.

At 6.30am, he walked to Gowan Avenue. Everything was ready. He intended to check everything out before returning at 8.30am, knock on her door and blast her. However, her car was not there. He began hanging around. Everything was set; she had to come back. He had on a wig and his Crombie overcoat; but as the hours passed, he began to panic, especially when a postman eyeballed him. He abandoned his vigil.

He went back to his flat in Crookham Road, but he was so agitated that he could not stay indoors. He was standing around when, on the corner of Fulham Palace Road, he suddenly saw someone who looked like Dando walk into Copes, the fish shop. He could not believe his luck. He walked over to check out if it was her. It was. He dashed back to his flat. This time he put on his fake Barbour jacket, the wig and surgical gloves. Again, he intended to knock on her door but when he walked down Gowan Avenue, she was driving up. His timing was perfect; there was no one in the street. He knew he had to take the moment even if it was not the plan.

She had left the gate open and he walked up her pathway towards her as she fumbled for her keys. She looked at him and said, 'Yes?' He told her that he was a detective making an enquiry about a car theft in Gowan Avenue.

As he got close to her, he pulled out the gun. He muttered, 'I won't hurt you, I just want your bag.' She was frightened but calm. He had to shoot her in the back of the head. He was 'The Hitman':

Don't get me wrong
I'll be your hitman
A fool for your love
I'm the head shredder

[From 'The Hitman',
words and music by Queen]

And in *Highlander*, the final immortal Ramirez dispatches enemies with a bullet in the back of the head. However, George also had to put her on the floor; Freddie would like the symbolism of killing her in the same position as the band on the cover of the first issue of 'Bohemian Rhapsody'.

There were other symbols, too. The six marks on the cartridge would bring him luck; the yellow bullet; changing into a yellow blouson. As he started to push her on to the ground, she began screaming. It seemed to go on for ever but he couldn't execute her until she was in the right position. Finally, she was where he wanted her.

Then he put one in her nut. She just gurgled as she dropped. Doing it was easiest of all. She would never scream again.

He turned and walked out, shutting the gate behind him. As he walked down Gowan Avenue, he kept glancing back and he saw a man opposite her house staring at him. He must have spotted the body, so he started running. He crossed over to the other side to shut off the man's vision. But no one came after him and he calmed down. He crossed Fulham Palace Road hurriedly, nearly getting run over, but he made it without being followed to the park and round the back of the old park offices. He put the gun in its prepared hole and patted earth over it, then went into the office and changed into his jeans and yellow blouson and collected his plastic bag of papers that he was going to use at HAFAD. He stuffed these inside his blouson.

He then went to HAFAD. He thought he played it perfectly at HAFAD — just made himself busy about his problems. He knew they would all remember him and what he was wearing. He was there for about 25 minutes, but when he came out there were helicopters hovering above the park. He became frightened that his hidey-hole had been spotted and that the helicopters were directing the search parties to it. He saw a middle-aged woman also glancing up. As a way of appearing normal, while thinking what to do, he made a credit call check on his pay-as-you-go mobile phone. Then he thought that the best way to see if his hidey-hole had been spotted was to attach himself to the woman who was walking towards the park. Just to allay any suspicions she might have had, he spoke to her about the helicopters, telling her about his having been in the Territorial Army. He walked with her down to the park and it looked OK. She wheeled off to her house, so he crossed over and walked alongside the park, scrutinising where he had hidden the gun and change of clothes. It was fine. There was no need to panic. He walked a little way alongside Fulham Football Ground before walking to his next planned port of call, London Traffic Cars. He used to support the club when he was a kid ...

He knew that eventually he would have to return to his flat, where he would change very carefully on some newspapers. These, with the clothes he was now wearing, would go into a knapsack. That evening he planned to go to Bishop's Park to collect everything he'd left there that morning. He had decided to cycle over to Wimbledon Common ...

In 1996, Robert Charig had told the police that he suspected

George of killing Rachel Nickell and he had been pulled in for it. Charig didn't know that George knew of his treachery. But Wimbledon Common was a good place to break up and bury the gun. On the way there, he planned to stop near rubbish bags and bins to dump items of clothing.

The next morning, he brought some yellow daffodils for Dando and gave them to a copper manning the cordon at the top of Gowan Avenue. Then, nearby, he saw George Coward who was once a very close friend of Freddie's. He often spoke to him about Freddie and the music. He went up to him and began asking him about how he could buy a Rolls-Royce Spirit of Ecstasy mascot for his bike. Coward owned a white Rolls-Royce, so he was the person to ask. He told Coward that he wanted it to mount it on his pedal bike as a tribute to Freddie. Freddie had owned a Rolls-Royce for a while and he loved Ecstasy. It was one of his favourite drugs. Coward was sceptical, even dismissive, about the possibility of buying a Rolls-Royce mascot if you didn't own a Rolls-Royce. George knew that Coward thought he was an idiot.

But Coward didn't know that he had executed Jill Dando the day before and that the reason he was talking like this was because, after a kill, Ninjutsu warriors always put a trophy of their victory on their horse or chariot. Maybe he'd change his tune when he eventually found out.

It was a perfect murder. He'd done it; finally he'd pulled something off. But society and people like Coward who dismissed him as nobody would eventually get to know ... he wanted them to, but no one would be able to prove it and they would never, ever know why.